aphrodite

in bloom

aphrodite

in bloom

anonymous

Entangled Publishing, LLC
10940 S Parker Road
Suite 327
Parker, CO 80134
rights@entangledpublishing.com

Amara is an imprint of Entangled Publishing, LLC.

Visit our website at www.entangledpublishing.com.

Edited by Liz Pelletier and Lydia Sharp
Cover design by Bree Archer
Cover images by Podraboty/Depositphotos
Interior design by Toni Kerr

ISBN 978-1-68281-523-6
Ebook ISBN 978-1-68281-599-1

Manufactured in the United States of America

First Edition August 2021

10 9 8 7 6 5 4 3 2 1

on imprint of Entangled Publishing LLC

Every once in a generation, a compilation of stories comes along that empowers readers and emboldens them to explore their sexuality.

These are those stories.

What's Your Fancy?

The Gift

A virgin receives an especially satisfying gift for her masked coming out ball, but the benefactor remains a mystery.

One Night with a Duke

To settle her husband's debts, a wife agrees to one night with a duke where his wish is her command.

Bosom Chums

A widowed baroness succumbs to her hidden desires and joins her best friend in her marital bed.

The Grand Ball

A country estate becomes the setting for all of society's darkest and most ribald fantasies.

Standing In for an Earl

Devoted to his nubile wife, an earl teaches his estate manager how to pleasure her most thoroughly.

Stepping Out with a Stable Boy

A pastor's wife with five children enjoys a tryst with a well-endowed younger man.

One Night as a Woman

As an introduction to a secret club, a viscount's heir is made over into a woman—and discovers her true self.

Love Letters with a Governess

A governess happens upon her employer's collection of erotic fiction and is drawn into enacting scenes with him.

A Glimpse of Her Groom

On the eve of her wedding, a young bride observes her groom in a compromising position with his best man.

A Lady for a Highwayman

Robbed at gunpoint by a female highwayman, a young lady loses her locket but gains self-knowledge in a stolen kiss.

An Evening of Cards

A French courtesan passes herself around a poker table during a high-stakes game played with explicit cards and rules.

The Baker's Man

Ordering his sister's wedding cake brings a nobleman to a gruff baker who gives him exactly what he needs.

The Gift

The Gift is a fun little tale of a sexually curious virgin that will leave you grinning, however the story includes one brief incident of a man striking his nephew, so readers who may be sensitive to this, please take note.

CHAPTER ONE

L ady Elizabeth's aunt always turned up with at least one gift for her favorite niece. This latest offering was the most surprising and generous ever—a coming out ball *and* the name of a potential husband.

Lizzie's mother did *not* approve. She blistered the ears of Lizzie's father, the Duke of Knightsmoore, behind the door of his study, insisting he put a stop to Auntie Blythe's interference.

Auntie Blythe had outlived two husbands and birthed a son to each, securing two fortunes in the process. It made her, as she described herself, that most fearsome of creatures to men—an obscenely rich woman in possession of beauty, intelligence, and influence.

She wanted the same for Lizzie.

"The Marquess of San Teodoro is a perfect match for her," Auntie Blythe declared, as if it were that easy to snare a proposal from the richest, most notorious rake to set foot in London in decades.

Victor the Virile, as he'd been dubbed behind society fans, was twenty-four. He'd brought his inherited fortune to England, where he could invest in trade ships that weren't taken by pirates as quickly as they appeared on the horizon. His holdings included land in the Kingdom of Sardinia, America, and India. He was nephew to the Prince of Carignano, a close friend of the Prince Regent's.

Lizzie may be the daughter of a duke, but a marquess of his connections and wealth was out of her league. And, as her mother screeched at her father, he was wildly inappropriate. He was *foreign*.

Victor was also reputed to have serviced a scandalous number of women since his arrival, not that her mother said that part out loud. Lizzie had heard it from friends. She had pretended to be scandalized, as any virgin should be, but she'd glimpsed Victor from afar once. His dark, arrogant looks had caused a tingle between her thighs.

Her infatuation was futile, though. She was doomed to accept the suitor her mother had picked out for her.

Lizzie loved her mother, but she was hideously practical. Auntie Blythe, on the other hand, was worldly and witty and yes, given to drowning Lizzie in presents and treats and tête-à-têtes that were *very* enlightening.

"Let me tell you what happened on *my* fifteenth birthday," Auntie Blythe had said three years ago as she and Lizzie celebrated Lizzie's special day with brewed chocolate adorned with whipped cream and orange blossoms. "A man was staying in our home—I won't tell you his name, but he had very close ties to the court in Vienna. He seduced me. Now, you might wonder what is involved in such a thing. I will tell you."

Lizzie had learned, as Auntie Blythe had called it, the "ins and outs" of marital relations. She spared no details on how a man's body fit with a woman's and how his caresses might stray in exciting and shocking ways. She had explained that a woman should find pleasure in it, but that a powerful man with charm and experience could use the intriguing, mysterious pleasures of her response to coerce her into believing herself in love. Before she knew it, she was ruined.

Lizzie's mother had nearly suffered apoplexy when she realized what Auntie Blythe had revealed.

"I don't want Lizzie taken advantage of the way I was," Auntie Blythe said without remorse.

There had been a *huge* row. Auntie Blythe had left for the continent, only returning recently.

Lizzie had been punished, too. Her friends had begun coming out, but her mother had made every excuse to keep Lizzie from balls and parties and *fun*. She wouldn't have her turn out like Auntie Blythe.

It would have been a dreary punishment indeed if Lizzie had not taken Auntie Blythe's advice. *"Take matters into your own hands. Understand the power of your own pleasure so no man can use it against you."*

Lizzie didn't have words for the rush of urgent joy that overcame her when she touched herself late at night, alone in her bed. How could anyone describe it? It was no wonder her aunt had been overthrown when that older man made her feel such things.

Two things brought Auntie Blythe back to London. Ostensibly, she returned to attend the Prince of Wales's fete at Carlton House, celebrating his assumption of the Regency.

Lizzie believed, however, it had been her mention of "David" in her letters. At thirty-two, he had inherited a healthy earldom and a seat in the House of Lords. Lizzie's father was mentoring him. Lizzie's mother threw him at Lizzie every chance she found.

Auntie Blythe wasted no time in offering to host her niece's coming out ball, setting a date after Easter, effectively blocking Lizzie's mother from marrying Lizzie off before she'd had a proper season to *"See for herself what's out there."*

Her mother was incensed. "This is how she behaves," she had railed behind the door to Lizzie's father. "And you *let* her!"

Lizzie had tuned out the shouting. She was ecstatic to have a ball. She had kissed David and let him squeeze her breast, but she felt cheated at having no other experience, especially when the mere thought of Victor excited her far more than the real-life attentions of dull David.

Her ball became *the* event of the season, mostly because Lizzie's mother ruthlessly vetted the guest list, making it very exclusive. Victor the Virile would *not* be invited. She had stroked a line through his name three times to be sure.

Lizzie was annoyed by that, but her aunt proposed at the last minute it be a masked ball. The party became more anticipated than ever.

•••

The day arrived and Lizzie was a bundle of giddiness, but she had no one with whom to share her feelings. Her friends were in their own homes, preparing for the evening. Her mother was lying down with a headache. Lizzie's three older brothers were the furthest thing from interested. Only Auntie Blythe would find all of this as diverting as Lizzie, and Lizzie wouldn't see her until tonight.

With a sigh, she dismissed her maid and indulged herself with opening all the gifts and parcels and packages that had arrived for her. There were new petticoats and hose and the satin dancing slippers that her aunt had ordered from London shops and forwarded on to her. Friends had sent her hair ribbons and eau de toilette, sheet music and embroidered handkerchiefs.

Lizzie spent ages opening and admiring all of it, feeling spoiled and special and wondering if this was how her wedding day would feel. She was about to ring her maid to put everything away when she shifted a hatbox and discovered with delight that it held one final gift. It was a pretty ebony box with gold initials from a jeweler she hadn't heard of.

Inside, she found two gold charms about the size and shape of robin's eggs. They each had a slit in the narrow end for the accompanying ribbon to tie into. As she handled them, she realized each held a weight of some kind, one that moved freely to cause a fine vibration in the golden shell.

The ribbon was a lovely, soft silk in pale blue, and there was a full ream of it. Why so much? Was it a necklace? A chatelaine? And who was it from?

Ah. A note.

Drat. Latin.

Well, thanks to Auntie Blythe, she had been educated in Latin along with Italian, French, and German. Still, it took her a few minutes to work out that the note advised her to *Measure two loops of ribbon around the woman's waist. That length should secure the eggs and provide enough slack to introduce them into her passage.*

Into her—? That couldn't mean—?

Lizzie nearly crumpled the note in her guilty haste to hide from the explicit thought that leaped into her mind, because *it couldn't be true*!

She searched the box but couldn't find anything to identify who might have sent it.

Were these eggs really meant to be *introduced into her passage*? She read and reread, growing less scandalized and more intrigued. The more she thought about trying it, the more a tantalizing dampness settled in *her passage*.

Swallowing, she went so far as to cut the recommended length of ribbon. She tied off the eggs with a firm knot. Where would they go if they came loose from the ribbon? She doubled each knot then tied it around her waist overtop her dress. She let the eggs dangle against her skirt as she considered whether to do as the note suggested.

Was this a rite of passage—ha ha—that no one had warned her about? Had her friends done it and not said a word? Lizzie didn't talk about anything deeply personal with her friends, only with Auntie Blythe, whom she trusted to always be honest and forthright.

Why hadn't she warned her of this?

Well, considering the eruption after Auntie Blythe had enlightened her on marital relations, Lizzie had her answer.

She put the eggs back into their box and tucked it away, then called her maid to tidy up while she took tea in the drawing room, pondering what to do.

As she sat there, she realized her mother wasn't lying down.

She was berating her father. Again.

"David is a good match," her mother insisted. "He's *English*. You *agreed* when I suggested him. Yet you'll allow her to parade other men before her. What if she changes Lizzie's mind?"

"She wants to give our girl a night of dancing," her father said in a beleaguered rumble. "You're overreacting. Nothing will happen."

"You always take her side against me!" A door slammed and a potent silence reigned.

Lizzie let out a despondent sigh, fearing her father was right. Nothing would happen. She would be boxed into a life with David, arguing with him about her own daughter's prospects, and never know the independence and empowerment Auntie Blythe enjoyed.

Unless she took matters into her own hands.

CHAPTER TWO

S ome hours later, Lizzie was dressed as far as her petticoat when she dismissed her maid on a benign errand and retrieved the eggs from where she'd hidden them. If she'd been wearing a busk in her corset she might have needed her maid to help her, but she was able to gather up her petticoat herself. She set a foot on a chair and brought the linen beneath her armpits as she tied the ribbon around her waist. Then she set the first cool golden egg against her mound.

She'd been thinking about this all afternoon, so she wasn't surprised to find her curls were damp. She caressed into her slit with her finger first, parting her slick folds and searching out the source of her wetness. There. She often imagined what it might feel like to have a man's thick member pushing into that tight, wet aperture. The fantasy never failed to stimulate her to the point of delivering the rush of deliciousness she so enjoyed.

She didn't have time this evening to soothe her tingling flesh. She pushed the first golden egg into her cavity. What a strange sensation! There was a pinch, then an awareness of the cool weight sitting at her entrance. She might have given herself more time to debate whether this was a good feeling—or even a good idea—but her maid would return any moment. She pushed the second one in.

It forced the first egg higher, tightening the pinch. It wasn't unbearable and quickly faded to a dull ache. That vague discomfort and the light pressure of the ribbon sitting in the channel of her slit trained her focus firmly on her loins. The sensation of fullness was pleasant, and she was teased again with the idea of a man moving within her.

Flushed with a type of heat she only ever incited in herself when she was abed, she hurried to drop her petticoat and rinse her hands at the basin. As she crossed the room, something happened. It wasn't the cataclysm that happened when she touched herself, but it was a suggestion of that climactic feeling. She was instantly primed for wanting to rub herself while shivering in something like the aftermath of having done so.

It was so startling and lovely, she stood still to absorb it, only coming back to herself when her maid returned. Lizzie schooled her expression while she allowed the girl to help her finish dressing.

The act of raising her arms and shifting and turning became a fine torture that redoubled her stimulation. She ought to remove the eggs. If this went on all evening, she was liable to betray that she was affected, but this sensual awareness was appealing, too. She felt as though she'd drunk a full glass of unwatered wine — something she'd done on a handful of occasions when her mother wasn't looking. It always warmed her beneath her skin and made her think scandalous thoughts.

As the maid put the final touches on her dress, Lizzie gazed at her image in the mirror, but she could barely focus. Her satin gown was white with a sawtooth trim in a color inspired by the chartreuse liquor made by French monks. The sheer silk overlay was embroidered in a similar way, and her wrap was that same matching green. Her silky brunette hair had been skimmed into piles of curls atop her head surrounded in bright leaves and white roses. It had seemed very virginal and girlish when her mother had pressed her to agree to it.

Lizzie put on her mask of green feathers, however, and now all she saw was a forest nymph with flushed cheeks and plump lips and a sheen of exhilaration in her dark brown eyes.

She looked like a dryad who enticed peasants into sinning against the gods.

"Your parents are waiting, miss," the maid reminded.

"Of course." In a haze of prickling awareness, Lizzie moved

down the hall and descended the stairs. The tiny eggs sat inside her like the iniquitous knowledge instilled by Eve's apple.

Her mother frowned as Lizzie appeared. Her father said an absent, "You look lovely. Very grown up," and offered his arm to take her to the carriage.

Her brothers were making their own way to the ball separately, so, minutes later, they were away—which was when Lizzie realized what a horrific mistake she'd made. The pitch and roll of the carriage over the cobblestones set the eggs to jiggling inside her. If they hadn't been muffled by her flesh, she was sure they would have sung pretty notes. She certainly felt the joyous tune they produced.

Thank goodness it was dark. She closed her eyes several times but had to focus on keeping her breathing steady and not gasping as the subtle vibration subjected her to unrelenting stimulation.

She heard her mother at a distance, lecturing that Lizzie must dance with David and never another man twice. And she mustn't talk about...

Lizzie's ears seemed to fill with water. She clenched her inner muscles, trying to resist the tension coiling within her. That only seemed to intensify the feeling, pushing her to greater heights of yearning. Her breasts felt as though they wanted to burst from her bodice. Her loins were growing wet enough to dampen her petticoat. What if she soaked through her gown?

Culmination remained frustratingly out of reach, though. She began to obsessively think of lifting her skirt to rub away the liquid ache thrumming in her flesh, but here they were now, slowing outside her aunt's home. She had to depart the carriage and climb the steps.

"No need to be nervous, pet," her father said, making her realize she was trembling and clinging to his sleeve.

"I'm fine," she lied, but thought everyone who saw her must know she verged on sexual culmination.

Her aunt gave her a warm embrace. Lizzie longed to ask

her about the eggs but was forced to collect herself and stand in the receiving line with her aunt and parents. She was so self-conscious she could barely pay attention to which names were said in relation to which masked faces as the season's crop of eligible bachelors arrived.

All she knew was that Victor's name was not spoken, but David's was. His dark blond hair and smooth, square jaw were impossible to disguise anyway. He paid her some ridiculous compliment about how she was glowing. She was so abashed, she blushed, which made him smile in a way that suggested he thought he was having an effect on her.

She was such a fool! Why had she worn this silly device?

The house became a crush of warm bodies. Auntie Blythe wanted to open the doors to allow people into the back garden, but first she brought Lizzie to the ballroom.

The crowd "oohed" as they encircled the edges of the floor where mythical creatures had been chalked onto its surface.

"It's too pretty to ruin, Auntie," Lizzie insisted, and heard someone bemoan a new pair of satin slippers.

"If it's not erased by the end of the evening, it won't have been a successful ball."

A country dance began, and David appeared before Lizzie to claim it.

Lizzie had been refining her footwork these last weeks but struggled to remember the steps. She was so stimulated by the eggs inside her that she flushed with heat as she gave David her hands.

They stepped in and then away, side left, brought their shoulders into line, then back, side right and shoulders in line, then away again.

"You look very beautiful," David told her, flickering his gaze to her bosom.

Her neckline was the latest cut—wide and straight to expose her upper chest and shoulders. She was very aware of the air caressing the swell of her breasts where her corset pushed them up. Her nipples felt as though they sat beneath hard buttons and protested the restriction, aching to be freed. Her stomach was a whirl of sensual tension.

Lizzie was working so hard not to betray herself, she almost forgot to say, "Thank you."

Her loins were soaked, her inner thighs slippery with her juices. She began to fear the eggs would slip free, but almost longed for that to happen. The ribbon was rubbing in her folds as she moved.

They took each other's right arm by the elbow and circled. Lizzie managed to say, "You dance very well."

"You're so graceful you make me look better than I am." It was outright flattery, but she was so mindless she only took his left arm and circled, then went back to her position.

The lively music forced the next move, which was a snaking figure-eight through the line of dancers, while she maintained her eye contact with David. His gaze stayed pinned to hers in such a way she feared he could see how precariously she balanced on the brink of release.

"You're incandescent," he told her when they came together.

She felt herself completely engulfed in flames and clung to his hands an extra second before they quickly had to spin away and travel down the line where they met again.

They were back to the beginning, repeating the first steps, clasping hands to step left and right, aligning their shoulders—

It happened. *Finally.* Yet it didn't. In a frustrating twist of yearning and fulfilment, a gratifying rush of well-being rolled through her abdomen. The walls of her sheath shivered against the eggs lodged within her, but the usual flood of wet release didn't happen. The most intensely pleasurable pulses failed to manifest.

She felt as though she'd caught a breath but was instantly drowning again. Her gaze fluttered, causing David to raise a quizzical brow.

She ought to be glad she wasn't completely overcome while on a ballroom floor. She wasn't relieved, though. She was clamoring with the same level of desire while flushed with the peak she had reached. It was as delightful as it was vexing.

The dance came to an end, thank heavens. They bowed, and David escorted her back to her mother.

"I'll call on you later this week?" The avid light in his eye was self-congratulatory. He assumed his dancing had caused her flustered reaction.

Lizzie was still aroused enough that she wouldn't object to being deflowered right here in the middle of the ballroom, but she wasn't about to let him think he had won her so easily.

She offered a cool smile. "If I miss you, we'll certainly see each other again this season. Now that I'm out, I'll attend all the parties." And she intended to, *Mother.*

His swaggering confidence dimmed. He nodded and disappeared into the crowd while her mother glowered.

"Don't toy with him, Lizzie." Her gaze narrowed. "Are you feeling yourself?"

If only, Lizzie thought wistfully. "It's the heat. May I stand outside? I see Clair." She nodded at a friend who chatted with a mutual acquaintance.

Her mother gave an impatient nod, and Lizzie slipped out to the terrace where she joined a group of young women who cooed over her dress and hair and the ball in general.

Lizzie calmed a little as the damp night air cooled her hot cheeks and swirled beneath her dress. She made a point of standing quiet and still amid the gossiping women who were trying to guess the identity of masked guests. Her loins relaxed and settled, allowing her to almost forget the small eggs inside her.

• • •

Victor slipped into the party through the garden, easily blending in with the guests who were strolling the grounds in search of darkened bowers where they could fondle and fuck.

He noted the shoes of a man poking from beneath the voluminous skirt of a woman's billowed gown. She sat on a bench, head thrown back in ecstasy, so she didn't notice Victor. Such a lovely picture. Here he'd feared this party would be a dead bore.

Anticipating a similar experience with a specific woman was the reason he'd bothered to turn up, despite his uncle explicitly warning him against showing his face.

Easy to hide it at a masked ball, but Zio Piero had meant it. They were at odds lately. His uncle might be a prince and still lusty and distinguished, but Victor's youth and endurance had usurped his uncle's lifelong reputation as the most vigorous cock in town. He kept telling Victor he should be looking for a wife, since his fortune needed an heir, but how could Victor imagine settling for one woman when he was sought by all— crones, widows, mothers, newlyweds, and virgins. Anyone who possessed a pussy and even some men were throwing themselves at him.

Meanwhile, Piero was still trying to seduce the one woman *he* wanted. Two weeks ago, at Zio Piero's musicale, Victor had crossed paths with the object of his uncle's desire. Lady Blythe Lavenham had asked Victor if he would like an invitation to her niece's coming out ball.

The idea of attending one of these over-chaperoned, non-tippling socials where virgins were paraded beneath the noses of men ready to shackle themselves was a firm, *no grazie*.

"Did my uncle ask you to invite me?" he had surmised.

"He's otherwise engaged," Zio Piero had cut in firmly and drew the very comely Lady Blythe away, making it clear he feared his nephew had caught her interest.

She was in her thirties and definitely intriguing, but one of the other women in attendance had soon begun a correspondence

with him. She'd urged him to meet her at this party, unaware
he wasn't invited.

But what else was he to do with his evening? Anyone of
consequence was here. And much to his delight, it wasn't nearly
so tedious as he'd expected. The music was lively and, judging
by the volume of conversation and laughter, alcohol was being
served.

Plus, there was a tantalizing mystery in not knowing who
lurked behind the masks.

His quarry had written that she would wear—a white dress
with green trim and a green feathered mask.

There. That dark hair of hers was impossible to mistake.

• • •

"I wonder if I might claim a dance?"

Lizzie was abruptly transported back to a state of
heightened awareness by the masculine voice behind her. His
English held the barest hint of an Italian accent and a velvety
tone that seemed to resonate against her golden eggs.

She turned and her stomach tightened. She couldn't place
him, which was startling because, even though she'd been in a
state when she'd met all the guests, she would have remembered
him.

He was remarkable for his sheer presence—tall and wide-
shouldered in a beautifully tailored dark blue coat over snug
buckskins. He had black curly hair and possibly swarthy skin.
It was difficult to tell in the filtered light of the terrace. He wore
a closely trimmed beard and his brows were strong. Behind his
black mask, his eyes appeared to be such a dark brown as to be
ink black. And his mouth. She wanted to sigh as she gazed on
his wide bottom lip, thicker than the top. Was that a diamond
winking in his ear?

Her friends gave muted squeaks of delight. Lizzie instinctively knew any of them would accept in her place if she turned down his invitation, but as she glanced toward the ballroom, she also knew she would embarrass herself if she had to skip and spin to such a merry tune.

Her mother's attention was averted, so she suggested, "Perhaps a turn in the garden?"

Her friends gasped, but the paths were well-lit with torches. Several couples were meandering among the roses and sculptured bushes.

"I'll challenge you to the center of the hedge maze," he suggested, gaze going to where laughter emanated from the shadows of the twelve-foot-high labyrinth.

Her mother would kill her, but Lizzie knew it like the back of her hand. She couldn't be trapped there. And she couldn't resist seizing this chance to do something Auntie Blythe would do.

She took the arm he offered and they moved onto the path.

CHAPTER THREE

"**A**re you enjoying your evening?" he asked as they walked.
"Perhaps too much," she admitted ruefully. The eggs
were nudging her back to a state of arousal. It made for the most
captivating and sensual stroll. "You?"

"I am now I've found you." He spoke as though he'd sought
her out. "Thank you for inviting me. You look lovely."

She was tempted to tell him flattery didn't work on her, not
that she'd had any suitors to practice resisting. Auntie Blythe had
warned her to be wary of charm, though. Plus, Lizzie knew the
real source of most men's interest would be her father's wealth
and title.

She paused as they reached the mouth of the maze, nerves
jangling more than the eggs inside her as she realized something
else. He had thanked her for inviting him.

That meant he wasn't Victor. How disappointing. Given his
accent and light beard, she had begun to think…

"Is something wrong?"

What could she say? That she had hoped the most infamous
rake in London, whom she had never met, had come here to
find her?

But who needed a disreputable marquess when she had an
intriguing bachelor?

"I thought I heard someone coming," she said belatedly.

"Give us time, *gioia*"—he took her hand and bit the tip of one
finger of her glove, giving it the slightest tug to loosen it—"and
I'll ensure that someone is *you*."

The tiny action knocked her breath out of her. His promise
was so wicked the hairs along her nape rose and a shiver accosted
her.

Perhaps it was the eggs. Tendrils of pleasure were wending their way through her breasts and belly and thighs after their short walk, but there was something about *him*. His confidence. He made her inner muscles clench with anticipation of something—a kiss, a caress. She instinctively knew he could seduce her and discovered a fervent hope that he would.

A couple spilled out of the maze. They were falling into each other as though drunk. Their clumsiness forced him to drop her hand.

"Shall we?" He invited with a wave.

It was impossible to read his expression, face half covered and shadowed by the tall hedge.

She ought to retreat, but she led him in, tantalized by the idea of being seduced. The pungent scent of cedar closed around them. The crunch of their footsteps struck her heightened senses.

They had made several turns when they heard a feminine moan around the next corner. He touched her arm and drew her close enough to whisper, "Someone else is about to come."

She might have laughed nervously, but he tugged her into the alley on their left. It was a dead end, but she let him steer her around the two corners into its deeply shadowed alcove. She was away from her mother's watchful eye, exhilarated to be doing something so brazen.

"Perfect." His hands came to her arms and he drew her to his strong frame.

She could have stopped him, but she wanted him to kiss her. She blamed the eggs and her aunt's bad influence and whatever that other couple were doing for her wanton behavior. Her imagination was running away with "ins and outs" as the other couple's moans rose in concert.

Besides, this was only a kiss.

Except it wasn't. He seemed to envelop her. His mouth closed over hers, his arms came around her, and he crushed her to his chest and thighs. The scent of cologne and wool filled her nostrils.

His soft beard scraped her chin in a silky abrasion that was very pleasing. His hands roamed her back and pressed her tighter, straying low enough to capture her bottom through the folds of her skirt and force her hips against his.

She gasped, not expecting him to be so forward, but her hips instinctively followed the command in his hands. She pushed her pelvis into his and let her arms wrap around him. She clung and drew herself even tighter against him, enjoying the pressure of his flat chest against her breasts.

Through the layers of her gown, she thought she felt hardness. His sex? Was he engorged the way her aunt had warned her men became? That ought to have frightened her, but it was so intriguing, and her mons grew so needy, she rubbed against him.

He released a gruff moan into her mouth and hardened his hands on her backside.

It was both delicious and torturous. She was soothing the ache while causing the eggs to vibrate. Tension quickly mounted within her while his strength and heat drew her more than anything she'd ever encountered. She couldn't help but continue rubbing herself against him in all possible ways while the thrust of his tongue between her lips caused a sumptuous curl of anguished pleasure deep in her belly.

They were dancing, she realized. The music was only in her head, but they were moving in concert, writhing against one another in something far more unseemly than that scandalous new waltz. If anyone caught them, she would be ruined.

Lizzie didn't care. She would be damned if she would stop before she achieved—

There.

She managed to lock her scream of pleasure in her throat, but her hissing breaths and shuddering body told its own story. He stiffened in surprise as he realized what was happening to her. The grip of his hands eased into a gentling caress. He moved his mouth to her ear and said something that wasn't English. It sounded like encouragement. An endearment. She was drowning in sensual pleasure and couldn't make it out.

While she reeled from her release, his fingers delved into her bodice. His fingertip was naked, she realized dimly. He had removed his glove and was exposing her breast to the cool air. A muted growl of pleasure sounded in his throat as he fondled her, lips trailing down her neck and—

She put her hands in his hair, thinking she ought to push him away, but wet heat enveloped her nipple. She touched his head, wanting the feel of his hair against her palms.

In a shocking abandonment of any sense of propriety, she yanked her own gloves off and let them fall, then stabbed her fingers into the luxury of his thick, silky hair, holding him as his suckling sent threads of fresh pleasure shooting like bolts of lightning from her breasts to her loins, reigniting all the pathways of ecstasy that had just burst with delight.

"I'm dreaming," she whispered, because every other time she had found satisfaction, she had rolled over and gone to sleep. She hadn't stayed in this state of greed and heightened stimulation. "This can't be happening. It shouldn't."

Yet she freed her other breast herself to offer it to him. He shifted to pull at her nipple with such gusto she gritted her teeth to hold back her moans of pained pleasure.

"Are we doing this here, *gioia*?" He kissed his way back up her neck. "I have a sheath."

This was everything her aunt had warned her about. She could feel the ridge of his turgid sex through the folds of her skirt and should push him away, but instead she whispered, "Can I feel it?"

"*Mio cazzo? Sì.*" With a flick of his wrist, he opened the fall of his breeches.

What little light penetrated from the path through the thick walls of the hedge had all but disappeared in the narrow space between their bodies. She could hardly see anything but a shadowed elongated shape. When she touched it, she drew in a breath of sheer wonder.

So did he.

He had more girth than she expected and was *very* hard. And so alive. His hot flesh leaped in her hand, startling her at the power he seemed to contain. Then his hand folded over hers, urging her to stroke so his velvety skin moved against what felt like iron-hard muscle beneath.

There was moisture similar to the kind her own body produced. She gathered it with her thumb and moved it around the tip of him, thinking if she liked such a thing, he might.

He did. He made a ragged noise in his throat and sought her mouth again.

For long moments, she caressed him that way while he kissed her and moved his hands to her breasts, pulling forth her desire with light pinches of her nipples and the sweetly aggressive play of his tongue against hers.

She didn't realize he had dropped his hand to gather her skirt until the swirl of cool air against her upper thighs brought her back to a semblance of reality. She let go of his sex and caught his hand before he was able to get it under her skirt.

"Don't," she murmured, mortified by what he would find.

"I want to feel your *gnocca*. We don't have to fuck, but I want you to come again."

"I can't let you," she said with deep regret, even though she was nearly blind with desire.

"Is it your time? I don't mind."

"No!" She nearly laugh-cried at that. "No. Something else." She pushed at his hand until her skirt fell down again.

"Are you a man? Given the pleasure we're giving each other, I wouldn't mind that, either." He licked beneath her ear, then suckled her nipple once more.

He sounded so sincere she thought he might not be terribly shocked by the truth. Perhaps she was justifying his touching her when they only had a little more time before someone was bound to search for her.

"You'll keep my secret if I reveal it?"

"Anything," he groaned. "Just touch me again. It feels so good."

They kissed, and she closed her hand around him to begin stroking again. He fondled her backside through her skirt, slowly gathering it. When his bare palm found the back of her thigh and splayed over her cheek, they both released a shaken sigh of pleasure. He pushed his sex into her clenched fist and kissed her very deeply, both of them stroking their tongues against the other's.

As his hand strayed around her hip to her sex, however, she tensed.

He lifted his head, crooning, "I won't hurt you."

"I know, but... That's a ribbon," she said as she felt him discover it.

He traced it into her fine hairs, following the path into the moist depths of her slit. He gave a shaky sigh against her mouth as he rubbed his touch against it.

"You've soaked it. Why are you wearing it?"

"Do you know what it is?"

"A chastity device? I don't think it works," he teased. "I wish I could see it."

"It's—ahh."

"You like that." He had found the sweet, plump bud that was the source of her deepest pleasure, caught in the vise of the ribbons.

"I do," she gasped, distantly trying to please him with her slow strokes, but it was next to impossible to concentrate when he circled and swept his touch, varying the pressure, and then dipped, following the ribbon where it went inside her.

"Why does it go in? Does that hurt?" His finger penetrated alongside the wet ribbon, thicker than the eggs. Thick enough to tease her with a fresh stimulation that made speech nearly impossible.

"There's something attached," he murmured.

"Charms. They give me pleasure—" She sucked in a breath as his finger slid deep, forging a space beside the eggs.

"Do you like that?" His finger moved in and out of her, stimulating her while he tapped the eggs inside her, causing them to reverberate against each other.

Her head lolled onto his shoulder. It felt incredible.

Her hips rocked, as did his, and he pushed into her hand. If she was holding him too tightly, he didn't say, but she could barely track what they were doing, moving against one another while kissing again. Now his thumb joined the play. He pressed it against her bud while his finger delved alongside an egg. The cacophony of sensations within her reached its limit and she was suddenly in the throes of another powerful release.

His hand firmed as she ground herself flagrantly into his palm. His free hand clamped over hers where she still clutched him, moving her hand as his rod throbbed in her palm the way her own body clenched in joyous squeezes around his finger. They muffled their cries of joy by sealing their open mouths together. For several heartbeats, they were caught in a remarkable, shared ecstasy, shaking and moaning and pulsing.

Then she slowly became aware of being in the hedge maze. Voices passed beyond the thin wall of branches with a crunch of footsteps. Music drifted in the distance.

His mouth released hers, and she listened to his unsteady breaths slow against her ear. Her skirt was up, her legs chilled, his finger still buried within her alongside the golden eggs. The hand that crushed hers relaxed, and she realized something like cooling custard coated her fingers.

He eased his finger from her, lingering to explore her wet folds. The strip of silk was uncomfortably tight after his touch had forced the eggs higher within her. As he attentively drew it slack, one egg slipped free.

He captured it in his palm and they both looked down at the wink of gold reflecting the moonlight.

"Should I put it back?" he asked.

"*No.*"

He chuckled and let it fall, then reached into his pocket for a handkerchief. He let her dry her hand on the soft linen before cleaning his own.

She shakily pushed her breasts back into her bodice and wondered if her dress was stained or her hair mussed.

"That was the most exquisite thing I've ever experienced," he told her as he placed a soft kiss on her lips. "Thank you."

"I think it was very sinful, but I can't feel sorry." She was beginning to tremble in reaction, though.

They kissed once more, sweet and lingering.

When he took her hand, she was starkly aware that their skin held the essence of each other's bodies. It didn't seem to bother him. His thumb made a caressing sweep across the back of her knuckles. He handed her the gloves she'd dropped and she clutched them in her free hand.

"Which way should we go?" he prompted as they moved out of their dead end.

"Oh, it's easy." She began to lead him, legs still weak. She was aware of the loose egg batting against the front of her thigh while the remaining one had slid low to sit at her entrance. Likely her powerful release had left her sheath slippery and relaxed. Her muscles no longer had the strength to contain it.

"You know the way?"

"Like the back of my hand. This is my aunt's home," she reminded.

He stopped and released her. "You're Lady Elizabeth?"

Perplexed by his shock, Lizzie paused to glance back. "You knew that. You said you were looking for me."

Her stomach clenched with instinctive apprehension as her

lover allowed a silence between them that filled with the noise of the party and a nearby strangled groan of pleasure.

"I mistook you for someone else," he confessed after an interminable length of time.

"But—" The receiving line. She had *not* met him in the receiving line. "You weren't invited," she realized. "That was a lie."

"I was not formally invited," he confirmed. "Someone asked me to meet her here. I thought you were her."

Oh God. She'd let a perfect stranger—who could very well be a vagrant for all she knew, one who didn't even want *her*— Who *was* he?

She knew. The accent. The skillful way he'd seduced her. *Victor.* She began to feel sick as it hit home that she'd allowed herself to become his latest victim. Far more mortifying than giving too much of herself to an infamous rake, however, was the fact he knew who *she* was. He knew what she'd been hiding up her skirt. *Inside her body.*

The most exciting, gratifying experience of her life became tawdry and humiliating. He would do worse than ruin her. He'd make her a laughingstock. She was so horrified, she did the only thing she could do. She ran.

CHAPTER FOUR

The ball was a roaring success. The Prince Regent himself made a brief appearance, so even Lizzie's mother had to concede that Auntie Blythe had done well.

Lizzie almost missed being introduced to him. She'd left her seducer in the maze and slipped up to a bedroom where she quickly removed the second infernal egg. She tucked both charms under the restrictive bottom edge of her corset so she wouldn't be so distracted, then waited in dread through the rest of the evening.

The more she thought of it, the more she was convinced that she had succumbed to Victor the Virile's wicked charisma. Everyone of consequence had been invited except him. He had admitted he hadn't been *formally* invited. If it wasn't him, someone else here knew who she was and could expose her. He had promised he wouldn't reveal her secret, but could she trust him?

She kept an eye out but didn't see him again. No one pointed and whispered, either. She did see a woman in a similarly colored dress and mask as her own. She'd been pouting and craning her neck as though searching for someone.

How debasing. That was the woman he'd really wanted.

Once home, Lizzie quickly hid the eggs inside a compartment of her dressing table where even the maid wouldn't come across them. She never wanted to see the eggs, or that odious man, ever again.

•••

The next day, she began receiving calling cards. It should have been thrilling. Lizzie had longed to be the most popular debutante in London and now that she was, she felt as though she walked on brambles.

Would he reach out and—ha ha—reveal himself? Start rumors about her?

As days turned to weeks, she worked herself into such a state of anxious dread, even her aunt noticed.

"Darling, I would have thought you would be in more lively spirits. You haven't seemed yourself at all. Did something happen?" her aunt asked with concern.

It had been a full three weeks, two trips to Almack's, one theatre performance, and countless quarter-hour visits since her ball. Her mother was out to chair a committee, and Lizzie was playing lady of the manor, ordering tea and scones for her aunt.

Lizzie absolutely refused to confess what she'd done, even to her beloved confidante. She pretended to be more interested in dissecting the hypocrisy of various lords and ladies who had crossed their path.

When they had declared themselves superior to all and laughed at themselves for it, her aunt steered the conversation back to her previous question.

"Is it anything to do with David? Your mother favors him, but do you?"

"He's a good match," Lizzie conceded, growing somber. She ought to marry him quickly, before gossip reached him that she had loose morals and deviant habits.

"But you can do better than an *earl*, Lizzie," her aunt insisted. "Especially one in politics. Have you listened to your father at a dinner party? They're dead bores, and you'll only leave London for summers in a country house."

"You're still pushing me toward the marquess?" The challenge burst from her lips while the mere thought of Victor made a streak of angry lightning spark through her. She sat straighter and felt as if her hair stood on end, almost wishing he would expose her and put her out of her misery.

"He's rich, titled, and far more worldly than smug David ever will be." Her aunt didn't pretend not to know which marquess Lizzie referred to. "Your mother is afraid he'll take you away and poison you with confidence and self-reliance. Which is exactly what should happen."

"He's reputed to be a libertine, Auntie." *What does that make me?* Lizzie wondered. She clenched her hands in her lap and looked to the window to hide her guilt from her aunt.

"Young men sow oats. Young women should be allowed to do the same. Why do you think I insisted on your having a proper coming out? I hope you've kissed a few men since."

"Auntie." The heat of a bright, culpable blush suffused her.

Her aunt must have believed kissing was all she'd done, because she only tapped her fan on Lizzie's wrist and said, "Good for you!"

It wasn't good. Lizzie was driving herself mad. At the very least, she needed to know for certain the identity of her lover. If it truly was Victor, she wanted to confront him and learn what he meant to do with his knowledge. Blackmail her?

If it wasn't him but someone else… Her stomach roiled even harder. If it wasn't him, she had no idea what she'd do.

"Is he still in London?" Lizzie sipped her tea, pretending only casual interest, when in fact she had been searching fervently for a sign of him. "I haven't heard any gossip lately or seen him in the park."

"The marquess? He's been indisposed. Or so the prince informs me. I tried every way I could think to get him to your ball, but he didn't come." She *tsk*ed with pity.

While Lizzie choked on the words, *He did. He most certainly did*.

"I'll work on the prince, see if we can arrange an introduction. We have time."

"Are you going to marry him?" Lizzie asked curiously.

"The prince? No, I don't wish to be tied down again. But don't let my aversion deter you, Lizzie. My first husband was a healthy young man who made love to me constantly until his untimely demise. This is how I know you want an experienced, attentive lover. Given his reputation, the marquess definitely is one."

Lizzie bit her tongue against confirming it.

She kept trying to convince herself the golden eggs had made their encounter so remarkable, but she hadn't worn them since. Even so, she continued to suffer debauched thoughts and fantasies about how it would feel to take his hardness into her passage. She woke and caressed herself and even went to her room in the middle of the day to rub away her obsession with finding out how lovemaking with him might feel.

"Even if you arrange an introduction, the marquess won't consider me," Lizzie said, as much to remind herself as curb her aunt's expectations.

"You don't know that."

She did. Victor knew who she was. If he was inclined to court her, he would already be here, speaking to her father. At best, he had decided her easy virtue made her unworthy as his wife. At worst, he would reveal her as aberrant and she would wind up committed.

"Leave it with me," her aunt said with a pat of her knee.

Lizzie bit back a sigh. What else could she do?

• • •

The day after the ball, while lingering over a late breakfast with his uncle, Victor had received a note from the woman he was supposed to have trysted with the night before. She said she was sorry to have missed him and suggested they rendezvous later in the week.

Normally, he would set that up immediately, but he took his

time replying, unsure why. As the week had worn on, he found he had little appetite for her or anyone else. Which wasn't to say he wasn't horny as hell. No, he was in a constant state of erection, but his mind returned again and again to the beguiling Lady Elizabeth.

He longed to feel her golden eggs against his finger again as her pussy clenched, soaked and twitching, while her fist milked him of every ounce of strength in his body.

Why had she been wearing such a thing? Was it an English habit? Victor was sexually experienced, but he'd never encountered anything like it. He was tempted to ask his uncle, but Zio Piero was in a filthy mood.

It crossed Victor's mind to call on Lady Elizabeth or send her a note, but they hadn't been formally introduced. She wasn't the sort of woman he dallied with anyway, despite reports to the contrary. Virgins from well-to-do families expected marriage offers. Victor was content as a bachelor. He wore a sheath to avoid the clap but took every opportunity to enjoy the variety on offer.

Lately his romantic adventures had become very predictable, but Lady Elizabeth had surprised the hell out of him. By all accounts she was a virgin, but one with a sexual curiosity that matched his own.

"Did you take it?"

Victor snapped to an awareness that he was brooding like an operatic castrato. He only needed the accompaniment of a cello to fill out his aria.

"Take what, Zio?" Victor was genuinely perplexed, but perhaps he didn't show his uncle the deference Piero thought he deserved.

Zio Piero's mouth flattened and he shut the library door. He was the older brother of Victor's deceased father and third in line for the throne at home. For most of their lives they had got on well and Victor respected him, but living together in London was testing their relationship. The lion was feeling threatened by the growing cub, and the cub was weary of his uncle's pissy moods.

"The ebony box?" his uncle prodded. "If you took it, say so."

Victor shrugged, completely at a loss. "Have you asked the servants?"

"It's a delicate matter. I arranged for it to be delivered in a hatbox, but she didn't receive it."

"Who? Lady Lavenham?" Oh shit. Victor knew where this was going. Shit, shit, shit.

"Yes. And she hasn't received it, so it's been mislaid. Or someone took it." He narrowed a suspicious gaze on Victor, sensing the wariness that had come over him.

"What exactly was in the box?" Culpability must be coming into his face. Victor knew what had been in the box. He'd *felt* it.

"Charms." His uncle spoke through his teeth, glowering at him. "A goldsmith back home makes them on commission. They're difficult to replace and *very* expensive."

"Egg-shaped," Victor deduced, closing his eyes with comprehension. How had they found their way up the twat of Lady Lavenham's virgin niece?

"You did take them! Where are they?"

Shit, shit, *shit*. If he admitted where he'd found them—which woman, which party—there would be hell to pay all around. Piero would tell Elizabeth's aunt, and Victor couldn't betray her that way. She'd been self-conscious that night but so passionate. Her ardent response had been captivating.

He made the only decision he could.

"I took them," he lied. "I gave them to a woman I was fucking. I can't get them back."

He braced himself, but his uncle's backhand still knocked him to the floor.

•••

When her aunt informed her with great satisfaction that a day of rowing had been arranged at the prince's country house, Lizzie had mixed feelings.

Her usual circle was invited, with the addition of the marquess. Everyone was feverish at the chance to be in his company, but Lizzie had an ache in the pit of her stomach and a hot lump in her throat. Yes, she might be able to reassure herself once and for all whether he intended to expose her to great humiliation, but he might very well make that announcement there.

As she turned up on the shores of a sparkling stretch of river and circulated among the merry group, her belly fluttered with anxious awareness of Victor. He looked very handsome and his silhouette was unmistakable. The way his subtly accented voice teased across her skin when they were introduced convinced her that he surely was the man from the maze.

If that hadn't done it, meeting his gaze would have. His eyes were every bit as dark and liquid as she had remembered them, but her skin tightened as they sustained the stare. He seemed to search her gaze, perhaps wondering if she knew who *he* was?

She had to look away or embarrass herself with a blush of mortified lust. She wasn't wearing the eggs, but his proximity made her feel as though she was. She couldn't do this!

She would make an excuse of illness and ask her aunt to take her home.

But it was too late. Names were being pulled from a hat to determine which lady should occupy which man's boat. To Lizzie's complete lack of surprise, she was paired with Victor while David frowned and helped her friend Clair into his boat.

Victor the Virile removed his coat in preparation for the activity of rowing. His shirt strained across his shoulders, and his waistcoat accentuated his trim waist.

It took everything Lizzie had to pretend disinterest as he helped her into his boat. Her blood was sizzling against the underside of her skin, all her senses heightened. She sat very straight and stiff, unable to look at him.

He settled into position at the oars, nodding to be pushed off.

The agreed upon strategy was to row upstream until the rower tired, then let the water pull them back downstream. The varying strengths of the rowers quickly pulled the boats apart, affording them some privacy.

"Your aunt speaks of you often," Victor said. "It's nice to finally meet you."

She flashed him a look. Did he think he was kidding anyone?

His mouth pursed. "I wondered if you had guessed who I was." He sighed at her affronted glare. His one eye looked bloodshot. "Are you wearing it today?"

"No," she hissed, knees locking together as if she feared he would check.

A pulse of yearning accosted her at the thought of him checking. Looking and touching— She averted her face.

"Why would you ask me that?" she spat.

"My uncle is looking for it," he said dryly. "He intended it for your aunt."

She gasped and covered her mouth with both hands, horrified as she recalled all the gowns, hats, and hose that had been on her aunt's account and delivered to her aunt's house first, before being forwarded to Lizzie. The hatbox with the gift inside it must have been caught up in the confusion.

"Did you tell him?" She was going to jump into that cold, dark water and let herself sink to the bottom.

"No." His mouth twitched. "I said I gave it to a paramour."

Lizzie was instantly, irrationally piqued. "*Who?* A woman in a white dress with green trim, perhaps?"

"I couldn't tell him the truth, could I?" One black brow quirked. "But there is no need to be possessive, *gioia*. I haven't seen anyone else since meeting you. I've been indisposed." His bloodshot eye ticked.

She wanted to deny his accusation of jealousy but realized

there was a lingering puffiness to his eyelid and a faint yellow that might be a fading bruise. Her stomach clenched.

"Did he *strike* you?"

"It doesn't matter," he dismissed.

She swallowed, stunned to realize that while she'd been terrified he would blackmail her or turn her into a laughingstock, he'd actually protected her.

"He shouldn't have resorted to violence."

"It was overdue. I've been needling him. Ignoring his advice. Advice I have decided to take," he said firmly. The way he looked at her became very focused. Intimate. Sensual. As if he was remembering their night, but also— She must be imagining it. He almost seemed to look on her with warmth or fondness.

She was being silly. They barely knew one another.

And yet, in one particular way, they knew each other very well.

Now she was thinking of dunking into the river to cool off. She became lost in watching the flex of his chest and shoulders as he pulled at the oars. His manly strength was drying her mouth and wetting her loins. All she could think about was being with him again. Alone. In the dark.

When she caught him smiling, clearly aware of the direction of her thoughts, she self-consciously brushed at her skirt.

"I presume you offered to pay him back? I'll reimburse you." She could hardly speak, her throat was so tight.

"Let it be my gift to you," he said in a voice that made her feel as though they were back in the hedge maze, driving each other mad with pleasure.

While shivers of anticipation chased over her, hot emotion pressed behind her eyes.

"You're not going to tell anyone?"

He gave one final pull, then drew in the oars and dropped the handles down by his feet, setting his elbows on his thighs as he leaned forward to gaze steadily into her eyes.

"That night was the most singular experience of my life. *I* feel very possessive when I think of anyone else learning how uninhibited and sexually adventurous you are. I want the charms to be an engagement present, Elizabeth."

She sat straighter, astonished. "You don't wish to marry *me*."

"I just said otherwise." He was looking at her as though she were the most fascinating woman alive. "My uncle has been telling me to find a wife. I thought marriage meant settling for someone who would bore me to tears, in and out of the bedroom. I already know we're compatible in one of those areas. I'll make every effort to keep you happy. Shall I talk to your father?"

Her cheeks were trying to pull her unsteady mouth into a joyous smile. She thought of her mother and sent a brief glance at David, who was trying to row his way out of an eddy.

"Yes," she told Victor, wishing she could lean forward and kiss his mouth. "I would like that very much."

• • •

Four months later…

"Show me," her bridegroom demanded as he closed the bedroom door of the house he had leased until they left for Sardinia later this summer.

"Show you what?" she asked over her shoulder, even though she had to cling to the bedpost for balance. She was so mindless with lust, she could hardly speak. "If you think I wore them to the *church*—"

"I know you did." His hands came around her from behind, gently squeezing her breasts as his breath warmed her nape. "You just promised to obey me and I asked you to wear them."

She made a strangled noise of protest and almost didn't hear him say against her skin, "Also you tried to suck my tongue out of my mouth in front of the bishop and your family."

"I'm dying, Victor." She turned in his arms. "I cannot wait to feel you inside me."

"Neither can I." He kissed her with as much urgency as was clawing at her, moving her to the bed to press her back upon the mattress. He lifted her gown to reveal her bare legs and the ribbons that disappeared into her wet curls.

With a groan, he sank to his knees and began to lick and caress, thumbs riding under the ribbons against her skin, parting her swollen folds so he could move his tongue freely against satin and flesh, unerringly finding her nub and making her come with barely little more than the flat of his tongue pressed against it.

She burst apart with one powerful throb after another, her only thought that she could have stayed exactly like this for the rest of their lives, with her fists in his hair and her hips lifting to his avid mouth.

But even though they'd spent the weeks leading up to their wedding kissing and fingering and even licking and sucking when they could manage enough time and privacy, they had teased each other by putting off this one act. She had yet to feel his cock inside her.

He was as impatient for it as she was. He left off circling his tongue around her pulsing nub as she was beginning to feel the tingles of arousal mount anew. He rose and gently eased the eggs from her pussy, then used one to trace her flesh, not allowing her to close her legs against his blatant scrutiny. Around and around he went, telling her how pretty she was. How she filled him with lust for all the things they would do to one another.

"One day," he told her as he bent her knee and opened her legs farther. "I'll push these into your ass and we'll see if you like it as much."

"Maybe I'll push them up yours," she said on a gasp of wicked anticipation.

"Maybe you will." He dropped the egg and bared his cock, not bothering to finish undressing either of them before he notched the head of his cock against her entrance. It was easily twice the size of the eggs put together and not nearly so shiny smooth.

She bit her lip as she felt the pressure of his flesh demanding admittance to hers.

"Maybe I'll even fuck you when they're inside you."

The idea caused a gush of wetness from her, but she gasped, "You're too big. There isn't room."

"Fuck, you're right," he groaned as he backed off before pressing in a little more.

She tensed, waiting for the pain she'd heard was inevitable, but there was only a small sting of stretch and an enormous sensation of being spread open. Breached by heat and strength as he sank deeper and deeper.

His arms were straight as he held himself above her. "You're so fucking tight. Can you take more?" He was being careful. Tender. He dropped his head to kiss her. "Does it hurt?"

"No, it feels..."

He sank a final inch and his nest of curls were against the delicate tissues that were stretched to accommodate him. His flesh twitched inside her.

"It feels like the eggs," she breathed in dazzlement, clenching around him and feeling him pulse in response. "Only better."

A dark smile widened his lips and he began to fuck her in earnest.

The End

One Night
with a Duke

One Night with a Duke features a married woman, who is sexually intimate with a man other than her husband, and while this is consensual between all persons involved, readers who may be sensitive to this, please take note.

CHAPTER ONE

W hen her husband told Clara they'd been invited to stay at the Duke of Covington's country estate on their way back to Rosewick, she assumed they were part of a large party but the massive stone hall looked deserted as the carriage drew to a halt in front of it.

"The thing is, Clara," Eddie said with his most remorseful brow-crinkle. "I'm in debt to a creditor. The duke has offered to bail me out."

Clara's heart copied the carriage as it jerked to a halt, then swayed in her chest like a pendulum while a cold sensation swept over her. Everything dimmed to profound silence.

"H-how? Why?"

He didn't get the chance to answer. A footman trotted out to open the door. A warm, summer-laden breeze wafted in. Eddie cleared his throat and exited. He stationed himself across from the footman and held out his hand to help her, but his gaze swept over the other man's livery.

The young man was admittedly handsome with a dark brown complexion, solid shoulders, and a tall bearing. If he returned Eddie's interest, he was subtle about it—not that it was any business of hers. She'd known about Eddie's partialities to men since before she understood his desires were supposed to be wrong.

There wasn't a wrong bone in Eddie's body. He was a dear, sweet, caring man who had saved her from penury. Their marriage was a meeting of minds, not bodies, and together they had managed to cling to Eddie's small, entailed estate.

Or so she'd thought. Her stomach roiled with misgiving. Normally they told each other everything. She wished he'd been more forthcoming about *this*.

She took in Scarsdale Hall towering three stories above her. The front was dominated by six massive columns and three tall windows on either side. From the wide entrance doors, a pair of curving staircases came down like arms. She couldn't tell if they were reaching out in a welcome embrace, or attempting to seize her and drag her into its maw.

The footman directed them up the right-hand side and showed them through a silent marble hall filled with alabaster columns. It was lit by a dome of glass that threw splashes of color across the floor. He brought them to a library where books lined the walls of two floors and announced, "Lord and Lady Halton, the Baron and Baroness of Rosewick."

Tall and broad shouldered, the duke rose and came around from behind a massive desk. He buttoned his coat over his green waistcoat and buff leather breeches. The starched collar of his shirt stood in points against his clean-shaven jaw.

Clara should have been mindful of the power he held over both of them, but she stared openly, startled by recognition. She'd seen him a month ago in London while she had been browsing the Pantheon Bazaar. She couldn't afford any of the jewelry or dresses, but it had given her something to do while Eddie took his meetings, trying to better their situation.

Somehow, she had wound up in the back of a stall full of novelties from the Far East. She'd poked through a basket of fur scraps, withdrawing an object that had mystified her. The polished marble had a girth about the size of her two crossed fingers and was about as long as her hand. One end flared and went abruptly flat, as though it was meant to be stood upright on display. The rest was a smooth rod with a tip that flared to a worn plum-like bulb—

It was a phallus!

She had nearly dropped it, she was so shocked. It wasn't like the small dangling thing she'd seen on a statue. This one was erect.

She ought to have shoved it back into the furs, but curiosity had gripped her. She hadn't gotten a good look at Eddie the few times they'd had intercourse. She was fascinated.

More importantly, though, why did such a thing exist? Did people—women—purchase them? Congress with Eddie had been awkward and distinctly uncomfortable. She didn't understand why anyone would penetrate herself intentionally.

Yet she had found herself caressing the phallus with her gloved fingertips, imagining the feel of it pushing into her channel. A strange, pulsing heat had come to life in the notch between her thighs. A dark craving to try it and see how it would feel.

At that lascivious thought, she had come to her senses and thrust it deep beneath the scraps of fur, glancing around guiltily to be sure she hadn't been observed.

She had. Her stomach had dropped to her toes as she realized a well-dressed man had been watching her from beneath half-lowered eyelids. He gave her a slow, knowing smile, one that made her cheeks catch fire with mortification while her nipples tightened and that low ache intensified.

He wasn't handsome in the way Eddie was, with long lashes and curly hair and fine-boned features. This other man's hair was black, his face rough-hewn, his nose hawkish and fierce. Even his mouth had a brutish look to it. He stood close enough she could tell that his eyes were blue. Such a vivid blue, she fancifully thought that shards of the sky must have broken away and struck him as he fell like an archangel from the heavens.

The proprietor had swooped over to ask in an alarmed voice if she needed assistance. He had quickly thrust the basket under a table and she had made her escape, hoping to never see that stranger's smirk again.

But now, here he was.

It wasn't easy to hold that knowing gaze of his. He was a *duke* for heaven's sake! One to whom Eddie might soon be indebted. But she had learned to be self-assured when her father had been ill. Then Eddie had taken her in and, well-meaning as he was, was forever being taken advantage of. *She* was the one who had to be firm with the staff and chase up late rent payments from the farmers, so she managed to keep her chin high and pretend she wasn't dying inside.

"Your Grace," Eddie said with a nervous glance at the footman who left them and closed the door. "I'd like you to meet my wife, Clara."

She held her breath, wondering if the duke would reveal that he'd seen her in a most compromising situation.

He only took her fingertips and bowed over her hand. "An honor."

Was it? Her palm was clammy inside the glove, but the heat of his touch penetrated and left her fingers tingling as he released her.

"Sit. Tea will take time. Most of my staff is at my newly acquired estate in Somerset. Once they have things in hand there, they'll be back, but I wanted privacy for this conversation."

"Your wife is there? Or joining us?" Clara asked nervously.

"She passed two years ago. Pneumonia."

"I'm so sorry."

The men waited until Clara had sunk onto the edge of a settee. Eddie sat beside her. The duke took the throne-like chair to her right.

"How much do you know of your husband's situation?" the duke asked without preamble.

Clara longed to say, *Everything*, but the truth was, "Only that he owes a sum of money and you've offered to cover it."

"Eighteen thousand pounds. And no, that's not what I said."

She did everything in her power to keep the shock off her face, but that was nearly ten times Eddie's annual income! She went cold all over and the duke no doubt saw how she paled. Bright sunlight streamed in from the south-facing windows. He probably spent eighteen thousand pounds in window tax alone, but she was absolutely sickened. They had no means of repaying such a sum!

"You've never been a gambler," she murmured in bewilderment to her husband. "Have you?"

Eddie was green beneath his normally creamy complexion. "It was an investment," he mumbled. "Supposed to be a sure thing."

"Don't judge him too harshly," the duke said. "The man who took his money was a charlatan. He duped many. I've put pressure where I can to bring him to justice, but the scoundrel has fled to the continent. It's doubtful the funds will be recovered."

"I see." She was amazed her voice worked. All she could feel in her chest was gravel. Her pulse quivered in her throat like a hummingbird's wings. "Did you also lose money?"

"No," he scoffed.

Silly Clara. How could she think such a man would be so stupid?

"Are you having this conversation with all of the victims?"

"No."

"Why not?"

A faint smile pulled at the corners of his mouth before he set his finger along the line of his lips. "You're very direct."

"Are you not?"

One dark eyebrow went up at her temerity, but she kept her spine straight, her gaze level, and hoped he didn't notice she was sucking in her stomach so hard she could barely breathe.

"Your husband got drunk at Brook's a week ago. The sort of drunk where he was confiding things that shouldn't be revealed without due regard for the consequences. You may not remember all you said."

Eddie was glowing with a sweat of panic.

"I ensured our conversation was kept between us," the duke said with a casual flick of his hand. "But you were concerned for your wife. You said you had promised her a secure future and showed me her portrait inside your pocket watch. I decided I had to meet her."

His gaze swung back to Clara. She understood he had decided to meet the woman he'd seen fondling a stone member in public. All things considered, revealing her brazen behavior wasn't the worst thing that could happen to her right now, but she still felt the way a mouse must when cornered by a cat—the kind too lazy to do her in quickly, not when he could taunt and toy with her first.

"I'd like to offer you fifty thousand pounds to achieve the security you both desire. All of your debts would be cleared. Future worries would be resolved. You could begin spending the season in London."

"What would you get? The estate?" Eddie frowned. "It's entailed."

"I would like one night."

The chill that hadn't left Clara's chest intensified, turning her limbs to ice and seeming to freeze her lungs solid.

"To do *what*?" Eddie asked with not nearly the level of outrage one might expect.

Clara dropped her gaze, already knowing the answer. The duke thought her some sort of trollop because he'd seen her acting so improperly. She was mortified and overcome with trepidation. He didn't look the type to be apologetic and quick when he mounted a woman. More like he would expect things she couldn't even fathom.

Her mind batted like a fly at a window, urgent for an escape, but there wasn't one.

"To do whatever I want." She heard the dark humor in the duke's voice as he replied blithely. "With your wife."

Her heart lurched while Eddie shot to his feet.

"Your *Grace*." Eddie's hand protectively landed on her shoulder. "I'd rather lose my estate."

"Eddie." Clara covered his hand, reeling, but she couldn't let him make things worse by calling out a man of the duke's station. Eddie in a duel? She would be widowed in the blink of an eye.

"No, Clara," Eddie said emphatically. "I would *never* ask you to do such a thing."

"You're not asking," she pointed out weakly. "His Grace is."

For a moment, there was only the distant tick of the clock on the mantel on the far side of the room. The duke didn't move, but she sensed a wave of intense satisfaction emanate off him.

"You're not considering this," Eddie huffed with disbelief.

She was, but her heart was thunking so loudly in her ears she thought her skull would crack. Women did worse for far less.

"It bears considering. It's very generous." It was only one night.

"It's bribery. Extortion. He knows we're in dire straits."

"Would you accept another arrangement, Your Grace?" Her voice was even, if faint.

"Do you have one to offer?" he asked with polite interest.

She didn't. Only a request for a loan that would be paid off in pitifully small amounts. It would mean at least the next few Barons of Rosewick would struggle worse than they did.

Whereas, she could spend a single night with a stranger and completely resolve all their most pressing problems. What would he do to her?

"One night?" she clarified, curling her fist in the folds of her skirt. "Will you..." She cleared her throat. "Will you be more specific as to what it would entail?"

"Since you've asked me to be direct... I want *you*. Naked. In my bed. Submitting to my every carnal desire."

Her skin tightened and there was an inexplicable quiver in her intimate flesh, like the vibration of a plucked harp string.

She shouldn't feel this wicked tug of curiosity in her belly as she held his steady gaze. What sort of woman was intrigued by the idea of spending a night with a man who wasn't her husband? With this particular man? She had the sense there was darkness in him. Not evil, but profligacy. He was exploiting her, wasn't he? He could ruin her in a thousand ways.

But she stood on the brink of ruin regardless.

Eddie took a half step to insert himself between them. "I won't have you debasing her for my mistake."

"There won't be any debasement, Edward." The corner of the duke's mouth dug in with that same knowing smile he'd worn the day at the bazaar, his gaze not leaving hers. "She'll enjoy every moment as much as I do. Isn't it time she did?"

Now his gaze rose to Eddie's.

"That's unkind." Clara pushed Eddie aside and rose, feeling her husband take her by the arms so they were one unit.

"Is it not the truth, Lady Halton?" The duke spoke her title facetiously, as though he knew exactly how superficial some parts of her marriage were. "Edward seemed to think that night at the club that he was failing to satisfy you."

It should have made her indignant that her drunken husband had been so loose-lipped, but she suffered a pang of melancholy. Longing. The way she'd felt at the bazaar. As though there were secrets to learn if she dared move past her own inhibitions.

She linked her hands before her, refusing to beseech him, but she had to stand up for dear Eddie. She could tell by the way he was clenching her arms that he was wondering what else he might have revealed.

"If you're serious about not being abusive, you will not insult either of us," Clara said with far more hauteur than she was entitled to, given the circumstances.

"Forgive me." He was droll now, still seated, legs crossed negligently. "When I want something, I become ruthless about getting it."

He wanted her? Enough to be ruthless about it? Her stomach flip-flopped in further consternation.

"I have a gift for you," he coaxed in an intimate tone. It was as if Eddie had ceased to exist and they were alone. "If you accept."

She knew he was talking about the phallus. The lewd ache it had provoked in her that day returned tenfold, making her intimate flesh pulse wantonly while the rest of her flushed with shameful heat. Why did she respond so acutely? The phallus had felt cold and heavy, not seductive at all, but something deep inside her tightened like a fist, yearning to clench around it. Her breasts tingled and the heat suffusing her became more than embarrassment. It was libidinous. *Lust.*

"Clara." Eddie squeezed her arm. "Don't even think it. We'll find another way."

"I—" She licked her lips, aware of a culpable hunger teasing her throat and filling her chest and ringing low inside her. "I want to."

Eddie sucked in a breath of shock. When she looked at him, his gaze dropped. He knew how dismal their bedchamber was as well as she did.

She wanted to reassure him, but the duke spoke again.

"Tonight." His tone was crisp and sharp, his attention honed on her. The energy in his body shifted from watchful tension to a readiness to pounce. It was distressing…but exciting. "I leave for France in a few days."

"I'm at your disposal," she said with as much confidence as she could muster, even as her knees grew weak.

CHAPTER TWO

This was the moment of no return.

The footman opened the door to the bedroom as if he showed women—gently born married ladies—into his master's chambers all the time. It was enough to make Clara's feet turn to blocks of stone.

The glow of the small fire drew her, though, the same way a moth might be lured. Did those silly creatures know what they were in for? She wasn't sure she did.

The door closed behind her, leaving her with only the knocking of her heart in her chest.

"It's only one night," she had reminded Eddie when they'd been shown to their rooms.

"It's indecent. I didn't exactly prepare you for anything like this." He gave his dejected face a swipe with an anxious hand.

"It's a chance for a life free of constant worry." She was trying to focus on that and the duke's promise there would be no debasement.

She ought to feel debased regardless, but there was a part of her that was intrigued. Shame nipped at her when she acknowledged that. She was breaking her wedding vows, entering this room that smelled of masculine scents like hair powder and cigar smoke and a faint whiff of spicy soap, but despite all that, she was here voluntarily.

As she stared into the fire, a flutter of anticipation, delicate as butterfly wings, filled her middle. Lower, even. Her pulse hammered in her wrists and throat and *there*, between her legs.

Which only mortified her further.

The blaze died to a mellow glow that cast ominous shadows into the corners and across the mattress of the wide bed. She couldn't see much else. Wallpaper with a stripe, an ornate mantel with a clock upon it, ticking quietly. A chair with a velvet footstool. A table that held a tray, a glass, and a bottle of brandy.

A side door opened and the duke entered, wearing a quilted banyan that closed on the right side of his chest. His hair was damp, his bare feet in slippers. A scent of freshly washed skin came in with him.

She had bathed, too. It had felt odd to do so, taking her time with it as though preparing herself for something special. For him. Each stroke of the cloth across her skin had been an admission that she wanted to be at her best when she was naked before him. That she wanted his hands on her body and his thrusts inside her.

She dropped her gaze to hide those betraying thoughts, trying to catch her breath.

"So shy," he mocked. "As though you've never seen a man in nightclothes before."

Words tangled on her tongue. Something about how unusual it was to see a stranger this way. To be in her own dressing gown as they met for…

"What exactly is going to happen?" she asked huskily.

"That's part of the excitement, isn't it? The not knowing?"

She lifted her chin, frowning at him, but stopped short of denying it because that piercing sensation was back, making her inner muscles tighten—which was deeply confusing.

His slow smile seemed to reach out and wrap around her, squeezing her breath from her lungs. "My impression is that you're often burdened with taking the lead. Allow me. See if you like it."

"Trust you?"

"Yes. Is that the nightdress I gave you? Take off the dressing gown. Let me see it."

To call the sheer muslin confection a "dress" was to call a cloud a wall. His note had read, *Wear only this.* She had half expected the phallus when she opened the box, so she'd done as he asked but balked at revealing it.

"Clara." His voice emanated from deep in his chest. It was both endearment and warning, strumming that fervent tension inside her.

"I don't even know your name. Perhaps if we get in the bed first?"

He closed in on her and took her jaw in a gentle grip, tilting her face up toward the light from the fire. His hand was warm from his bath, each fingertip seeming to brand her skin.

"My name is Stephen, but don't call me that. It reminds me of a tutor I hated. My friends call me Covey, but don't call me that, either." He shifted his touch to gently pinch her bottom lip from either side. "I don't want to think of anyone but you right now. As I have since the day I saw you discover your sexual curiosity." His finger and thumb squeezed a tiny bit more, not hurting but firmly plumping her lip. "I've been obsessed about finding you and witnessing your explorations of that part of yourself ever since. So kindly do exactly as I say and remove your dressing gown."

She started to draw back a step, but he didn't let her. Their gazes clashed as she asked a silent, *Now? Like this?* With his hot hand making her mouth feel swollen and tender?

She moved her trembling hands between them, the backs of her knuckles grazing the cool silk of his banyan, aware of the firmness of his torso beneath.

When she let her dressing gown fall down her arms and to the floor, he finally released her and said, "Yes. Come by the fire." He moved to feed a few sticks of kindling into it so it flared brightly, illuminating her nudity beneath the gown.

The exposure made her feel intensely vulnerable, especially when he shifted the chair and sat, kicking one foot onto the stool while he unabashedly ran his gaze all over her.

"Take down your hair."

It was only loosely gathered for her bath. She did, aware

that it caused her breasts to thrust against the thin muslin. She didn't want to think of how the tips must be as clear as a dark pinch of nutmeg on cream. That her nipples must be standing up against the fine fabric.

"Lovely. Now fondle your breasts."

"Why?"

"Do you not feel a desire to?"

"*No.*"

He frowned. "You're not a virgin?"

"I'm married," she reminded.

He tilted his head in consideration. "You've consummated your marriage but haven't made love. Is that correct?"

Was there a difference? "You're being very personal," she said and crossed her arms.

"I haven't even started," he assured her and chucked his chin at her. "Do as I say. Hold your breasts. Weigh them in your palms."

Think of fifty thousand pounds, she thought, but that wasn't her motive. Despite her discomfiture, her whole body tingled in a way that made her want to use her hands to smooth the sensations away. She shyly covered her breasts with her splayed hands and, without thinking, massaged lightly, trying to appease the orbs that felt swollen and hot.

"Don't close your eyes. Look at me while you do it. Play with your nipples. Pinch them."

It was both mortifying and exciting, watching his lashes flick as he swept his attention to her hands, down to the shadow of her thatch at her thighs, then back up to her flushed face. When she pinched her nipples, the heaviness in her loins grew. Her mind traveled to caressing herself there, too, to soothe, which felt like a very wicked thought. She bit her lip, hoping he couldn't read her mind.

"Are you wet?" he asked in a low growl.

"From the bath?"

He husked a laugh that was almost cruel and rolled his wrist to beckon her closer. "That wasn't what I meant, sweet thing. Your pussy. Are you wet here?"

With one hand he took hold of her nightdress and pushed his fist between her knees, forcing her legs apart so the thin fabric pressed taut against her loins, blatantly revealing her mound.

She *was* wet there. She felt the change in temperature as the cotton grew damp. Latent moisture from the bath? It didn't matter why. Wet muslin hid nothing, especially if it sat flush against a part of her body she'd never examined as closely as he was doing right now. She trembled in both apprehension and... arousal?

"Do you feel a desire to touch yourself here?"

So much. There was a dull agony throbbing there that called to her like a drumbeat, but she couldn't bring herself to admit it.

"Trust me. Hide nothing and I promise I will reward you," he said in that voice like earth and coffee and sin.

"Yes," she admitted reluctantly. "I want to touch myself there."

He shifted slightly so he could lean forward. He used both hands to carefully roll the front of her nightdress up and up and up, until she was completely bare to him from the waist down. Her thighs trembled as he pressed one of her own hands over the bunch of cotton, pinning it to her middle.

"Touch yourself. Lightly. Follow the line of your lips... Yes, like that. Slowly."

It wasn't enough. It made it worse. The faint, tickling touch of her fingertip caused the yearning sensation to deepen.

His foot went back onto the stool, his other knee crooked and splayed wide. He pushed his hand into the opening of his robe and she realized he was caressing himself as he watched her. A fresh rush of damp heat released, and her inner muscles reacted in a pinch to try to catch it back.

"Press a little harder," he commanded. "So your lips part."

They both moaned slightly as she did. It felt better. Good.

Really good.

"Follow down to where you're wettest, then spread that slickness around."

She did, hitting a place that caused such an intense shock of pleasure, she jolted and gasped.

"You've never done this to yourself?"

"No." She was barely able to comprehend words or form them as she rolled the tip of her middle finger over the small bump where all of paradise seemed to be located.

"I know you want that, Clara, but do exactly as I say. Go back to your opening. Push your finger inside yourself, as far as you can. Does it hurt?"

"No," she breathed as she explored the hot, slick channel that ached so.

"How does it feel?"

"Good." She wriggled her finger as much as she could and used the heel of her hand to press that place at the top of her sex. "But not as good as the other."

He smiled. "Go back to the top of your notch."

She did, moaning with relief as she rubbed firmly on that swollen bud. This was remarkable!

"You like that."

"I do," she admitted helplessly, varying the pressure and speed, seeking the most intense spikes of pleasure between the waves.

"Stop," he commanded. "Remove your nightdress."

A sob of deprivation left her. Betrayal. She didn't want to be at his mercy, but she did as he asked, even stepping out of her slippers in hopes he would let her go back to relieving the throb in her loins.

He shifted to pull something from the pocket of his banyan. The edges parted to reveal his turgid sex, thick and dark, the tense shape of him arrowing up from a nest of hair toward his belly. His bollocks hung heavily between his open thighs.

She ought to have been terrified, but her intimate flesh clenched in a fresh, silent cry of longing. She swallowed.

He withdrew the phallus from his pocket, but didn't bother closing the edges of his banyan. Rather, he lined the marble replica alongside the real thing. It was significantly smaller than his.

"A more ladylike size than a real cock, but it's meant to be versatile. I warmed it in the bath for you. Put your foot here." He patted the narrow space on the chair next to his hip.

He expected her to expose herself so blatantly? She had never thought herself a debaucherous person, but the fleshly pleasures he had offered so far were an inducement. And there was something deeply satisfying in watching his cruel mouth soften into a libertine smile when she did as he ordered.

He hadn't even used that mouth to kiss her! In fact, he'd barely touched her and she was naked and doing vulgar things at his command.

"Part your lips for me."

She did, fingers trembling. He took his time tracing the path her fingertip had taken with the hard, warm bulb on the tip of the marble phallus. He circled it first over the nub at the top, then gently forced it against her entrance.

She tensed, expecting the pain of lovemaking, but her wetness allowed it to slide in easily. It was heavy and deep and *so* hard. Her eyelashes fluttered.

"Tell me how you like that." He used his hand to hold its flared base against her flesh. His thumb played across the tender, slippery tissues that surrounded the implacable penetration.

"I like it...very much." She caught her breath as he skimmed his thumb across that beautiful, tiny knot of heaven.

"Play with your breasts. Move however you need."

She did, swaying weakly and discovering the shape of the phallus shifted inside her as she moved, pressing and caressing, intensifying everything. When she pulled at her nipples, her inner muscles gripped onto the phallus and the most incredible need filled her.

"C-Covey," she managed to gasp.

"You've never been this aroused?"

"No. And I don't think I can bear it—"

He leaned forward and replaced the rough pad of his thumb with the hot, wet circling of his tongue. He *sucked* on her.

She did the only thing she could. She grabbed the back of his head to stay upright and ground her hips into his face, screaming as she came apart.

CHAPTER THREE

Covey was a gentleman. He carried her to the bed, careful to keep her thighs together so the phallus stayed inside her.

She was still trembling and dazed when he threw off his banyan and joined her.

She kissed like a novice, but she wasn't prudish. When he thrust his tongue between her lips, the taste of her still in his mouth, she unabashedly sucked in a way that had him groaning at the effort to keep himself under control.

Everything in him wanted to withdraw that false prick and insert his own to pound away this itch that had been nagging at him since the day he'd seen a *lady*, in *public*, caress a tool for ass-fucking while wearing a dreamy smile.

It had taken a few weeks of discreet inquiries to learn who she was then cross paths with her husband at one of the clubs. The part where the Baron of Rosewick had tried to drink himself to death, mumbling about debts and "the only true friend he'd ever had" and his sexual preferences? That had been pure chance. Divine luck.

Covey *was* ruthless. Secrets were power and he never let an opportunity go by, but he drew the line at destroying lives simply because he could.

Once he'd realized her husband didn't give her the pleasure she clearly desired, he'd been determined to take up that cause. He could have seduced Lady Halton and left her to the destitution her husband was headed toward, but she didn't seem to deserve utter ruin.

He'd struck upon the idea of requesting a night of pleasure. Eighteen thousand pounds would only take the pair back to the edge of insolvency. He'd sweetened the pot to get what he wanted. Because he wanted *a lot*.

"Was that your first orgasm?" he asked between their languorous kisses.

She blinked at him, flushed and sated the way a woman ought to look when she was in a man's bed. Her arms were loosely twined around his neck, her body pliant and lovely.

"I thought only men did that." She looked down between them. "But you didn't. I thought you said I would enjoy it as much as you did."

"I enjoyed your pleasure very much. And we're far from finished, but I want to ask you a few questions first. When you first saw this…" He slid his hand down her stomach to where the marble protruded from her sheath. He gently withdrew it, pleased by the heat it retained and the glistening coat it wore. He touched the tip to each of her nipples, coating them in her flavor. "What did you think it was?"

"I didn't know. I guessed it was for sexual purposes, but I didn't know why anyone would want to do that."

"Now you do." He dipped his head and suckled each of her nipples clean.

"Now I do," she agreed on a luxurious moan as he took his time returning to the first breast and lingered there.

"I believe it's meant to be used elsewhere, though." He lifted his head, then set a kiss on her chin as he waited for her reaction.

"Where?" She frowned in confusion before her eyes popped wide. "The bottom?"

"You've never done anything like that?"

"No! With who?" She quickly pinned her mouth shut and her brows lowered in suspicion.

He kept his face deliberately empty of expression, not willing to betray her husband if she didn't know how he leaned. Or bent, as it were. Her reaction when he'd remarked on her husband's inability to satisfy her could have simply been loyalty.

But she knew, he realized. And she was realizing that *he* knew.

"If your curiosities lie in that direction, you've picked the wrong Halton to invite into your bed," she said with tart humor.

He chuckled and ran a hand from her breast to her mound, touching the fine hairs that were damp with her latent arousal. His cock quivered and his nostrils flared, seeking more of her scent.

"I am curious," he admitted. "But I'm too enamored with tits and cunt to bed a man. Yours are particularly fascinating." She was sensually curved and responsive enough to shift restlessly under his caress as he swept his hand over her body. "The way you smell and feel and moan is intoxicating."

"Thank you for saying that." She petted the hairs on his breastbone, bottom lip quivering. "Eddie doesn't find me—any woman—attractive in this way. I didn't mind when I didn't know what I was missing, but..."

Her light touch went lower, grazing the twitching tip of his cock. She discovered the pearl of semen and absently painted it around his head with a single fingertip—driving him insane and likely not having any sense of it.

"He won't give me a baby, either. Which I thought was best while finances have been so dire, but... You could finish inside me, if you like," she offered with bashful sweetness, bringing her gaze up to his. "Unless— Do you have an heir?"

"And a spare." A barony in the north was a decent situation for a third son of a duke, if it came to that. "And I will come inside you if you want me to, but I want to come in your mouth first."

Her pretty mouth went lax as her jaw dropped open in shock.

"You asked me to be direct, Clara."

"And you asked me to do as I was told." That magical inquisitive smile pulled at the edges of her lips.

He bit back a groan of anticipation and dropped onto his back. She ran a questing hand across his chest, pulling up her palm when she scraped across his beaded nipple and he sucked in a breath.

"I'm sorry. Should I not touch you like that?"

"Do whatever you want. I'll let you know if I don't like it."

She rose on an elbow and kissed his mouth, beneath his chin and into his throat. Her hair spilled across his chest as she licked at each of his nipples. Sucked them.

He gritted his teeth, wanting that stimulation on his aching cock, but she took her time getting there, breasts brushing his swollen member as she painted a line with her tongue down his middle before shifting to kneel between his legs. After a brief, puzzled look, she dabbed a few hesitant licks at the length of his shaft.

His cock twitched and he pulled a pillow under his head so he could watch.

"You don't have to be so careful," he growled when she apprehensively wrapped a finger and thumb around the base of his cock. "Use your whole hand. A tight grip is nicer."

She met his gaze as she squeezed him.

"And move it up and down," he coached.

She did, watching as the skin gathered and pulled against his head. Her movements drew a fresh bead of milk to the eye of his cock and she lowered her head to flick at it with her tongue.

He groaned, then groaned again as she licked her lips and seemed to weigh whether or not she enjoyed the flavor. She gave him that witchy smile again right before she took him into her mouth.

In the same way she'd picked up kissing very quickly, she explored with her tongue, learning how he felt in all corners of her mouth. She tried to take him down her throat, gagged, and he soothed her, petting her hair and giving her pointers about keeping her teeth out of the way. It was both the sweetest and most torturous experience of his life. He loved it.

Her tongue discovered the tip of the arrow and he grunted. She seemed to understand immediately that digging her tongue against that spot would drive him wild.

It did. *And that,* he thought dimly, *was worth fifty thousand pounds.*

Her free hand drifted down to explore the shape of his bollocks, stimulating them into contracting. The tingle of climax beckoned. He fought it, not ready to lose this pleasure so soon.

She stopped. Sat up on her heels, one hand still fisted around his shaft. "You said I should do whatever I want."

"Yes," he said raggedly, uncertain how he'd allowed himself to wind up so completely at her mercy.

Her free hand reached out for the phallus. She sucked the bulb into her mouth.

That wasn't the sort of curiosity he'd had. He'd wanted to insert it into her ass, but as she fucked the decoy prick between her lips, coating it in spittle, a forbidden thrill kept him silent. In fact, he drew his knees up.

A moment later, there was a kiss of wetness and pressure. It threatened pain and felt instinctually wrong, but his cock hardened more than ever. All of him was going taut with excitement as the phallus entered him.

"Fuck!" He couldn't help the near shouted profanity. An intense sensation fluttered directly from where the phallus brushed something inside him.

"Should I not—"

"Keep it there. *Fuck.*"

She dipped her head and her hair caressed his stomach and thighs. Her mouth returned to anointing his cock. Her hand bobbed up and down his shaft in the same rhythm as her head. The texture of her tongue swept along the sensitive point on the underside of his cockhead while that fullness in his ass made every sensation so acute, he felt his entire being seem to gather like a storm. He couldn't contain the force.

"*Fuuuck,*" he shouted as he spurted his come deep into the back of her throat.

CHAPTER FOUR

lara left the phallus in the wash basin as she rinsed her mouth. She wasn't sure what to do after that. When she glanced at the bed, the duke had his arm across his eyes. His abdomen was still shaking, his chest heaving with unsteady breaths. His sex was still elongated, but spent and lax against his thigh.

She was pleased she'd given him such pleasure. Fifty thousand pounds worth, hopefully, but she was despondent, too. It wasn't because she was feeling debased by this arrangement, either. She probably should be questioning her morals, but she would have done all of this for free, it was such an incredible experience.

She was blue, though, because she had thought he was genuinely attracted to her. It was just her luck to become mixed up with another man who had yearnings for other men. Did they all? Or did she turn them that way?

"The night isn't over yet." He sounded positively lethal.

She hugged the nightdress she'd absently picked up and shrugged defensively. "I wasn't sure…"

He slid his arm to the edge of the mattress, fingers crooking to draw her closer.

She kept the protective shield of the thin material in front of her and allowed herself a moment to memorize the virile state of him, all wide shoulders and powerful chest, his flat stomach and thickly muscled thighs. She had never considered the male form beautiful, but she felt rather weak, looking at him lying there, satiated by her bawdy act.

"You enjoyed that?" she asked timidly.

"I think that's obvious. Did you?"

"Yes." It had been exhilarating to steal that moment of control and undo him so thoroughly. "But I really do think you invited the wrong Halton," she added sadly.

"Do you." His eyes narrowed and he tugged at the muslin until it was dragged from her grip and fell to the floor. "I don't like my words to be second-guessed. I should spank you for it." He dragged the pillow from beneath his head and threw it away. "But I'm too weak from having my cock sucked dry. Are you aroused? Put your hands on the wall." He glanced toward the headboard. "I'll bring you off."

"What?" Her hands had tightened into fists of protest at the threat of being spanked, but her thighs pinched together at the same time, trying to ease the streak of excitement that pulsed there. Now she was utterly confused.

"I said I wish to correct your misguided assumption about the sort of partner I desire. Toying with my arse was a delightful experience, but it's not something I'll request often. Eating, however, is necessary for my very survival." He licked his lips. "Put your hands on the crosspiece and sit on my face."

"You're not serious!"

"A spank or a thank, darling. Your choice."

She obediently moved onto the bed, kneeling beside him before she hesitated again, unsure about more than an awkward physical position. She frowned at her own hands tangling in her lap.

He slid his arm alongside her thigh and caressed her hip in a surprisingly tender gesture. "You're really bothered by my enjoyment of that? Why did you do it, then?"

"I don't know," she mumbled miserably. "To test you, maybe?"

"And I failed?" One of his dark brows went up in offense. "I plan to use that thing on you, you know. Maybe fuck you in the ass proper. Not tonight. Another time. It doesn't mean I want to fuck men. It means I want to fuck *you* in every way I can think of. I want to fuck your tits as badly as I want to fuck your cunt. Can't do either of those things with a man."

Her belly swirled in wicked delight at the potent things he was saying, but, "There won't be another time," she reminded in a near whisper. He was leaving for France. She was headed north.

He went very still, not saying anything. His cheek ticked.

She bit the inside of her cheek and felt a different sort of sadness. A wistful yearning to have unlimited time with him. It was impossible. She was married. This wasn't a love affair, just a night of bawdiness in exchange for a future that suddenly looked very empty.

"Come," he coaxed with a nudge of his hand against her hip. "Ride as long as you like. I never tire of it."

• • •

Covey left Clara dozing in his bed and moved to rinse her essence from his face. She'd come four times, each more powerful than the last and all with complete lack of inhibition. She had ground her cunt against his chin and lips and tongue in a way that had had his cock recovering faster than he ever had before.

He gave it a squeeze. His hand was cold from the water, which cooled his ardor a few degrees. Enough he could think past the urgency that had released into his blood when she'd said, *There won't be another time.*

Why did that bother him? He'd taken married women as paramours several times since his own wife had died. His very first lover, before he married, had been a countess who'd been well into her thirties, eager to teach a young man of eighteen the fine art of making a woman scream with pleasure.

It had been more than an act of generosity or affection. She'd used her sexual wiles to manipulate him into marrying her niece. He'd been young enough to fall for it.

At least she'd been correct in that securing his title at an early age had left him free to do as he liked in his thirties. He was stalked by matrons eager to pin him to their young charges, but he wasn't under the same pressure to marry as other men his age.

Covey hadn't enjoyed marriage. He'd vowed to be faithful and was, but despite his best efforts to seduce his wife, she'd been lukewarm. She hadn't liked him to eat her muff and had little interest in exploring other pleasures.

As things had declined, he'd grown into the cynical bastard he was today, paying a perfectly charming woman to sit on his face and shove a chunk of marble up his ass.

"If you..." she spoke hesitantly. He'd thought she was asleep but now realized she'd been watching him. "If you want to do that to me, in the bottom, I'll let you. This is your night, not mine."

It was as much her night as his and he didn't hear desire in her voice. More like sacrifice. He *did* want to do that to her, but she seemed in deep need of being appreciated as the woman she was.

He moved to the fire and fed it a few sticks of kindling so the room brightened and warmed once again. Her eyes were wide and vulnerable, her bottom lip caught between her teeth.

He joined her and tucked her beneath him, one thigh pinning hers, bracing himself on his elbows over her.

"Is your pussy too sore to take me?"

"A little tender, but I could."

He was tender in his ass, but he liked it. He would feel it when he sat on the hard chair behind his desk tomorrow and wrote the draft to her husband.

"I want you to promise me something." He nuzzled his lips down to her ear and blew softly, intent on teasing her senses awake.

"What?" Her voice held a distracted little pang that pleased him.

"I want you to pleasure yourself every day. Use the phallus and think of me."

"I will," she swore, growing breathless as he tantalized her nape. Her nipples were erect and all of her was flowing beautifully into the river of pleasure they gave each other.

He couldn't wait any longer. He mounted her, using his thighs to push hers apart, then guided the head of his cock against the growing moisture in her folds, seeking her entrance. She was tight. *Her sheath hadn't seen much use,* he reminded himself as he varied the pressure, teasing her muscles to let him into the wet core that enticed him.

"Do it now," he commanded. "Play with your button so you'll soften and take me in."

She did, the brush of her fingertips teasing them both. She bit her lip and moaned softly. The swollen crown of his cock gained entry and a satisfied noise left him.

Her eyes widened in apprehension.

"Hurt?" he asked gruffly.

"A little. You feel very big."

"I'll go slow," he promised and dropped his head to lick at her lips, coaxing her into a passionate kiss as he gave small pulses of his hips, easing his way into her a fraction at a time. The slow give of her tense, wet flesh was exquisite. She was breathing in jagged little pants, growing hotter and slicker, clasping him in a different, more deliberate way when he backed off, sighing with welcome as he buried himself deep again.

"I didn't know," she said in a voice that rang with both joy and dejection. "That it could feel so *good*." Her fingers weren't just caressing for her own pleasure but exploring and sliding around the base of his shaft, spreading her lubrication, then sweeping back to fondle her nub.

He shifted, bringing his knees under him and guiding her legs around his waist, spreading her legs farther so he could rock himself to the very depths of her cunt, until the hair of their sex meshed and there wasn't room for her to force her hand between them.

"Toy with your nipples. See if you can come without rubbing your notch." He tested her with a gentle withdraw and thrust.

Her pale hands cupped her pretty tits, erect nipples poking from between her fingers. He fucked her lazily as he watched her grow flushed with arousal, fondling herself and biting her lip again. When she grew restless with increasing desire, he leaned down to close his mouth over one of her nipples, sucking hard.

Her sheath tightened around his cock and her legs vised his waist. He smiled, using his teeth to stimulate her nipple. Her hand fisted in his hair, pulling enough to sting, but she was encouraging him to keep at his rough play. Her pussy had grown so wet his bollocks were coated with her juice.

It was the best kind of fucking. Messy and lush. He kept his pace slow, building that wall of arousal higher and higher so, when it burst, it would be all the more explosive.

"I can't reach my peak like this. I need—" She tried to slide her hand between them.

He caught both her hands and pinned them to the bed on either side of her head, pumping his hips to hold her on that plateau of intense pleasure.

"Covey, please," she begged.

"Does it hurt, sweet thing?"

"No." She thrashed her head side to side. "It's so good, but it's *torture*."

"Is it?" He chuckled and withdrew completely.

"What's wrong?"

He dragged a pillow closer and rolled her stomach onto it, urging her to bend her knees so her ass was in the air.

Her hands clenched into the sheets and she turned her head so she could eye him warily. He positioned himself behind her. Her arsehole winked at him. *Another time*, he promised himself grimly. For now...

They both groaned lustily as he drove his cock back into the wet heat of her cunt.

"I'm going to get rough now, Clara. Tell me if it's too much." He braced one hand on her hip, the other caught her shoulder and he let her feel the full power of his thrusts.

She cried out again, but it wasn't pain. She clenched her hands tighter in the blankets and held herself still for his thrusts. "More," she gasped.

He gave it to her. Unleashed the beast in him and fucked her until she came and came again. Hard. Screams muffled into the mattress. Only then did he let loose with his own cry of triumph as his release threatened to blow the knob right off his cock.

CHAPTER FIVE

They made a subdued pair as they left the duke's estate. Eddie said a remorseful, "Clara," but she shook her head.

"It's fine. Truly. I have no regrets." Not quite a lie. She'd caught the besotted glance Eddie had sent the footman as they'd taken their leave and had a feeling her face was just as long. "I should like to settle all our debts immediately then see if we can make some investments that aren't quite so risky."

His cheeks flushed. "You don't hate me?"

For introducing her to a man who had changed her life? "Never."

The next weeks were busy with closing out their accounts in London and then traveling back to Rosewick for the summer. They settled up with the merchants in the village, then arranged for a handful of much-needed repairs on the manor.

She and Eddie fell back into their comfortable friendship, even confiding a little about their night at the duke's country home. He *had* dallied with the footman, Horace. In fact, they were maintaining a correspondence.

The duke wasn't as eager to stay in touch with her. She tried not to let it bother her, but when she discovered she was carrying his child, she decided she would write to him once the baby arrived.

Eddie, the silly dear, was beyond tickled with her quickening. He brought tears to her eyes with his proud announcements that *his* heir was on the way. She had teasingly asked if he understood how babies were made, but she knew he was ensuring there would never be any doubt that he claimed the baby as his own.

They didn't bother with the season in London and had the first lavish Christmas Clara had ever experienced. After a lifetime of fretting about money, it was strange to worry instead about how best to manage an abundance of it. Together, she and Eddie made sound investments. By the time "their" son was born, she felt secure and truly optimistic about their future.

Thanks to her night with the duke, Clara had everything she'd ever wanted.

So why did she feel like crying every day?

●●●

With the war over, Covey's wife's family had returned to their home in the south of France. His sons hadn't seen their grandparents since their mother had passed, so he took them for the summer. His father-in-law's unexpected death then forced him to travel to India to fetch his brother-in-law back to France to run the estate.

The journey should have been a welcome absence from England's wet winter, but Covey wore a soggy, gloomy mood the entire time.

He hadn't been homesick. It was worse than that. No matter what he did, or how far afield he traveled, he couldn't shake thoughts of Clara. It had nothing to do with the ribald acts she seemed up for, either. Perhaps that was part of it. Rather than seek fresh female company, he preferred his fist and a recollection of their night, but there was more to his melancholy. He couldn't shake a sense that he'd overlooked potential for something rare and precious.

When he finally returned to England and made inquiries, he learned she and the baron had a son. By all accounts, they were comfortable and needed no further assistance from him.

Disgruntled, he attempted to pick up the threads of his old life, but shortly after he arrived in London for the season his butler offered him two letters on a silver tray. Each bore the Rosewick crest.

My Lord Duke,

It was my intention to deliver this message in person if you were in London, but I'm informed that you are out of the country and not expected soon. We are not planning to stay the entire season as I am already missing our dear son, born on Easter Day this year. I wished to name him after his father, but we have called him Robert. He is strong and healthy and my dear husband wears paternal pride with unbridled enthusiasm.

I wish to thank you again for your generous assistance in various matters last year. I think of you often.

Yours,

Clara Halton, Baroness of Rosewick

That was what he was missing. That cheeky wit as she informed him she had had his son and masturbated to thoughts of him. A throb of sexual delight struck his loins and a shout of achievement at having another son lodged in his chest.

He opened her husband's letter with more circumspection, wondering if she was overstating her husband's acceptance of the situation. Perhaps this letter contained demands?

He read it. Read it again, then rang for the butler.

"I'll be at the club— No." Hell, he wasn't sure which way he was going, only that his coat was on. "I'll be out."

●●●

Clara was reading *The London Advisor and Guide*, trying to better her understanding of the lease process now that Eddie had left the running of their properties in her hands.

After a long talk, they had agreed that even though they loved one another, her night with the duke had revealed they both had needs the other couldn't fulfill. They settled on a plan that would allow them to find their own version of happiness and had signed papers in London allowing her to act on Eddie's behalf. Eddie had taken quick steps to secure his heart's desire and had left for the continent.

Clara was glad for him, but she didn't possess his courage. She had written to the duke but kept her letter very simple, not wishing to burden him with a sense of obligation. Perhaps the difference was that Eddie had known he was loved, whereas she didn't have that same assurance. She had told Eddie it didn't have to be the duke, that she only wanted a man in her life who wanted her, but she did want it to be the duke. The fact Covey had made no response to her letter left her feeling very bereft and blue.

At least she was comfortable here in Rosewick—

"The Duke of Covington is here to see you, my lady," the housekeeper announced in a sudden flutter.

Clara shot to her feet in a soar of joy, stammering, "Show him— Oh. You didn't wait."

He shouldered into the second-floor reading room behind the housekeeper, his hair damp and mussed from the light summer squall outside.

"The parlor is much nicer," she said, brushing at her plain gown and touching her hair. She hadn't been expecting visitors. "Please let me show you to it."

"This will do." He glanced around the tiny space at the back of the house overlooking the garden where good reading light came through the single window. "We'll ring if we need you." He practically shoved the housekeeper from the room, firmly closing the door and turning the lock.

"You'll cause gossip." She could hardly speak, she was so overwhelmed by his presence. Recollections at what they'd done to one another a year ago were flooding into her head, imbuing the air with sensual memories and crackling in her voice.

"I don't care." He came toward her and set his hands on her hips, thumbs drawing the fabric of her gown taut against her stomach where it still retained a slight fullness, as did her breasts.

"Are you upset?" She tentatively set her hands on his sleeves. "Should I not have said anything?" She had dithered for weeks over when and how and whether to tell him. "I wasn't asking for anything. We are very well situated as you can see." Rosewick was small but quaint and now in good repair. "Are you here to see him? I only thought you should know."

She had wanted an excuse to reach out. That was the painful truth of it.

"I did want to know." He sounded upset. Grim. Or something. He kissed her. Hard. As though he was reprimanding her, but there was a sweet greed beneath it.

She was so surprised, she submitted with a lax mouth, hands clinging to his sleeves for balance before she felt the fire catch in her and began to respond with a hunger of her own. Oh, she had missed him!

When she was dizzy with want, leaning against him, he finally lifted his head.

"Your Grace," she gasped, trying to assimilate that he was here, that he was touching her the way she'd been longing for him to touch her again.

A cool swish of air warned her that he was lifting her skirt along with her chemise.

She set her hand on his, glancing with alarm toward the door.

"I'm starving for you, Clara." He made another of those primal noises as he caught sight of her thatch. "Don't make me wait another second."

She was so startled by his urgency, she let him back her into the chair she'd been using and bunched her gown to her waist. He knelt at her feet and scooped his arms beneath her bared legs, dragging her hips to the edge of the chair. She clutched at the arms as he bent his mouth to her sex.

They'd barely said hello, but his tongue was tracing her slit, quickly bringing her alight. A gush of her fluid response rushed to her loins. She combed her fingers through his damp hair as his wicked tongue delved deeper and his mouth opened wider to heat her tender flesh.

"I missed you, too. So much," she confessed on a pang.

Her tension soon mounted, but just as her peak began to tease her, he straightened and opened his breeches, revealing his turgid member. He poked at her, drew her another inch off the edge of the cushion, and drove into her. There was a sting, but the way he filled her made her arch with sheer indulgence.

"I missed *this*," she moaned.

"Me, too." He kissed her, spreading her own essence across her lips as he made love to her mouth while making love to her body. Within moments, he was down to the short strokes, but she was there, too. She dug her heels into his flexing buttocks, encouraging his quick thrusts. Whimpered noises in her throat begged him to hurry.

They came in a rush so perfectly timed she couldn't tell which pulses were hers, which throbs were his. It wasn't the most powerful of orgasms, but it went on forever, leaving them shuddering against each other as though taking shelter from a storm.

As they came back to reality, she was overwhelmed by tenderness.

"You didn't have to come," she murmured.

"That's what you think." They both chuckled and he slipped free of her. "I shouldn't have come inside you. Not when it only took the once before."

He stood to close his breeches and she lowered her skirts. They shared a somber look.

"Eddie doesn't mind babies that aren't his," she said with a wavering smile. Eddie wasn't here.

"Your husband isn't coming back. Do you know that?" He withdrew a letter from his jacket and waved it. "He said he was in need of a valet on his grand tour of the continent. Since Horace accompanied me on my recent travels, he has hired him away.

Your husband has run off with my footman, Clara."

She pressed her lips and folded her hands. "I did know, yes. Are you upset? May I compensate you for your inconvenience?"

"No. That's not why I'm here." He looked insulted. "This letter also suggests, if I am so inclined, that I check on you from time to time. Your husband deeply respects my expertise when it comes to maintaining the security of an estate and believes his son could learn from me, should I wish to be a guiding influence upon him."

Oh, Eddie.

"That's no obligation on you," she insisted, cheeks stinging at her husband's matchmaking efforts. "Things are very well in hand. Eddie has acknowledged Robert as his heir. I have everything I need. You needn't worry that anything will reflect on you *at all*."

"I want you and the boy to come live with me and my sons, Clara."

"But you don't have to—"

"Clara." He set his hands on the arms of her chair so his nose was practically touching hers. "We've talked about how ruthless I am when I want something. I want *you*. Is there some reason you're not doing as you're told and beginning to pack?"

She took hold of his cravat and swept her lashes down to shield the yearning in her eyes. "If I ask what will happen, will you tell me it's more exciting to wait and see?"

"You're a quick learner." He stole a kiss. "I like that about you."

"Really, Covey. People will talk," she said anxiously. "They'll say I'm your mistress."

"And we'll pretend to be outraged by the very idea, exactly as others have done before. If you're slighted, I will fight a duel to restore your honor, but I am a duke, Clara. Most will pretend to believe that I am looking out for my dear friend's wife and son—and any other children your husband might conceive with you while he is off exploring the ruins of Greek civilization," he added dryly.

"What happens when he returns?"

"Will he?"

"He plans to be away for two or three years, but he didn't want to leave Robert without a father."

"The boy has one. Come," Covey commanded quietly.

She hesitated and he crouched before her.

"What?" he demanded, but his tone was gentle. "Tell me and I'll solve it. I want you to be happy, Clara."

"Do you? Because..." She cleared emotion from her throat. "I mean, I would hope that someday, do you think you might, at some point..." She felt very defenseless, but she needed to know. "Do you think you might love me a little? Sometime in the future?"

"I think I'm halfway there," he said solemnly.

A smile trembled on her lips before he kissed it away.

"Well, you're not letting me pack, are you?" She playfully nudged him to hide how moved she was. "Why don't you come and meet your son while I do?"

• • •

After a busy season, they were finally settled in at Scarsdale Hall, where Robert slept down the hall from his two older half brothers. Arrangements had been made for Rosewick to be managed by an estate agent and the income was piling up since Covey insisted on supporting her.

The first time Clara had accompanied him to a play in London, she had suffered a brief assault of smirks and titters before they'd been firmly stifled by Covey's powerful, arrogant stare. Then she'd been befriended by a marchioness who lived with her husband's brother in a similarly flagrant, yet unspoken arrangement. Clara was reassured that she had at least one ally and knew any social awkwardness that arose in the future would be quickly overcome.

Best of all, this morning a letter had caught up to her from her husband advising her he was well. Eddie enclosed a book of poetry and some silk ribbons from Paris.

She thought back to when her husband had proposed, vowing to give her a secure, happy life and resolved to write and thank him for providing her exactly that.

Her gaze meandered to the man behind her reflection in the mirror.

Covey liked to sit in his chair, nursing a drink and reading his letters while she brushed her hair and readied for bed. He'd had a mirrored table and bench brought in especially for her to do it here, seeming to find her ritual titillating.

She sometimes drew it out to tease him, but tonight his gaze met hers in the mirror. Her skin tightened with anticipation.

"What are you thinking with that hedonistic smile on your face?" he asked in the low voice that told her he was growing aroused.

"I'm thinking of the first night I was here." She only hesitated a moment before she reached to the lower drawer and withdrew an object lovingly wrapped in velvet. She pivoted on her stool to face him. "I'm thinking that I haven't used this since Rosewick. I haven't needed it because I've had the real thing."

"Is that so?" He rose as he spoke, setting his drink on the table with a soft clunk.

Her heart soared as he seemed to swoop down upon her, bracing his knuckles on the table behind her. They were nose to nose, his masculine scent surrounding her.

"But now you do need it?" His blue eyes were *so* bright. He was laughing at her. Laughing at their game, delighted with her, but also growing heated with that exciting intensity that made her stomach flutter in response.

She loved him for that hidden tenderness inside the animal desire. He always made her feel safe even when she felt at her most vulnerable. She felt very vulnerable right now, expressing her desire, even though she was confident he would be receptive.

"I don't need it." She did. Dampness was gathering between her thighs at the thought that had been teasing her for a while now. "But I wondered if you might *want* to use it?"

"If I want it, I'll ask for it." He lightly nipped at her mouth with his lips. "If *you* want it, you'll have to ask for it."

Nervous excitement made it impossible to do anything, but creak out, "I do."

"Where?"

That deep rumble of his voice demanded that she be as brazen as he was. It put her into a kind of freefall so she had to clutch at his shoulder as she implored, "Surprise me."

He chuckled but cut it off as he gathered her up to carry her to the bed. They kissed and caressed, removing their nightclothes and growing more and more aroused. Just as she was about to abandon fantasy and grab him by the cock to guide him into her, he reached a long arm to the pillows and dragged one into the middle of the bed.

He rolled her onto her stomach across it.

She tensed and looked at him over her shoulder.

"No? Are you frightened?" He stroked her round cheeks, squeezing them in a way that teased her into moving against his touch.

"A little."

"Here. Warm and wet this." He rolled the phallus free of its velvet and nudged it into her wet channel.

"Mmm," she moaned. It felt narrow and not as nice as his thick, hot cock, but she squirmed a hand beneath her so she could move it within her the way she liked.

"Don't you dare." He caught both her hands and moved them to above her head. "I will watch you do that another day. I can't believe I haven't already," he added in a bemused mutter. He rose off the bed.

"Where are you going?" She turned her head on the mattress to watch him.

"As I learned when you did this to me, my dear, a bit of spittle is not enough lubricant. I have some oil that should do nicely." He came back and made her bend her knees beneath her, raising her ass a little more and fully exposing her to his view.

She twitched and bit her lip, feeling very defenseless, especially when his slippery touch rimmed her tightest aperture. She clenched her hands in the blankets, unconsciously tensing as his finger prodded.

"Relax," he murmured. "We'll take it slow."

His finger was soon fucking her ass, gentle and thorough. Her pussy clenched around the phallus and she pushed her face into the blankets, groaning at the conflicting sensations that were good and sweet and dark and sharp. Her stomach was in knots, the rest of her slithery and restless.

"Do you like this? Can you come like this?"

"I don't know." Her hips were dancing to follow his touch, tension mounting within her, but the sweet pleasure of climax was tantalizingly out of reach.

"I'm going to move it into your ass now. Relax. I won't push it too deep."

She whimpered as the hardness of the phallus left her pussy, leaving her feeling empty and bereft before the warm tip nudged the slippery opening he'd greased with his touch.

It felt so big! She tasted blood on her lip as she bit down hard while concentrating on relaxing and accepting.

The bulbous tip was in her, the shaft holding her open. She shivered in reaction.

"That's all you get for now, love." His hard fist was against her, keeping the phallus from penetrating more than a couple of inches. His warm body settled half over her and his mouth kissed across her shoulders and nuzzled through her hair to reach her neck. "You like it?"

"Yes." She didn't know why, but it was incredibly exciting. She shifted, trying to gain the stimulation she needed.

He gently began to fuck her with it. His whole body brushed her as he did. "One day this is going to be my cock. Does that excite you?"

"Yes," she gasped, so aroused she was nearly wild with it. She was writhing, pussy empty and dripping with need, ass aching and full, all of her going hot and cold, quivering with sensation.

"Let me do this." He carefully rolled her off the pillow onto her back. He slid down to hitch his arm under her thigh. "This is all I thought about when I was in France and India, doing to you what you had done to me."

She let her other leg fall open in offering, groaning, "Yes, please."

He gave her pussy the attention it was begging for, licking up her juices and sucking at her nub and giving her those abbreviated pulses of the phallus in her ass until she clamped her thighs on his ears, certain she would die from the coiling tension in her belly, but never wanting it to end.

It was more than she could sustain, though; the white-hot sensations began to engulf her. Suddenly her release struck in a burst, shattering her so completely, she screamed and thrust against his mouth, pulling his hair before drowning in wave after wave of intense pleasure.

When it abated, she was limp with gratification. A latent pulse of orgasm hit as he eased the phallus from her and kissed her pussy one last time.

"Fuck, I love you," he told her.

It wasn't the first time he'd said it, but it made her smile and glow as if it was.

Then she had to warn, "Don't throw it off the bed. It might crack."

"If it did, I would buy you a new one." He set it upright on the stand, though, and came back to cover her. "You always have this, though." His turgid cock slid against her still soaked folds. He made a noise of pleasure, grunting as she easily took his cock in one deep thrust. "So wet and ready. You liked having your ass fucked, didn't you?"

"I did," she groaned, wrapping arms and legs around him and instinctually lifting her hips to receive his thrusts.

"I liked doing it." His hand went low, finger seeking her arse and penetrating the still tender flesh. "Scream for me again."

She did.

The End

Bosom Chums

Bosom Chums will open your mind to a scintillating world of possibilities within a marriage and embraces polyamorous relationships, however, one of the main characters is a widow, so readers who may be sensitive to this experience, please take note.

CHAPTER ONE

When Lavinia's letter broke into Maude Cavendish's bleak winter with an invitation to "join me and my dear John in Bath for the season," her flutters of anticipation had an embarrassing tickle to them. A sense of possibility she didn't wish to examine too closely.

She told herself it was the opportunity to scout for a potential second husband and quickly replied that she would be honored.

By the time she was traveling, however, nerves were assailing her. She hadn't seen Lord and Lady John Sutherland in two years and hadn't known them very well beforehand.

They had met in London the year Maude married. Lord John, the virile and handsome younger son of a duke, had been a dashing presence at all the balls. He'd asked Maude to dance once and nearly caused her heart to stop, brushing against her gown and looking at her in a way that had softened her knees.

Lavinia, his wife, had noticed and teased Maude afterward, seeming almost pleased by her reaction.

Maude had felt very callow and baffled that Lavinia had befriended her. She and her husband were beautiful and wealthy and socially in demand. Maude was only the second wife of a baron, unknown in society, and rather shy.

She'd been complimented by their notice and had enjoyed spending time with someone her own age. Her husband had been much older than she was, which was how she wound up abruptly widowed. Her budding friendship with Lavinia had been cut short and, secretly, she had mourned losing that more than she had her husband.

She did wish she had managed to provide him the heir he had desperately needed. The title went to his great-nephew and

Maude had been living in a drafty dowager cottage ever since, trying to survive on a penurious income. She'd been convinced her life was over.

But here she was, now arriving in Bath! Her stomach churned with anxiety, nervous that she would disappoint the two people who had grown to savior status in her mind. What if they realized she wasn't nearly as interesting as they recalled?

She entered the town house and Lavinia's, "At last!" echoed the flood of relief that Maude experienced on finally seeing her friend again.

Lavinia didn't look any older. Her skin was still as pristine as a drift of snow, her red-gold hair like a warm, beckoning fire. She was shorter than Maude, but so filled with confidence, she seemed ten feet taller. Her brilliant smile near broke Maude in half and the strength in her welcoming hug squeezed the breath out of her. She smelled of crushed flower petals and the press of her curves filled Maude with that remembered sense of being special and valued.

Happy tears struck her eyes and filled her chest with a wonderful ache.

When they stepped apart, Lord John gave a gallant bow over her hand.

"Since the moment Lavinia suggested you join us, we've been counting the days," he said in the deep voice that made Maude's skin feel tight.

We? Maude wouldn't dare question her host, especially when his green eyes met hers to underscore his sincerity.

His charm was legendary, but her heart swooped in a flattered delight anyway. How was she even here? They were two bright stars and she an unremarkable moon shadow. As happy as she was to have been invited, she had to wonder if they had a reason for opening themselves so generously. For now, she took Lavinia's advice to settle in, hoping all would become clear soon.

• • •

An hour later, Maude had freshened up and came down to the parlor. She heard the couple speaking as she approached.

"You can't show me my gift then tell me to wait until Christmas to open it," Lord John grumbled.

"Blossoms aren't meant to be opened, darling. You have to let them flower on their own. *Then* you can push your nose into it," she added with a gusty laugh at her own joke.

Lord John seemed to think her remark worth a good chuckle, too.

Maude didn't get it, but entered the parlor with a smile on her face—only to discover the couple were in an intimate embrace.

"Oh, I'm so sorry!" Maude turned away, flooding with embarrassed heat, but the vision of Lord John clutching Lavinia's bottom through her gown was imprinted behind her closed eyes. More disconcertingly, she didn't know who she envied more, Lavinia for receiving his touch, or John for being able to give it. Her heart lurched in confusion at that realization.

"Oh, Maude, please stay," Lavinia said. "Lord John is leaving us for the evening." She sounded more rueful than embarrassed.

Maude turned to see the pair exchanging a look she couldn't interpret. Scold and satisfaction, perhaps? After a brief moment, Lord John kissed his wife once more. Maude was quite certain she caught a glimpse of Lavinia's tongue stealing between his lips.

A curl of intrigue settled into her belly, and Maude became very aware of her most private flesh. Inner muscles clenched of their own accord, sending little shockwaves of tingling sweetness into her thighs and upward. Her nipples stung.

She dropped her gaze to the floor as Lord John approached, terrified she would betray herself. She'd suffered this same thing when she'd met them in London but had told herself that had been from the excitement of a proper season. It wasn't, though. It was *them*.

"It's our habit to be very open with our affections," Lord John said as he came even with her. "I hope we haven't offended you?"

He barely touched the backs of his knuckles to her elbow, but she felt it as though he'd wrapped his hand around her entire being and squeezed, leaving her breathless.

"No, of course not." Maude found a shaky smile to send upward. "It makes me want the same thing for myself."

The silence that crashed down nearly had Maude choking on her own tongue.

"I mean that you have a very happy marriage," she stammered. "I hope now that I'm out in society again, I might find a prospect for a similar, happy union."

"Ah."

"That's what we want for you, too." Lavinia hurried forward, gracefully smoothing over her faux pas. "A happy union." She sounded as though she was strangling on a laugh.

Maude wanted to die.

"Your artlessness is very charming, Maude." Lord John made no effort to hide his amusement. "I'm glad you're here to entertain us."

"Really? Because I feel like a twit," she mumbled, tying her fingers together.

He chuckled, but Lavinia protectively scooped her arm around Maude's back.

"You mustn't feel anything but comfortable around us. Express yourself however feels right." She flashed her husband a glance before guiding Maude toward the sitting area.

Lavinia's hold gave Maude a jolt behind her navel that had nothing to do with feelings of inadequacy. The way Lord John watched them gave her another. It made her feel like the flower Lavinia had alluded to—as though something was blooming within her that was sweet and receptive and enticing.

She again lowered her lashes, unnerved by her unseemly reactions.

"I would stay to enjoy more of this stimulating conversation," Lord John drawled, "but I'm expected elsewhere. I won't be late." That, too, seemed to have some significance for Lavinia, but he bowed and left.

Maude's thoughts were a jumble of innuendos that were so far-fetched, she had to dismiss them before they became something they weren't. She didn't want to go down a wrong track and expose herself in some uncomfortable way. She could pick apart the exchange later. For now, she let Lavinia put her at ease.

They talked for hours, as if they'd never been apart.

At one point, Lavinia gave a throaty chuckle and tossed back her head so her red-gold curls danced, and she stole Maude's breath. Maude had forgotten how entrancing her friend was, with her porcelain skin and even, pearly teeth, her forget-me-not eyes and her Cupid's bow of a mouth.

"What's wrong?" Lavinia asked when she realized Maude had gone quiet.

They held a gaze that was... It was the feeling Maude had experienced in London. As though magic surrounded them.

"Nothing." Maude felt mousy and silly. She was still at a loss as to how Lavinia had ever noticed her, let alone wished to continue their friendship. "I'm just very grateful to be here."

"I'm glad you're here, too." She sounded very sincere and inched her bottom along the cushions so they were sitting closer. "It's always bothered me that we didn't have enough time in London to get to know one another properly. I felt we had a very special connection."

Her hand came to Maude's knee, sending the most exquisite swirl of delight through Maude's thighs and pelvis.

It was almost as if Lavinia's words were literal and she purposely demonstrated their invisible connection. Lavinia was looking into her eyes and for the briefest moment, Maude thought Lavinia must know how she made Maude feel. Trepidation quivered through her, but also—

There was a noise at the door. Lord John had returned. He came up short as he entered the drawing room. His gaze flickered to how close they were sitting and his expression shifted to one of consideration or—

Maude wasn't sure. She couldn't look at him and instinctively inched away from her friend, but Lavinia didn't remove her hand.

Flustered, Maude made a point of noticing the hour. "Look how long I've kept you talking." Her voice was sore and she was still feeling bewildered by her moment of connection with Lavinia. By all of this. She rose and announced, "I'll wish you both good night and retire."

The married couple exchanged another of those looks that made Maude feel both an outsider and part of the conversation. Then her friend warmly embraced her and said good night.

Maude was aware of Lord John watching her as she passed him at the door. He said again how pleased he was to have her join them, forcing her to say another flustered, "Thank you. Me, too," before she hurried up the stairs.

● ● ●

A quarter hour later, as Maude waited for sleep, mind still awhirl, she heard the pair in the room below her.

"Did you broach the idea?" Lord John asked in a rumble.

"Not yet," Lavinia murmured.

"Do *you* still want—?" What was that last low word he'd said? This? It? *Her?*

Lavinia said, "More than ever."

"Good. So do I."

There was a longer silence when Maude only heard her heart hammering in her ears. Was she imagining things, or did they have an interest in her that went beyond friendship?

As she called herself a fool, she heard a rough male sigh. The frame of their wooden bed began to creak.

Her eyes snapped open before she clenched them closed again and quickly pushed her hands against her ears. Curiosity immediately got the better of her, though. Was that really lovemaking she was hearing?

She took her hands away and heard Lord John say a distinct, "Fuck, you feel good. Your cunt is so hot." Lavinia moaned unabashedly.

Maude should have covered her ears again, but her friend's enjoyment piqued her curiosity further. Maude hadn't been touched intimately since the first weeks of her marriage three years ago. Her husband had been considerate enough. He had always taken a moment to pour a small measure of oil into his palm and rub it into her passage and on himself so his entry was smooth and only a little uncomfortable. After a few minutes of thrusting, he would make a strangled noise of completion and leave her.

Sometimes Maude would then soothe her used flesh and, if she did it long enough, found the sensations to be *very* pleasant. She hadn't imagined a woman could feel that way with a man, though.

She heard Lavinia moan, "Harder. Oh fuck. Don't stop."

The bed thumped the wall in swift, repetitive bangs that matched Maude's increasing pulse. Lavinia's voice broke into sounds that were pure, tortured joy.

Maude squirmed in her bed with sweaty, guilty excitement. She was tempted to let her hand stray to between her thighs, but that would be indecent to touch herself while imagining she was in her friend's place.

The noises eased and Lavinia sighed with gratification.

Lord John sounded tense as he said, "Turn around."

What did that mean?

Maude wished she could see them, wished she could feel what her friend was experiencing.

The bed noises started up again. This was going on a lot

longer than her own husband had ever taken to finish. Lavinia began to moan again in mounting pleasure.

How did she look as he made love to her? She sounded as if she were in heaven.

As an image of Lavinia's parted lips and naked chest appeared in her mind's eye, Maude quit fighting her urges. She pulled up her nightgown and secretively touched herself, discovering her lips were as slick as if her husband had spent himself inside her. She searched out the little nub where all her sensations originated and circled it, enjoying the ripples of pleasure as she tried to imagine Lord John thrusting into her.

Somehow, she conjured *Lavinia*. Maude knew it was terribly wicked to picture her, but she rolled onto her stomach so she could thrust against her hand, as though she could somehow thrust her sex against Lavinia's and kiss her mouth and feel her breasts against her own—

As the groans beneath her reached a mutual culmination, she muffled her own cry of release into the mattress. Contractions of pleasure overwhelmed her and dampness pooled into her palm.

CHAPTER TWO

T he next morning, Maude washed the guilt from her face and met her hosts for breakfast.

"Did you sleep well?" Lord John turned the full force of his inquisitive gaze on her, almost as if he knew what she'd done last night. She flushed hotly.

"Yes. Thank you." Maude could hardly look at either of them. She'd woken in the night from a dream where she'd been sandwiched between the two of them. She'd been in such a state of arousal, she'd had to stroke herself *again* to settle her restlessness and get back to sleep.

"So did we," Lavinia said with a smoky look at her husband. "Better than we have in ages. We've wanted this a long time, haven't we?"

"We have. And it's nice to have our desire within reach."

"This house? Are you thinking to purchase it? It's beautiful," Maude said.

"More what's in it," Lord John said with a bland look.

Lavinia tilted her chin in a scold at him. "This trip to Bath."

"And *you* want a husband." Lord John teased Maude, eyes dancing over the rim of his teacup, reminding her of yesterday's misspoken comment.

"Of my own," Maude asserted with a fierce blush, though it felt untrue. She did feel attracted to him, a married man. She was equally attracted to his wife. It was very confusing.

So she focused on explaining her situation with the new baron, her late husband's great-nephew. "He was sympathetic at first, but his wife doesn't care for me."

"You're young and lovely. He must have noticed." Lord John's gaze flickered over her with unabashed assessment, adding more dryly, "And she must have noticed that he noticed."

Maude didn't know how to respond to such a blatant compliment, especially when it provoked a sensual glow in her abdomen and brought fresh visions to her head of joining them in their bed.

She shot an apprehensive glance to Lavinia, fearful she would be offended at her husband lavishing praise on her, but Lavinia only traced absent fingertips on her husband's sleeve.

"You really are lovely," she murmured to Maude, head cocked in admiration while she let her gaze travel lazily from Maude's face to her throat to her breasts. "They clearly don't appreciate you."

A fresh blush of pleasure flooded her with heat, but Maude felt incredibly self-conscious. Her heart pounded as if she'd run to the top of the house and back, fearful they would realize she was entertaining prurient thoughts about them, but also wondering what they would think if they knew.

"I really am hoping to find something like what you two have," she managed to say in a strained voice, trying to cover up her hidden desires.

"We've made it our goal to ensure you do," Lord John said.

Lavinia squeezed his arm, murmuring, "Flowers," before shifting the conversation to visiting the Pump Room.

The Pump Room was the morning ritual for all visitors to Bath—a glass of the mineralized water and a stroll around the room while the orchestra played. Maude and Lavinia made the pilgrimage an hour later, and Lavinia made a subtle face as they sampled the water.

"It tastes as though they've boiled eggs in it," Maude said with a grimace.

"I was trying to place it. That's it exactly," Lavinia agreed with a bright laugh.

Each time she amused Lavinia, Maude felt a sting of pride and wanted to hug her. Everything about Lavinia tempted Maude to touch her and stand close, put her arm around her or set her cheek on her shoulder. She wondered again how Lavinia had looked when her husband had taken her last night and experienced so much longing to see them that way, she could hardly breathe.

She kept control over herself, though, and allowed Lavinia to introduce her to her circle. Lavinia remained well-connected, quickly gaining the best information on private bathing.

"I'm sorry, I didn't hear what her ladyship said." Maude leaned close to Lavinia, who was quite a bit shorter than she was, to be heard over the din of music and conversation.

"She warned us *not* to visit the public baths." Lavinia touched her shoulder as she lifted her chin. Her lips grazed Maude's cheek and her breath tickled her ear.

All the hairs on Maude's body stood up. Even her nipples tightened and a fresh desire to rub herself as she had last night accosted her. She had to get control over her desires!

"She directed me to one with women only."

Maude nodded. Her voice had completely deserted her. Fortunately, they were distracted by the approach of another acquaintance.

•••

They went to the bathing pool the next day, each in their own sedan chair. It seemed a ridiculous expense, but Lavinia insisted on paying for it so they wouldn't be seen stepping into a carriage still soggy after taking the waters.

They wore caps into the pool but were each helped into a dark green linen petticoat. Maids then tied a ribbon around their necks that supported a shallow bowl suspended against their upper chest. The bowls held pomanders of cloved oranges that would release scented vapors as the bowls floated on the water before them.

The water was hot, but the experience of sinking into the pool, gown billowing around her, was very pleasing. An orchestra played a soothing melody behind a screen and Maude immediately grew languorous, especially when Lavinia sat next to her, her shoulder brushing her own.

"Are you serious about marrying again?" Lavinia asked after a time.

"What choice do I have? I could live with my sister and her husband if things become very dire, but married couples don't want an interloper underfoot." Maude tipped a little closer in a nudge, pretending playfulness when she really just wanted an excuse to touch her. "You and Lord John are too kind, suffering my presence while I search."

"It's no imposition, but did you enjoy being married?" Lavinia didn't move away. In fact, she settled closer despite the tremendous heat. Her thigh was against Maude's and Maude held very still, thrilling at the feel of her.

She was so caught up in how delightful it felt, she took a moment to understand the question and form an answer.

"Oh, um, not the way you do. My husband was much older and we had different interests. We didn't speak much beyond what was necessary."

"So you didn't *enjoy* it." A delving light entered Lavinia's side-eyed gaze.

Through the melancholy over her short marriage Maude tried to discern whether Lavinia was really asking her whether she had enjoyed her marital bed. And because she was in a stupor, she repeated, "Not the way you do."

It was basically an admission she had listened to them, but Lavinia only offered a sympathetic smile-frown that was earnest and filled with caring.

"You ought to enjoy it, Maude. You know you don't *have* to be married to find a certain 'happy union'?" she asked tentatively.

Maude's response caught in her throat. Lavinia wasn't suggesting—

They were interrupted.

"Lavinia?" Another woman spoke, startling them from a conversation that had become so intimate, Maude had forgotten they were in public.

"Wallis!" Lavinia appeared disconcerted. She glanced at Maude with something that almost struck Maude as guilt before she quickly found a smile. "How lovely to see you after all this time. This is my dear friend, Maude."

The dismissive glance Wallis sent Maude reminded her she was suffering from hallucinations if she thought there had been some sort of invitation in Lavinia's words.

Lavinia and Wallis were soon embroiled in lighthearted gossip, leaving Maude feeling excluded. She knew so few people here.

"I don't know how much more of this heat I can take," Lavinia said mid-conversation, moving to sit on the edge of the pool. She removed her bowl from around her neck and held it under her chin, closing her eyes to inhale the aroma off the pomander.

From her position in the water, Maude watched Lavinia's breasts lift. The linen of her petticoat was plastered like a second skin all the way to the mound at the juncture of her thighs.

The sight of her near nakedness had a heady effect on her. She stared at the jut of her nipples against the linen and suffered a most unladylike desire to suck on them.

With a surreptitious glance around, she hoped no one had noticed her lusty interest. These inappropriate impulses had plagued her most of her life. She had them about men, too, often entertaining lurid curiosity about sucking a man's member or bending over so he might thrust into her from behind like an animal. At the same time, she just as often saw a comely woman and imagined lifting her skirts and licking her slit.

She didn't know where these thoughts came from. It was

a bewildering desire she had always tried to ignore. It was especially concerning to think those things about her *friend*.

"I'm wilting, too," Wallis said to Lavinia as she began to climb the stairs beside her. "I leave tomorrow, so we won't have another chance to visit. Would you like to join me for a cool drink?"

Wallis stood on the steps with her petticoat stuck unabashedly to her voluptuous figure, making no effort to draw the fabric from stealing into every crevice—which struck Maude as deliberately provocative.

Lavinia's lashes flickered as if she took in the sight with appreciation. A knife of irrational jealousy sliced into Maude's belly. Maude was so mortified by her possessiveness, she dropped her gaze rather than see what was in Lavinia's eyes.

"I'm here with Maude," Lavinia said. "I'll catch up with you another time. Write me."

Wallis made a huffing noise and left.

Maude was so relieved that Lavinia had chosen her over someone who seemed very special to her the backs of her eyes stung. "I didn't mean to come between you two," Maude said, moving closer so they could speak privately again.

"You didn't." Lavinia's smile was strained. "Lord John did."

"She had designs on him?" Why that took her aback, Maude couldn't say, but it was the last thing she would have guessed.

"Not at all," Lavinia said with a humorless chuckle. "Wallis and I were close during the season that I came out." Lavinia licked her lips as though trying to decide how much to say. "John and I found each other fairly quickly and became engaged. I was falling in love with him, but Wallis didn't understand my desire to have a man in my life. She has a good situation, so she doesn't need to marry and never wishes to."

Given her dead husband's oblique attentions, Maude saw Wallis's point of view, but Maude didn't have the luxury of a "good situation." Most women had to marry, and it was rarely as loving a partnership as Lavinia's and John's.

"Lord John isn't just any man. Is he?"

"He is not," Lavinia said firmly. "At first, he felt threatened by my intimacy with Wallis, but then he came to understand it. She didn't feel as tolerant of him, though. There are still hard feelings." She frowned pensively.

Maude considered that Wallis hadn't asked after Lord John. She had barely acknowledged Maude, all her attention on Lavinia the whole time. The way she had displayed herself so wantonly before Lavinia seemed almost defiant, while Lavinia had looked on her with familiarity and something like nostalgia. Had they had an *intimate* relationship?

Unreasonable jealousy dug its claws into her again and her mind whirled, trying to dismiss the suspicion.

Lavinia suggested they leave, and Maude absently agreed, moving to the changing rooms with her mind still trying to find simple explanations for her outlandish thoughts.

The maids were busy elsewhere, so they went into a single curtained chamber and helped each other from their wet petticoats.

It was a torturous process that shortened her breath. Maude tried to keep her gaze off the soft curves and lush pink nipples she exposed as she peeled away Lavinia's gown, but her head was filled with wondering if Wallis had seen her this way before. Had they stroked and kissed and suckled at each other's breasts?

When Lavinia dropped a dry petticoat over Maude's head, she swept her hands down Maude's body to smooth it, and a bizarre helplessness overcame Maude. A yearning she couldn't put words to. It made her stand like a flame before her, flickering and twisting with conflict, hot and transparent as she silently begged Lavinia to continue touching her.

"Darling," Lavinia said with a tender, concerned frown. Her hand, soft from the bath, cradled the side of Maude's face. "Don't look so distressed."

Perhaps she meant to reassure Maude about her marriage

prospects. Maude would never know, because she did the stupidest thing. She dipped her head and set her mouth against Lavinia's.

She didn't know why she did it, or even what she was doing when she got there. She was compelled by a potent mix of dreams and longing and envy of a stranger who may or may not have done this to Lavinia herself. She wanted to flick her tongue into Lavinia's mouth the way she'd seen her flick her tongue into Lord John's.

She wanted more. So much more.

As her mouth moved instinctively against Lavinia's soft lips, Lavinia's lips parted with surprise. Her tongue brushed Maude's and white light seemed to streak through Maude. She forgot anything but the feel of Lavinia, overwhelmed by the faint scent of cloves and oranges and the latent heat of the bath through the thin layers of their petticoats.

She was aware of sweetness and thrill and nothing else. Lavinia sighed and stroked her back and everything was right. A shudder of pure joy went through Maude. Possibility opened and seemed endless.

Then a gaggle of excited female voices entered the outer room. Maude yanked her head up, stepping back as reality slapped her.

This wasn't a dream.

She had just kissed a woman. Her friend. Her *married* friend. While they stood nearly naked. In *public*.

Maude snatched up her gown and hurried to another closet.

CHAPTER THREE

"**W**here's Maude?" Lavinia asked her husband the moment she climbed from her sedan chair and entered the town house.

"She said the waters had given her a headache and won't be down for supper. I thought the bath was supposed to cure such ills."

Lavinia *tsk*ed and tilted her head toward the library, urging John to follow her into it. The moment he closed the door, she confessed in a whisper, "Maude kissed me."

"Good." A slow smile spread across his face. "Did you like it?"

"Like" wasn't a strong enough word. Maude had been shy, but the sheer intensity of her desire had imbued her kiss with a thrilling, trembling urgency. Lavinia had been sweetly agonized by it, wanting to reassure her, but so eager with passion, she'd wanted to make love to her right then and there. It had taken everything she had not to reveal her greed by pressing her to the wall and lifting her gown.

Then Maude had pulled away, stricken by what she'd done.

"I did like it," Lavinia said in a still-affected voice. "But she was upset. I couldn't reassure her. There were too many people around." She frowned, wondering if she ought to go talk it out with her or give her time to reconcile her feelings.

"Are you sure *she* kissed *you*? You can be very aggressive when you want to be." It was a backhanded compliment. John loved when she proved how much she wanted him by demanding his cock or insisting he let her sit upon his face.

"I'm sure," she said, heart flip-flopping at the way Maude had swept down on her as if her life had depended on it. The connection between them rivaled what she had with John but,

"I think this is very new to her."

"It's new to us."

"I mean sex. Enjoying it. Being with a woman." Lavinia removed her bonnet, annoyed with herself for misreading Maude's signals.

When they'd first met, Lavinia had been certain their attraction had been mutual. It had been so tangible, she'd felt compelled to tell her husband that she was likely to take Maude as a lover.

Once Lavinia drew his attention to her, John had taken an interest in Maude as well, flirting and asking her to dance. He'd teased Lavinia, asking, "Are you sure it's you she wants?"

It had been the first time they'd competed for a lover, and it might have become an issue between them, but Maude's husband had died. Maude had gone into mourning and Lavinia had only received intermittent letters. She had tried to put Maude out of her mind but hadn't been able to stop thinking about what might have been.

"Wallis was at the pool today," she mentioned, more because she didn't keep secrets than because it bore relevance to this conversation.

"Oh?" He came across to help her remove her pelisse. "Will you see her again?"

"No."

Her former lover was not a sore point exactly, but Wallis had caused them strife in the early days. Lavinia and John had come to an arrangement where they occasionally spent time with other people. They were always very honest with each other about it, but they didn't flaunt their lovers beneath each other's noses.

Thus, it had been a delicate conversation when Lavinia had said, "I'm thinking of inviting Maude to join us in Bath. How would you feel about having her in the house?"

"About *you* having her in the house?" had been his dry rejoinder. "So long as I can, too, I think it's an excellent idea."

He'd been joking, but it had only taken a moment for both of them to make the leap to sharing a lover. At the same time.

"Would it make you jealous to see me making love with a woman?" Lavinia had asked him curiously.

"I'd be titillated. I've thought of it often. Would it bother you to see me fucking another woman?"

"I've thought of it often." They'd laughed and quickly had to fuck away the lust their talk had inspired.

Later they'd discussed it more seriously. Both were resolved to trying it. Their planned visit to Bath made it ideal. They could quit the city abruptly if things weren't working.

Maude had seemed the perfect person to approach. They didn't want someone like Wallis who had no interest in men. Lavinia wanted someone like herself.

"Maude was attracted to both of us," Lavinia had said with confidence.

She was still certain of it, but she hadn't realized how sexually sheltered Maude was. She was responsive, but she hadn't found fulfillment with her husband, let alone with a woman.

"Do you want me to speak to her?" John offered.

"You don't want to speak to her. You want to seduce her," she accused with a light bat against his chest.

"What's wrong with that? If I'm not mistaken, you convinced me that we should try this arrangement after a strong orgasm and some pillow talk. Fucking solves a lot of problems. Shall I demonstrate?"

"You're excited by the fact that she kissed me, aren't you?"

"I'm out of my mind with it. I want you over the desk. Right now."

Since she was equally aroused from Maude's single, hungry kiss, Lavinia set her elbows on the mahogany and welcomed the lift of her gown.

•••

After a restless night, Lavinia had the maid deliver a note to Maude with her breakfast. She said that Lord John was out for the morning and most of the servants were on errands. It was a good opportunity to speak privately if Maude wished to. Lavinia awaited her in the small parlor.

Lavinia was half-convinced Maude would appear at the bottom of the stairs with packed bags. She came in wearing a plain day dress and a wan expression. The dark circles beneath her eyes suggested she hadn't slept well, either.

Lavinia's smile faltered. She set aside the book she hadn't had the concentration to read and took refuge in manners. "The tea is fresh. May I pour for you?"

"Thank you," Maude murmured.

Lavinia nodded at the maid to close the door as she left.

For a few moments, there was only the clink of china and the stir of spoons and the snap of the morning fire.

"I want you to know that yesterday has not impacted my regard for you. In fact, I feel closer to you than ever," Lavinia began carefully.

"May I say something?" Maude's voice sounded papery and dry.

Lavinia folded her hands in her lap, pretending utter calm. "Of course."

"I always thought…" Maude frowned as though suffering from a splinter that was being picked out of her. "I thought the feelings I have sometimes were make-believe. Something that could only exist in my mind, like flying. Flying is impossible, but it's fun to allow yourself to believe you could. You imagine the wind rushing across your face and how the ground would look below and how dizzy and free you would feel to tumble in the air… But sensibly, you know you can't really do it."

Lavinia's eyes grew hot, but she didn't let herself blink. The sun was dawning inside her, filling her with pressure and light.

"It didn't occur to me that the way I feel about women…"

Maude's mouth quirked sheepishly. "The way I feel about *you*, could be something that could become real. Is it?"

Lavinia did blink then, only to discover her eyes had grown so wet, her lashes knocked tears onto her cheeks. Her vision blurred further.

"It's very real." A laugh of surprise and relief and excitement was caught somewhere between her chest and her throat, trying to escape. She bit at her lips to try to stop their trembling, but she was smiling like a fool, she knew she was.

Slowly, shakily, Maude's shy smile appeared. "I thought you would be angry."

"No," Lavinia said, feeling so tender toward her, she wanted to cradle her. "I was confused, too, when I realized I felt the same way about women as I do about men. Growing up, I would giggle and shriek like the rest of the girls over a young man on his horse, but one day the butcher's daughter looked at me a certain way and my knees went weak. Is that how you feel?" She had to be sure. "About men *and* women?"

"I do." Maude looked bewildered by it. "I'm sure the church would say it's a sin."

"Do you think me sinful?" Lavinia asked. She knew how hard it was to unlearn those dictates.

"No," Maude said, quiet but firm, mouth curling in a small smile of affection.

Lavinia squeezed her hand, remembering how painfully exciting her own awakening had been when she'd had to share a bed with a French governess while she'd been traveling with her family at sixteen. The truth about herself had come into focus very gradually as curiosity tugged and inhibitions had slowly succumbed to desire.

"You mustn't feel bad about something so natural." Lavinia moved to sit next to her so their knees touched.

"But I kissed you," Maude said with grave remorse, voice thin as an onion skin. "You're *married*."

"I wanted you to. And John doesn't mind. Oh, darling, don't be upset!" she urged as Maude's face fell. "We invited you here *together*."

She was handling this badly. Moving too fast. Her hand unconsciously pressed Maude's knee, silently begging her to stay and listen.

"We are friends before anything, Maude." It was the most difficult thing Lavinia had ever said when she wanted more, but seeing so much of herself in Maude, she was coming to care for her very deeply. This wasn't the randy desire that had driven her into Wallis's arms years ago, excited to have a lover who understood her even though they hadn't meshed in other ways. She wanted to know everything about Maude, including what she liked in bed, but, "I would never ask you to do anything you don't want. I know your situation is very tentative. I won't compromise your future."

Maude gave an abbreviated laugh. "The new baron and his wife would love an excuse to cut me off. A salacious rumor would do it. Lord John really knows that you...?"

"Like women? Yes. We've both taken lovers at different times, but this is the first time we've wanted the same person."

"Me?"

"Why is that so shocking? You're lovely." If she only knew how hard Lavinia was fighting the urge to lean across and take her by the shoulders, plant her open mouth across Maude's unsteady lips, and kiss the life out of her.

"It seems impossible," Maude said, gaze flickering around like a nervous bird. "I don't know what to say or do."

"You could let me kiss you again." Lavinia smoothed Maude's hair off the side of her face. "If that's something you want?"

The air crackled as their gazes held. Maude's was like a glittering amber stone, filled with mystery and magic. Anticipation manifested between them.

Maude glanced toward the door to ensure it was still firmly

closed. Lavinia's heart began to race with excitement.

"If you really want to," Maude breathed.

"I do." She leaned in.

As their lips touched, a spark snapped between them, making them start and draw back. They each licked the sting from their lips before pressing their smiles together.

They sighed.

Lavinia made herself work her lips across Maude's very gently. Maude had one of those bee-stung mouths that was small and plump, and the way it trembled with excitement made Lavinia lightheaded with desire. She wanted to be graceful with Maude's initiation, but the passion rose so quickly between them, she was sucking on Maude's lip before she realized what she was doing.

And Maude's hand was at her shoulder, silently urging her closer. She stabbed her tongue into Maude's mouth and Maude sucked on it before drawing back with a dazzled look. They were both panting.

"Am I being too aggressive?" Lavinia asked.

"I'm still astonished you want me the way I want you." Maude kissed her again.

"I want to feel you," Lavinia breathed when Maude's mouth trailed into her neck. "Will you come to my room? I'm going too fast, aren't I?"

"I want to feel you, too. But perhaps my room? In case Lord John comes home?"

Lavinia wanted to reiterate that John would love to join them, but one step at a time. They hurried to Maude's room.

●●●

Maude was sure she was dreaming but hoped she never woke. Lavinia was in her room, turning the key in the lock and reaching for her with hands that were as tender as they were greedy.

Who knew kissing could be such a wonderful experience? Not a smear of dry lips across hers once or twice, but a lengthy, loving anointing that had no hurry. The dance of Lavinia's tongue into her mouth made Maude's breasts feel hard and her loins pulse a throbbing signal. A plea for this delicious kiss to last forever.

They undressed one another between kisses, peeling away layers, caressing where a wrinkled bit of muslin or a tight lace had left a mark against pale skin. Maude touched her mouth to Lavinia's wrist and inside her elbow. Lavinia left damp kisses along Maude's collarbone to the point of her shoulder.

When they were naked, they embraced torso to torso. Their breasts brushed and compressed against the other's, nipples catching. Maude shook with want. She cupped the swell of Lavinia's heavy breast and toyed with her nipple, fascinated by the way touching Lavinia seemed to cause echoing sensations deep within her. As she circled Lavinia's nipple with her thumb and watched it grow tight and ripe as a berry, the tips of her own breasts stung with desire. Before she could think twice about it, she bent to suck Lavinia's nipple into her mouth, letting that hard bead roll against her tongue.

Lavinia gasped and her hands firmed on Maude. She roamed her touch down to Maude's hips, taking handfuls of her bottom and inciting swirls of wicked pleasure into recesses that called for touch. Longing had Maude nearly begging as she dabbed kisses up to the perfume in Lavinia's neck and sucked the dangling fruit of her earlobe.

Lavinia did not disappoint. She strayed her touch across to Maude's belly and down. She was confident, so deliciously knowing as she combed her fingers into the fine hairs and parted Maude's folds. Her fingers slithered with a firm touch along the slick petals of her sex, sliding low to claim her channel and coming back to toy with the throbbing knot that incited Maude's deepest hungers.

They stood in the middle of the room, sharing carnal kisses, breasts lightly bumping, their shaken breaths the only sound. Slowly Maude worked up the nerve and let her own hand trail to the fine hairs of Lavinia's mound. She adjusted her posture, opening her legs to welcome Maude's timid caress.

She hadn't even touched her husband so intimately, only herself. How soft she was! It was a remarkable experience to explore, discovering the abundant moisture gathering the way her own had the other night. Her scalp tightened and a moan of intense feeling escaped her.

She was so overcome with wanton lust her knees couldn't hold her. All Maude wanted was to worship her for the gift she was giving her.

As she dropped to her knees on the floor, the scent of Lavinia's arousal seemed to inebriate her. She looked up at Lavinia to see her rolling her fingers on her tongue, tasting the juices she'd gathered from touching Maude.

"Your curls are red. I've never seen a woman's sex," Maude said huskily. "Not even my own."

"Darling." Lavinia stroked a hand down Maude's hair in an affectionate caress. "Say cunt or pussy if you want to." She drew apart her folds to reveal the glistening inner flesh.

Maude licked her lips when, really, she wanted to lick *those* lips. "May I?"

"Of course," Lavinia said, petting her hair again. She wore a gentle smile, but her whole body trembled, even her smile. "But we can do that to each other. On the bed."

Maude could barely rise. She still felt as though she was dreaming as she joined Lavinia on the bed. They embraced again. Kissed and fondled each other and then Lavinia kissed down to her breasts, suckled and toyed until Maude was mindlessly running her hands into Lavinia's hair, fingers catching on pins they hadn't bothered to remove.

"I'm sorry."

"No, I want to eat all of you at once." Lavinia shifted and

now they were top to toe, except Lavinia's hips—her pussy—was in front of Maude's nose.

"Take your time," Lavinia assured her in a voice that rang with desire. "But I can't wait." She nuzzled all around Maude's mound, nose playing against her thighs, tongue dabbing into the creases on either side of her patch, breath heating flesh that grew swollen with need.

Maude was so paralyzed by anticipation she could only press her forehead against Lavinia's thigh and try to remember to breathe.

With the same assurance she'd had with her touch, Lavinia gave Maude's pussy a firm, luscious, unhesitating lick. Maude began to shake. Part of her wanted to close her thighs against a sensation that was far too intense, but her legs fell open.

Lavinia laughed softly and did it again, sending what felt like a burning light into Maude's abdomen. She wanted nothing more than to lie here and passively enjoy what Lavinia was doing, but she desperately wanted to give her new lover the same pleasure. She copied what Lavinia had done, sweeping her tongue through the sweet and salty flavor of her cunt. The taste went into her like potent liquor, spiking heat through her and making her feel drunk. She wanted *more.*

Maude explored the silky, slippery textures of her pussy, searching out the hard bead where she knew her own pleasure was centered.

Lavinia groaned with all the abandoned pleasure Maude had heard when Lavinia was in bed with her husband. That, more than anything else, encouraged Maude to keep making love to her with her mouth.

Lavinia's arms curled around Maude's thighs and she applied herself with such gusto to Maude's cunt, Maude couldn't help but make equally lewd noises. Soon they were both sucking flagrantly on each other's swollen buttons.

It was a singularly wicked experience to writhe this way,

with her own arms curling naturally around Lavinia's thighs, the growing abundance of juices against her tongue thrilling her as they signaled Lavinia's climbing excitement. The tension within her was mounting to the point she was grinding in pleasure against Lavinia's mouth, the rest of her taut with approaching crisis.

If she hadn't been so determined to pull Lavinia into the same storm with her, she would have tipped back her head and screamed out her pleasure, but she kept hold of Lavinia's bucking hips until they both stiffened with climax.

The moisture against Maude's face became a flood. Lavinia's swollen bud pulsed back against her tongue while Maude's entire being seemed to hollow out before a powerful earthquake rolled through her.

Sharp waves of pleasure crashed over her, striking like delicious hammer blows through her abdomen and sending shockwaves of joy to the ends of her limbs. It was so intense all she could do was keep her face buried between Lavinia's thighs and moan her exaltation.

CHAPTER FOUR

"Oh. I thought Lavinia was here," Maude said when she came upon Lord John in the parlor. She had been dreading facing him but had at least expected Lavinia to be here as a buffer.

He looked very handsome and intimidating wearing a blue coat over a dark green waistcoat, snug breeches, and a knowing smile. Her heart seized in her chest.

"She was fast asleep when I went to her room. She's getting ready now."

They were supposed to attend a soiree this evening. Maude was in her best dress, but a mantle of self-consciousness weighed her shoulders. She didn't know what to say or do. Did he know? This was excruciating.

"Let's have sherry in my library while we wait."

Please no, she silently begged. Her feet were like lodestones as she moved into the room ahead of him.

He closed the door. "My wife and I don't keep secrets from one another."

"She said." Maude wanted to bury her face in her hands but instead sank into a chair and swallowed back her gross sense of exposure, trying to keep her head up while he moved in her periphery. Glass clinked against glass.

"Did she also tell you that what happened today is something we both want?"

Did he mean he wanted Maude to make love with him, or that he wanted her to have an affair with his wife, or...

Maude found the idea of lying with both of them incredibly erotic, but the reality was daunting. She had slept a little after Lavinia had left her, but mostly her mind had been too busy replaying Lavinia's parting remark of, *I can't wait for John to see you like this*.

All she could think was that Lord John could have Lavinia. Why would he possibly want *her*?

She accepted the glass he gave her and watched him settle comfortably on the divan. He was the epitome of confidence and vitality with his long limbs and wide shoulders and steady gaze.

"Do you wish to call me out?"

His laugh was a bark of surprise, then a warm smile.

"No. I am very confident in my marriage." His mouth twitched before he sobered and gave a small nod of acknowledgment. "I wasn't always. You met Wallis today." There was no rancor in his voice, but his expression was forcibly held bland. "She tried to persuade Lavinia against marrying me. Took a 'him or me' attitude. I was wildly in love and didn't understand how Lavinia could want me *and* share my taste for women. It made for a rocky beginning, but we found our way. No one could come between us now. Unless it's someone we want between us," he added suggestively.

Maude felt as though she was back in the hot pool, she simmered in such a scorching blush. "I don't understand why..." *You would choose me*, she almost said, but her voice gave out.

"I want to keep my wife happy." His grin grew wicked. "And I would love to *see* her happy." His gaze was traveling over Maude, setting alight all the tender erogenous zones his wife had touched a few hours ago. "She tells me your husband didn't give you any joy in bed. That is an absolute pity, Maude. I would like to correct that."

A curl of erotic desire twisted low in her belly. How could she experience such a sharp reaction when she'd been so satisfied mere hours ago?

"Come here," he invited.

Maude couldn't help feeling she was a bit of a lark they were chasing, but after the extraordinary pleasure she'd discovered with Lavinia, she couldn't bring herself to turn down this opportunity. She did want to enjoy lovemaking with a man. And when would she have another chance to explore lovemaking with two people who appealed to her?

"I only want to kiss you," Lord John coaxed.

Maude shyly stood and moved across to him. She would have sat beside him, but he casually caught her wrist and eased her into his lap.

She sat there nervously, spine stiff, unable to look anywhere but at the wide, masculine mouth that wore a ghost of a smile.

"I find I am a little jealous," he murmured, opening his thighs and shifting her deeper into his lap so he could nuzzle his lips against her ear. "That my wife has seen you naked and I haven't. I'm dying to know how you look. How you feel. What you like."

His fingertips grazed the tip of her breast and sparks of renewed arousal glittered through her, making her gasp.

"Sensitive," he murmured in a tone of discovery. "Is that because she sucked them so hard?" He continued to caress her through the layers of her gown, his touch firming enough to tantalize her.

Maude's breathing grew uneven with anticipation. Her hand curled into the velvet of his coat and her loins tingled and dampened. She unconsciously shifted on his thighs, working her backside against his hard thighs, seeking pressure on her aching flesh.

He made a crooning noise. "Does your pussy need petting?" He pushed his hand into the folds of her skirt until he was cupping her mons.

She caught her breath, legs falling open a bit so he could rock the heel of his hand against the ache.

"Kiss me when you're ready," he said in a jagged voice.

She looped her arms around his neck and sought his mouth with her own.

He took control immediately, lips slanting firmly across her own. His free arm tightened around her hips to draw her bottom against the hard shape in his lap. His tongue stabbed into her mouth.

She instinctively pressed her thighs together, but his hand was jammed between. He refused to give up the territory he'd claimed. She whimpered and grew so damp and aroused her hips gave muted thrusts against the firmness of his touch.

He made a satisfied noise and his hand on her hip encouraged her movements.

Their tongues slithered and stroked and she felt her arousal mounting, but Lavinia's footsteps on the stair treads, and her voice asking if they were in the library, sent a bolt of shock and guilt into her. Maude scrambled to her feet, panting.

Lavinia entered and paused as she took in their tableau, Maude looking very caught in the act, Lord John sprawled on the divan, thighs splayed, making no effort to hide his erection.

"Is everything all right?" Lavinia closed the door.

"We were just getting to know one another." John rose and made a casual adjustment to the cock pressing firmly against the fall of his buckskins.

Lavinia appeared before Maude and dipped her head to force Maude to meet her gaze.

"Darling?"

"This is just very strange," she tried to explain, hands splaying then clenching. "I like you both very much. I admire how close you are and I don't want to be someone who causes trouble between you."

"You're not. I promise you." Lavinia caressed her arm where it was bare between her glove and the cap of her sleeve. "John is happy that you and I were together this afternoon. I'm glad you two were finding your way here. It doesn't impact what John and I have. Does it, darling?"

"Only in a good way. I love you all the more for wanting to try this." He cupped Lavinia's cheek and kissed her deeply to underscore his claim.

Maude didn't avert her eyes. She watched unabashedly, heart pounding, but had to shift to try to ease the slippery tickle that watching them caused between her thighs.

John lifted his head and brought his hand to the side of Maude's neck. "And I'm delighted you're willing to try this with us. I find you infinitely fascinating, Maude."

He dropped his mouth over hers and kissed her with the same passion he'd shown his wife. Maude felt so wanted, so cherished, her knees weakened. Her lips clung to his as he lifted his head.

She fluttered her eyes open to see John look between them with a hint of challenge. He'd kissed her deliberately, perhaps to test their resolve.

She looked to Lavinia. If she had changed her mind, everything would be ruined. The memory of all they'd done this afternoon would be tainted and she would be on the street.

Lavinia stepped closer and wound her arm behind Maude's waist, lifting her mouth.

With desire sparking through her, Maude met Lavinia in a kiss that exactly mirrored the heat they'd each shared with John.

Somehow it was all the more exciting for his having stoked their fire. His witness to this kiss, proving nothing was hidden, made it all the sweeter. And his groan of enjoyment at watching them made the kiss all the hotter. She and Lavinia drew it out to please all of them.

"We're not going anywhere except upstairs to our bed," John growled.

Lavinia broke away with a soft giggle. "So impatient." She touched one more soft kiss to Maude's mouth before releasing her and reaching for her husband's crotch, giving him a friendly squeeze. "No, darling. We'll test you to the limits of your control before we allow you to see what you missed today."

CHAPTER FIVE

Lavinia wanted to be sure Maude was as enthusiastic about their arrangement as she and John were. They spent the next few days stealing kisses and petting in front of each other, allowing the passion between all of them to reach incendiary levels.

Lavinia and John slept apart to heighten their own anticipation, and soon Maude was less bashful about watching their interactions or reciprocating their intimate touches in front of the other. She even confessed that she'd pleasured herself when she heard them in bed.

"Do it now," John said in his commanding way.

Maude turned her gaze to Lavinia in a coy, *Should I?*

They were ready.

"Let's meet in the bedroom for that," Lavinia suggested breathlessly.

When John arrived in his banyan, she and Maude were in their petticoats. He kissed Lavinia in greeting and reassurance, silently telling her they were in perfect accord with what they were doing. Then he moved to where Maude sat in the chair, wringing her hands. He gave her cheek a small caress so she would look up at him.

"Need more time?"

"I'm nervous." She kept her chin dipped while her lashes came up. "I'm quite sure you'll live up to my expectations. I'm worried I won't live up to yours."

"I'm barely hanging on at the *idea* of what could happen between the three of us." He opened his banyan to reveal his engorged cock.

"Oh, darling," Lavinia said, unable to resist wrapping her

hand around him. He was hot as a fire poker and twice as hard.

He sucked in a breath and hooked his arm around her, familiar and possessive. His cock pulsed in her hand as he offered his hand to Maude, inviting her to join them.

Maude dragged her attention off the dark crimson head of his cock and, after the briefest hesitation, rose to stand with them.

John caught a hand behind her neck. He pulled her close to plant a long kiss on her, the sort of lazy but thorough seduction Lavinia knew well. Watching him do it to Maude, feeling his cock tugging with pleasure in her hand as he did it, made her grow wet with anticipation for all that was coming.

Maude's nipples tightened and pushed against the muslin of her petticoat, urging Lavinia to reach out and caress one.

Maude drew in a startled breath and broke her kiss with John. She was flushed and dazed, panting in an effort to catch her breath. But as natural as water flowing downhill, she slid her arm around Lavinia and sucked her bottom lip in a voluptuous kiss, then dragged her teeth as she very slowly released her.

"Oh fuck," John breathed, cock leaping and pushing into Lavinia's grip.

He muscled them toward the bed.

• • •

Maude had been nearly sick with nerves and still was, but now her trembling was also excitement. She was thrilled by Lavinia's intuitive caresses and found Lord John's strength and masculinity very alluring. The impact of both nearly undid her.

Lord John urged them onto the bed and Lavinia rolled Maude close, gathering her in as they kissed and ran their hands over each other.

Lord John threw off his banyan and stood by the edge of the mattress to slide his hands up both of their thighs, bringing their petticoats to their hips. His touch strayed around Maude's bottom cheeks and perhaps Lavinia's as well. As his fingertips sought the damp, plump flesh in Maude's warmest shadows, making her gasp in surprised pleasure, Lavinia also opened her mouth to release a moan of delight.

"Take these off. Let me see you," John commanded.

"He likes to be very bossy," Lavinia said, rising to her knees to obey. "One time I refused and he spanked me."

"It was a very playful spank," he assured Maude who hadn't moved because his hand was still firmly on her backside and she rather liked the tantalizing way his hard hand cupped the back of her thigh and his fingertip toyed at her entrance. "Why do I get the feeling you need very little seducing, Lady Cavendish?" His finger circled and slithered in the abundant moisture.

"Perhaps I've thought about this a little. Or a lot." She looked at Lavinia while John's finger probed deeper within her. She stayed very still, trying to keep her eyes from fluttering shut so she could enjoy the sight of Lavinia on her knees like an Amazon goddess above her.

"Us, too." Lavinia smoothed Maude's hair off her face and bent to kiss her.

Maude's mind was split with yearning to lose herself in Lavinia's hungry kiss and the fact that her nightdress was going up to her waist. Lord John adjusted her knee, pushing it higher so her ass and pussy were fully on display to him. He continued to caress her with a proprietary touch, his thick finger delving along her slit, working up her juices until he could push his fat thumb into her and roll his finger to tease her nub.

Maude groaned into Lavinia's mouth.

"I told you," Lavinia said, continuing to smooth aside her hair so she could kiss all over her neck. She drew the nightdress higher up her back and her soft hand moved to caress Maude's bottom, squeezing as she asked, "Don't you think she's pretty?"

"Beautiful," John said in a guttural voice, increasing the pressure of his touch. "Creamy and— Ah, you *have* been thinking about this, haven't you?" His thumb deepened inside her and his finger rubbed harder as if he knew her crisis was rising.

Perhaps it was because Maude was pinching at his thick thumb with her inner muscles. She stroked her tongue into Lavinia's open mouth, greedy for their dual attentions. She clutched at Lavinia, roaming her hands over her as Lavinia cupped her breasts and pinched her nipples then sealed their mouths as Maude's climax struck. Lord John kept up his rhythmic caresses all the way through and only gentled when her shudders began to recede.

Maude fell onto her back, stunned.

Lavinia stood on her knees at the edge of the mattress, curling her arm around John's shoulders. "You're happy, darling?"

"So fucking happy."

Lavinia took his hand and sucked his thumb and finger, the ones that had pleasured Maude. She was being very blatant, holding his gaze as she did it.

Maude's gaze slid down to the effect Lavinia's sucking was having on Lord John. His cock was dark red, thick and veined with a dark crown. It was bouncing with excitement.

"Can I suck it?" she asked, startled by how badly she wanted to.

He dragged in a breath as he noted where her gaze had strayed. "Fuck, yes." He came down on the bed between them, settling on his back.

Lavinia joined her as Maude set her mouth at the base of his cock. They kissed each other once across it, then Lavinia ran her tongue along her husband's shaft. They dueled tongues at the tip, making him groan with ecstasy. When Maude slid down to explore his testes, sucking them into her mouth, Lavinia sat up and squeezed his cock, saying, "He'll come if you keep that up. He's getting close. You want to fuck her, don't you, darling?"

"I want to fuck every part of both of you. Why do I only have one cock? Sit on my face, love." He strayed his touch between

Lavinia's legs, making her freeze then writhe and moan. "Let me lick you while she rides me."

"I want to watch the first time you fuck her," she said on a whimper.

"You're soaked." He removed two fingers from her pussy and pushed three in.

"I know, but..." Lavinia held his cock and shakily motioned for Maude to straddle him.

Slowly, after Lavinia had rubbed his cock against her folds and made John bite back an agonized curse, Maude impaled herself with his thick flesh.

She couldn't help tipping back her head to moan in luxury. Her husband's cock had never felt like this. Nothing had. John's thick shape stretched and filled her, so hard as to be nearly bruising and so hot as to sear her inner flesh.

She gloried in it.

Lavinia gave a joyous laugh. "That's how you should feel, darling. Oh, I'm so glad I can share him with you." She danced her fingers over the taut flesh stretched tight around his intrusion then dipped her head and tickled her tongue along where they joined.

John clamped one hand on Maude's hip, the other in his wife's hair. His lips peeled back against his teeth in a sensual snarl and he lifted his hips as though he couldn't help it.

Maude tightened her muscles around him, hips grinding, seeking the flick of Lavinia's tongue against her nub while the steely shape of him shifted inside her.

Her blurred gaze locked with John's slitted eyes. It was a startling moment of affinity. He loved Lavinia. She saw it in him. She was falling for both of them and, locked as she was with him like this, was almost certain he felt something for her, too.

It was the most exalting feeling, to be joined and attuned to both of them as sensual tingles raced over her whole body.

Lord John reached out with his long arm and caught at

Lavinia's thigh. He rearranged her until she straddled his mouth, facing Maude. Lavinia smiled with seductive pleasure and took Maude by the shoulders. They exchanged a kiss that tasted of Maude's juices and a sharper, more masculine essence.

As Lord John's hips began to buck beneath her, Maude slid her hand down to play with her button. Lavinia's hips ground against his face and within moments, they all came in a rush that Maude would have easily heard if she'd been in the bedroom above.

But she was here, adding her voice to the choir.

CHAPTER SIX

The next two weeks were the most exquisite of Maude's life. Like the hot water at the bath house, she steeped herself in her time here, making no inquiries about what would happen when they all had to leave.

As they made their social rounds, however, she wondered if she should seek a husband who ran in Lord John's circles. Would that provide a nice proximity to her lovers or would they prefer not to have any reminders dogging them back to London? Would they even want her if she was sleeping with a husband of her own?

It was complicated, so she tried not to think too much about it, but she ceased to have a choice when a letter arrived.

"Maude? You've gone white," Lavinia said as the three of them took tea in the library.

"It's from the baron. He, um. He has negotiated a match on my behalf." The arrogant bastard. "An earl who lost his wife in childbirth. His son survived. He'd like a mother for the boy and more children." She'd been barren in her first marriage. Did they not realize she was a poor bet?

Lavinia's mouth hung open with outrage. Lord John had gone very still.

"Tell him 'no,'" Lavinia finally sputtered.

"I don't think I can, Lavinia." Maude wished with all her heart this were a cruel joke, but, "It sounds like a very advantageous match."

"John!" Lavinia demanded of her husband.

"What do you want me to do?" he snapped with uncharacteristic impatience. "Offer for her myself? I'm already married."

"Don't be obtuse. Do *something*."

It was the first time Maude had seen them at odds. Guilt stole over her for being the cause of it.

"There's nothing I can do." John was still speaking harshly. "He's a damned *earl*. She could do worse." He flung a hand out to encompass their unconventional arrangement.

Lavinia went gray. "That's cruel."

"Lavinia," Maude said, heart hollow. "He's right. I have to at least go and learn more. Perhaps I'll...see you in London." She was trying to sound optimistic, but her voice trailed into nothing as she realized how hard it would be to have more than a fleeting tryst with them if she did. She'd had her flux once and Lord John had been very careful since, but she couldn't risk pregnancy if she was marrying another man.

"Do you *want* to marry a stranger?" Lavinia demanded, sounding appalled.

"Of course not." Maude's eyes welled. "But I don't have an alternative. And this... It was only meant to be..." She didn't know what to call it. "I'm leaving early. That's all."

"Do something, John." Lavinia rose in fury.

"Lavinia, I *can't*."

"You're not even trying!" Lavinia threw her cup at the fire.

Lord John shot to his feet. "Take hold of yourself!"

One of the servants burst through the door, wide-eyed in shock.

"You're being a heartless bastard," Lavinia said on a broken sob and stormed out.

"Please don't be angry with her," Maude begged, rising to catch his sleeve. "She's far too kind and doesn't realize..." She gave a wobbling smile at what had transpired between the three of them. "This is more than I deserve."

"Don't say that," he muttered through his teeth, though he had moments ago intimated they should be ashamed of themselves for their arrangement. His gaze shifted from hers.

"I'll help her see this is for the best," Maude murmured, circling him, needing Lavinia as much as her lover needed her right now.

He caught her arm, forcing her to look back at him. His expression flexed with frustration and regret. "I'm sorry, Maude."

"I'm not," she said with a poignant smile, longing to kiss him, but the servants were hovering. "I'll leave in the morning."

•••

Maude urged Lavinia to forgive Lord John. He was as helpless as she was in this situation. "I'll write to you as soon as I can," she promised.

Lavinia nodded, chin high, but her sadness was absolute, as was Maude's.

Maude's trip back to the dowager cottage was arduous and she arrived to disarray. The new baroness was redecorating for her own mother and had made a start while Maude was away. Wood shavings and bits of plaster were everywhere. The fire hadn't been lit in weeks. Maude barely slept in her ice-cold slab of an empty bed.

A week later, she met her prospective husband. He was an absent-minded man of forty-something who was decent enough to look at and didn't have bad breath. That was the best she could say of him, especially since she doubted he was any good at fucking.

Funny how she'd gone from thinking wicked things about everyone she met to feeling no interest in anyone but a woman with copper-gold locks and her stallion of a husband who had last fucked her bent at the edge of the bed because she'd asked him to. She had wanted to bury her face in Lavinia's cunt and they'd all been in a delirious sea of pleasure.

Dear Lavinia, she sat to write several times. The words wouldn't come. She should tell her things were not terrible, but they were. The two people she had come to love were not here. She could tell Lavinia that she missed Lord John as badly as she missed her bosom chum, but she had never wanted to impact their marriage and feared she had.

She should tell her that all had worked out for the best, but that would be a lie and she didn't want to lie to the woman she loved.

Finally, she sent her a short note that the wedding date had been set. She advised the formal invitation would be sent forthwith and she hoped they would be free to attend. That was another lie. She feared if she saw them again, she would never recover enough to bear the touch of her new husband.

Less than a week after sending her letter, she was called to the manor house. The new baroness would have some bone to pick with her, she supposed. Maude had dared to sweep the nails into a corner and moved a bucket of paint out of the middle of the floor. She was likely to be accused of hindering progress.

The handsome man who rose when she was shown into the baron's study had her heart lurching and stumbling into a gallop in her chest.

"Lord Sutherland." All of her swelled with happiness to see him again. She rushed forward to offer her hand even as she looked for Lavinia.

"Lavinia isn't here, but she's anxious to see you."

Her heart lurched again, this time stalling. "Is she well?"

"Please don't be alarmed." He kept her hand and squeezed it. "But she's been listless, not at all as fit as we were in Bath. I hoped you could come and attend to her as you did while we were there. It made all the difference."

Maude's jaw went slack with shock.

"I've explained to the baron that it would be my privilege to provide you a home and look after your needs if he would be so kind as to continue the income that was awarded to you by your deceased husband."

"And *I've* explained that you're about to be married." The baron was stewing red-faced behind his desk. "And that you'll have a better income from the earl."

"You keep saying that, but I assure you the earl is broke." All the warmth disappeared from Lord John's demeanor. "As broke as you will be if I repeat what I know of your dodgy dealings when I visit my club next month. I am offering to ensure your late uncle's wife is properly cared for so that my own wife might be well cared for. When you have women counting on you—" Lord John released Maude to lean on the man's desk.

The baron went white.

"—you ensure their health and happiness as best you can. So do it. Release her to me." He turned back to Maude with a pleasant smile as if he hadn't threatened to ruin the man. "I'll wait while you pack. The rest of your things can follow."

Maude stood frozen in shock, stunned speechless. Lord John owed her nothing, yet here he was. Why?

"No?" Lord John asked with a rare shadow of self-doubt in his eyes.

"I— Of course. Yes." She was trying not to cry, she was so touched by his rescue.

A short while later, her two cases of necessities had been loaded into his carriage. That was her first opportunity to speak to him.

"I don't know what to say."

"Say you forgive me." He tugged her across to sit in his lap. "Lavinia is not the only one pining into nothing. Her heart is broken and, frankly, our bed feels empty without you. I don't know how you made yourself such an integral part of our lives, but I cannot live without you any more than she can." He kissed her in one of his rough, hungry kisses that made her heart leap.

"I really don't have to marry the earl?" she asked when he let her breathe.

"I've never even met the man and want to kill him for thinking he could touch you."

They stopped at an inn a short time later. Lavinia was waiting to greet her.

The rush of gladness that hit Maude stung her cheeks like a slap. She flew into Lavinia's arms and it was all they could do to keep their lips from joining. They hurried to the private rooms Lord John had arranged for them.

"I can't believe you did this for me," Maude said as she and Lavinia breathlessly laughed and kissed and pulled at each other's clothing, needing to touch and make love and reconnect.

"We were both so miserable, you'll never know! Everything was empty. Our house, our bed, our conversation. He would start to ask, 'What does Maude think?' and we would both feel as though you were dead."

"I've been so miserable without you." She hugged her naked body to Lavinia's. "I kept telling myself that even if the earl was not a good lover, I would find one, but I couldn't imagine being with anyone but you and Lord John."

They fell together on the bed and couldn't take their lips off one another, even when there was a rap against the door.

"It's me," Lord John said through it.

Maude kept twirling her tongue in and around the tangy folds of Lavinia's cunt, reacquainting and loving and pleasuring and claiming.

They heard the floorboards creak as if he was settling into a more comfortable position. "Are you punishing me?" he asked against the door.

"We should," Lavinia murmured, equally lavish in her quest to bring Maude pleasure.

Maude couldn't. Not when he had saved her from such a grim destiny. She left the bed and padded across to unlock the door.

Lord John slipped in and locked the door, then he cupped the back of her head and kissed her, groaning with discovery when he tasted his wife all over her lips. He tapped her backside. "Get back there. I want to watch."

"He says that now," Maude said knowingly as she rejoined Lavinia. "We know he won't last."

He was patient enough to let them shudder in release twice before he said, "All right, I can't take it." He began pulling at his clothes. "Tell me you missed my cock at least half as much as you missed her cunt."

"I missed all of her." Maude sat up and realigned herself so she was nose to nose with her darling Lavinia. They kissed and Maude rose atop her, on her knees so she could tilt her hips up for Lord John as he stationed himself behind her.

"I missed you both," she said with a sigh as his cock slid into her from behind.

"We missed you." He braced on one hand and covered her to press his open mouth to her nape. His free hand reached to fondle his wife's breast.

"We love having you between us," Lavinia assured her as she cupped Maude's head and drew her to press their blissful smiles together.

That was fortunate because this was exactly where Maude wished to be.

The End

The Grand Ball

The Grand Ball is a party that many won't want to miss, where a variety of appetites are fully satisfied, however, these may not be suitable for every reader. The story includes age difference & grooming, sex work, verbal abuse in a sexual role-play setting, sexual acts performed in front of onlookers, multiple sexual partners for a single woman in a single night, and puppy play. Readers who may be sensitive to any of these, please take note.

B efore today, the farthest distance Ester had traveled was her fall from her cozy room in the attic of an inn to the flea-infested room her mother had rented in Lant Street when her father was sentenced to Newgate.

Her innkeeper parents had taught Ester to change sheets and tend fires as soon as she could manage it. They'd been an honest, hardworking family, but her mother's best efforts to persuade a solicitor to defend her father only got Mum pregnant with Ester's half sibling.

Ester had been seventeen and on the brink of marrying the blacksmith's son. With such a blight on her, no man would look at her. She resigned herself to making her way as other fallen women did, the ones she'd seen visit the inn with men who weren't their husbands. Her mother had always said those women lived off their "wits and charm," leaving Ester with the impression that bosoms were called wits and the thatch between her thighs was her charm.

Her mother hadn't been wrong, Ester learned on her first visit to the solicitor's office. Ester told him she was a virgin and a good girl, but her mother needed money for the baby he'd put in her. Ester had let the man stick his hand up her skirt and suck at her wits. Eventually she knelt to take his bludgeon in her mouth and swallowed when he finished.

Despite the indignity, she hadn't minded. It answered a lot of questions. Plus, the solicitor had given her enough money to keep the three of them for months.

All was well until her mother died in childbirth, taking the babe with her. Ester used the last of their money to buy her father a better situation in the prison. He had a cough and wouldn't last long, but at least he would be comfortable in his final days.

With no prospects left, she gave her virginity to the solicitor. By then she had learned of something called a "sheath." He used one, then put her in a room above a greengrocer and used them often.

Ester was content and was even starting a flirtation with an undertaker's son, in hopes of securing a marriage proposal, when the solicitor brought another man to see her. He said he couldn't keep her any longer, but his friend here would do so.

The other gentleman was younger, but still seemed old. Thirty-five to her twenty. He was titled and wealthy, though. He promised her a nice room in a better part of the city, so she let him tumble her to see how they got on.

They got on very well. He was attentive and brought her astride him, then caressed her in such a way she discovered she could have the same experience as a man.

That made her very happy! He put her in a room at a town house and came two or three times a week. She came at least twice that, welcoming him gleefully when he turned up.

"You like to fuck, don't you?" he said one evening as she washed his sheath in the basin and left it to dry.

"I like to fuck you," she assured him, returning to the bed and kissing all over his chest. "Why? Does your wife not like it?"

"She likes to fuck, but not me." He curled one arm behind his head. "I can't stand her, but our parents have the marriage they wanted." He used his other hand to toy between her thighs as she knelt beside him. "There's a costume ball I attend without her. You might enjoy it. It's in the country, invitation only. They're always looking for enthusiastic young women to even out the numbers. They'll pay you." He slid one finger in and out of her at an idle pace, his touch making her squirm with renewed desire. "You'd have to let other men do this to you. Not all of them. Only the ones you like, but you have to fuck a few of them. Suck them off and let others watch. I'd very much like to watch other men fuck you."

"It sounds indecent."

"It excites you, though. I can tell by the way your pussy is melting and clinging to my fingers." He wasn't even playing his thumb against the place that made her moan, but she was dancing her hips, growing very randy and soaked at the wickedness of his suggestion.

"These balls are where I learned to frig a woman and make her come," he continued. "You'll find even the most depraved requests very satisfying."

"How much do they pay?" She could hardly speak, she was edging so close to climax.

He told her and the number undid her. Her peak arrived and she humped into his hand, moaning, "Yes. Take me to the ball."

So here she was, arriving at an inn that was well-to-do. Her patron was staying at the manor house, as all the invited guests did. She was given a room and a light meal and instructions to nap off her travels. She woke when a box arrived with a note telling her when to expect the carriage. It said she should wear only her costume, no chemise or hose or other types of undergarments.

The box contained a cloak and a mask with a cat's eye shape. Beneath it was a gown in marmalade-colored velvet with white trim. There was also a device she'd never seen, a silk-wrapped sponge with a string that she was instructed to soak in the accompanying solution and insert to prevent pregnancy. How ingenious! She bathed and fitted it before she tried on the gown.

The gown was far more of a surprise than the sponge. The high-waisted bodice was little more than a pair of cap sleeves and a shallow pair of cups for her breasts that barely shielded her nipples. The skirt was sewn as though it had been constructed backward, with the seam in the front, except there was no seam. It overlapped a tiny bit where it attached beneath the bustline, but the width of her hips caused the slit to open, revealing her legs to the middle of her thighs. When she walked, it fell open to expose all the way to her patch.

Doubt inched into her. This inn was much like the one she'd been raised in. She had expected to grow up and marry a working man and live a respectable life like her parents, not go to a salacious ball wearing an outrageous costume that invited anyone and everyone to see her intimate flesh. To touch her and defile her.

Yet even as she considered strangers fondling her so blatantly, tendrils of curiosity tickled at her pussy. When she put on the mask, she felt emboldened. She threw the cloak over the dress and went down to await the carriage.

"You're one of us," a young woman said, beckoning her toward the carriage that was arriving. She was with two other women who wore cat masks.

"A pussy girl," another explained with a playful hiss and a claw of her hand in the air.

"Have you done this before?" Ester asked as the carriage crunched rocks beneath its wheels.

"We all have," the third said. "I don't even do it for the money anymore. Pace yourself," she cautioned and the three women erupted into gales of laughter.

Ester wasn't sure what that meant. "How many guests will be there?"

"Ooh, forty or fifty? It's hard to keep track. Some of the very rich have private parties within the party, if you know what I mean."

Ester didn't, but one of the girls eagerly enlightened her.

"I did one of those last time. He was a foreign gent. Barely spoke English. It took me forever to get that he wanted me to tie him to the leg of the bed and whip his arse with the riding crop, even his balls! Then I had to rub liniment on the welts and hand him off. He pushed a gold crown up my cunt after. Seemed quite happy. I was!"

Ester swallowed nervously, wondering what she'd got herself into.

They arrived, and as they stood in the receiving line, she saw people wearing costumes, milling through the lower floors. Most wore animal-themed disguises, but there were some highwaymen and jesters. One woman wore a painted Venetian mask with only a corset that lifted her breasts, but left them mostly exposed. The cage of a short crinoline rocked like a skeletal bell around her naked hips as she walked.

Ester arrived to meet the hosts, two men wearing simple cloth masks. The first was tall and strapping, with exposed arms and shoulders that belonged on a blacksmith. He wore only a waistcoat decorated with the shield of a lion over buckskins. Ester wondered if it was a family emblem or a clue to his identity, but with his wild dark-blond mane flowing freely around his face, perhaps a lion was merely his nature.

His friend was slighter and not as tall, a dandy with lace cuffs beneath a dark blue waistcoat over inexpressibles that were so tight, his todger and bollocks were clear as day. He had a heart-shaped mole on his cheek and greeted each person with warmth and kisses.

"Welcome, you beautiful pussy darlings. Oh, this little minx again. Can't get enough of us, can you? And is this a new pussy in our midst?" The dandy took Ester's hand and twirled her so her skirt fluttered open.

She had been expecting her lover to greet her, but she didn't see him. Instead, she was being singled out and, even though it was with admiration, her stomach knotted with self-conscious nerves, especially as she felt the brush of air tickling the curls on her mound.

A few people looked and she *felt* their interest. Spirits were high and everyone seemed good-natured, but she was daunted. Where was her lover? How long would she be here? What would happen before she could leave?

The lion gave her an appreciative nod. "Come see us later. Tell us how you're enjoying yourself."

She nodded, finding a smile of false confidence before following the rest of the pussy girls. They showed her the room set aside for them to leave their things and where she could retreat if she needed to wash up and tidy her hair.

"You will," one assured her with rueful amusement.

The other women rushed out, but Ester moved at a slower pace, wondering if her lover was in his room or what sort of costume he wore.

The house was the most astonishing thing she'd ever seen, with high ceilings and grand rooms full of pretty furniture and fancy clocks. She poked along a gallery, admiring the tapestries and paintings of staid old gentlemen framed in gold filigree. The wealth in owning so many fireplaces and colorful rugs and chandeliers with fat candles burning brightly was staggering.

She heard a giggle and peered into a small parlor where a ruddy-faced man sat on a footstool before a pussy girl. He had her bare foot in his hands and was sucking her toes while her other foot massaged into his groin. His eyes were closed in ecstasy.

Ester backed away, unsure if she was supposed to watch such things or give them privacy. Her lover had warned her she would have to let a few men fuck her, but given what the pussy girl in the carriage had said and what she'd just seen, she was realizing she may have to do other things.

You'll find even the most depraved requests very satisfying, she recalled her lover saying. Was that what he'd meant?

She wanted to look again, but a voice called across the gallery, "We need another woman for Last One Standing— Ah! Pussy girl. Come. We need you." A man dressed as a fox beckoned her.

Her stomach swooped with nerves.

Ester warily came around to him and he took her hand, drawing her into a music room where a man on the pianoforte diddled lively tunes from the keys, while four women stood on a round rug. They were knocking away the hands of three men playfully trying to get under their skirts.

The musician stopped abruptly when Ester entered. "We have enough?"

"Yes. Find your partners," the fox said.

Two of the women were pussy girls, but neither were the ones she'd met. One had dark brown skin, the other was a fair-skinned redhead. The third woman was older with a white streak in her black hair. She was very voluptuous and began gathering up her blue skirt with the help of an eager young man wearing a mask that rose high over his brow in a horse's head, like a chess piece. The last woman wore a man's riding habit and began releasing the buttons on her breeches to drop the flap and expose her loins.

"I don't know how to play," Ester said, glancing around nervously as she realized she would be expected to allow some kind of public intimacy.

"It's easy," the fox said—which everyone seemed to find highly amusing. "It *is* easy," he insisted. "Stand still and don't make a sound. The first to make noise must step away from the game and watch. We play until—"

Several voices chimed in, "Last one standing."

"I see," she said cautiously. "And why is it difficult not to make any noise?"

The fox set his finger against his smile to insist on silence. Then he went to his knees before her, as did all the men before the other women.

Oh.

Without hesitation, her partner lifted the panels that made up the front of her dress and tilted his head as he gazed on her. He gave her a small smile that suggested he was pleased with what he saw, then clutched her hips beneath her dress to hold her skirt open and blew softly against her fine hairs, waking up her flesh with tingling sensations that made her sheath tighten.

She drew a breath of anticipation and the warmth of his wet mouth settled against her pussy.

Oooh. It was all she could do to hold still and bite back the sigh of sweet joy that rose in her throat as his wet tongue lazily traced her slit. He was in no hurry, but he knew exactly how to seek out her nub and dandle the tip of his tongue against it, then swoop to poke at her entrance and come back.

Ester stood in a circle with the other women, watching a pair of eyes close across from her, watching one man's head nodding in a slow rhythm that she swore she could feel in her belly as tugs and swirls. Next to her, she watched the man use his thumbs to press back the woman's outer folds to distend her glistening inner lips. When he went back to slurping them with his tongue, that woman gave a jagged moan that was immediately followed by a cry of defeat and a rush of laughter from everyone else.

Ester caught her breath and touched a hand to where her heart was racing. A flush of relieved heat washed through her, but what now?

The woman who'd broken walked away and now there were only four women and five men. How would this work?

"Ready?" The woman who'd been sent away took a seat on the bench of the pianoforte and counted to ten. "One, two, three..."

The men walked inside the circular rug. One of the pussy girls parted her dress in invitation. The woman in the riding habit set her legs apart in an aggressive gesture that suggested she was determined to win.

"Ten."

Ester had a new partner, a man with brown skin and big, soulful eyes that peered at her from behind a tiger-striped mask. He had two round ears atop his head covering and a warm touch that stroked up her thighs from her knees, drawing back her dress to reveal her.

He circled his nose in the air around her thatch and inhaled, smiling as if he was most pleased to meet her in this bizarre, wordless way.

Her arousal had receded a little during the intermission, but it returned threefold as he licked into her still wet folds. He had a long, agile tongue, one he used to lap and lick, then fuck her. The light stabbing sensation made Ester want to shift restlessly and grab at his head to insist he let her grind herself against his face.

It was maddening, yet exciting to grow so aroused, yet be forced not to move, not to make a sound.

She looked across at the brown-skinned pussy girl who was being licked by two men. Her breasts were heaving against her dress. She was biting her lip, but one of her hands moved to the back of one man's head in encouragement and they immediately stopped.

"Noooo!" she sobbed.

Ester wanted to cry as well as her own partner immediately pulled away. Her stomach panged with an ache of loss as all the men released good-natured laughter and rose. The pussy girl pouted as she joined the voluptuous woman on the bench and began to count.

This time, as the men paced slowly in front of her, Ester's cunt throbbed with anticipation in time with their steps. "...five, six..."

She looked at their mouths as they passed, longing for each. The fox's knowing smile and the tongue tracing the sensual lips on that intense young man—

"Ten!"

Two men dropped before her. Ester drew a surprised breath and held it, standing very still.

They knew how to work in tandem. Each took hold of her hip in one hand to open her dress, then used his free hand to draw her plump folds apart to expose her most sensitive flesh. They had no inhibition with letting their tongues run freely against one another's as they swept them along the delicate inner lips they'd exposed, first getting to know her with flagrant licks, then sucking at her lips and growing more insistent.

Her legs trembled. Last one standing, indeed. She had never felt anything like this and feared she would collapse. The hot penetration of a tongue pushed into her. The other circled her button and here was the head bobbing that had so fascinated her when she'd seen him do it to the other woman. His tongue lapped rhythmically at her nub, driving her excitement steadily upward. Her crisis began to gather within her. She was going to come and when she did, she would scream with pleasure and relief.

"Oh fuck," the fair-skinned pussy girl sobbed.

"Oh *fuck*," Ester complained as she was abandoned as quickly as the other women. She dropped her head into her hands, shaking with desire.

The other pussy girl had had two men on her as well. She staggered away, bemoaning, "I hate this game."

Ester was barely able to keep her knees locked. The tough-looking woman in the riding habit moved so she was right across from her. She smiled and said, "I love this game. I always win."

Five mouths on her? Ester was trying to imagine how she would handle three if she wound up so lucky. Unlucky?

"One. Two..."

Her stomach tensed and her pussy lips felt weighted like rain-soaked snow. Her skin was too tight. All of her wanted to burst and she had a shameless urge to fondle her breasts and beg all of these men to fuck her senseless.

"Ten!"

Three men dropped to the floor at her feet. She nearly groaned at that outcome alone, but she held very, very still. Her original partner and one of the men who'd slicked his tongue against her a moment ago parted her dress and then her folds.

The musician was her third. He drew the edge of her dress even farther to the side, lifting it to expose her backside. His firm hand took hold of her bottom cheek and lifted to expose her arsehole. His tongue swept all the way down her crack until he was pushing his face deep into her ass so his tongue could reach where his friend was already claiming her entrance with the thrust of his tongue.

Ester couldn't take it. She nearly buckled and made a garbled noise of overwhelmed senses as she grasped at the nearest shoulder for balance. All the men stood, but her original partner stayed close and caught her arm to steady her. Her legs were trembling and there was so much slickness between her thighs, it was as if all these men had deposited their come inside her.

"I thought we might have a new champion." He kissed her, tasting intensely of cunt. "We each make her come now in whatever way she likes. Stay and watch. I'd love to fuck you after."

That sounded amazing when she was so aroused she was nearly mindless with it, but she recalled rather dumbly, "I'm looking for someone. Perhaps later?"

He nodded and she slipped away, still feeling dizzy and so aroused, the friction of her wet lips rubbing together as she walked filled her with lust.

She heard moans and entered a parlor where two artists were hard at work while their models were hard at play. A painter had his easel set up next to a divan where a knot of human flesh writhed. Four—five?—naked bodies were arranged in various states of fingering, tonguing and penetrating. They were moving, but only a little while he hurried to capture the vision.

On the settee, a sketch artist balanced a pad on his crooked knee and was capturing a close view of a turgid penis. A woman knelt with her mouth open to it, tongue reaching for the underside of the man's tip.

They all ignored her as Ester quietly entered and perused the sketches left on the table, all graphic depictions of sexual congress. The visions of cocks stuffed into pussies only served to keep her desire acute, but she wouldn't find satisfaction here. They were all occupied.

If she found her lover, she would fall on his cock so hard and fast!

Ester crept up the inside stairs to the bedrooms where most of the doors were firmly closed. No one was around, but behind one she heard what sounded like a crop against skin and a man's cries of pain in response. Farther along, she heard nothing but groans of pleasure.

The eerie quiet and faint noises set weights in her stomach while her wanton lust stayed lodged in her loins.

As she reached the end of the hall, she found one door had been left cracked open. She halted, quietly positioning herself to see the woman tied to the four corners of a bed. She struck Ester as a lady of quality, given her finely painted mask and sparkling earrings and what looked to be a diamond necklace. Her lips were painted bright red, but the color was smeared. Her indigo gown was torn open and in tatters around her.

A man sat atop her, naked from the waist down. He was rubbing his cock between her very large tits while pulling at her nipples, and saying nasty things like, "You want my prick in your hot little cunt, don't you? You are my hot little cunt. Every part of you."

Her pale globes were shiny and he moved with so little friction, Ester thought he must have oiled her chest before he started. As she watched, the man increased his speed and came with a shout, spilling his cream all over the woman's necklace.

The woman pulled at her bindings and said, "You animal. You've ruined it. It was a gift from my husband."

"Your husband doesn't know what a slutty cunt you are." He moved up to set his cock against her painted lips.

Ester heard a noise and her guilty conscience forced her to slip away. She fanned her hot cheeks, so anxious to climax she would take any solid object up her cunt right now if it would relieve the ache. She returned to the gallery and thought about the man who'd offered to fuck her, but a moan from the main staircase drew her.

The stairs were a grand affair with mahogany rails and two separate landings. On the lower one, she discovered two people coupling.

The woman wore an ornate mask bedecked with diamonds.

Her dress was an outlandish affair in bright yellow with purple lace and orange ribbons. The front of her dress was open, her breasts swinging freely as she bent and kept a low grip on the rail. The back of her dress was rucked up to the middle of her back, exposing her ass to her partner, who was giving potent thrusts into her cunt from behind.

He had quite a cock on him. With the build of arousal still concentrated in her loins, Ester couldn't help but stop and gaze enviously at the way that thick, glistening cock worked the woman's pussy. Ester's mouth watered and her inner muscles clenched in agonizing emptiness as she watched his long member slide in and out.

The woman turned her head to look at her, a dreamy smile on her face that quickly fell. "Marmalade cat."

"I'm sorry," Ester said, clearly intruding. "I only wanted to pass by." It was a lie. She'd been drawn by their noises of pleasure.

"No, I know who you are." The woman wriggled a signal that she wanted the man out of her.

The man—he was dressed in an elephant costume with a snout making an upward S from between his brows—drew his shiny cock free of her, but it continued to stand like a trumpeting trunk.

"I'm sorry I disturbed you," Ester mumbled. The woman was furious.

"I saw his receipt. Payment for one cat. *Marmalade*. He thought he could invite *you* and leave *me* at home, the bastard."

Oh *no*. Ester's heart plummeted. She didn't know what to say or do as she confronted her lover's wife.

"Don't deny it," the woman said, skirts swishing as she advanced on Ester. "He bought you for a night here. I know he did. But he won't be seeing you. I gave him a sleeping draught. He'll be abed all night. *Alone*."

Ester was backing away as the woman advanced and suddenly hit the stairs that went upward behind her. She stumbled, winding up on her ass on a carpeted step. She set a hand on one behind her, a foot on another, ready to scoot up the steps in escape.

"Should I leave?" the man asked.

"No," both women said. Ester spoke in fear while the other woman wore a sinister smile.

"No, you should watch," the woman said. "I'm going to give her something my husband never will." She dropped to her knees on the stair below her and brushed Ester's split skirt open.

Ester had her feet on different stairs and was so startled she didn't know what to do when the woman stared at her slit, still shiny with her unsatisfied arousal.

"Look at that little pussy, all wet with no tongue to clean her," the woman mocked. "Don't you worry. I'll help."

The next thing she knew, to Ester's complete shock, the woman dove her head between her thighs. Ester didn't fight her. How could she? She was so aroused from the silly game and then watching the couple on the bed and then seeing that huge cock that was still bobbing in front of her with its pulsing purple veins. She was *aching*.

The woman burrowed her lips into her folds and Ester tipped back her head, groaning loudly enough to shake the crystals in the chandelier. She relaxed onto her elbows on the steps behind her and spread her thighs wide, letting that angry woman have her way right there.

As she suckled and tortured Ester's button, the woman pushed two fingers into her. Three. She began to move them with a little dance that pressed up behind her belly button. It was so glorious, Ester lifted her hips into her sucking lips with utter abandon. She had never felt such tremendous waves of pleasure. They seemed to roll all the way up to sting the tips of her tits and return like thunder into the middle of her back.

As the woman worked on her, Ester felt herself growing tighter with anticipation. She clamped down on the woman's fingers with her inner muscles, bit her lip, and sought the finish that eluded her. She was so close, yet not close enough. What was this woman doing to her? She was cruelly teasing her by keeping her on this fine edge of acute need, building her desire until Ester was sure she would die if she didn't—

Her body did something it never had. An urge to bear down overwhelmed her. She clenched and her climax hit her so hard, she screamed. As she released, she thought her very soul might be shooting out of her body from between her legs. Wetness squirted from her in rhythmic pulses. Her stomach ached with the power of her contractions. The euphoria that stung through her was more potent than hot brandy on a cold day. It was a messy, all-encompassing ecstasy she'd never experienced.

"Oh fuck," the elephant man said with astonishment.

Ester collapsed like a wet rag while the woman chuckled with vicious enjoyment and withdrew her fingers. Ester dragged her eyes open and weakly whispered, "Thank you."

The woman's face was dripping with fluid. She used the edge of Ester's skirt to dry her cheeks and mouth.

"Has my husband ever given you that?"

"No," Ester had to admit, still breathless, still splayed and weak.

"I want to fuck her," the elephant said in a guttural voice.

The woman pouted briefly, then rose to move from between Ester's open knees and waved her partner into place. The elephant man dropped to his knees on the stairs, staring at her cunt. He used a finger and thumb to part her and guided the crown of his massive prick to her entrance.

"Just a little," the woman warned, touching his shoulder. "Just so she knows what else my husband will never give her."

Ester didn't protest. She was too limp and, frankly, highly curious how it would feel to—*oh*. "Sweet fucking horse cocks."

Having just come, she was still juicy, but not as slick as when she'd been dripping with desire. And he was *huge*. The stretch stopped just short of hurting, but it had her holding very still while his slow, steady penetration seemed to go on forever. In and in and in, stuffing her full and there was still more of him.

"It's nice, isn't it?" The woman played with the man's ear as she watched.

Ester was so astounded that he fit, she touched where they joined. Her flesh was stretched thin to accept him, and the tautness of it meant it only took a light play of her fingers across her button to have her juices flowing again. Her sheath softened around his fat intrusion.

"No," the woman said, batting at Ester's hand. "You may have my husband's useless cock. This one is mine." She made the big man remove his member and follow her up the stairs.

Ester stayed where she was, legs still open, her sex still recovering from that remarkable cock. She'd had it in her just long enough to inspire a fresh spark of randiness. She gathered herself and stood, taking a moment to find her balance on her soft knees.

She briefly thought of looking for her lover in the bedrooms, but she would have to ask someone which one he was using. Who? The crowd from when she had arrived seemed to have dissipated, people pairing off into couples and groups to enjoy their parties within the party.

She finished descending the stairs and wandered into a banquet hall with a long table of delicacies. Toward the end, a man had a naked woman on a table. She was decorated with various delicacies that he was in the process of sampling off her, one by one.

Ester ate a small cake from the table and was inordinately thirsty, so she had a glass of wine. She passed a small parlor where she saw the most amazing sight. A woman had a stone phallus dangling from a harness that went around her waist and upper thighs so she appeared to have a todger. As Ester stood in the doorway, the woman mounted another woman who reclined on the divan. They made love exactly as a man would with a woman.

The one with the todger lay atop the other and kissed her as she thrust, making the other woman groan lustily.

How did one acquire such a thing? How did it feel to have a woman do that to her? Or to be the one who did that to another woman?

So many things she wanted to know, but she left the pair to their enjoyments and followed the sound of voices speaking casually. Finally, a place where people were merely having a conversation and she wouldn't be confronted by pure carnality!

She entered a library with a billiards table in the middle of it. There was a small sitting area off to the side where a naked woman sat in a chair with one leg over the arm. A man knelt before her, eating her pussy. Three men were at the billiard table, two holding cues. The game seemed to have stalled and turned to betting on whether the white ball could go into the pocket of the naked woman who was on all fours on the table.

The dandy man was running the ball along the woman's open crack from her shiny pink lips to her tailbone and back to her notch. "But *which* pocket?"

"The lower left without question," the lion-dressed man said from his position in a throne-like chair near the woman being eaten. "The top right would be a very easy shot as well."

"You're so mean." The woman on the table was one of the pussy girls Ester had met in the carriage. She looked over her shoulder at the lion and wiggled her ass. "Just because you've been in both doesn't mean I'm loose."

"I've seen a man's fist disappear into both those holes— Oh, hello. Our new kitten. How are you liking your first ball?" the lion asked her.

"It's been...educational," Ester said.

"Has it? Come sit on my cock and tell me what you've learned." His buckskins were already open and he only had to flick them aside to reveal his cock, which was mostly hard. He squeezed it and it went red at the tip and lengthened, looking quite inviting and not nearly as challenging as the elephant's.

Ester didn't waver long. He was her host, after all. Or one of them, she supposed.

He slouched a little and got her knees beside his hips on the cushion of the chair. As she took him in and sank down, he shifted again and she was really quite pleased with the thickness of him tucked warm and firm inside her. She rested her arms on his shoulders and they kissed a little, which was very nice while he drew absent circles on her backside beneath the fall of her skirt.

"How many times have you come?" he asked casually, glancing toward the woman who began sobbing with release in the chair. The man followed the buck of her hips, hands tucked beneath her cheeks, tongue firmly in play while he rode out her climax. "That's eleven for our caged Birdie. We challenged her to see how many she could have without leaving that chair."

"I've only had one," Ester confessed. "But it was a very, very good one, so that is no reflection on my enjoyment of the evening."

"No? Because that sounds as though you've been shy or neglected. You say it was *very* good?"

"Two verys," Ester assured him, thinking it the oddest thing to banter with a stranger while she had his cock twitching inside her.

The talk at the billiard table continued. "There's no question it could go *in*. I'm asking how you get it *out*?"

"Put it in a sheath?" someone suggested.

"Still," the lion said with lazy confidence, ignoring them. "I'm sure we can do better than *one*. What sorts of things do you like?" He let his head tilt against the back of the chair to regard her.

"Well…" Ester was feeling cheeky now, since he was being so amiable and attentive. "Again, this is no criticism of your delightful ball, but do you know that I've had half a dozen tongues beneath my skirt and you're the second cock to fuck me, but not one single person has asked to see my titties? I saw a man fucking a woman's tits, but no one has offered to fuck mine. I rather think they're my best feature."

"Let me see." He drew the cups of her bodice down to expose her pale breasts with their beige circles and stiff pink tips. "They're very pretty. Let me taste."

She rose a little on her knees, feeling his cock slide to nearly leave her. He tightened his hands on her hips to keep the tip of his cock inside her while he sucked her nipples, one and the other and back again. He sucked hard, sending a runnel of heat into her loins. She could feel herself growing slick and hungry for the sensation of him thrusting.

When he lifted his head, he let his hands move to the backs of her thighs and gently rotated out as she lowered to take him in again. It had the effect of making her feel spread wide for his penetration and he hitched a little in the chair so he landed a little deeper, creating a sharp sensation that sent delightful tingles through her whole body.

Catching her breath, she rose to let him do it again, but this time, he reached his fingers in from his grip on the back of her thigh. His fingertip played in her juices, rubbing the moisture all over the sensitive flesh around her entrance.

When she came down again, his wet finger prodded—

She gasped and stilled, staring wide-eyed as his fingertip pressed insistently until he was penetrating her arsehole.

"What's wrong, little cat? Has no one played with you like this before?" He gave an experimental wiggle.

She shook her head, wide-eyed and unsure, but grew wetter as the sensation of what he was doing became more undeniable. It didn't hurt, precisely, but made her wary it might. At the same time, the profound filthiness of it made her pussy clench on the throbbing stick inside her. She was pinned like a butterfly, helpless.

A slow smile of satisfaction spread across his face.

"Did you know that my friend has a cock perfectly sized for initiating virgins to having their asses fucked?" He worked the tip of his finger a little harder, giving her the sense of what it would feel like. Strange, dark music thrummed in the deepest caverns of her loins, making her quiver in wicked anticipation.

"It's true." The dandy fellow came over and showed her his cock. It was smooth and dark pink, significantly thicker and longer than the finger inside her, but no elephant or even a lion. "I've fucked nearly every ass here. Even his. He lets me fuck him on my birthday."

"It's true," the lion said, finger still working in her arsehole. "I like it as a special treat. And it's a known fact that if he initiates a virgin, the ball will be a roaring success."

"Have any been dismal failures?"

"No." The lion showed his teeth in a wide grin. "But a good public ass-fucking sets a tone. What do you say? We can sweeten the pot." His finger gave a final poke that made her sit up straighter. Everyone laughed at his pun.

"I promise it will only hurt a little and in a way you like." The dandy stroked her hair.

"You'll have at least one more orgasm," the lion assured her.

Someone near the billiards table said, "I'll place five on her having two."

While betting began, Ester had a lingering thought that the wife of her lover would probably tell him what she'd done to Ester. He might well turn her out. Ester would need as much money as possible to make a fresh start. If she earned enough tonight, she might never have to take a patron ever again, only lovers when she wanted one.

Beyond that practical inducement was the thinking that she had come this far. The evening had already been something of a hallucination. Why not engage in one more exceptional act?

She nodded. "Yes."

A cheer of "Huzzah!" went up.

As the cheer died, the dandy threw up his arms and shouted as if commanding an army. "Bring me...my oil!"

Another roaring cheer went up and the lion gave her bottom a pat before he cheerfully lifted her off his cock.

As she stood, the dandy took her hand and lifted it, giving her a dizzying three twirls for their growing audience before he led her to a small couch. It had sturdy mahogany legs and carved scrollwork below and above the cushioned arms and back. It was covered in red damask with patterns in silver threads.

"Kneel here, my dear. And hold on tight here." He guided her hands to smooth knobs on the carved backing.

Ester did, now positioned to look at the billiards table. The pussy girl who may or may not have a billiard ball rolling around inside her climbed off it.

Ester wasn't sure what to expect, but the dandy didn't even lift her skirt. He was distracted by a challenge from one of his friends who asked if he thought he could produce four orgasms in her while his cock was lodged up her arse.

"Were she a man, I would say, 'no,'" the dandy said. "Women are far more resilient. Where have they gone for my oil? Italy?"

"Excuse me," Ester said as a man emerged from beneath the billiard table, naked but for a collar of linked chains around his neck. He was on all fours and stared at her with a blank look on his face.

"Yes, darling?" The dandy set his hand on her lower back and leaned close to hear her over the betting chatter.

"Who is that?"

"That's the dog. Chester. He might have to pee. Can someone take him out? Use the leash. Keep an eye on him or he'll run to the neighbors and eat their chickens."

Ester could only blink in bemusement while the "dog" came up to sniff her hands.

"Your oil, milord," someone said, coming in with a stoppered bottle upon a silver tray and making a flourishing gesture.

Another cheer went up and the man on the floor barked exactly like a dog.

"You'll have to put him in one of the bedrooms," the dandy said to the lion.

"He barks until the guests complain." The lion crouched to comb his fingers over the man's head and neck. "There's a good boy." Someone brought him the leash and he clipped it to the man's collar. "If he doesn't need to pee, leave him in the kitchen. He won't bother anyone there."

The man pretending to be a dog was led away and the lion clapped his hands to get everyone's attention. "All bets are closed?"

Ester had forgotten she was about to have her arse deflowered, but as a final few bets were placed, butterflies began to invade her stomach. Her pussy tingled with nervous tension.

"Ladies and gentlemen, cats and dogs," the dandy said. "I present to you..." He slowly drew her skirt up the backs of her thighs, revealing her nude bottom, inch by inch. "A virgin ass!"

Everyone clapped and cheered. The dandy gave each of her cheeks a warm greeting with a circle of his flat hand, lightly squeezing as though appreciating a particularly nice piece of fruit.

"Now, I like an ass with a bit of color. This spanking isn't meant to hurt or punish, kitten, only wake up your senses. You'll tell me if it's too much. This usually helps." He shifted to the side a little and ran one hand from the front of her thigh to her stomach then combed his fingers down into her pussy. His fingers splayed enough to catch her fat lips between his fingers. Her swelling button was firmly trapped in the notch between his middle fingers. He had definitely done this many times.

His other hand began to slap her bottom. The noise made her jump, but the sting wasn't bad. It did wake up her senses, drawing heat into her rear and making her grow wet as each strike caused her pussy to rub his palm, pulling lightly at the hairs. It wasn't comfortable, but it was oddly exciting to be held so, forced to endure the tanning of her cheeks.

Just as she was about to protest that the sting was growing too acute for her to bear, he stopped and soothed her with firm, circular strokes. This time as he squeezed, she felt it all the way up to her shoulders. His hand on her pussy moved in her folds, grazing her notch, but he seemed to deliberately avoid making any effort to give her an arousing caress.

"Such a pretty pink, yes? Who wants to kiss this virgin ass for luck?"

The gathered crowd began queuing. Some gave a modest peck, others took advantage of the moment to lick deep at her crack and taste her arsehole.

Her grip on the mahogany tightened as the kissing went on, seeming to fill her pussy with a weighty hunger that would remain unfulfilled. That's not where the dandy would fuck her. She grew both impatient for his penetration and increasingly aroused with anticipation.

The lion was behind her now, crouching to push his face deep into her spread thighs. His tongue lapped at her button and licked a generous taste from her cunt, then traced a wet line all the way up her crack. He left a kiss on her tailbone.

Then he stood beside her and said, "You *do* have nice tits. Once he's in, I'll play with them while he fucks you."

That earned protests of rigging the bets until he was forced to concede. "Sorry, kitten." He patted her. "Next time. I promise."

Ester wasn't sure she could take too many points of stimulation anyway. Her nipples felt hot and sharp, dangling in the cool air. The sense of exposure from having her ass out this way, damp from the licks and kisses made her nubbin throb. It was all nearly more than she could take and it hadn't even started yet.

"Oil, my good man."

She looked back to see the dandy hold out his palm. A small amount was poured in.

"Breaching a virgin, especially for you more endowed gentlemen, should only be attempted after an appropriate massage of the purse, yours and the one you intend to breach."

A ripple of laughter followed, then his slippery fingertip began circling her back entrance.

"Take your time. She's excited, but apprehensive, so she's puckered up and doesn't want to relax. We're in no hurry, little puss." The dip of his finger dabbed and circled and dabbed with a little more insistence. "When you're ready. You liked my friend's fat finger up your tight ass, didn't you? This will feel even— Ah. There. You see?" He worked his oily finger into her hole with slow power.

Ester let out a breath, stomach jittering with tension. Her pussy ached, but now so did that other channel.

"Oil," he murmured.

She didn't open her eyes but felt the cool oil pool behind her tailbone and slide down her crack. As it reached where he was fingering her, he drew free of her and gathered it, then slid two fingers into her.

She groaned loudly at the dull ache and intense sensation, quivering as he continued to press and drag his fingers in and out of her.

"How are we doing, little puss?"

Ester couldn't speak. Her hole stung and the neck of the bottle touched her ass cheek as he poured more oil into his hand and worked it into her. The sensations were so clear and sharp, she could swear she felt each finger separately.

"She likes it," the lion said in a warm voice of approval. "You should see her face."

Ester licked her lips. They were dry from panting and she dragged her eyes open. The lion was lazily pulling his cock and she licked her lips again, thinking how much she'd like to swallow that into her mouth as his friend kept up the lovely abuse of her behind.

"You see how she's bowing her back and lifting her ass, begging for more?" the dandy said. "It's time."

Ester was unconsciously offering herself in the most feral and brazen way, but because she longed for his cock to jab into her pussy.

The dandy's hairy thighs brushed the backs of hers and his hot cock rested in the crevice of her cheeks. She gripped harder to the carved wood as the cool sensation of oil poured over him and ran down her crack and seeped down the insides of her thigh.

"There is no such thing as too much oil," he assured the onlookers and massaged much of it up and into her cheeks, pressing them apart to further expose her arsehole. "Assistance, my good man?"

Another hand came to her cheek to hold her open while the dandy withdrew enough to slide the tip of his cock to the center of her hole. "Are you ready, little puss?"

"Yes. Do it," she said, clenching her eyes and trying to relax her hole.

There was pressure and stretch. It began to hurt, but along with the dull ache was a heavy feeling deep in her pussy, a place that was being touched for the first time.

A soft moan emanated from her throat. This was much like the elephant cock going into her cunt. It went on and on until she thought she couldn't possibly take any more, filling her to her limits, but it was so remarkable, she held still and took it. *Wanted* it.

"Huzzah!" The dandy's belly came flush against her hot ass and his bollocks nudged the sensitive skin near her pussy entrance.

The crowd shouted, "Huzzah!" and clapped and money changed hands.

Ester barely had any sense of what was going on around her. She clung to the wood and panted, impaled in a way she hadn't even known was possible. Everything about this moment was darkly forbidden, yet she reveled in it.

"Now the good bit begins, little puss." The dandy roamed his slick hands over her ass. He reached to play his fingers through her pussy folds and as she clenched in reaction, she felt a wave of pleasure jolt through her.

"Ha ha, you see?" He didn't move within her, just diddled her folds and circled her nub until she was the one who moved restlessly, urging him into motion.

Then he took hold of her hips and began to fuck her. She thought she would die from the heaviness. The fullness. It hurt, yet felt so incredible she could hardly breathe. Her sweating hands could barely hold on and the build of excitement within her seemed to gather from every part of her body.

She moved with him, utterly caught up in the filthy act, soon crying, "Harder, faster. Fuck my ass! Fuck me hard."

People were cheering and he gave it to her with firm, measured thrusts that weren't the same as being fucked in her pussy, because suddenly she was screaming, flying, her entire body convulsing with a climax that had struck from nowhere. From *there*.

He slowed to hold himself deep in her and petted her hips while she endured wave after wave of an orgasm that shook her very bones.

Slowly, she came back to herself. Money was changing hands and people were toasting her and one man had dropped his breeches to take a woman against a wall.

"You see?" The lion caressed her cheek and tilted her chin up. "I told you he would make you like it."

"Would you like another, puss?" the dandy asked as he massaged her cheeks and let his thumbs run against the tight ring clinging to his cock. "Would you like me to fill your ass with my come?"

"I don't think I could take another like that," she said in a daze.

"That's all right. Best to treat a newly fucked arse with some tenderness." The dandy gave a final squeeze of her cheek as he eased out of her. "Someone else will want my load."

"I do," several voices cried.

Ester slowly lowered onto her hip and rested there, ass sore, but she wasn't the least bit sorry. She watched a man kneel before the woman in the chair and pull her hips to the edge. He brought her ankles onto his shoulders and began to fuck her. Another man wrapped his lips around the lion's cock and she felt forgotten until something nudged at her hand.

It was the man with the collar. The leash dangled loosely behind him.

"How did the dog get back in here?" the dandy asked with annoyance. He had a man bent against the billiard table and was thrusting into his ass.

"I don't mind," Ester said and petted the man's head and ears while he licked her hand and wrist.

The panting and groaning resumed around her, but she remained in a daze. When she felt she could walk, she took herself to the pussy girls' room and cleaned herself, tidied her hair, and wondered how she could still feel sexy and curious, speculating on what kind of partner she might yet find for herself when she'd been so thoroughly caught up in so many debaucherous sex acts already. Perhaps because she hadn't been properly fucked in her cunt?

As she left the room, she found the dog-man had followed her. She was dying to ask why he pretended to be a dog but decided to make him happy and play along.

"Has no one taken you out yet? I will. Come." She picked up his leash and took him down the servants' stairs, through an empty kitchen, and out the back of the manor. It was a fine night with a high, bright moon and the air was pleasantly warm.

The man sniffed around the hedges exactly like a dog and even lifted his leg to pee.

Afterward, she sat on a bench on a square of lawn where the roses filled the night air with their perfume. He set his head in her lap and she combed her fingers through his hair.

"I wish you could talk and tell me how you came to be in this strange place," she murmured. "I'm a woman with no means. I had little choice but to take the opportunity. I don't regret it, though," she realized. "I will probably come back, but this isn't the way I expected to live my life. I don't suppose this is the way you meant to live yours, either, but we all wind up where we are, don't we?"

She told him all the strange things that had happened to her this evening, stroking the back of his neck under his heavy collar.

Talking about it made the embers of desire in her begin to glow hot and she glanced toward the house, wondering very belatedly whether her lover might have awakened and wish to fuck her.

The man before her snuffled his nose in her lap and she let her legs part so he could dig his nose into her crotch. He began to lap his tongue against her slit. She sighed in bliss, but she was dying for a good fuck. She noted he was hard and, impulsively, went down to her hands and knees on the lawn. She swept her skirts aside and asked, "Do you want to mount me?"

He understood perfectly and growled as he caged her smaller body with his long arms. His weight forced her to crouch onto her elbows and submit beneath him. His cock poked around until she guided him to her entrance. Then he thrust in and began humping her vigorously. She'd had much more sophisticated fucks tonight, but this one was so animalistic and thorough, she was soon coming with deep gratification.

He growled again and set his teeth against her neck where it met her shoulder, pumping furiously as he filled her pussy with the wet heat of his come.

Afterward, he held her tightly as they lay on their sides on the lawn, recovering. Each time she moved, he growled and set his teeth against her neck in warning. Why she found that endearing, she had no idea, but she eventually relaxed and waited until he disengaged himself.

He gave himself a shake and she picked up his leash to bring him inside. He stayed by her side the rest of the night, growling at anyone who approached her. When she agreed to pose in the art room, taking a straddled position over one man's face while sucking another's cock, she was encouraged to hold his leash so he was included in the piece eventually labeled "Her Loyal Companion."

When Ester took her leave, she petted him lavishly and said, "I wish I could take you home with me, but I can't. Perhaps I'll see you next time." She wondered if there would be a next time, seeing as her lover was liable to be very angry with her. She had no idea whether the dandy or lion would know how to reach her to hire her again.

At the inn, she found a heavy purse full of gold and silver coins waiting for her. It was such a fortune, she secreted it all over her body when she traveled back to London, terrified she would be robbed if someone heard the jingle.

She didn't wait for her lover to show up and turn her out. She removed to a room in a house of spinsters and widows in a quiet, respectable neighborhood. She claimed a false name and a husband lost in the war. She took in sewing for pin money and lived very frugally, as one would in her situation, while hiding her fortune in the floorboards.

One day, she was called to the parlor and discovered a smartly dressed man waiting for her. She didn't recognize him.

He grew redder and redder as her face remained blank. Finally, he stammered, "You may not remember me. My friends introduced me as Chester. I've, um, changed quite a bit. But I so enjoyed our conversation in the garden, I wanted to track you down."

"Oh," was all she could say as she realized he was the man who'd pretended to be a dog.

She had been trying to leave that strange night and the life it entailed behind her, so she probably should have been alarmed that he'd tracked her down, but she was surprisingly glad to see him. Respectability had its advantages, but she missed getting roundly fucked. Was he an agent from the lion and dandy, here to issue an invitation?

"Let's walk in the garden." They could speak with a modicum of privacy there while still being in full view of the house.

He was a banker, he told her, and was under much pressure to marry, but he hadn't found a woman with whom he could properly be himself.

"You seemed to accept my"—he swallowed—"predilection. I wondered if I might court you?"

He was not handsome or even boyishly cute. In fact, he was rather depressed-looking with his hangdog expression, but something about the earnest devotion in his eyes went straight to her heart.

Ester agreed, and within the year they were married. With their combined fortunes and his sensible head for finances, they were extremely well situated. In time, he gave her three children, whom they privately called their litter. Most days, Chester was an upstanding husband who toiled at the bank and was a doting father and bought the children a sweet after church on Sundays.

Some nights, though, because it made him so happy when she did so, Ester ordered him to sleep on the floor at the end of the bed. When he fucked her, he nearly always did it from behind. He would nip and lick at her neck afterward and he loved to lick her and make her come again and again, especially when his come was dripping out of her.

They returned as often as they could to the dandy-lion parties where she always held him on a tight leash. She would make him watch while she engaged in the most licentious acts with other guests and he only wet on the carpet once. She thought they would be banned for life, but the lion said she would be forgiven if she took both him and the dandy at once, pussy and ass respectively.

They made a ceremony of it and that ball was pronounced, as every single one of them was, The Grandest Ball Ever.

The End

Standing In
for an Earl

CHAPTER ONE

David Fitzwilliam was hardly the first child born to a nobleman and a freed slave, but he did have the advantage of being given a decent education and arrangements for his future, even if his father hadn't publicly acknowledged him. A bastard was a bastard and men tended to disguise such inconvenient details when their wives were still alive.

Nevertheless, his father had quietly ensured his mother received a small pension and the use of a cottage near where David was provided a living. David assisted the aging manager of a forgotten property in Cornwall. It belonged to the family of an earl David's father had known at Oxford. David's legitimate brothers received far more generous inheritances and appointments, but many a fourth son of a viscount received nothing at all. David appreciated what he had and was determined to make the most of it.

Five years later, his superior, Mr. Carew, died. David was allowed to rise into the position of manager but knew he would have to prove his worth. To that end, after walking a stretch of fallow land that had been deemed too much work to reclaim, he began to excavate an old pig sty with a thought to repair the abandoned cottages. If he could rent them and sharecrop a little barley or allow sheep to graze, it would increase the estate's profits.

He no sooner started than he made a discovery that forced him to do something he would have preferred to avoid—he had to write to the earl.

The reaction to David's letter could have gone either of two ways. The earl might have politely thanked David for keeping him informed, asked him to ship the items to London, and told him to carry on as planned. That was what David hoped for. He would much rather keep his head down and go about his business.

But Henry Quigley, the Right Honorable Earl of Wolfrik, was a noted antiquarian and enthusiast of historical discoveries. He replied that he would arrive in the first week of June to view the find himself.

All field work stopped. David pitched in to ready the manor for the earl and his wife. A stooped housekeeper had been in residence for forty years, but the butler had long passed and hadn't been replaced, because no one in the family had visited for upwards of a decade.

David combed the village for bodies willing to dust and air out the house. They cleaned windows and mended moth-eaten linens, polished silver, washed china, and swept the chimneys. He found a retired cook to stock the pantry with whatever fresh produce, wine, meats, and cheese the village shops had in store.

Anticipating the earl would bring an army of staff and provisions, David dismissed all but a few lads to help with unloading when the post chaise arrived. Only one carriage turned up, however, and no servants occupied the bench seat at the back. A trunk was tied there and the postillion was from a posting inn.

The housekeeper nudged a boy to step forward and open the door. A rumpled but fit man of thirty-something emerged and offered David a friendly nod. He had a dark tan as if he spent much of his time outdoors. Or had heritage not unlike David's own?

He must be a manservant come ahead to ensure things were in order. His clothes weren't that of an earl. He wore baggy breeches with tall boots and an unbuttoned coat without a waistcoat. He clapped his hat on his wavy, light brown hair and beamed happily at someone in the carriage as he held up a hand of assistance.

A well-formed ankle and calf above a short walking boot

appeared. Then a confection in pink poured out in a waterfall of silk and frills.

Bloody hell. Was that the countess? The housekeeper had told David the master remarried after his first wife had died sometime after birthing their second son. This woman was David's age or younger and stunningly beautiful. Her round face of clear, dusky skin and plump lips was framed by the wide ribbon of her pink bonnet. A few tight, dark brown curls were decoratively pulled to frame her temples.

She was very sweet looking as she gazed adoringly at the man, smiling her thanks for his attendance on her.

He escorted her forward. David took his cue from Mrs. Grimsby's curtsy and bowed.

"Mrs. Grimsby. I haven't been here since I was a child, but you haven't changed a bit," the man said. "Please meet my wife, Lucrezia."

Wife. This was the earl? David worked to keep his shock off his face.

"My lord. It's a pleasure to see you again. My lady." Mrs. Grimsby curtsied again.

"It's very nice to meet you," Lucrezia said in a voice that held the sensuous huskiness of a Mediterranean accent.

She turned her bright-eyed attention onto David. He felt the sweep of her curious gaze like a spring breeze that drifted across his exposed skin to raise all his most masculine desires. His throat dried and his scalp tightened. A pleasant shiver slid down his spine, leaving a heavy prickle in his loins that threatened to draw forth a bulge in his breeches.

He dropped his head in another abbreviated bow so he wouldn't be caught ogling where the swells of his employer's wife's breasts rose against her neckline.

"May I introduce you both to David Fitzwilliam?" Mrs. Grimsby said.

"The man we've been anxious to meet." The earl eagerly

thrust out a hand and shook David's with enthusiasm. "Old Carew never gave me such a thrill! We've been counting the days until we could see what you have for us, haven't we, darling?"

"We have." Now the lady was offering her hand with a pretty smile. "It's a pleasure to meet you."

She wasn't wearing gloves. David bowed over her hand, regretting his calluses, but she didn't seem bothered while the tingle in his crotch rose through his belly and chest and tightened his throat.

As he released her and glanced at the earl, expecting to be frowned at for touching her, David caught...something. The earl's attention was closely trained on his wife. She met her husband's gaze for the barest hint of a second, then dropped her lashes. It wasn't guilt. Self-consciousness, perhaps?

David was still trying to interpret it when he realized the earl had turned his gaze back on him. David braced himself, but there was no hint of accusation or hostility. If anything, he appeared to reassess David in a way that suggested he saw more than had first met his eye.

It caused David's heart to take a strange bounce in his chest. The kind that happened amid danger, but the thrilling kind, like taking a leap from a height into a pile of hay.

He didn't know what to make of it, so he cleared his throat and indicated the carriage. "We expected you would bring staff. I'll send word to the village that we'll need assistance."

"No, no! We're used to living rough," the earl assured him. "The countess and I met in a remote camp in Tuscany where her father was excavating an ancient village. Lucrezia has a great passion for relics, don't you, darling?"

She smiled at what might have been a joke at their age difference. She had to be fifteen years younger than her husband, but that wasn't unusual among the aristocracy.

"What can I say? I'm drawn to the richness of history."

Oh. *That* was a bold cheek.

The earl chuckled with enjoyment, but David forced himself to keep a straight face. They were the most eccentric couple he'd ever met. Thankfully they were the housekeeper's problem, not his.

"I asked Mrs. Grimsby to lock the Roman coins with the silver in the butler pantry. It's too heavy for her to manage. Shall I bring it up for you to examine once you've settled?" David offered.

"Is it far to the site? We've been stuffed in a carriage for days. We'd like to stretch our legs. Yes, darling?"

"Oh, yes please," Lucrezia said.

Shit.

"Not far at all." David dug up a smile. "Let me show you."

•••

Lucrezia and her husband might have been drawn to Cornwall by their shared passion, but they hadn't come here with the inkling that *all* of their shared passions might be indulged.

An ache of sexual need had struck like a blow the moment she had glimpsed Mr. Fitzwilliam. He was tall and muscled and had a bearing of quiet confidence that unfurled a sharp yearning in her, one stronger than any she'd ever experienced—even for Henry when he'd been helping her discover her capacity for passion.

Her astute husband had noticed her reaction, too. Thank goodness he was not only observant, but also devoted and doting. She really did love him to distraction. How could she not when he was so generous and willing to facilitate her every whim?

She let herself fall back so she could trace the line of Mr. Fitzwilliam's broad shoulders with her gaze. His shiny black hair was gathered so tightly, he had pulled almost all the wave out of it and secured it with a lace of leather that wrapped and restrained the short tail.

She imagined releasing his hair and feeling it against her breasts and stomach and inner thighs. Would he like that as much as she would?

Men frequently made overtures to Henry Quigley's nubile wife, but very few understood—or embraced—that their relationship was actually very close and intimate. Her husband might be unable to make love to her the way he wished, but that didn't mean he didn't want her to have pleasure or witness the lovemaking she did enjoy.

Not all men wanted to be part of *that*, however.

As they strolled beyond the outbuildings toward what looked like a bluff overlooking cliffs, Henry attempted to put Mr. Fitzwilliam at ease. "My last visit here was the summer before I started at Eton. Since then, I've been seeking treasures abroad, never imagining I had such rich history at home."

He related how he'd developed an interest in antiquities through his grandfather and furthered his studies during his grand tour after he left Oxford. He married abroad, much to his father's dismay. His first wife had been the daughter of a Tuscan vicomte and they quickly secured the title, which redeemed him. His two sons were at Eton now.

"I was inconsolable when she passed, but then I met Lucrezia."

That was almost five years ago. Lucrezia had been nineteen. They'd been called home three years later when Henry's father died. She was still trying to find her way in his circle. Most of his peers presumed she had married him for his money, but she and Henry were well-matched intellectually. If he hadn't had the responsibilities of his title and Napoleon hadn't been encroaching, they would still be in Italy, cleaning, examining, and recording their finds.

"And you? Married? Children?" Henry asked with his natural affability.

"None, my lord. My mother keeps our cottage and it's a very small village. Few prospects, but I'm content to focus on my work, especially now that full responsibility for caretaking the estate has fallen to me."

Lucrezia tucked a smile into her neck, admiring the way Mr. Fitzwilliam cemented his position so smoothly.

"Call me Henry. We don't stand on ceremony when we're in the field, do we, Lucrezia?" He glanced back, steady gaze asking, *Are you pleased? Shall we continue?*

Very pleased, she said with her smile.

"Are we walking too fast? Come." Her husband held out a chivalrous arm, drawing her into the space between the two men so her awareness of the tall David beside her nearly overwhelmed her. "Tell our new friend about some of your most salacious discoveries."

"My husband wants me to shock you," she told David with a rueful glance upward.

"I pride myself on being broadminded and unshockable." He was very appealing with his strong jaw and wide mouth. The way he watched her so closely from beneath his spiky dark lashes caused a sting of excitement to heat her blood. "But please dare try."

"I grew up among forthright men who uncovered naked sculptures and explicit murals," she said without a shred of qualm or regret. "I not only made detailed notes describing the finds, I also held them and cleaned them and made sketches. It's the sort of art study few students could boast of receiving, but London society judges me very vulgar. I can't help that the Romans were free-thinking and graphic, though, can I?"

She waited for David to ask, *How graphic?* People hated to admit how intrigued they were by the libidinous and indecent, but they always were.

"I will have to see the sketches to judge for myself. Here. Watch your step." He slipped ahead of her down four long, shallow steps overgrown with grass. Turning back to her, he held up a hand.

She took it, gaze drawn to the walls of stone surrounding the depression, taking note of the configuration obscured by centuries of Mother Nature trying to reclaim the land. As David's steady hand folded over hers, however, a frisson went through her and she felt the reflexive jolt in David. Their gazes clashed into one another's as her feet came even with his. She had to consciously catch a breath, because hers had been punched out of her.

"This is a much more significant discovery than you realize, my friend." Henry halted on the last step so the top of his head was even with David's ear. He clapped his hand on David's shoulder. "It will take all summer to explore what we have here."

CHAPTER TWO

A ll summer? David did not look forward to being at the beck and call of spoiled nobs, but Henry wasn't afraid to get his hands dirty on a pickaxe or other implement. Lucrezia was practical and bright and sketched incredibly well.

She was also an exhibitionist, wearing plain gowns without corsets that grew damp in the mist. When the sun came out, she lifted her skirts to her knees and rolled up her sleeves. She was beautiful as hell, though, so how could he complain that he had to milk himself twice a day just to stay sane? If David had met her on the obscured terrace of an abandoned seaside villa in a place he'd never heard of, he would have married her as fast as he could, too.

He was growing infatuated, thinking of her under him in his bed. Or in the grass. Or against a wall. He might have somehow conquered his obsession with her if he hadn't caught them in a moment of profound intimacy.

His fault, he supposed. Mrs. Grimsby had passed along an invitation that David lunch with them the following day. He had sought them out to accept in person. So he could see her.

Which he did.

As he wove through the site, he heard a noise and stopped at a gap.

Lucrezia sat on a stone bench built against a rock wall. Her seat was cushioned by centuries of thick moss and grass. Her skirt was up around her waist, her bare legs over her husband's shoulders, her hand in his hair. Her buttoned neckline was open, exposing her voluptuous breasts. Her bonnet was off and kinked strands of hair were wafting free of her thick plait as she tilted her head back and moaned at the sky.

David stared a long time. He'd heard of such a thing but never done it. He was frozen by a voyeuristic thrill and uncontrollable jealousy. Not envy. He didn't wish he had something like what Henry had. He coveted the man's wife. He wanted *her*.

It was such a shockingly acute emotion, he strode all the way back to the dairy barn and worked like the devil all afternoon, trying to feel shame for watching them. For wanting her. Instead, he simmered in a strange combination of lust and excitement. He envisioned the lascivious act a thousand times, of putting himself on his knees. *Craving* it.

He wanted to hate the both of them for this cruel longing they'd inspired in him. The memory of her, so beautiful in the throes of passion, had him stroking himself into a powerful orgasm that night and again in the morning. His cock was still twitching with anticipation when the luncheon hour arrived. He couldn't wait to see her again even though he feared he would embarrass himself by staring or growing hard.

The kitchen and hall were empty. He found the earl and his wife in the sitting room. She wore a lightweight white gown with a pale yellow sash below her soft breasts. Her hair was loosely gathered atop her head and she had her legs curled beneath her on the divan as she sketched in her book.

"David." The earl stood at the window in his typical half dress of a shirt without a neckcloth or waistcoat. He turned at the sound of David's footsteps and smiled.

The countess moved her feet to the floor and set aside her book to pick up what looked like a glass of brandy.

"I didn't see the cook or Mrs. Grimsby." It struck him that he might have misunderstood. Was he here to *serve* lunch? How humiliating when he'd gone to the trouble of scrubbing up and putting on his best clothes.

"Both gone to the village. We're having a cold lunch, I'm afraid, but we had things we wanted to discuss with you in private. Will you have a glass of brandy?"

"Thank you." He accepted the glass warily. "Concerns about the site? My work?" He forced his gaze to hold the earl's, hoping he hadn't betrayed his interest in the man's wife and was about to be called out.

His stomach knotted as he recognized knowledge in the older man's hazel eyes. *Your lust is obvious.*

"I'm extremely happy with your work. Your employment is not in question." Henry cleared his throat. "No matter whether you accept the offer we make you today or not."

David took his first sip of alcohol. The fiery trail went down the back of his tight throat while every muscle in his body instinctively tensed.

"Lucrezia and I discovered very quickly that we are perfectly suited to one another." Henry held out a hand and she rose to join him, taking Henry's hand and gazing up at him with the adulation David had seen several times.

It put that sick, possessive knot in his gullet while his libido took one look at her breasts, unconstrained by a corset, and his cock nearly exploded.

"Something happened shortly after we married, however. I had an inflammation in my throat. Mumps? Are you familiar with that contagion?"

David gave a vague nod. He'd heard of it.

"You're in no danger. I'm fully recovered," Henry assured him with a raised hand. "But at the time, it affected other parts of my body." His hand indicated the fall of his breeches. "The physician who treated me attempted to help, but it seems to have caused irreparable damage. I am no longer able to make love to Lucrezia the way I most wish."

David bit back a curse and moved several steps to the side, partly to keep from revealing where his mind leaped. *I'll do it.* He set his drink on the nearest flat surface and said, "That's very unfortunate." What a conversation. He looked to the door.

"We've misunderstood?" Henry asked, frowning with concern.

"You're not drawn to her the way she is to you?"

David snapped his head around. Lucrezia stood with Henry's hand in both of hers, eyes limpid and filled with a come-hither yearning that stoked the furnace of heat in his loins.

"It's not easy to find the right match, but you excite Lucrezia and you and I have a good rapport. I'm confident you'll be discreet, whether you join us or not."

Us? David picked up his drink and swallowed it all in one gulp. It left a scrape in his voice as he asked, "You've done this before?"

"Twice." Henry brought his wife's hand to his mouth and kissed the back of it while gazing lovingly into her eyes. "I adore seeing her abandoning herself to pleasure and want to provide it to her any way I can."

"You watch." David didn't bother trying to sound outraged. The image of Lucrezia's bare legs slung over Henry's shoulders and her naked breasts arched to the sky hadn't left his mind's eye. Apparently, he liked to watch, too.

"Have you had many lovers, David?"

"Excuse me?" Even within the context of this bizarre discussion, that felt like an overstep. And no, he'd had fewer than Lucrezia, given her vast experience of three. He had only the housemaid who had initiated him and the widow he'd visited for a few months before she left to live with her sister.

"I'm only asking if you've developed skill with the art of lovemaking." Henry released Lucrezia to bring the bottle of brandy across. "And whether you're liable to have the pox?"

"I don't," he growled, accidentally answering both questions.

"Good. We've considered many times that she might simply take a lover, but she feels safer if I'm there. And I like to direct things. Make love to her *through* you, if that makes sense."

Why did that titillate him? David was an independent, headstrong man. He'd barely suffered the supervision of old Carew and only because the payoff had been worth it. Still, it annoyed him to no end when he was the one at work and others stood around.

He held out his glass, but the earl only splashed a little into it.

"I won't be accused of getting you drunk to talk you into this. It has to be your choice," Henry said with a wink. He returned the bottle to the sideboard then stood behind his wife, hands on her shoulders while Lucrezia demurely kept her lashes lowered. "But look at her. Don't you want to make love to her? Don't *you* want to know how best to pleasure her?"

David looked into his drink without tasting it, thinking he must be drunk because he had already made up his mind. His hands were aching to touch her. His rod was growing stiff in his breeches.

"Lucrezia?" David's voice originated in the bottom of his chest.

She lifted her depthless gaze, dark eyes promising all sorts of paradise.

"You like what he's offering? It's something you want?"

"I do," she said with a pang in her voice that begged for understanding. She tilted her cheek against her husband's hand on her shoulder. "It makes me feel very close to him."

His scalp was so tight with excitement he could barely think, but he forced himself to address the practicalities. "What if you fall pregnant?"

"That would be a blessing we didn't expect," she said with a quirked smile up at her husband. "Since he can't make one with me."

David's breath backed up in his throat, pushing pressure into his chest. "Is that what this is about?"

"No!" Henry looked shocked by that. "No, we're only saying we would welcome a child and would happily raise one with you. Lucrezia's mother came from Tunis and I have a great-grandmother who was Greek. Many in my family are very swarthy, so there wouldn't be any awkward explanations. And you have noble blood, David. It would only be right that your child enjoy the appropriate privileges of our class."

David ran a hand down his face, more shocked that the earl knew who his father was than any of the rest of this conversation. It reassured him, though. Made him feel less of a hired hand, more of an equal.

As anticipation began to overtake him, his mouth wanted to form the word, *When*?

He only had to look to where Henry was removing pins from his wife's hair to know the answer to that. He swallowed.

"Isn't she the most beautiful sight?" Henry unwound her hair so her plaits fell in long, dark lines over her breasts. "Come closer."

David was drawn by an invisible force. By unfettered *want*. He found himself standing right in front of her. A light scent rose off her that he couldn't name, but it went straight to his head. Her cheeks darkened with a blush and her breasts were lifting in subtle pants of excitement. He hesitated, then let his hand curl around the plait where it hung next to her neck.

From a long way off, he heard Henry's quiet command to, "Pet it all the way down."

He felt himself almost in a spell as he loosened his grip and let his hand pet the silken path over the swell of her breast and pressed the tail into her rib cage beneath it, continuing until he found the tension of her stomach.

His hand shook. He fisted it in a bid to take control over himself.

"Would you like to kiss her?"

David dragged his gaze up to her mouth, round and plump and tempting as a ripe plum. He wanted to *devour* her. He blinked, trying to clear his blurring vision.

"If you do everything he says, it will be lovely for both of us." Lucrezia set her hand on his cheek, cool and soft. "You'll see."

"Do it gently," Henry said in that voice that seemed to seep from his own inner thoughts. "There's no rush. Let her know you want to be sweet with her. Tender."

Did he? He didn't know what he wanted. So many imperatives were clashing within him, he couldn't make sense of them, but she licked her lips in anticipation and he couldn't resist. He had to taste her.

Her mouth was firm and luscious, her breath scented with brandy, her response like sugar that melted under the press of his lips. He cupped her neck and took his time getting to know every quiver and tremble of her beautiful mouth. So heady while the pulse in her throat hammered against his palm, exciting him. Her hand moved from his cheek to the back of his head, encouraging him to kiss her more deeply.

They kissed so long he forgot Henry was there, losing himself in the bliss of it, but when the other man spoke, his quiet voice didn't startle him. In fact, he found it added a taboo element to what they were doing that spurred his arousal.

"Give her your tongue. Let her know how much you're looking forward to filling her in other ways."

He was. So intensely, he plunged his tongue deep between her lips and felt hers swirl around his in greeting. In reception. It was exquisite. *She* was. His chest stung and his cock was so hard he ached.

He shuffled closer, moving his free hand to her waist and drawing her closer so he could kiss her harder. But carefully. He schooled himself with brutal control. Everything in him wanted to consume her, but oh, he wanted to cherish her at the same time.

"And her neck," Henry murmured. "She loves to be kissed here." He drew a line down the side of her neck and Lucrezia shivered, lifting her chin as David sought the tender area with his mouth. "And across here. Kiss all of this. You'll have to hold her up."

Henry turned her so David could taste the tendons at the back of her neck and the bump at the top of her spine, exposed by the wide neckline of her gown.

She grew weak, drooping her head and gasping out the most delicious noises as he set his open mouth along her nape.

"And her earlobe."

He had never sucked a woman's earlobe. It made Lucrezia moan and squirm in his hold. The soft give of her ass pressed through the layers of her gown into his upper thighs. He rooted his feet and tightened his arms.

"Are you hard? Let her feel it."

She couldn't mistake it. His cock pressed into her supple ass. She pushed back in welcome. One arm reached back to twine around his neck. The other dug nails into the back of his wrist.

"Am I hurting you?" He started to ease his suffocating hold across her waist, but her nails dug in more sharply, keeping him there.

"No. It feels good," she said in a voice husked by growing passion.

"Look at her nipples," Henry said. "She loves this. Don't mark her, but let her feel your teeth on her neck. And hold her breast if you want to. Feel how lush and warm she is."

He'd already been staring down at the way her nipples stood against the light muslin. As he closed his hand around one globe, she arched into his touch, pushing her ass into his cock with even more vigor. He set his open mouth on her neck and swirled his tongue against her skin, groaning with enjoyment.

"Put your hand in her dress. Pinch her nipple. Not too hard."

No corset, just the warm weight of her breast filling his palm and the stiff berry of her nipple rolling between his thumb and fingertip.

"Henry, please," she moaned.

"Is he making you wet, darling? Move your hand between her thighs, David. Feel how hot she is."

She was. He pushed his fingers against her gown, enthralled by the plump shape of her mound and the intense heat in that condensed notch. She covered his hand and encouraged him to press harder as she moved, writhing in his hold.

"Don't come, David, but help her find release. Lick into her ear and tell her how badly you want to fuck her."

"I wish I was inside you right now," he confessed. "Feeling this heat around my cock." He ground his hand against her.

Suddenly she was crying out and shuddering in his arms. A flood of heat soaked his fingers. It was incredible. He clenched his teeth, damned near coming in his breeches. Somehow, he kept his fingers rocking into her notch until Lucrezia hung weak and panting in his arms.

"That was the most exciting thing to ever happen to me," he whispered.

"I liked it, too," she breathed, setting her hand on his cheek and kissing him over her shoulder. "I'm so glad we found you. That you're willing to indulge us."

"Are you?" Henry asked. "Do you want to continue? Should we go upstairs?"

David wanted to have her on the floor. He was hard as a rock and shaking with arousal. His heart was knocking so hard she must feel it against her back.

He scooped her up and looked at Henry. "Let's go."

CHAPTER THREE

Lucrezia wore only a chemise beneath her simple gown and she wanted to tear both from her body, but when David put her on her feet in the bedroom, she stood acquiescent as Henry pulled the bow on the sash and took his time undressing her.

He liked undressing her. He had said once that it was like knowing a treasure lurked beneath layers that had to be removed carefully, to ensure he did no damage. On a day like today, she knew he was giving her time to be sure, but she suspected he also wanted to watch her new lover's reaction to the slow revelation of a shoulder, a brown nipple, a wink of navel, the line between her ample bottom cheeks and the appearance of her black bush at the tops of her thighs.

The two previous lovers he'd found for her had all shucked their own clothing in a rush, betraying their impatience.

David was different in so many ways. She had urged Henry to go slowly from the start, unable to tell if David was as intrigued by her as she was by him. He was a quiet, subtle man. Controlled. She had felt incredibly safe, falling apart in his arms a few minutes ago, and longed to know what might crack his composure as completely as he'd destroyed hers.

He set aside his boots, then removed his jacket and waistcoat and shirt very absently, all of his attention on her. The heat in his gaze was as lust-inducing as his wide shoulders and muscled chest and flat stomach sprinkled with black whorls of hair.

Henry was a very thorough lover, though. Whether he was using his hands, or his mouth, or another man, he ensured each moment was drawn out to the height of its ability to imbue her with pleasure. He stood behind her as he dug his fingers into her hair to unplait it before he swept it in frothy curtains down the front of her naked shoulders so the tails tickled the swells of her breasts.

"Is this not the most erotic sight you've ever seen?"

The tip of David's tongue wet his lips before he said gruffly, "Almost."

"Oh?" Henry's voice cooled, but the lust in David's gaze left Lucrezia in thrall.

"I saw you yesterday." He dragged his gaze from scouring the depths of Lucrezia's soul and said to Henry, "Licking her. You should have seen her face. *Should*." His voice lowered into a graveled note that curled her toes. "Tell me exactly what you were doing."

"Oh, darling." Henry's voice held an uncharacteristic quaver. He gave her upper arms a reflexive squeeze. "We have found the right man, haven't we?"

She trembled in reaction, inner muscles clenching so hard with eagerness, a latent drip of juices wet her lower lips.

"Come. Kiss her. Tease her. Seduce her," Henry invited.

And here was David looming before her, a wall of strength and heat. His mouth enveloped hers and the tips of her breasts were stimulated by the springy hair on his chest.

She let her arms go around his neck and he took her weight, the wool of his breeches coarse against her naked belly, but she liked the subtle torment of roughness and denial coupled with the brush of his chest against her naked breasts. She liked the way he gathered her hair and tightened his fist around it, forcing her head back so he could kiss down her throat and across her collarbone.

"Suck her nipples. Make her beg you to lick her the way she begged me."

She'd been going out of her mind thinking about David and here he was, gathering her breast in his wide hand and closing his lips over her nipple to suckle and pull and flick his tongue against it. Another release of wetness struck as he shifted to torture her other breast.

His hips were eluding her as he bent. She couldn't feel that delicious thickness that promised to alleviate the deepest ache inside her.

"I want him now, Henry." She looked anxiously to her husband.

"Not yet, my love." He was watching with fervent pleasure. "I want to see what he saw. I want you to buck against his face the way you did mine. Bring her to the bed, David."

He did, picking her up like she weighed no more than his abandoned shirt, and sat her on the edge of the bed.

Henry touched her knee, urging her to spread her legs to show her pussy to David. She leaned on her hands and opened her knees wide.

"Pretty, yes?" Henry prompted.

"Fucking beautiful." David's nostrils flared. He licked his lips and swallowed, then set a heavy hand on her opposite thigh and stroked once along the sensitized length, restless. "I've never done this. I want you to like it."

"You always like it, don't you, angel? What did you ask me for yesterday?"

He was going to deny her, the wretch. She knew it. "Two fingers," she admitted.

"Not this time." He softened the blow by smoothing her hair from her brow. "I want your cunt so hungry for his cock you scream when he puts it inside you."

She whimpered and her thighs reflexively tried to close in an effort to ease the yearning in her empty sheath.

"Kiss her thighs so she knows what's coming."

David fell to his knees and began worshiping every inch of her inner thighs and down to her ankle, coming back to lick behind her knee, groaning, "You smell so good."

"Spread her lovely petals. Look how beautiful she is."

He used a gentle touch, delicately examining her most intimate flesh for a long minute before flashing her a wild look.

"I'm going to come in my breeches."

"Please don't," she pleaded.

His teeth flashed in a brief, tortured grin before he ran the pads of his thumbs in the abundant wetness, spreading her sex to expose her even more, like sectioning an orange.

"Taste her. Get to know all of her," Henry invited.

David leaned in and his tongue found her hole, pushing in with what was more tease than satisfaction. He made a noise that suggested he liked the taste and slithered his tongue in all the smooth little channels between her folds, kissing her the way he'd kissed her mouth—hungrily and thoroughly and with a delicate suction that made her blood run like fire.

"Look. You see this little bud peeking from its hood?" Henry framed it in a light pinch, making her thighs tremble all the more.

Her breath began to saw in anticipation.

"She's so sensitive here, she flinches if she's not ready for you to touch her like this, but anoint her with your tongue and she is lost. Start slow. You'll know when she wants more vigor."

His mouth returned, hot and soft. His tongue explored her slit again, this time with more confidence. He knew what she wanted and watched her with a merciless glint in his gaze as he avoided giving her what she yearned for most. Waiting until she whimpered.

Then—

"Ooohhh." She groaned from the depths of her soul as sharp joy struck the pit of her belly and flames licked up to her throat. She let her head fall back in bliss.

"Fuck you're beautiful," Henry said with dark satisfaction. He cupped her breast and squeezed, making her nipple sting. "You love being tongued, don't you?"

"I do." She moaned, wanting to tell David how good it felt, but oh, he was a quick study. She bit her lip and touched his head as the sensations intensified and he drew forth a fresh flood of juices. "Please let me have his fingers? Please?"

"No, my love." Henry stroked her hair with tender cruelty. "And keep your legs wide so I can see. Suck now, David. She'll come."

He did, seeming to draw her very life force out of her before it slammed back in a rush of ecstatic heat and shivering pulses that stole any strength or control she had.

She had no recollection of crying out or falling back, but knew from the faint rasp in her throat and the pressure against her shoulders that she had done so.

She came back to utter lassitude. David was placing tender, open-mouthed kisses on her thighs and sweeping his tongue across her spread pussy, not quite soothing, but not inciting, either. Like someone whose meal had been so good, he was licking the plate clean.

• • •

"Please can we fuck now?" Lucrezia asked from where she was still splayed, legs dangling off the edge of the bed.

David was still on his knees, shaken, cock leaking eagerly in his breeches. He was astounded he hadn't come when she had and was afraid he would lose it the moment he thrust inside her.

"Soon, darling."

A dampened towel appeared in front of his eyes. The earl had brought him a cloth to clean his wife's juices from his face.

David used it to blot away his utter bemusement at how he was here, eating the man's wife into ecstasy and about to fuck her.

He stood, damned near overcome with lust. She rolled her head to send him the most wanton, womanly smile he'd ever seen. Her hair splayed in every direction, framing her smooth shoulders. Her nipples stood erect atop her quivering breasts and her stomach still trembled with her recent climax. Her knees were open, her soft thighs beckoning.

He stripped off the last of his clothes as he gazed on the

bright pink center of her. His cock gave a sharp bob of longing and he clasped a hard fist around himself as he thought of the little bud he'd suckled to make her come. He hadn't known such a thing existed and would live the rest of his life in eternal quest for it.

"Oh." She sighed, hand opening in a plea for him to let her touch.

"I'm too close," he admitted starkly. It took all his control to keep his fist from jerking his length into spurting molten cream all over her.

"On your knees, darling?" Henry suggested. "So he can fuck you deep and hard, the way you like?"

"I want to see her," David blurted, voice near barbaric, but he'd made her come twice and hadn't seen her face yet. No guarantee he would last long enough to see it this time, but he wanted to catch her expression if he could.

"Here, then," she said, staying exactly where she was, smiling that beautiful smile.

The bed was a good height for it and her ass was already on the edge. He bent her knees up and rested his cock against her bush. The heat of her wet center scorched his tense balls.

"Go slow," Henry commanded softly. "Tease her with the end of your cock first."

"Henry, I'm so ready," she protested.

David was shaking, but he did it because it's what he wanted, too. His eyes nearly rolled back in his head as he touched the most sensitive part of his tip to the place that made anguished music pang in her throat. As he traced the weeping eye of his cock against her folds, they both grew more and more slippery. Her lips flowered open in reception.

In a kind of trance, the blunt tip of his cock found her entrance and he pressed against her slick, taut hole. Her supple flesh resisted briefly then swallowed him in. He watched as her wet heat engulfed his length in increments, the walls of her sheath clenching and clutching at his rod as she took more and more of him.

Her legs were shaking. He scooped his arms under them, clasping her hips and flexing his arms to draw her ass into a better angle. The action drove his cock deeper so his balls nestled into the open crack of her arse and her wet curls meshed with his own. He was buried so far inside her, he imagined he felt her heartbeat in the near-splitting head of his cock.

Did Henry tell him to kiss her then? He had no idea. He only knew he had to bend over her, untwining one arm from her leg so he could brace his elbow on the mattress beside her. They kissed in a long, luscious melding of lips and tongue. He could feel her getting hotter and wetter and softer around him, responding to the way he fucked her mouth with his tongue.

Her breasts. Maybe Henry told him to fondle them. He only knew he needed her dark nipples against his tongue. Needed to draw forth her exquisite moans. Needed to feel her writhe beneath him in heavenly persecution and gasp, "Fuck me. *Please* make him fuck me."

David straightened and looked down at where her flesh held his captive. Henry said something, but David only licked his thumb and circled her bud, sliding his touch to collect all the slippery juices that had leaked around the base of his shaft. He brought them back to rub them into that sweet nodule.

She arched and bit her lip and clenched her hands in the coverlet—so glorious he had to lock his jaw against climaxing at the sight. He steadied her hip with a firm hand and watched his shiny length come out of her, almost all the way, until she squeezed the tip with her inner muscles and he forgot how to breathe.

He plunged back in, forcing a ragged note of gratification from her.

He might have made a similar noise. He didn't know. He was lost then, lost to the friction of her clasping heat, the twist of her body, the feel of her heel in his ass and her sharp nails catching at his forearms to urge him on.

Harder. He didn't know if she said it or Henry or the voice in his head. It was necessary, that's all he knew. He braced a hand near her ribs and clasped her hip and pounded the cushion of her ass and thighs, nearly going blind at the intensity of pleasure. He managed to keep his eyes open, just enough so he could watch her expression grow anguished. When she clenched her pussy so tightly around him he thought he'd lose his cock, he nearly screamed at the intensity of it.

A broken cry left her lips and her inner muscles abruptly relaxed, then convulsed in a series of rolling squeezes.

He lost it. A shout of triumph scored his throat. His gut cramped with the force of his climax, damn near ripping him in half, but he loved it. He jammed his cock deep into her cunt, tip stinging painfully as his come spurted in sharp, hard bursts that bathed him in molten heat. It was like being burned alive, but so good. So fucking good.

He might have said, "Oh fuck." He only knew he had nothing left when it subsided.

He sagged onto her. Soft arms and legs closed around him. Her breasts pillowed his chest and he buried his nose in the intoxicating scent of her neck.

CHAPTER FOUR

The bed sagged beside them.

"Thank you, Henry," she said in a voice like velvet.

David picked up his head to see her turn her face to kiss her husband. David tensed, expecting a rush of possessiveness or resentment to wash over him. On the contrary, as he watched their tender, lingering kiss he felt as though he had genuinely delivered something on her husband's behalf that had made them both very happy.

At the same time, he wanted to thank *them*. He hadn't known this kind of sex was possible.

But it was over now and he refused to wait around to be told to leave. He gathered his strength and carefully withdrew his lax cock from her delicious heat.

"You don't have to go," Lucrezia protested, thighs trying to cage him as he gently broke away and stood. His knees were still weak.

"I'll let you two..." Do whatever they did after encounters like this.

"David." Henry's voice held a hint of reproach. "If you leave now she'll think you didn't enjoy making love with her."

David ran a hand into his hair. It had come loose from its leather tie and he absently gathered it, thinking Henry's remark sounded vaguely manipulative, but Lucrezia had a wounded look in her eye. Henry was climbing off the bed.

"Stay," he urged. "Hold her and kiss her." He went to the basin and came back with a damp cloth that he tenderly used to wipe David's leaking come from his wife's pussy. "Tell her how happy she made you. You're happy, aren't you, darling? Do you feel well fucked?"

"I do," she assured him with a blissful smile that she turned up to David. Uncertainty crept back into her expression. "Did you like it?"

"Very much." His stomach still ached from the force of his orgasm.

"I'll fetch our lunch. We'll eat here and talk." Henry tossed the cloth onto the wash table as he left the room.

David sent a bemused look to the bedchamber door Henry had left open. "By all means, let's have a picnic where we committed adultery in the most outrageous way I can imagine."

"You regret it?" Lucrezia's crestfallen expression kicked him in the chest.

"Not one bit." He couldn't help it. He had to hold her.

He climbed onto the bed and dragged her to the middle of it before settling her along his side. He pressed each of her curves into his chest and belly and thighs as if he could engrave her into his skin.

"You did like it."

"I like *you*." She was every bit the lady with her frills and ribbons and scented water behind her ears, but she was also earthy and outspoken and delightfully passionate. "You're lovely."

"I like you, too." She snuggled closer, head pillowed on his shoulder and thigh weighing across his own. Her wet pussy kissed his leg and her hair tickled his arm. "It's been hard to find someone we both trust and respect. Someone we feel we can spend a lot of time with. Like this."

He tucked his chin. "You want to keep doing this?" He had suspected that's what might happen and had recognized this was an audition of sorts.

"Don't you?"

"Yes." He probably should have given it more thought, but there was no hiding from the truth. He wanted to fuck her until there was nothing left of himself.

"Good." She lifted her smiling lips.

David gathered her for a kiss. It became a longer, more passionate involvement that brought arousal flickering to life in both of them. She gave a soft moan. He palmed her breast and felt a twitch of sensation zip into his cock.

He began to understand Henry's willingness to open his marriage like this. A woman with her sexual fire shouldn't be constrained by a man who couldn't extinguish it.

"That's better," Henry said as he returned with a large silver tray and a bottle under his arm. "I feel like the most selfish lobcock, keeping her tied to me when I can't satisfy her the way she deserves, but look at her glowing and lazy now. Well done, David."

He motioned for them to sit up so he could set the tray at the foot of the bed. He reclined on the far side of it. There were three fresh glasses amongst the cold cuts of meat, pickled beans, wild strawberries, chunks of cheese, and broken buns of dark bread. Henry filled the glasses and handed them out.

David stacked the pillows, then sat against them, naked as the day he was born, sipping potent brandy, the warmth of his married lover against his side as she gazed adoringly at her husband.

"I haven't been able to make her look like that since about six months into our marriage," Henry mused.

"That's not true. You're a very good lover. Ask David," she said with a teasing smile up at him. "How did I look when you watched us?"

"Rapturous," David said, which wasn't an overstatement. He caressed her cheek with the back of two fingers.

"I'm glad I can give her that much. We were devastated when we realized I would never fully recover," Henry said with a distant frown.

"He wanted to leave me and come home." She scowled at her husband, not seeming to have forgiven that suggestion. "He said I could say I was widowed and remarry. I didn't want any other husband."

"What did you do? Tell him," Henry prompted, smirking. "See if he's as broadminded as he claims."

"I brought him to look at a mural we had uncovered. It showed a woman with a man taking her from behind. There was a second man behind him."

"No, thank you," David said promptly and unequivocally.

"Couldn't if I wanted to, though your ass is not without its attractions," Henry said with laughter in his eyes. "I peeked."

"Fuck," David chuckled under his breath, turning his hot face to the sheer drapes lit by the sun beams against the window. "The day you two climbed out of the carriage, I thought you were the most unusual pair I'd ever encountered." He sobered, compelled to ask, "What exactly happened?" His hand twitched, instinctively wanting to protect his bollocks at the mere thought of suffering an injury there.

"It's unusual to have such a lingering debilitation, but I was very sick and very swollen. The physician gave me herbs and tried cupping." He winced in memory. "After the swelling went down, the more intense feelings never came back. I don't get fully hard, not even from sucking." He looked with regret at Lucrezia's pouted lips. "But I get very aroused watching. Sometimes I even have what feels like a release, but I don't spurt."

"Did you feel one earlier?"

"No, but I still enjoyed it." His eyelids were heavy with gratification.

Interesting.

"What happened to the others? Like me." It was bothering David, not knowing how he would be discarded.

"Paulo didn't want to come to England," Henry said with a fatalistic shrug. "Thornton left London for an opportunity in America. We were sorry to say goodbye to both of them. It's been difficult to find someone new. It's not the most conventional arrangement."

"No," David agreed, but it didn't deter him. He looked at Lucrezia, lolling so comfortably against him. "You want me to keep making love to you?"

"I do," she assured him.

"Now?" he asked dryly.

She glanced down and her brows went up with admiration at how ardently he'd recovered.

"Well, yes. I would like that very much." She glanced to Henry as if looking for permission.

David touched her chin to bring her focus back to him. It was a small test. If she had balked at that tiny bit of assertiveness from him, David might have backed off, but he saw the flare of excitement in her eyes and heard the small catch of her breath.

"Kiss her," he heard Henry say.

Lucrezia lifted her mouth and anticipation crackled in the air between all of them.

A small surge of power went through David as he considered that he was not really here to service Lucrezia at Henry's behest. He was here to make it exciting for all of them.

He took his time, making both of them wait as he braced a hand behind Lucrezia's rump while he slowly leaned in, not quite kissing her. His free hand went between her thighs, gently easing them open so Henry had a good view.

"David," she whispered, hand soft against his cheek as she urged him to kiss her.

He resisted but let his fingers draw aimless patterns where she was still creamy and plump.

"Lie back, darling," Henry said. His voice didn't sound as steady as it had the first time. "Tell him how many fingers you want."

She sank back, voice a sob as she said, "Three."

David gave her one and he was very slow about it. He kissed her and fucked her mouth with his tongue as he lazily slid his finger in and out of her, distantly aware of Henry's hissing breaths, but he was more caught up in the way her sheath clung to his touch and how she moved her hips and sucked on his tongue.

When she was wet and tense and nipping at his lips, he slid a second finger into her. With a slight curve of his touch, he pulled his caress forward. It only took a few of those to cause her to shudder and cry out and come wetly into his palm.

His experience with the widow had not been a wasted education.

"Fuck," Henry said, hand inside his trousers.

"Now we're going to fuck," he informed Henry who nodded.

David only had to touch Lucrezia's hip and she rolled onto her stomach. He helped her come up on her knees and she dipped her back, lifting her ass to offer her glistening pussy. She was shaking with eagerness.

He slid into her with one luxurious thrust and fucked her for what felt like hours, losing himself in their sopping noises as she came three, four times. Then once more when he came himself, spilling his soul hotly inside her.

CHAPTER FIVE

"**Y**ou're humming," Henry remarked. "Happy, darling?"

Lucrezia paused in wrapping a silk kerchief around the curls she'd finished pinning for bed.

"I am," she said, but even though Henry sounded pleased, she sensed a tension growing between them.

Was it David? They had fucked every day for the last fortnight, sometimes twice a day, always under Henry's keen gaze. David had stamina, control, and an uncanny ability to sense what she desired. He was pure delight, but did Henry resent how much she was enjoying him?

If he did, he had a strange way of proving it, since he seemed to be encouraging them at every opportunity.

Like today, for instance. They'd all been at the site. She'd been sketching on a grassy bench. The men had been discussing something innocuous. She had looked up and seen the two of them with their sleeves rolled back, wearing perspiration stains and squinting against the bright sun.

Lust had dug its claws into her at their combined masculinity. When Henry happened to glance her way, he'd noticed and stilled.

With only the slightest nod, he had drawn David's attention to her. David had locked onto her and wordlessly come to fall to his knees before her. He was gorgeous, especially when his face grew hard with intent. He had lifted her skirts and gazed on her like he'd found the most exquisite treasure.

As his head went down between her thighs, she had lifted her gaze to her husband. He'd been taking it all in with the alert indulgence he always did, nostrils twitching, breaths growing uneven with his growing excitement, especially when David lazily reached up a hand to bare her breasts and fondle her nipples.

When David made her come, Henry's lips pulled with gratification.

Through her fluttering lashes she had watched him watch David lift his head and open his breeches. As he thrust into her, she clung her arms across David's strong back and looked at Henry over David's shoulder, secure in a way she'd never felt with her other lovers. She could let David take control and release every one of her most instinctual responses and he would absorb them with his easy strength. Henry had given her this. She loved him for it.

But it was only now, as she thought back on it, that she realized Henry hadn't said a word. He hadn't given David one direction at all.

"Are you?" she asked, turning on the little bench at her vanity table. "Happy?"

He set aside the notebook he'd been writing in, his lack of answer more sobering and frightening than any words he might have spoken.

"Henry?"

"David isn't like Paolo and Thornton."

"No, he's not," she agreed. Paolo had been experienced and carefree, treating their arrangement as a pleasant game and she a game piece. Thornton had been young and eager to learn, sweet, but she'd known he was anxious to take his knowledge and move on.

David was intense. Attentive, but not biddable the way the other two had been. He wanted to give her pleasure on his terms. He wanted *her*. That's what made him so compelling to her.

"They needed guidance," Henry said pensively. "David does not."

"Does that bother you?" she asked as furls of apprehension crept into her belly.

"I'm more concerned whether it bothers you."

"No," she said with surprise. "No, I feel perfectly safe with him."

"Good." He smiled faintly. Sadly. "That means I'm not needed."

"Henry." Her apprehension grew to alarm. "Do not say it!"

"I'm going back to London—"

"No." She stood and stomped her foot. "If you go to London, *I* go to London."

"You're not even happy in London," he said shortly. "I *want* this for you."

"Do you think that's what I want for *you*?" She flung out her hand. "To be alone in that rainy, gloomy city with *no one*?"

He averted his face and a muscle pulsed in his jaw. "Obviously, you're not in a frame of mind to talk about this. I'm going for a nightcap." He took his empty glass out of the room.

• • •

David was starting his day in the barn, setting lads to mucking out stalls, when Lucrezia came in with puffy red eyes. Her hair was still wrapped in a kerchief of silk, a light coat wrapped around what he was fairly certain were her nightclothes.

"What's wrong?" he asked with alarm, quickly handing off a rake.

"Henry wants to go to London. If he goes, I go. Which means all of this…" Her mouth began to tremble.

Was over.

David took it like a kick to the stomach. He wasn't ready. Not at *all*.

"Come talk to him. Please," Lucrezia pleaded.

David followed, but he didn't know what he could say to change the man's mind. If Henry had had enough of this arrangement, he was completely within his rights to end it.

His next thought was that he might lose his position. That panicked thought became the first words out of his mouth when Lucrezia took him into Henry's bedroom where her husband was buttoning his quilted banyan.

"Lucrezia," Henry said wearily. His eyes were darkly sunken, as though he hadn't slept.

"Are you dismissing me?" David blurted.

"What? Never," Henry said firmly. "I told you from the beginning that your employment would not be affected by our arrangement."

"But did I do something to offend you? Is that why you're leaving?"

"Not in the least." Henry gave his hair a dismayed rumple. "I simply think it's best if I return to London."

"*You*," David repeated, glancing at Lucrezia. "Did I misunderstand? I thought you said you were both going."

"Where my husband goes, I go," Lucrezia said in a voice scratched apart by emotion.

Henry gave her a stern look and drew a patience-gathering breath. "I suggested she stay here, David. To be with you."

"And excavate the site herself? I can only help now and again between the rest of my duties. I wouldn't want her swinging pickaxes alone if a wall caved in. Do you have business in London? Why do you feel pressed to leave?"

"Don't be obtuse," Henry said in a small snap of temper. "I'm superfluous, David. I'm trying to clear the way for you to be together. Tell Lucrezia you want her to stay with you."

"I want you both to stay," David said, surprised at his own words given how odd their arrangement was, but he was telling the truth. "I know you'll both have to go back to London eventually. I've been bracing myself for it, but I would never ask Lucrezia to stay here without you, Henry. She wouldn't be happy."

Henry sent him a pithy look. "Don't patronize me."

"It's true," Lucrezia insisted. "David is very sweet and listens politely when I talk about historical discoveries, but—" Lucrezia held up an imploring hand to David, trying to stave off whatever offense he might be taking. "He doesn't care the way you do, Henry."

"I care," David assured her in a small aside. "But it's true, not as much as you two. But I don't think you care about barley yields on the south slopes, do you?"

"Not a wit. That's something that only interests you and Henry."

"This isn't about fucking barley," Henry said shortly.

"No," David agreed. It was about fucking. He licked his lips and ran a damp palm down his thigh, hating that it had come to this so soon, but he had to accept it. "If you want to end this arrangement—"

"I'm not going to say you should stop, am I?" Henry cut in. "Not when she loves it so much. But how can you say you want us both here when you don't listen or do what I say? You don't even know I'm there."

"That's not true." David was taken aback. "I always know you're there. I, uh—" He scratched his brow. "I get caught up in what we're doing and I'm always most focused on Lucrezia, to be sure she's enjoying it. *I* want to make love to her, but I like that you're watching." He was probably going to hell for that, but he couldn't find it in him to care. "There's always a part of me thinking about what you're seeing and whether it excites you. I want you to enjoy it in your way."

"I do," Henry admitted quietly, adding dryly, "It's like watching a fucking opera."

David didn't laugh. He started to say something but thought better of it.

"David?" Lucrezia prompted.

Ah, fuck it.

"I wish you'd let me watch you," he admitted to Henry. "I haven't asked because I thought it might be your private time together. That it was something you preferred to do without me, but—" His shoulder hitched defensively. He didn't want to admit he felt closed out by the fact they hadn't offered to include him.

"Really?" Lucrezia asked, sliding David a speculative glance.

"Of course. Why not?"

"But would you—" She looked to Henry and back to David, expression growing sensual the way it did when lust was creeping into her blood. "What if you both made love to me?" she asked hesitantly.

"Would you want that?" David wasn't sure who he was asking. He shot Henry a look.

Henry opened his mouth, flicked a considering look at David. "Would you?"

"Yes." David was a little shocked at himself that he not only accepted the idea very quickly, but also found the thought even more exciting than being watched.

Henry looked between them with hesitation and David realized the other man was suffering self-consciousness.

Lucrezia went to him and cupped the side of his face. "Darling, I want you to be part of this with us. Please?"

"Get her so wet and ready for me, she comes the second my cock slides inside her," David suggested, voice thickening with lust as he anticipated it.

Henry's arm tightened around his wife, drawing her closer. His eyelids drooped in the way that suggested he was becoming aroused as well.

"Would you like that, darling?" He grazed his lips against her ear, making her shiver. "Should I bring you to the brink then let him take you over?"

She nodded, wildness coming into her eyes. Her shiny lips parted in wonder.

"Sit back and let me show you how it's done, David."

David dumbly backed into a chair, dropping into it blindly as he watched Henry take his time unwrapping the silk kerchief from Lucrezia's hair. He slowly drew the pins out, kissing her neck as he went.

When they were gone, he moved on to pressing his mouth

to her wrist and brushed light fingers over her quivering breasts. He dragged her earlobe through his teeth and asked if she was thinking about his tongue tracing her slit.

Hardly able to sit still, David gripped the chair arm, cock growing thicker as he watched the way Henry seemed to know exactly how to tease and please. He skimmed away her coat and pinched her nipples through the cotton of her nightgown.

Lucrezia drew in her breath, face anguished.

Oh fuck that was gorgeous. David squeezed his prick through his trousers, gaze pinned to where the shadows of her limbs were visible through the airy fabric.

Then the pair were kissing. He glimpsed their tongues dipping and playing. Henry's hand went into the neckline of her gown. David knew what he was feeling. The impression of her nipple in his hand was something he knew intimately, and watching Henry palm her made him close his fist around the phantom sensation.

She would be growing slippery. He stared holes at the dark patch he could see through the translucent layer of white, knowing how soaked she must be, yet wanting to see the proof. He wanted the feel of her heat on his own hand, but he was equally excited by the sight of Henry pushing the fabric into her notch, creating a damp patch that made David's pulse throb in the tip of his cock.

"Another day we'll show him how you like to clutch that bedpost and ride my face," Henry said.

David made a tortured noise, incapable of even the basest words.

Henry sent him a merciless smile over his shoulder. "Not easy, is it?"

Lucrezia was humping herself against the heel of Henry's hand, lips parted, looking so close to coming, David almost tipped over the brink with her.

"It's so fucking hard." The heaviest form of heat was pooling in his cock and balls, making him ache with a need to do something. Undress, pull his cock, fuck her. Anything.

Henry lifted her nightgown so slowly it was a cruelty to all of them. Lucrezia husked out, "Henry." Her eyes were unfocused, her hands clutching at his arms for support.

"Soon, my love." He arranged her on the side of the bed and stood between her open thighs, teasing David with a glimpse of her pinkest flesh before he bent over her and began to kiss his way down her middle.

She wasn't shy about clutching his head and guiding him. David was familiar with that sensation, too. The clutch of her fists in his hair. His scalp tingled in parallel excitement.

Henry began to lick her, long lavish sweeps of his tongue along her inner thighs, then tracing around her thatch, making her jerk and twitch and whimper. "Henry, *please*."

When he arrived where she wanted him, she pressed her head back and let out a garbled cry. Her breasts quaked. Her stomach trembled. Her toes curled and her fists clutched the blankets.

When she began to take small, sharp inhales, David said, "Let her come. I want to see."

But Henry didn't. He placed an apologetic kiss on her pubic bone and rose.

"You wretch," Lucrezia said on a ragged, hopeless laugh.

"Soon, my love," he crooned, stroking her thigh. He looked to David. "Your turn."

David could barely stand let alone unbutton his breeches while crossing the floor. His head swam, but somehow he managed to do both.

This felt surreal, to be this ready. To see her writhing and eager for his straining cock when he hadn't even touched her. He desperately wanted to cover her, kiss her, suckle and bring her off with his tongue.

"Quit teasing," she gasped, staring ravenously at his cock.

Henry very carefully spread her lips. David gripped his

throbbing shaft and guided the tip of his cock against her slippery, anointed hole.

Lucrezia made a noise that was a growl of approval and a helpless sob.

"You're so fucking wet." He sank in with barely any effort, drawn in by a wave of slick heat that immediately began to tremble around his stiff shaft. Some inner part of her began to hammer the swollen head of his cock. He had to clench his teeth to endure it without losing his load.

"Oh fuck, David. Henry." She arched, eyes open but unseeing, breasts heaving as she came, mouth open in a silent scream. She was so fucking magnificent it was criminal.

"There you go, darling," Henry said, voice low and intense. He accentuated her orgasm, soothing and rubbing her nub, knuckles brushing against David's pubic bone.

It was so enticing, it took all his effort not to thrust and release deep inside her. When she finally began to calm, David was dizzy with lust.

"Fuck, that was exciting," he said, smoothing an absent hand on her thigh. "Tell me how you want it. Hard?" That's how he wanted to fuck her. Until they were absolutely shredded by pleasure.

"Pick her up and sit on the edge," Henry said, cheeks flushed and eyes bright. He kissed Lucrezia's hand. "I want to eat your ass while he fucks you."

Lucrezia's pupils dilated and David's probably did, too, because he lost his sight for a moment. Then, since she reached her arms up to him, he did as Henry asked. He gathered her up and she hugged her knees to his ribs, then straddled his lap as he sat.

They rocked slightly so he was buried as deeply as possible inside her. Then he opened his thighs as much as he could, kissing her and stroking her naked back down to her ass. He cupped her cheeks and spread them.

He felt Henry settle on his knees between his feet. He rested one elbow on David's knee. His hair tickled David's thigh, then Lucrezia nearly screamed as she jolted in his arms. Her cunt clenched around his cock, instantly thrusting David to the limits of his control.

He tightened his arms around her. She wasn't exactly trying to get away from what Henry was doing, but was so stimulated she squirmed and thrashed, cunt squeezing and tantalizing his cock as she did.

Henry's breath warmed David's balls. He felt the flick of his tongue, too, dancing near the root of his shaft. Deliberate? Who cared? David reveled in it. Everything in him wanted to clasp her hips and work her pussy on his cock, but he had to sit there and endure her slippery, condensed ride as she reacted to Henry's tongue lashing.

It was so lascivious, so exciting, David's control was falling away with no hope of catching it back.

"I'm going to come," he groaned.

"Me, too," she moaned.

They sealed their mouths together and seconds later, her pussy was milking his cock. A hard quake went through his balls and he was coming inside her with hot, ecstatic bursts.

As the shudders and waves of pleasure rolled through them, so powerful he thought his heart would explode, David was dimly aware of a jagged noise from Henry. His head pressed into David's inner thigh and his hand gripped the other like he was hanging on for dear life.

For long moments, David felt suspended with them in some otherworldly space, one where nothing existed but the euphoria of fucking to completion.

When his orgasm began to subside, he made a conscious effort to stop suffocating Lucrezia with the bands of his arms. He became aware of the way his thigh was being pinched so hard he was liable to have a bruise.

"Henry?"

"Fuck, that felt good," Henry said, hand relaxing and falling away from David's thigh while his weight increased against the other one.

"I think he came with us," Lucrezia said with a blink of astonished delight. "Did you come, darling?"

"So fucking hard."

"Oh, darling." She reached to stroke his hair. "Come onto the bed with us. I want to kiss you."

"I can't move."

David shared a smile with her and eased onto his back so he could help her lift herself off him. She sank onto her side with a blissful sigh and straightened her legs.

David sat up and clapped his hand on Henry's shoulder. "Come on, man. If you stay down there, she'll think you didn't enjoy eating her ass. And I'll be worried you didn't like the taste of my balls."

"You're a pain in my ass, do you know that?"

"No, thank you. Not even if you ask very nicely. But I enjoyed this."

"Me, too," Henry said, still sounding dazed. He accepted David's hand and came onto the bed to gather Lucrezia into his arms.

David rose.

"Where are you going?" Lucrezia asked drowsily.

"You two get some sleep." He squeezed her leg as he looked at them intertwined so lovingly. He really had a great affection for the both of them and liked seeing how he'd brought them together when Lucrezia had looked so devastated earlier. "No more talk of going to London," he said, as if he had the final word on the matter.

"We'll stay until we have no choice but to go back," Henry conceded on a yawn. "Thank you, David. You've been the real treasure we've found here."

• • •

They did leave for the season, but at Christmas they extended an invitation for David to join them at the family home in Kent. While there, he met Henry's sons and "consulted with the land agent," but he was really there to join them in Lucrezia's room every night.

The following summer, they returned to Cornwall with the boys and their infant daughter. It became their habit to spend as much time as they could there, especially when another son was born. It was, after all, where the three of them most enjoyed coming together.

The End

Stepping Out
with a
Stable Boy

Stepping Out with a Stable Boy shows how a mature woman, who is a pastor's wife and has been abandoned by her husband, learns what joys she'd been missing all her life, with a man much younger than her, however, readers who may be sensitive to sexual practices outside the marriage regardless of the circumstances, please take note.

CHAPTER ONE

Drat, drat, and drat. Her first morning to herself in ages and her boot had given up its sole. Winnifred Hornsby had been meaning to take them to the shoemaker, but given this muddy spring, she was always *in* them.

Now what? She removed her bonnet to look at the ribbon. Tying a bow onto only one foot would look ridiculous and both would be an outrageous frippery on a woman her age walking a country lane. Not that the women of London wore such sturdy, practical, and deeply unfashionable footwear in the first place, but they didn't have to visit every home in the parsonage at least once a month, did they?

The morning sun was strong enough—and her temper hot enough—she removed her spencer and threw it atop the heavy basket she'd been carrying. Her gloves and bonnet followed. She really didn't care to pick up any of it again.

For one wild moment, she imagined taking off the second boot and running in her hose down the grassy lane that wound into the green. She could hear a stream burbling.

When was the last time she had walked with empty arms and sun on her naked head and a spring breeze wafting over her face? When she'd been her children's age, she imagined.

She looked one way and another. It was a mile back to the village and a mile to her destination of Deerlane Park. There was a small cottage across the field behind her, but if there was an occupant, they weren't using the chimney. If she couldn't manage a walk on a well-kept road that had finally dried out, she had no business trying to cross acres of freshly plowed dirt to reach an empty cottage.

She huffed and looked again at the quiet lane used by a

gamekeeper, perhaps, or the occasional fisherman. She was so tempted! But if she left her things here, anyone coming across them would think her kidnapped by highwaymen. Although, why take a middle-aged mother of five when they could steal berry preserves and freshly baked scones?

What a fine picnic it would make! She was about to give herself the gift of enjoying her bounty by the stream when she heard the jingle of a harness and the rumble of a wagon.

She looked to where the road curved out from below the green, half expecting her husband, since her day was already going so poorly.

The children would like to see him, she supposed, even if she had no desire to.

His curate would love for Aldous to show his face. The poor young man, freshly ordained, barely managed to choose a sermon from the book each week. Winnifred made all the preparations for the baptisms and weddings and funerals. The curate only read aloud what she gave him and signed where she pointed in the registry. She set the meetings and agenda for parish business and arranged the church repairs and ensured the churchwarden election was conducted.

All this and she still kept up her duty as the rector's wife to visit the parishioners, especially the sick and elderly and the mothers with newborn babies.

She hadn't found the courage to tell the overwhelmed curate that her husband had misled him and wouldn't be returning. He had taken up housekeeping with his *other* family.

A year on from accidentally intercepting a letter and Winnie was still beside herself. Had she done right by telling him to go and live with the other woman who had birthed his children? All those sabbaticals and bible studies and inescapable meetings with the bishop!

She was such a fool. At least she had the parsonage house. Aldous paid the curate from his rector's income while Winnifred farmed the glebe and fed his children from the tithe barn. In exchange for his leaving her means, she maintained appearances, pretending Aldous was on a pilgrimage or improving his doctrinal knowledge. The scoundrel.

It wasn't Aldous who appeared with the steady plod of a horse, thankfully. It was Benjamin, their former stable boy, whose red hair she had once ruffled because he'd been so discomfited after witnessing the barn cat having kittens. She'd been pregnant with George at the time, and Benjamin had stared at her swollen belly in horrified fascination.

That had been ten years ago and there was absolutely no reason she should grow so flushed with heat at the sight of him. They crossed paths often. He was still a boy of twenty-one to her matron of thirty-six.

But she had *heard* things about him. Things that made her glance toward her discarded outerwear, suddenly feeling very exposed in her single petticoat beneath her muslin gown and her one unshod foot.

Benjamin had grown into a healthy six-foot. He had a wide, square jaw, sharp blue eyes, and a charming grin that awakened any woman to an awareness of her femininity. Over the last two years, he had worked alongside the other men who'd dug the extension of the canal that had brought all sorts of modern commerce to their village of Yardley on Tipplington. The hard labor had filled out his shoulders and thickened his thighs. He might not be rich, and he might have a younger sister to look out for, but by local standards Benjamin was one of their most eligible bachelors.

Winnie wasn't the only woman who had noticed. She'd overheard the blacksmith's girls squabbling over which of them might pursue him. The wives in the sewing circle were making very bawdy remarks, and this winter, the widow Grassley had had him in so many times to haul her ashes, she'd had to remove to her sister's in Norwich come spring to quash the speculation.

Winnie knew better than to give much credence to gossip, but she was still very conscious of the press of her breasts against her gown as she waved Benjamin to stop.

"Good morning, Mrs. Hornsby." He halted the wagon with KENT'S GENERAL STORE painted upon its side. "How are you?"

Far too elated. Her own husband had never made her feel so girlish and uplifted.

"I'm well." She cleared a telling thickness from her throat. "Except that I've lost a shoe." She nodded at the boot she stood upon.

"Shall I fetch the farrier?"

She kept her chin tucked and gave him a very stern glower. Perhaps he *was* a man if he had the temerity to tease her.

His crooked grin flashed and her heart turned a somersault at how handsome he was with his clean-shaven jaw and hair blown untidy from the breeze. It gave him a rakish look even though his features were the earnest type with high auburn brows, a straight nose, and wide cheeks.

"I'm delivering to the big house, then I will be at your service."

"I'm also headed there. May I join you?"

"Of course." He leaped down with agile grace and came around to take the basket from her to set it behind the buckboard. He held out a hand to assist her up to the seat.

She should put her gloves back on, but there was no point in standing on ceremony. A callused palm had never set her blood afire in her life.

Until today. Whew. She couldn't help a small exhale as she experienced a sharp thrill at his hand closing over hers, so strong and steady.

Her step up with her unshod foot caused the hem of her skirt to rise, exposing her calf. As she found her balance, standing in front of the wagon seat, she glanced down self-consciously and caught him eyeing her ankle as he set her broken boot beside her foot.

She ought to be affronted. She was married to the rector—even if her husband *had* made a mockery of their vows. Still, it gave her a distinct stab of delight to know she had the ability to catch a man's notice, especially a young, virile specimen like Benjamin.

So she allowed the long-forgotten, once very comely maiden within her to awaken for a brief moment to say a flirtatious, "You have grown up, haven't you?"

He noted by her elevated brows that *she* had noted where his attention had strayed.

He wasn't the least bit abashed, only offered a slow, admiring smile. "I have."

Well! She seated herself and adjusted her gown, willing the blush that stung all the way to her nipples to subside as he rounded the wagon and came up beside her. Perhaps she ought to set a more decorous tone.

"Your sister and the younger Mr. Kent are engaged," she noted. The curate had started reading the banns last Sunday. "That's happy news." It was the sort of remark she would make with any of the villagers.

"It is," Benjamin said warmly. "And your family? Everyone is well? Mr. Hornsby is still away?" He took up the reins and flicked them to urge the horse into a walk.

"Yes. And Michael is finishing at Eton. He has a scholarship to Oxford next year." She breezed past talk of Aldous and caught him up on all the children, practically stacking them like a wall between them.

"It's funny to think of little Eleanor old enough to mind the rest while you're out visiting," he said with absent affection.

"And the maid, of course, but she's a good help when I'm kept so busy. I imagine you're very busy as well, now that the roads are decent?" She glanced at the bushels of produce and crates that had come from much farther afield than London, judging by the stamps from the East India and Hudson's Bay companies. Why had she bothered packaging up her biscuits and jars of preserves when they had sugar and tea and spices en route?

"There are shipments off the canal every other day. Mr. Kent is pleased."

"Are you not?"

He side-eyed her. "Can you keep a secret?"

She placed her hand over her heart. "The wife of a clergyman must be an excellent listener and a very circumspect speaker."

"Pity. I should imagine you hear the tastiest gossip. But I'll add to your larder by saying I'm only here until Ingrid's wedding. I haven't told Mr. Kent yet, but the canal company has a job for me. Once I've saved up, I'd like to take a ship to America."

Her heart took an inexplicable trip. She wasn't sure why.

"I suppose a young man must explore his options." They had so many these days—enlistment, factory work, exploring the new world. "That's a good prospect for you, but it will be our loss."

"You're too kind," he dismissed.

"I mean it," she said on a burst of sincerity. "You're one of those rare young men who not only possesses ambition, but also the work ethic and patience and discipline to make something of yourself. I admire you for it." If she were fifteen years younger...

Better yet, if she were born male and had those same opportunities?

He might be a grown man, but he still had the capacity to flush with self-conscious pleasure. "Thank you. I've always had the utmost respect for you, Mrs. Hornsby. Those words mean a lot coming from you."

Now she warmed with a blush. Thankfully, they reached Deerlane Park and the awkward moment of mutual admiration passed.

•••

Benjamin pulled the wagon around to the storehouse. Word was sent to the housekeeper who brought out a pair of her own slippers for Mrs. Hornsby to wear into the house for her visit with the elderly baron and his wife.

"It will take time to unload. I'll wait until you've finished your visit and take you back to the village," Benjamin offered as he helped her down. He was trying not to be fresh about it, but her hand on his shoulder sent a bolt of sensation straight to his cock.

"That would be a good excuse to leave early," she said in a low voice as she stood before him. "Thank you." Her conspiratorial smile sent another pleasurable twinge into his chubbing todger.

He didn't let himself watch her walk away, but she made a fine sight any time he had. Today's glimpse of her ankle, her uncovered hair, and her breasts bouncing with the wagon's jostle had brought back his boyish crush with a vengeance.

Oh, he'd had it bad for her at fourteen. His pecker had refused to stay down when she was around. He'd been miserable over it, especially because Winnifred Hornsby was nothing but kindness. She had employed him in the stable and to help in the glebe when his mother had been sick, then ensured he learned to read and write. She'd talked their landlord into letting them keep the cottage once his father was gone, and even sold them a runt piglet on installments their first year they'd been orphaned. That sow still gave them litters that brought in enough at the fall market to keep him and his sister fed through winter.

Mrs. Hornsby was the one who'd put in a word for Ingrid, too, when Mr. Kent had needed a shop girl. Look where his sister was headed as a result. Into a better marriage than either of them could have dreamed.

So he definitely should not be thinking about fucking the fine Mrs. Hornsby's ample tits. He shouldn't be imagining plowing her loins or palming her soft round ass while she sat on his face.

Apparently, he still had it bad for her. So bad, the coolness of the storehouse did nothing to take the edge off his ardor and the flirtations of a kitchen maid did nothing for him. The girl was only fifteen or sixteen and positively juvenile, giggling and batting her lashes, incapable of stringing two sensible words together.

Maybe if he hadn't spent the winter enjoying the "mature conversation" of the widow Grassley—*that* woman knew what she wanted and how to ask for it—he might not be so drawn to Winnifred Hornsby. While most men spoke lustily about virginal, fresh-faced maids, he had been introduced to the delights of a woman with confidence and experience.

Which wasn't to say he was blind to a young woman's charms. When the maid arched her back and set her hand on her waist and hitched her hip to ensure he had a fine view of her figure, he drank it in.

Mrs. Hornsby returned at that moment. Her appearance caused him a fresh jab of carnal hunger while she only crooked a disdainfully amused brow, seeming to lump him in with the maid as a pair of adolescents bumbling toward a stolen kiss.

To hell with that. He knew how to fuck and did it very well, thank you.

"The baron's valet has repaired my boot." Mrs. Hornsby glanced at her ankle as she turned it to demonstrate. Her tone held a patronizing lilt as she said, "If you have other things you wish to attend to, I can make my own way home."

"Not at all. I wouldn't forgive myself if you were stranded again. Let me help you up." As he set the basket by her feet, he realized she had left a few items in it.

"Are you visiting someone else today?" he asked as they started back down the lane toward the village. He nodded at the basket when she looked blankly at him.

"Oh. No, I— I thought you could have them. You've been very kind." Her profile wore a hint of defensiveness and he sensed she wasn't being completely honest.

His stomach took a dip as he realized she might have kept some things for herself. The men at the canals clucked worse than any flock of quilting hens. Benjamin had heard a vague rumor that Aldous Hornsby had been spotted in a village some distance upstream with a woman Benjamin's age. She'd had a baby in her arms, a boy in short pants, and a tarnished ring on her finger.

Benjamin had put a stop to the talk, confirming it was absolute nonsense, since he was personally acquainted with the family, but it didn't change the fact that Aldous was gone and the rumor was likely true.

"Please save it for someone who really needs it, Mrs. Hornsby. Ingrid and I are very well situated these days."

She didn't say anything, but a moment later, quite out of the blue, she touched his hand, causing such a spark up his arm and into his groin, he pulled on the reins, halting the wagon at almost precisely the spot where he'd found her.

"Did you drop something?" He looked down on the dry track.

She tucked her hands into her lap, drew in a big breath, and let it go as though a decision had been made.

"Would *you* like to hear a secret?"

Shit. She was going to tell him about Aldous.

"If you want to share it," he said warily.

"Earlier, as I stood on my broken boot over there, I was tempted to take my basket down this track." She pointed into the trees. "And have it as a picnic next to the stream. I never do things like that. Even saying it sounds very self-indulgent." With an annoyed little purse of her mouth, she said, "No. Forget I said anything. Please carry on." She waved ahead of them.

Benjamin looked to the basket and then back to her. She sat very straight and wore an expression of discontent. He wondered if anyone was as generous to her as she was to everyone else.

The lane was overgrown, but the weather had been dry enough the horse and empty wagon could manage it.

"Perhaps I will accept your offering, Mrs. Hornsby. And perhaps I will sample it by the stream. I'm happy to share them with you if you care to join me, but you're free to walk home if that's what your sense of duty demands."

Her look of exasperation turned to suspicion, as though she guessed that he knew something of her husband's abandonment.

"Are you feeling sorry for me?"

"May I be frank, Mrs. Hornsby?"

"Yes." She seemed to brace herself, biting her lower lip in a way that sent a thorn into his cock.

"I'm grateful for all you've done for my sister and me. You know exactly how dire things were for us when we were younger. It feels good to talk to you as a man who doesn't need your charity. I would love to give you a picnic by a stream as a thank you."

"It's not charity to help where I can. It's my role in the village," she murmured.

Because she was a clergyman's wife.

"Still, I'd like to. If you'll allow it?"

She cut him a conspiratorial glance that was suddenly full of excited impulse. After a swift look around, she said, "Yes. Quickly. Before anyone sees us."

He gave the reins a light snap to send the horse down the lane.

CHAPTER TWO

It took a few minutes to turn the wagon in the small clearing alongside the stream, but Benjamin soon set the horse to grazing. They made themselves comfortable on the lowered gate on the back of the wagon and watched the sparkling water as they consumed the reserved biscuits drizzled with strawberry preserve. Benjamin even had a jar of cordial he carried in case thirst got the better of him while he went about his day, so they shared it.

"This is the most peace I've had in years. Thank you." Winnie had removed her bonnet and was tempted to take off her boots. "Not that I wish to sound ungrateful. I know I have a very good life."

"You've been lucky with your children."

"I have." She understood what he was saying. His mother had lost two before she'd passed from an extended decline.

"Are you looking forward to having a family of your own— Good heavens!" A thought occurred and she blurted it out. "That's not why Devina Grassley had to leave for her sister's, is it?" Winnie clapped her hand over her mouth. "I'm so sorry. That's— I shouldn't—"

Benjamin's hearty belly laugh drowned out her stammers, allaying her suspicion. Although, she could see what might have attracted Devina. He was so handsome as he laughed, he blinded her like the sun's reflection off the water, shearing off a piece of her heart.

Nevertheless, she was embarrassed at saying something so personal. When he finally stopped laughing, she said, "I shouldn't listen to gossip. Please forgive me."

"It's a requirement of your position," he reminded her, amusement dying away into a sober expression. One that held concern. "I hear things, too."

His compassion made her flinch. The bite of biscuit in her mouth became a lump that clogged up her throat.

"Does everyone know?" she asked, wetting her throat with cordial.

"No. Would you like to talk about it?"

"No."

He accepted that and they ate in silence a few more minutes.

"Devina's sister wrote that an old beau of hers had lost his wife. She went to see if there was a chance at rekindling things."

"Oh." She studied his profile. He looked unbothered. "I wish her luck. You weren't...in love with her?"

"I liked her very much. She seemed to enjoy my company, but we, uh..." He scratched his upper lip. "We were very careful not to let ourselves be tied into the future by any sort of..." He cleared his throat. "Lasting consequence."

"Did you buy from Mr. Kent's back room?" she asked in another leap of suspicion. "I *knew* he was selling sheaths! Do you think he will admit it to me?"

"You asked him?" Benjamin manfully kept a straight face.

"For a friend." There were several women in the parish who couldn't afford another baby, financially or physically.

"You can mail away for them, you know. That's why they're called 'letters.'"

"And they work? Well, obviously," she muttered.

"Or a man can pull out."

"Can he, though?" she asked with scathing sarcasm.

Benjamin ran his tongue over his teeth behind the smile he wasn't quite able to suppress. "Says the mother of five children?"

"Says the woman married to a man with *seven* children. That I know of." She closed her eyes in mortification. "*Promise me* you won't repeat a word of this," she said on a morose sigh, trying to think what had come over her that she was allowing herself to be so frank.

"Not a one," he vowed, leaning back on his elbow. "But do you miss him? You must have loved him?"

"Oh, girlish love, I suppose, when we married." She kicked her feet where they dangled. "He was a good match, as my mother told me a thousand times. I think I just told myself what I needed to believe." She made a face at herself. "And I probably spent too long only seeing what I wanted to see."

"But a woman who's had five children..." He was shredding a leaf, tearing the blade from the veins. "You must have enjoyed the intimacy of marriage?"

"That's a very personal question, Benjamin," she said with mock outrage. "What makes you think you can ask the *rector's wife* such a thing?"

"Mmm. Sheaths are never purchased for our own use. They're always for a friend," he said with facetious bite. He set the stem of the leaf's skeleton between his teeth as he gave her a knowing smile.

"Are you trying to ask if I want to feel like a woman without becoming a mother again? Who wouldn't want pleasure without consequence?" She scowled in contemplation at the water, muttering, "This is the most ridiculous conversation. I don't even talk this openly at sewing circle. I have no idea why I'm admitting such things to you."

"Don't you?"

His voice struck her ears like a deep chord. She looked over her shoulder again. Her heart felt snagged by the heat and promise in his gaze. Her skin tightened all over her body.

"I can give you pleasure without any consequence."

"Do you have a sheath?" she asked with a lofty elevation of one brow, as if she would only deign to entertain the idea if he did.

She was already entertaining the idea. And he knew darned well that she was, despite the affront she was pretending.

"As it happens, I am fresh out. But there are other ways."

Her heart sank and rebounded, leaving her more curious than

anything else. Sexually curious. She was tingling all over, legs kicking with nervous agitation, mind whirling with possibility.

When the silence became an overloud rush of water and the chirp of birds struck her ears like a cacophony, he said abruptly, "I didn't mean to make you uncomfortable."

He leaped out of the wagon and walked toward the edge of the stream. He threw the remains of the leaf into it and stared broodingly as it circled in a tiny pool, saying quietly, "We can leave."

"I—" She slid off the wagon, telling herself to be sensible and agree that they should leave. But she would never have another stolen moment like this with a man who appealed to her so strongly. "What...um..."

This picnic had felt terribly hedonistic, but she was so sick of being selfless and taken for granted. She had made a good home and supported her husband and birthed his children and what had she got in return? Infidelity. Increased responsibility and the distress of telling lies to protect him and her children.

No. Surely sauce for the gander was sauce for the goose!

She lifted her chin. "What were you thinking?"

He picked up his head and looked over his shoulder. As he sauntered toward her, she realized exactly how imposing a man he'd grown into.

She fell back a step, not alarmed precisely, but he did have an undeniably sexual air about him.

"I'd rather show you. But I can describe it in detail first. If you like." His gaze slid down to her neckline. Further. As if he was looking through her skirts at her thatch.

It was indecent but caused her inner muscles to clench with forbidden longing.

"Benjamin." Her hand found its way to his chest, which must mean her feet had propelled her toward him. It should have been a defensive touch. A resistance.

But it wasn't. She *wanted* to touch him. She wanted him to touch her.

"Winnie," he whispered as he very slowly dipped his head. He held her gaze the whole time. Her heart seemed to hammer for release behind her breastbone, perhaps trying to reach his. Two, three, four, five—

His mouth settled on hers and a jolting thrill shot through her. Her hand tightened into the rough cotton of his shirt and her breath hissed in through her nose.

All her senses came alive as she let her mouth part beneath the pressure of his, opening in reception as he rocked his firm lips across hers in a thorough claiming. A soft rumble of satisfaction filled his throat and he shuffled closer. One of his heavy hands came to rest on her hip. He tilted his head and their kiss deepened even more.

She felt so young! So utterly free of constraint except for the raw desire that wrapped around her and squeezed all thoughts from her mind.

She twined her arm around his neck and let the other trail around his waist until she was plastered to his front, mouth tilted up in offering. Her lips pulling at his, sucking the bottom one in and tasting it with her tongue.

His arms, *so* strong, tightened around her. He crushed her curves into the hard planes of his chest and plundered her mouth with his own.

The thick evidence that he found her desirable was a sweet discovery against her mound. She rocked invitingly, feeling one of his hands come into her hair while the other splayed against her tailbone, pressing her harder to that ironwood shape.

When his tongue came into her mouth in a blatantly carnal way, thrusting the way she wanted his thick member to push and drag at her intimate flesh, she moaned, lost.

As his mouth trailed hungrily down her neck, she whispered, "If you want to…do it. You can." It was bad. So bad. But *so good*.

He lifted his head and his eyes blazed with lust beneath heavy lids. His mouth pulled at one corner in something between boyish charm and manly satisfaction. It made slithers of apprehension and anticipation move through her middle.

His hands hardened on her waist and he picked her up, setting her on the end of the wagon again. The sun-warmed boards radiated through her gown against her bottom.

"I promised pleasure without risk," he said in that graveled voice that made her nipples sting. His hands found her calves and swept up to the backs of her knees, revealing her shins. "Lie back."

"What—"

He was opening her legs, skimming his touch to her bare thighs, taking up her gown.

"Benjamin."

"Lie back. You'll like it. I promise." He looked at her. Looked right at her sex and licked his lips.

He wasn't thinking of— It was the worst type of sinning. "You can't—"

"I want to." He bent to blow against her curls, making her folds feel heavy and plump, like her breasts. Like she would burst if he didn't do more. *Soon.*

With a helpless whimper, she let herself sink back against the hard bed of the wagon, biting her lips in embarrassment that young Benjamin had his face between her legs. That he was using his thumbs to part her and was making a noise as though the sight of her pleased him.

There was a soft, wet dab. Cool, but not. Just enough to have her inner muscles clenching in mortified pleasure while tingles raced along her inner thighs, causing her legs to instinctively try to close.

She couldn't. He was caressing her and there was another more confident sweep of his tongue, one that was so blatant in his quest, it made another noise of torture rise to her throat. She twisted her hips, certain she couldn't bear this intimacy.

His hand shifted to her stomach, urging her to stay flat. Then he angled his hand so he could use his finger and thumb to splay her folds. "Tell me if you like it when I do this."

His tongue swirled in a spot that made her stomach contract. All her senses seemed to coil into a knot that originated in that one place. Hot pleasure pooled in a way that made her want to spread her legs wider for more of it. It was the slippery response that, when it happened, made conjoining sweet and ultimately very satisfying.

That gratifying culmination took time to achieve, though. She had only occasionally experienced it, but what Benjamin was doing had her swiftly scaling the mountain toward that peak. She held her breath, tensing as she both sought and waited for it.

He lifted his head. "Should I stop?"

"No," she moaned. "Please. It feels so good."

"Do you like this?" One finger slid easily into her slick canal. He grunted with animalistic pleasure. "You're so wet, Winnie." He withdrew, fingered her again, then returned with two long, wet fingers. He watched as he moved them in and out of her. His tongue touched his bottom lip. "I can feel how hard you're squeezing my fingers. I'd love to feel that on my cock."

He shouldn't say that word, but she was too mindless to scold. In fact, she said, "You can."

"I promised, Winnie. But fuck, I want to. You're so pretty." His fingers went deep and scissored open as he set his mouth on her again.

His free hand came up and fondled her breast, pinching her nipple through the muslin while she writhed in acute pleasure. Her inner walls had never quivered like that, holding her on a precipice, shivering with glorious promise. Her body had never felt so molten. Her inhibitions had never been so far abandoned that she lifted her hips and groaned, "Keep licking me. It feels so good."

He did, keeping the pace slow so she stayed on this plateau where all of her felt as though she floated above the world, while her blood thickened in her limbs and need coiled tighter within her.

His fingers slipped out of her and she made a noise of loss, but now a third joined the first two and she felt stuffed full, making a guttural noise of joy as the tension of being so thickly impaled shot her right to the edge of gratification.

And now he was sucking blatantly. Loudly. The sensations became more than she could take. Her limit was reached and her whole body clamped down in a way that would have alarmed her if she'd had time to recognize what was happening. Her heart and lungs seemed to seize, then her body bore down for a contraction that was so strong, it should have been painful.

Her sex gripped and pulsed and shivered around the fingers he kept tucked deep inside her and her body did something it had never done during the throes of passion. She released a stream as a profound climax exploded within her.

CHAPTER THREE

Everything in him wanted to crawl atop her and bury himself balls deep in her soaked, pulsing cunt.

But Benjamin didn't want scandals or obligations any more than she did.

As her cries of startled pleasure receded, he gave her a final, loving lick and withdrew his hand. He straightened and flicked open his breeches, staying between her splayed knees, but pivoting slightly. He used the hand still slick with her juices to clasp his straining cock and jerk it. He was so ready, it only took a short, swift hammering and he was thickening and throbbing with release.

He ground his teeth, but a guttural shout still left him as his buttocks clenched and his come shot like an arrow that seemed to originate in his arsehole and land halfway to the burbling water. He kept milking his cock, watching his own spurt until it was a last drizzle against his swollen, purple cap.

As he came back to himself, he wiped his sweaty face, still damp with Winnie's juices, in the crook of his elbow. His heart pounded with exertion as he looked at Winnie.

Her legs were weakly splayed open. There was a damp patch on the back of her gown beneath her. Her cunt was still flushed and shiny, lips and hole pouted open.

Fuck, he could eat that all day. His cock gave a latent twitch, wanting in there.

"I'm so embarrassed," she moaned, shakily trying to sit up and close her legs, but he didn't move, so he was in her way.

"Why?"

She gave him a wild look that held guilt and shame and confusion as her gaze struck her gown. She threw the top of her skirt down to cover her knees. The way her breaths were so shaken, he feared she was about to cry.

"Winnie." He set a gentle hand on hers to get her attention and dipped his head to try to see her eyes. "Did you not know a woman could come like that?"

Her lashes came up, revealing wary brown eyes. "Aldous never kissed me there. Maybe he knew and that's why. Oh no! Did I get your shirt wet?"

"Hell yes, you did." He plucked the front of it where her scent would stay with him the rest of the day. "You were supposed to. I wanted to make you do that."

She only stared with horror at the stain.

He tried not to laugh at the irony as he tenderly cupped her cheek and asked, "Do you remember the time you told me where babies come from? *Exactly* where they come from?"

She clenched her eyes shut. "You're not helping me feel better about *any* of this."

"I'm only saying it's nice to be the one educating you for a change." He was unable to stop his wry smile. "I was trying to make you do that. I haven't been with enough women to know if it's something every woman can do. It doesn't happen every time, but I thought you would like it. No?"

"I'm so weak, I can barely move." She hung her face in her hands. "I think I should feel very bad about all of this."

"But you don't? Please tell me you feel very good, Winnie."

"I do," she said, mouth pulling with more rue than remorse.

She started to slide off the wagon and he helped her to her feet. She shook out her gown and brushed at the damp stain on the back of her gown before sending him a look that was vulnerable, but also held the sort of womanly satisfaction that fed his pride.

"Thank you, Benjamin."

"Anytime." With a slow, wicked grin, he added, "I mean that."

•••

Very early in her marriage, Winnie and Aldous had attended to a family burying their daughter, a woman close to Winnie's age at the time. Winnie had been feeling off-color and emotional, not yet aware she was carrying their first. Condoling had been very new to her and the family's loss hit her profoundly— especially when the young woman's mother confided her daughter had accidentally poisoned herself with pennyroyal attempting to stop a pregnancy.

Deeply affected by that dark secret, Winnie had always been reluctant to try "regulating her courses" with herbs. But as her mood stayed light for days, body pleasantly humming with the memory of her tryst with Benjamin, and her mind completely at ease because there was no fear of pregnancy, she began considering how she might enjoy lovemaking without procreating.

Not that she would have Aldous in her bed if he came back to her on his knees, but Benjamin? Absolutely. Maybe even another man after he was gone. She *liked* pleasure without consequences.

So, when she had the opportunity a week later, she spoke with the midwife about recipes for herbal remedies.

"I know they can be dangerous," she said with apprehension. "That's why I won't try a recipe from a book, but I thought with your experience, you might know of something that is safe to take?"

"Is your husband back?" the midwife asked with surprise. "I hadn't heard."

"No. I'm inquiring for someone else." *They're always for a friend.*

"I see." After a long pause in which Winnie bit her inner lip, the midwife said, "Well, it's important you understand that husbands find such tonics very threatening. They view having a big family as a sign of virility. Any man who learns a woman is taking steps to prevent a pregnancy will question why she feels a need. I should never wish to be accused of promoting infidelity. I would be run out of the village in the middle of the night. So I *must* tell you, Mrs. Hornsby, that I *never* recommend such measures. Which is the message I would ask you to pass along to your friend."

"Of course. I understand." She did. With absolute clarity. The woman was protecting herself and her practice. "Forget I mentioned it."

"Of course. Now…" She rose and went to a cupboard. "As a mother of five with a husband often away, I imagine you feel very weary at times. Perhaps agitated at other times? Let me give you a tisane that I prepare myself, one that will keep you robust and energized. Have you had your courses since weaning your daughter? A spoonful of this twice a day will ensure your cycle *always* arrives." She offered a small tin.

"Without unsettling effects?" Like pregnancy?

"None. Several women in the village use it. In fact, the widow Grassley swore by its restorative properties."

Winnie smiled. "I can't wait to try it."

● ● ●

Now protected against consequences, Winnie tried to think how she could arrange another rendezvous with Benjamin before his sister's wedding.

Divine intervention arrived when she was asked to the solicitor's office. Mr. Middling was a diligent man when it came to drafting a contract or pursuing a point of law. He was much less so when it came to dirtying his hands with manual work or throwing an extra coin into a hat for charity.

"Mrs. Hornsby. I have a favor to request." He invited her to sit before he took the chair behind his desk. "You're aware the widow Grassley is my tenant? She has written to inform that she will remain in Norwich. She's remarrying."

"Ah. Happy news," Winnie said brightly.

"Yes. And she has asked me to arrange for her things to be shipped. I have a comprehensive list of the furnishings that were let with the cottage, but I shouldn't like to muss with a lady's mementos or have any issues arise later that this or that went astray. I could think of no one else so far above reproach to take on such a task."

Or anyone else who would charge no fee, she suspected, but kept her smile firmly in place. "Of course. I imagine there will be glassware and other fragile items. Let me ask Mr. Kent if he has some ideas on how best to pack them for transport. No doubt his wagon could be of assistance, too."

Happy news *indeed*.

• • •

Mr. Kent promised to have Benjamin drop some wooden crates and straw for packing at Mrs. Grassley's. Once Winnifred had everything ready, Benjamin could come by to collect it and Mr. Kent himself would make the arrangements for the outgoing manifest.

She met Benjamin at the rear door of the cottage two days later. It had been two weeks since their day by the stream and she'd only seen him from afar. Heat flooded into her cheeks as she met his polite smile. Had she imagined the whole thing, or was he being discreet in not greeting her more warmly?

The ladies from the sewing circle chattered behind her, determined to help her with her chore. They watched with great attention as Benjamin brought in the crates.

He touched his cap as he took his leave. "I have a delivery now, but I'll check back in a few hours to see if you need more boxes?"

"Thank you. We should have a good sense of things by then," Winnie said.

Several hours later, the crates were full and ready to have their tops tacked closed. The ladies had all returned to their own homes to feed their families while she waited for Benjamin.

"You didn't bring the wagon?" she noted when Benjamin turned up at the door.

"Is this not what I think it is?" he asked quietly, his gaze moving beyond her into the empty cottage.

Since they didn't have time for prevarications, she let him read the wild delight in her expression. "It's exactly what you think it is."

He stepped in and closed the door, dragging her into his arms as he did. His mouth came down on hers with greedy passion, instantly setting her alight, but she had to tear her mouth away to say, "The window."

He turned her back to the door and reminded, "This isn't my first time in this cottage. I know how to avoid being seen." His open mouth went down her neck while his hands roamed, shaping her hips through the fall of her gown, clasping her buttocks as his mouth came up to suck her earlobe, weakening her knees. "This is all I've thought about since that day."

"Me, too," she admitted.

They kissed again, without restraint, mouths open and tongues plunging against one another's. She twined her arms around his neck and arched her back as his hands came to her breasts.

When he exposed one and dropped his head to suckle, she flinched at the strength of his pull, but it sent such a tug into her loins. She'd been damp all day, awaiting his arrival and now her desires intensified. She wriggled in anticipation.

"You can do it this time," she whispered, running her fingers through his thick hair, not sure how to broach the topic of the tea she was drinking. "Be inside me."

"I'll pull out," he said, lifting his head. "I don't mind."

She nodded, smiling shakily, pleased he was willing to take

that extra step.

A slow grin spread across his face, so handsome she had to kiss him again.

He framed her head with his forearms against the door and kissed her senseless while the rough linen of his shirt abraded her exposed breast.

A moment later, amid their moans of passion, she heard a soft click near her hip. She glanced to see he had turned the key in the lock. He did know this cottage well.

"Bedroom," he said, wet lips against hers. "If this is my only chance to fuck you, I want you naked on the bed so I can do it right."

With a small whimper of helplessness, she ghosted through to the widow Grassley's former bedroom and ensured the curtains were firmly drawn over the tiny window. It meant that only a faint, late-afternoon light came in, which helped greatly with her sense of modesty. She divested of her gown and petticoat and was removing her hose when he came through the door and dragged his shirt over his head.

He threw a pair of linen hand towels on the bed.

She faltered.

One arrogant auburn brow went up. "I want to make you come like I did before."

The thought made her dizzy, especially when he nudged her to turn and quickly unlaced her stays for her. Seconds later, her chemise was gone and she was shivering, naked in the cool, darkened bedroom.

His breeches hit the floor and his big frame crowded her toward the bed, making her shiver in a different way—with awareness of his hot, bare skin with its layer of rough-soft hair. The strength in his hands as he pressed her onto the bed was both alarming and reassuring. She knew she could trust him, he wouldn't let her fall, wouldn't force her, but he was a very big, solid man. His weight came down alongside her and rolled her against him on the mattress.

"I'm nervous," she confessed, touching his erection with equal parts trepidation and longing. He was well-endowed and very hard. Her folds were weeping with desire for his thrusts, but despite her five children, he was much better at this than she was.

"That's all for you." His open mouth was at her neck and shoulder. "I'm like this every time I think of you. I can't keep the fucker soft."

She would have laughed, but his mouth was pulling at her nipple again and his hand crept between her thighs. He groaned as he discovered how slippery she was. His touch glided along her folds, making her scalp tighten while the pull of his mouth on her breast had wetness pooling against his fingers.

"I'm like this for you," she moaned, crooking her knee open so he could finger her more deeply. "Wet all the time because I can't stop thinking of you."

"Mmm." He withdrew his hand and sucked her essence from his finger. "I want to eat you again, but let me inside that heat first. Do you want my cock in you, Winnie?"

It was a rhetorical question. He was rolling atop her and she was opening her legs to offer herself. The wide dome of his member pressed her hot entrance, slipping and sliding against her a moment, then pushing in to sink deep within her channel in a long thrust that filled her up, making her groan in gratification.

He growled and hooked his arms under her knees, lifting her legs so she was fully open to his first careful thrusts. "Look," he commanded.

She picked up her head and watched the thick, gleaming length of him ploughing the damp hairs of her furrow. It was the most licentious thing she'd ever done, if one didn't count releasing against his mouth. The sight was so blatant, shivers chased across her skin and her inner muscles pinched him tighter.

She dropped her head back and he adjusted slightly, nudging his knees closer on either side of her hips. The way his member rubbed against her elongated folds caused her desire to take a sharp upswing. She groaned and tried to twist away from the intensity, but found herself pinned by his hard arms holding her legs open. She was completely helpless to his mercilessly delicious lovemaking.

"Hurt?" he paused, his sex buried deep inside her, twitching in a way she felt most intimately.

"No, but it's…a lot. I feel too much."

"You're supposed to." He moved again, watching her as he thrust, slowly building his speed and power, dragging her along with him so her insides were beginning to quiver the way they had that day by the stream.

"Benjamin." She tried again to twist away from the intensity, feeling too exposed that he was watching her endure the pleasure he ruthlessly inflicted.

"Your cunt is holding me so tight, Winnie. Let it happen. Come," he coaxed grittily. "Come hard."

The slap of their flesh grew louder and the rub of his tip hit something inside her that had her bearing down. All of her locked up as it happened again. She felt the contraction and the spurts of wetness. A barbaric noise was torn from her throat as her womb contracted and her body shuddered under waves of pleasure while he kept her caged in the vise of his lovemaking, thrusting through all of it, keeping her in that state of climax as long as possible.

Gradually, when she was a quivering mass, he eased up. He slowed to play her sex like a violin with his bow, drawing out the sharp notes and vibrations for a long time until he settled with his iron hardness still lodged deep in her relaxed and twitching sheath.

They were both shaking. She was boneless while he was taut and hard, controlling himself with supreme effort. He shifted onto one elbow, still inside her, and ran one of the linen towels between them. Only then did he let his thick, hard sex slip from her body.

She lay quiescent with her legs still open while he knelt between them.

"Do you want me to touch you?" She eyed his slick, thrusting sex, wondering if she dare use her mouth on him?

"I want you to roll over." He lightly stroked himself as his gaze traveled hotly over her. "In a minute. After I lick you back to excitement."

She couldn't help it. She set a protective hand over her mound. "I don't think I can take it."

"I think you can." He shifted, sliding down so he was half off the bed. He easily picked up her thigh to drape it on his shoulder. "If you want me to stop, say so."

His tongue began to flick at the seams between her fingers, so tantalizing, she groaned and removed her hand. Then he ran his tongue soothingly along her slit, kissing better the tender flesh that had received such a pounding. It was lovely and she found herself relaxing into his sweet ministrations, combing her fingers idly in his hair, accepting this as a type of affectionate caress that made her feel close to him.

Then he slithered his tongue to that spot.

"Oh, Benjamin." She closed her legs on his head, hearing him make a noise of cruel amusement.

He knew exactly what he was doing, reawakening her with a lazy suckle that made her loins grow heavy. She must be seeping juices all over him, but he didn't seem to mind. In fact, he ran his tongue all over her inner thighs and outer folds, making noises of luxury as he did.

When he finally lifted his head, his eyes were fierce with carnal delight, his lips and chin glistening.

"Do you want to climb onto your knees for a proper hard fuck?" he invited.

Heaven help her, she did. She had never done anything like it in her life and there was nothing the least bit decorous about it. Not when he set a towel beneath her and knelt behind her to finger her, making her tilt up her hips in blatant offering.

"I love how wet you get." He pinched and fondled and stuffed his thumb into her, stimulating her into squeezing and silently begging for more. "In another life, Winnie…"

She felt the same, moaning without constraint as she waited for him to fuck her again.

His knees moved between hers and the hot weight of his cock danced against her swollen folds. She rocked her hips, inviting him to guide his tip to her wet, clamoring pussy. She *never* thought such dirty words, but today they slid into her head the way his thick cock slid into her cunt.

She grunted and embraced him with welcoming squeezes and a moan of unfettered joy.

He made a noise of fulfillment and fondled her buttocks, saying, "You have a great ass, Winnie. And you feel so good. Do you like this? Does it feel good to you, too?"

She couldn't speak. After a moment, he offered a few light, steady thrusts. Ones that claimed her and made tingles chase down her spine. She arched in delight and his cock found a spot inside her that made her choke out a guttural sound.

"That's what I wanted to hear." His hands clamped onto her hips. "Stay just like that, Winnie. Hear me?"

"Yes," she gasped, holding very still to receive his cock as he took up a quicker pace, continuing to stimulate that sweet spot so her pussy walls felt wide open, yet plumped to excess, so the friction of his hammering cock built the pressure within her all the more.

She was afraid to move for fear the flames that were swallowing her would smolder. She was caught in a stasis of absolute pleasure, distantly aware of their slapping flesh and her keening moans. She was being royally fucked in a way she hadn't known was possible and it was so *good*.

His hand slid down her stomach and two fingertips pressed

the top of her sex.

She couldn't move at all and didn't have to. The rapid pump of his hips caused just enough friction to scrub his fingertips against her nub and make lightning explode through her pelvis.

In a rush, she came so hard her body bucked and shook. Her pussy walls clenched and released that satisfying gush. Her arms wouldn't hold her and she sank onto her elbows, burying her cries of ecstasy in the mattress.

As it began to subside, Benjamin withdrew.

She made a noise of protest and he crooned soothingly. He kept his cock against her soaked folds as he shifted his knees to the outside of hers.

With a flex of his strong thighs, he brought her knees together so his cock was tucked into the slippery press of her thighs. Her juices ensured he was well-lubricated as he thrust his cock against her still sensitive folds. The movement teased out latent pulses of pleasure while he clamped a hand on her shoulder and his hips slapped into her ass and the backs of her thighs.

Within seconds, he was biting off a harsh curse as he came in a scorching river that painted her stomach all the way to her breasts.

How remarkable. She hadn't known *that* sort of lovemaking was possible!

As his orgasm subsided, she could feel him shaking behind her. Their skin adhered with sweat where they touched. His come cooled and drizzled along her skin while his hand absently pet the curve of her hip and thigh.

"Fuck that felt good, Winnie."

"It did." She was both ecstatic and melancholic as they carefully untangled and she brought the towel to her stomach.

They settled facing one another in the darkened room. He drew her close to warm her. The aromas of sex permeated the air. They both sighed.

"I'm tempted to stay for you. For that," he said, filtering her loosened hair through his fingers.

Much as she wanted to take that as a declaration of love, she reminded herself he was still very young. He had made love with another woman in this very bed.

"Don't. I'm married, remember? We couldn't live openly."

Even if they could, she wasn't certain she wished to be committed to a man again. Perhaps she would feel differently once the children were grown, but for now she was learning to appreciate the advantages of being married to an absent husband.

"You have a lot to contend with," he noted.

He had been responsible for his sister a long time. He wasn't the type to leave a woman to fend for herself, she understood that, but, "You have so many opportunities, Benjamin. The world is full of men who are given more than they deserve and squander it. You have a good mind and a good heart. You can move so far ahead of where you came from. I want to see you do that."

"You've always believed in me." He tucked his chin to kiss her nose. "Do you ever wonder what your life would be like if you hadn't married and started a family?"

"Careful," she snorted. "You'll be accused of reading Wollstonecraft and upsetting the social order."

His mouth twitched. "I have read it. Someone left a copy in the circulating library." He eyed her. "Ingrid brought it home."

"Guilty. And my life is a good one. For a woman." She turned onto her stomach. "If I had options, however, I would exercise them. So I want you to do that for both of us. Please?"

His hand slid down her hair in an affectionate caress that ended with a light tug of a tendril. "Do you want to hear a secret?"

"No one asks me if I *want* to hear them. They simply tell me things and expect me to keep it to myself. I can't tell you how satisfying it is to have a secret of my own." She pressed her self-satisfied smile against the hollow of his shoulder, memorizing his scent. "I won't feel half so denied in life after this. Thank you."

"I've wanted to be with you like this for a long time." He

let the backs of his fingers caress under her jaw. "I wanted you when I was mucking your stable and you were already married with three children."

"You were a child." She dipped her chin.

"Not anymore." He gathered her atop him and kissed her.

"No," she agreed as she felt him hardening against her thigh. She opened her legs across his hips. A small adjustment later and they were joined, not moving as they simply enjoyed the connection while kissing.

Eventually he rolled her beneath him and made love to her with tender, thorough strokes that brought her to a deeply satisfying peak. Again.

When she had caught her breath, she finished him with her mouth, knowing she would regret not at least trying to give him pleasure this way. When he came, it seemed to startle them both. He said, "Oh fuck, Winnie, I'm— Oh fuck. Sorry."

His hot come filled her mouth so abruptly she wound up swallowing a little. She spit the rest into one of their towels, apologizing as she did.

"Why are *you* sorry? I didn't expect you would— I didn't expect *I* would lose it so fast. Not after you drained me dry earlier. I feel drunk, that was so good. Thank you." He dragged her close and kissed her, roaming his tongue into her mouth in reassurance that he adored her for what she'd done.

They made themselves dress then. It was growing dark and he let her leave first, staying back to move some of Mrs. Grassley's furniture pieces so they would be close to the door when he returned with the wagon in the morning.

CHAPTER FOUR

Though she looked for another chance for them to be alone, she didn't see him again until his sister's wedding.

"Benjamin," she greeted when they met outside the church. "If the gossips are correct, you've quit your job and your sister and her husband will take over your cottage."

"The gossips are correct. I'm leaving tomorrow by barge. I…" He squinched one eye shut. "I wondered if you would come see me off?" he asked quietly.

"Of course," she said with a touched smile. "If you'd like me to."

"I have an ulterior motive," he admitted, surreptitiously glancing around to ensure they weren't being overheard. "It bothers me you don't have anyone here to keep an eye out for you."

He was adorable. "I'm fine, Benjamin. Honestly."

"I know you're very capable, but… You deserve to have someone who appreciates you, Winnie. Someone you can trust. A man who makes you feel like a woman and isn't breaking your heart or leaving you." His brow lifted in self-reproach. "I want to introduce you to my friend. He works the barges, so he's away a lot, but he's kind and solid, a bit shy. Very funny once you get to know him. He's closer to your age than mine," he added ruefully.

"I don't need you to find me a lover," she hissed with exasperation.

"It's just an introduction. He doesn't know that you and I…"

She shook her head and they were interrupted at that point, but she was curious enough—and anxious enough to see Benjamin one last time—that she went to see him off.

She was feeling forlorn as she said goodbye to him, wishing

she could kiss him, but it was impossible.

At the last moment, he introduced her to Holden.

Holden blushed bright red as he tipped his cap in greeting. He was close to thirty, strappingly built from the hard work he did, and he had the most charming smile.

Thankfully, Benjamin had given her the perfect excuse to seek Holden out a few weeks later. She asked him if he had any word on their friend.

It led to regular conversations where they discovered they both liked books. She came upon him singing one day and told him his voice was a gift. So were his fingers, as she discovered when they finally found a moment of privacy. One kiss and a straying touch beneath her gown and she was coming in a rush into his palm.

He had a lovely fat cock, too, and wasn't shy with his tongue.

By the time she received a letter from Benjamin, stating he was about to board a ship to America, she was able to reply that she was managing very well. The curate was taking on more of his proper duties, freeing her up to enjoy time on personal pursuits. She looked forward to the barge every week as there was always something on it she wanted. She wished him well and urged him to stay in touch.

Not long after that, her perfidious husband turned up. He was in a lather that the appropriate amount of the tithes weren't reaching him.

Winnifred left him to sort it out himself, generously blessing him with their children for the day while she spent a satisfying few hours sucking Holden's cock and sitting on his face.

The End

One Night
as a Woman

One Night as a Woman is a tender romance between a man and a woman, who was assigned male at birth, and a touching story about acceptance of self and others, however, it includes certain elements that might not be suitable for some readers. A hazing ritual, outdated views of sex and gender, and the unintentional misgendering of one of the main characters are included in the story. Readers who may be sensitive to any of these, please take note.

CHAPTER ONE

L eigh Rempleton had survived Eton and Oxford. One might have believed that was enough to prove one's mettle among one's peers, but no. Here came yet another challenge.

Lord Somerfair,

Being as you are a man in good standing and health, demonstrating all manner of loyalty, intelligence, and strength of character—

This accolade surprised Leigh, given the attention those who demonstrated none of those qualities seemed to earn. What exactly was this letter trying to sell?

—you are herewith and cordially invited to join the Knights of Ribaldry, a society dedicated to furthering the enlightenment and ambition of Great Britain's finest. Fear not. This is not a dry evening. Ennui is the foe we combat at every gathering!

Your initiation test commences Friday hence at eight p.m. Present this letter at the Cocksblood Inn an hour beforehand. Instructions will await you.

Sincerely, and with much anticipation of your joining our esteemed ranks,

—Chancellor, Knights of Ribaldry

"Fuck me." Leigh sighed, glancing to the smoldering fire with an urge to throw the letter onto it.

There was no getting around it, though. Leigh had completed the epic poem of "school" by accepting two things: That any dismay or dissatisfaction Leigh felt with a system that awarded a title and fortune based on an accident of birth was irrelevant. And the dangling bit of flesh between the legs of the Viscount Somerfair's issue awarded Leigh power and privilege that couldn't be squandered, not when Leigh's twin sister would kill to possess the same.

What was the alternative? Move to France for a life of penury as an artist? No, the whip of duty to birthright was one that Leigh wielded in self-flagellation, if only to ensure Devona would receive as much of an equal share as Leigh could squeeze from the entailment.

Not that Devona was in dire straits. She had married well and held the title of duchess above even their father, but that was all she held. Her marriage settlement would come to her if her husband died. Ideally, her two sons would ensure she was comfortable in her old age, but if tragedy caused the title to slide to a distant cousin, Devona would look to her twin. She had every right to expect their father's fortune to support her. She was older than Leigh by nearly an hour. Leigh must claim it for both of them.

Thus the letter couldn't go into the fire, even though Leigh already knew the ceremony would involve some humiliation or other with wine, whores, and other levels of fuckery, all in the name of promoting a fraternal bond.

As tedious as that sounded, however, connections would be formed. Later, when a favor or support for a venture was needed, members of the club would be there. That's how this worked.

Leigh sent regrets to the evening of cards offered by a favorite cousin and, at the appointed time, turned up at the Cocksblood Inn where Leigh was conducted up the stairs to a guest chamber.

Two other initiates were there, stammering with excitement. Leigh was acquainted with one, Alistair, the son of a baron who'd been a year ahead at Oxford. The other, Neville, was the son of a colonel stationed in Bath.

They introduced themselves and poured glasses of the wine

that had been left for them, speculating on what might await them.

Soon, a woman entered. A prostitute, Leigh surmised, judging by the amount of stocking she showed and the way her bosom looked ready to spill over the wide neckline of her gown. Was she the test? Because Leigh wasn't interested.

"I'm Kitty. I'll help you dress." She nudged Alistair off the trunk on which he sat and began pulling out women's clothing. "Let's see what fits."

"Oh fuck no," Neville groaned, but he was already grinning at the adventure.

Leigh sighed. So infantile, but fine. They were each made to strip behind a screen and come out in a chemise. Kitty named all the pieces as she directed them to put on a corset and then a petticoat over it, insisting they play lady's maid for one another.

"You learn to put these on, you'll know how to take them off—and how to put them on again in a hurry," she added bawdily.

The other initiates laughed, but this was why a sense of being "one of the boys" eluded Leigh. For years, remarks on pretty tits and ploughing a particular furrow had hit Leigh's ears without ever prompting similar fiery fantasies. Once or twice Leigh had considered visiting a prostitute to learn what all the fuss was about, but pox was rampant in London. Since a viscount's heir did not sow oats in the fields at home, Leigh was a virgin, resigned to fumbling through the basics on some distant wedding night in hopes of producing the required future viscount.

After stuffing the hollow cups of the corset, they pulled on gowns. Alistair wore green, Neville blue. Leigh was given a pale yellow with a pink overskirt that fluttered like a cape off the back of the high waist. It was very constrictive yet graceful, making Leigh feel sensual and conscious of standing tall and moving with fluid care.

"You've quite a mane, don't you?" Kitty pushed Leigh onto the corner of the bed to fiddle with the heavily waxed locks atop Leigh's head. "We can do something nicer than a bonnet, I think."

A ribbon and pins were procured and the bulk of Leigh's hair pulled back and up. Face-framing ringlets were formed with hot tongs.

Leigh sat very still for a brush of white powder across brow and cheeks and jaw. Afflicted with a narrow chin, Leigh had tried growing a beard to broaden it, despite the fact beards were no longer in style. Mother Nature had not deigned to adorn Leigh with heavy whiskers, though. A fresh shave had been more affectation than necessary this morning. Even at twenty-two, when most of Leigh's peers shaved daily, it was a once per week occupation for Leigh. Sideburns? Nothing of consequence had arrived, so the effort had been abandoned.

"Rouge," Kitty said. "And lip salve. My, you *are* a pretty one."

Alistair and Neville already had their final touches and looked exactly what they were, young men in ill-fitting gowns with garish cheeks and lips. They stopped knocking elbows and stared when Leigh stood.

"Do I look that dreadful?" Leigh asked, glancing for a mirror and finding none.

"You actually make a fine woman." Neville sounded sincere but looked uncomfortable for having noticed.

Leigh's stomach took a swoop, the kind that was habitually suppressed and ignored. In response to Neville's "compliment," Leigh blew a kiss at him.

"Oy. I do the flirting here." Kitty gave Leigh's ass a dull thwack. "Sounds like your lot are arriving. Come on, then. Yer the barmaids 'til the meeting's called to order."

● ● ●

Ulysses York, Earl of Mesterlyn, son of the Duke of Taymore, rarely attended these meetings anymore. He had come into the Knights of Ribaldry four years ago, believing the club would afford him a place where his political leanings would be supported. While he had formed good contacts and occasionally enjoyed enlightening conversation, the actual meetings were more often an excuse for young rakes to drink themselves into turning out their insides, failing to get it up for the prostitute they'd bought for the evening.

With the season starting, however, there were new initiates to vote in, so he had his carriage drop him at the Cocksblood.

The meeting hadn't been called to order yet. The noise from the top of the stairs was worse than the rabble in the common rooms below.

As he climbed the stairs, Ulysses noticed a woman standing at the rail on the landing. She wasn't so well dressed as a proper lady. She'd fallen down on her luck, perhaps. He noted her soiled slippers while admiring her slender ankles. Her gown looked worse for wear, too, but there was a definite air of quality about her. Something elegant yet delicate that kicked him in a place he made a point of keeping guarded, having learned caution with matters of the heart.

She didn't notice his ogling. She was staring across the well of the stairs to the uncovered window. It was dark outside. She couldn't possibly see anything through it, but she was fixated.

Ulysses was about to tell her she had wandered to a wrong floor when he noted the shocked look on her face. She'd either suffered a *terrible* turn of fortune or—

Ulysses's heart lurched.

"Miss, has something happened?" He turned at the top of the stairs to face her. "Did one of those men upset you?" He pointed to the noise at the end of the hall. He would kill them. Each one of them, one by one. Slowly.

"What? Fuck." She touched her trembling lips and blinked rapidly. "I'm such an idiot."

Ulysses didn't know what took him aback more, the curse from a lady or the voice that was deep for a woman, masculine yet husked with so much emotion, the hairs on Ulysses's arms stood up.

"I'm one of the initiates." She pinched the bridge of her narrow nose. "I came out and saw myself in the window. Saw my *sister...*" She looked to the ceiling, revealing an Adam's apple.

He?

No initiate had ever turned himself out this well as a woman. This one was blessed with a slight build and a lack of bristly body hair on the upper chest. He made a very appealing woman, which was a strange thing for Ulysses to absorb when he had never been attracted to men. He was attracted right now, though. There was no denying that's what this prickly curiosity was.

"You're upset," Ulysses said, protective instincts stirred by the femininity and genuine vulnerability on display. "Has she passed? I'm so sorry."

"No." She shook her head, choking on a laugh. "She's perfectly fine. It's me. I'm—"

Still upset.

Ulysses angled himself to provide them some privacy while trying to search out what was causing this pull. He appreciated beauty, same as anyone, but as a woman, she was tall and lithe, not curvy. Her nose was big and angular. Short, spiky lashes surrounded the direct blue gaze that met his own, causing a hard thump in his chest.

That was it, wasn't it? It was that air of self-possession. Ulysses liked a woman with confidence. Despite clearly being overcome, there was no wailing for smelling salts or hysterical weeping. Only a tense smile with a narrow chin lifted in resolve.

He had to smile in admiration. Couldn't help it.

Her eyes widened as though she suddenly saw him. *Really* saw him. In a blink, something fiery and exciting flared to life in her blue eyes, something that just as quickly made her drop her gaze and blush hard enough he saw the color rise despite her layer of powder.

It was a reflection of this sexual awareness he was experiencing and it fed his own, filling him with further heat and a strange gratification.

"Why does it upset you to look like her? She must be beautiful." It was supposed to be a tease but came out with a rumble of truth from deep in his chest.

A determined throat clear, then, "We're twins. I'm very protective of her and wind up doing things that I've just realized are more sacrifice than she would expect of me."

That wasn't the whole truth, Ulysses suspected, but that deep voice reminded him the gown was part of the initiation, not a choice. He also heard averseness to this silly test, which caused him genuine alarm, because he was growing more and more intrigued by the minute.

"You can't leave. We haven't all touched pricks yet. Or frigged into the collection plate."

The cheeks beneath the powder blanched, the color that bloomed only moments ago fading. Painted lips made an *O* of horror. "Tell me that's a joke."

"It is." Ulysses couldn't keep the corners of his mouth from curving. "But give us a chance before you decide we're asking too much of our members."

"Christ." What was probably a very attractive smile was firmly suppressed. "I knew there would be nothing but assholes here. Leigh Rempleton." An ungloved hand came out.

"Ulysses York." Leigh's hand was narrow but warm, with a firm grip. Ulysses wanted to keep hold of it but only nodded toward the main room. "Let me introduce you."

CHAPTER TWO

The evening wasn't as interminable as Leigh feared, thanks in large part to Ulysses.

Leigh was forced to circulate with a jug of beer first. That mingling renewed acquaintanceship with a handful of existing members and revealed that a connection from Oxford had put forth Leigh as a potential member.

One man, already well into his cups, offered Leigh a guinea to go down the hall.

"You'll have a surprise there, my man." Kitty intercepted the exchange and took man and guinea to the room where the initiates had been dressed.

Leigh happened to meet Ulysses's eyes from across the room at that point. He sat at a table in the corner with two other men, but he was no less imposing or attractive as the first impression he'd offered. He wore well-tailored clothes and a brooding sternness. His tightly curled black hair was shorn close, his strong, dark brown jaw was clean-shaven. Though big and broad across the shoulders, his grin was quick, his air that of a wolf tolerating a litter of rambunctious cubs.

He was the heir to a dukedom, Leigh had since learned, but the deference other members showed Ulysses was as much personal regard as respect for his title. He was looked to as a leader among them.

Ulysses quirked a brow that was humor at the man's mistake, but there was something else in his silent query. Something that asked if Leigh was insulted or upset by the mistake. Protective?

Leigh had to smile at that, warmed, but no longer distressed at projecting a certain ambiguity, having learned to navigate it long ago. Leigh never felt true kinship when among a group of men, but no longer experienced profound loneliness, either. A handful of cherished confidantes were all Leigh needed. Devona knew the person deep inside, and two beloved cousins with their spouses were also very dear and close. The other initiates might be desperate to be accepted here tonight, but Leigh cared very little for approval by outsiders.

Perhaps that wasn't entirely true. When the meeting was called to order and Ulysses indicated the chair he'd saved at his table, Leigh was pleased to be invited to sit with him. It went beyond feeling flattered to have a highly regarded man offer friendliness and a seeming desire for further acquaintance. Leigh was reacting to Ulysses in a completely new way—with a sort of bubbling excitement in the blood and a deep craving to know more about him. It was as unexpected as it was euphoric.

Leigh accepted a tippling from the bottle of smuggled brandy Ulysses ordered, still reeling at the sight of Devona in the window. Because of course it hadn't been Devona. It was Leigh's true self, the person Leigh had always known lived inside the face reflected in the mirror, but who was suppressed for many good reasons—and perhaps some that were detrimental. That's what Leigh had been confronting when Ulysses came up the stairs.

Leigh's pulse was still uneven, tripping and racing at a sense of being discovered *like this*. Most of the men were treating Leigh like the other two initiates, as though this was all a big joke to put a man in a gown, but Ulysses had seen past the costume. It might have been terrifying if there hadn't been this sizzle of warmth between them. It was the last thing Leigh expected to find here, having braced for the Knights of Ribaldry to be a fatuous bunch of asses.

They proved to have some substance, however. Their first order of business was an announcement that, with Napoleon defeated at Waterloo last summer, a handful of members wished to revive the Grand Tour and travel to Italy next year. A list was being circulated to express interest.

The next thirty minutes were spent on the analysis of various properties and investment prospects, much of it hearsay, but it was helpful considering Leigh's father entrusted Leigh to handle much of the family's London business on his behalf. This was the reason Leigh was Leigh. The viscount had terrible gout and the family's circumstances were not so lofty and secure they didn't need constant tending. Leigh was learning the ropes of investment for all their sakes.

Ulysses rose next. He was a philosopher with a deep involvement in politics, Leigh quickly learned, and offered weighty insight on *D'économie Politique*.

"That's his idea of erotic literature," one of their tablemates, Edward, leaned over to say.

Leigh chuckled but thought Ulysses made a persuasive orator, taking complex ideas and breaking them down so they were easily digestible.

As Ulysses returned to his seat, the meeting relaxed. Leigh and the other initiates were made to stand and introduce themselves, then sing "A Lusty Young Smith." They had to scull beer if they stumbled the words, but that was only a warm-up to reading passages from erotic novels.

Ulysses handed Leigh a book with a few pages marked. It was a prank, of course. The minute Leigh began reading an essay railing against hypocrisy in the church, the members booed. "Get to the good part!"

Leigh sent Ulysses a mock-glower of betrayal and Ulysses chuckled. Leigh turned to a more lascivious passage on the deflowering of a woman's ass.

That had the effect of sending two men down the hall with Kitty and another prostitute, but the rest stayed for Neville and Alistair's tantalizing readings.

"Very funny." Leigh leaned a little too far into Ulysses, thanks to the beer and brandy.

"What can I say? I regard religious blasphemy as the good part."

"Ulysses is nothing but melancholy and weighty thoughts," Edward provided. "When you're having too much fun and need to be reminded of the world's dullest wrongs, he is the one to bore you into sobriety."

"How could there be room in this club for me if you've already taken that title?" Leigh asked, earning another warm chuckle from Ulysses and a glimpse of amused brown eyes that made Leigh's heart wobble.

Before the final votes were taken, each initiate was pressed to demonstrate a talent. Neville walked on his hands while balancing a glass of beer on his foot. Alistair belched loud enough to rattle the glassware.

Through the interminable years of school, Leigh had developed a gift for caricature, one that could be wielded as a weapon when necessary. Those who could withstand gentle mockery liked Leigh for the humor. The most loathsome tormenter, however, backed off under threat of being depicted fucking a goat.

Quickly setting pen to paper, Leigh soon rendered a knight in armor attempting to get under a woman's gown only to discover a man's equipment beneath.

"Bloody hell. You should sign that," Ulysses said, taking it for a longer study.

"Not since I got a round dozen, thanks," Leigh said of the flogging the headmaster had administered on seeing Leigh's name on a similar piece of vivid artistry.

Ulysses barely flickered an eyebrow, because who hadn't been bent across the block? He handed the page to circulate for every type of coarse yet appreciative remark.

Minutes later, votes were taken, and Leigh was inducted with the other initiates amid great applause.

•••

Ulysses had worn a reputation as humorless for most of his life. It wasn't inaccurate. While he was capable of engaging in amusing banter and lighthearted pranks, he was far more interested in exploring social thought, economics, and politics.

Which wasn't to say he preferred scholarly pursuits over carnal ones. He wasn't a virgin, but he had learned with his first romance that lovemaking had consequences. He had the good fortune to have a ten-year-old son as proof of that, but sadly that boy did not have a mother. She had died in childbirth. It was a consequence Ulysses had not even considered when he'd been losing his heart to her in his last year at Oxford.

He'd been with women since, but he took precautions against everything: pregnancy, disease, love, and loss. He didn't allow himself to tumble into deep feelings, which was why his attraction to Leigh was both exciting and troubling. He kept getting lost in Leigh's graceful movements and expressive face. His ears strained to hear husky-voiced repartee and well-informed opinions over the babble surrounding them.

Ulysses kept telling himself this was a budding friendship with a fellow Knight, nothing more. But when the black windows turned to silver and everyone was staggering and yawning, he still wasn't ready to give up his new company. Not yet.

"Part of the joke is to send you home in the gown. Come in my carriage. I don't want you accosted."

"I can fight. I'm a pew— What's the word?" Two clenched fists came up. "I pugil."

They were both drunk. Everyone was.

"If you can't talk, you can't fight." Ulysses easily tumbled the lightweight Leigh into his carriage, then pushed in to sit on a swath of gown. They jostled into one another as they tried to free the gown from his drunken ass while the carriage began to move.

"Gowns are fucking cold," Leigh grumbled.

"Here. Better?" He tucked Leigh under his arm, liking the trusting way Leigh leaned into him.

"Thank you." Leigh's voice turned soft and husky. Intimate. "I'm glad I met you."

"Me, too." Ulysses slid his hand along Leigh's bare arm, enjoying the firmness beneath smooth, warm skin, the flex that suggested a sensual reaction to his touch.

Leigh leaned more heavily into him. The implicit invitation had Ulysses dipping his head to find Leigh's mouth in the dim interior of the carriage.

Leigh stiffened in surprise, but then relaxed immediately and softly kissed him back. It was a shy kiss, one that grew deeper in stages. Pliant lips firmed. Ulysses licked to part the ones he kissed. A hot breath grazed his cheek. She sucked his bottom lip, pulling everything in him taut.

Ulysses bit back a groan and drew Leigh even closer. They both opened their mouths and found a tighter seal. Leigh's hand settled on his thigh, bracing to lean closer. They grew even more impassioned. He flicked his tongue deeper, thrusting for a lustier taste, catching a throaty moan in response that made him growl in pleasure.

He was hard, so hard. He gathered her up and into his lap and her arms went around his neck, clinging as she thrust her tongue into his mouth. He sucked, wanting to consume her. Her back was so narrow he could almost span it with his splayed hand. When he stroked across the silk, she arched into him, ass deliciously grinding against his cock.

He drew her deeper into his lap and slid his touch along her waist, up to her breast—

The cup was stuffed with fabric, not warm flesh. They both drew back in shock.

Ulysses's heart hammered with lust and surprise. He could feel the tension that suddenly gripped Leigh, the sharpness of an elbow that signaled a desire to retreat.

"I completely forgot," Ulysses said, shifting Leigh to the seat beside him so they were no longer touching.

"We're really drunk," Leigh said faintly, looking into the corner of the carriage.

Ulysses was definitely too drunk to know what to say.

The carriage stopped and Leigh said, "This is me. Thank you. Good night."

CHAPTER THREE

L eigh had thought impassioned poetry about urgent rushes of emotion were bullshit. Such feelings had never arisen in Leigh when in the company of a woman, so they must be an embellishment on the sort of pleasant fondness Leigh occasionally felt toward one of Devona's friends.

Of course Leigh experienced that frequent and irritating hardening of flesh suffered by every man Leigh knew. That's why men sought the company of women, Leigh had always believed. They were too lazy to take care of it themselves or were succumbing to the pamphlets that warned against "self-polluting."

Leigh had never correlated feelings of arousal with attraction to men, though. On the occasions when a particular man had struck Leigh as appealing, perhaps provoking a certain physical response, Leigh had blamed Devona's influence. She made a sport of pointing out a "delicious rake" or a "libidinous libertine." Since there had never been a reciprocal interest, whatever interest Leigh experienced had been suppressed and eventually ignored.

Until Ulysses. And their fiery kiss.

Leigh warmed thinking of it. Couldn't *stop* thinking about it. It provoked a hunger that was everything and nothing like an appetite for food. A craving for more of Ulysses's touch. To see him and suck on his full lips, stroke the hot back of his neck, explore further, beneath his clothes. That night, through the folds of the gown, Leigh had felt how hard Ulysses had been and yearned to touch his cock. Salacious thoughts consumed Leigh. Fantasies of setting kisses there, licking and sucking and doing all the things the morality pamphlets discouraged.

Leigh had always been aware of not being "the same" as the boys and men held up as role models. Those differences had never sliced too deeply because in other ways, Leigh had been exactly the same. *Everyone* hated school. Everyone was picked on by someone. Everyone had learned to combat the bullies in their own way, as Leigh had with caricature.

No one was loved by everyone, and Leigh was loved enough by Devona and other family not to feel any sense of deprivation— except possibly of the sensuous kind. That, however, had been rationalized away. Previous generations might have been debauched, but theirs was an enlightened one. Leigh possessed a mind of reason, not a body of carnal urges.

Such arrogance! Leigh was as capable of lusty thoughts as anyone, now that Ulysses had roused the beast within.

It was a thrilling discovery, one Leigh might share with Devona if the right moment presented. For now, it remained a billowing internal heat that kept Leigh from taking in the external world, lost in sexual fantasy while running errands in London.

Until a thirst for chocolate sent Leigh into a public parlor where Ulysses sat at a table near the window.

It had been more than a week since their meeting. They'd had no contact since, but aside from a note of welcome from the chancellor that listed the dates for future gatherings, Leigh hadn't heard from any of the Knights.

Leigh couldn't walk out without acknowledging Ulysses. It would be rude in the extreme and, despite a sudden burst of shyness, Leigh was excited to see him.

How Ulysses felt about their kiss was another matter. He seemed deep in thought, composing a letter or some other important document. His table was scattered with crumpled, rejected drafts—a testament to his wealth. Leigh and Devona still cross-wrote their letters to one another, their father's insistence on frugality alive and well in both of them.

Leigh refused to let nerves take hold. Eventually they would face one another again. Carpe diem and all that.

Leigh's self-consciousness intensified with each footfall toward Ulysses. He was even more handsome than Leigh had consciously acknowledged before they kissed. Today, he wore a blue velvet jacket that made his brown skin appear luminous. His intense concentration and firm scratches of his quill were pure intimidation.

Leigh stopped near the table and waited for Ulysses to raise his head, but he didn't. After a small throat clear, Leigh used as confident and respectful a tone as possible, saying, "Lord Mesterlyn. It's good to see you again."

Ulysses looked up with a scowl at being interrupted and held the scowl as his gaze went from Leigh's unruly curls to the tall boots that had picked up spatters of mud from the streets. As his gaze came back with complete lack of welcome, Leigh's insides knotted.

"Yes. You, too," Ulysses said dismissively.

What had been a genuine smile was maintained through sheer force of will. Leigh hovered for one more agonizing heartbeat, yearning for a hint of warmth, but Ulysses dropped his gaze back to his paper with disinterest. He definitely wanted nothing to do with the *man* he'd kissed.

Leigh found a shred of dignified courtesy and said, "I'll see you at a future meeting, then." It was a lie. Leigh would never go back. Not now.

Ulysses jerked his head up as Leigh started to turn away, expression stunned.

"Leigh. Christ. I didn't recognize you. *At all*." Bright color rose against his brown skin. "I'm in the foulest mood imaginable, completely wrapped up in— It doesn't matter. Sit." He waved at the chair opposite. "How are you? I've been meaning to send a note."

Leigh's heart lurched in confused surprise, then warmth climbed to soften all of Leigh's joints, making the offered chair very welcome.

"I'm fine." Now Leigh was embarrassed for not realizing these town clothes of double-breasted dark green jacket and closely-tailored trousers were a very different look from their last meeting. "Do you care to share what set you off?"

"My father." Ulysses glowered at what he'd written. "One day I'll have his seat and spend the rest of my life undoing the mess he makes by his sheer apathy and ignorance. Until then, I should probably guard against his disowning me. Will you read my draft? Advise where I could take a more circumspect tone?"

"Of course." Leigh took the offered page of scrawls and scribbles. "Swag-bellied boot-licker might be too strong."

"I crossed out 'quim,'" Ulysses said as if that had been a tremendous concession.

Leigh couldn't help laughing.

Soon they were discussing the points Ulysses wished to make and how best to phrase them diplomatically. Ulysses was a very serious fellow, Leigh realized, and extremely well-read. He wasn't simply digging into a position, but seeing many sides before advancing what he saw as the best way forward.

"This has helped me clarify my thoughts enormously. Let me get it down. Do you have somewhere to be? Will you stay until I've finished?"

"Of course." The viscount expected a report on recent meetings, but that letter could wait. Leigh sipped cooling chocolate and took out a pencil and a sheet of the drawing paper that had been purchased as part of this morning's errands.

As Leigh cast about for something to sketch, the scritch of Ulysses's quill commanded attention. He held it with a decisive grip, the conviction in his penmanship as compelling as the words he wrote.

Leigh didn't make it a caricature. Couldn't. Infatuation and esteem were growing into regard. It became an ode without Leigh realizing until the drawing was nearly done.

"That's beautiful," Ulysses said in a tone filled with humbled admiration.

Leigh hadn't realized Ulysses had looked up to notice.

"No, it's..." Leigh scribbled a self-deprecating title for it, signed it, and said, "Something to take to Parliament when you get there."

"'The Political Pugilist,'" Ulysses read, lips curling at the corners. "I suppose I am. Who's Dawn?" His inquisitive gaze delved into Leigh's.

"Oh." Leigh hadn't consciously meant to reveal her, but perhaps Dawn had insisted on identifying herself, needing Ulysses to see her. "I, um, told you I have a sister. Devona. When the midwife told our mother she was having twins, she picked out names for two boys and two girls, Liam and Leigh, Dawn and Devona. Leigh and Devona arrived. Growing up, painting and sketching were pursuits my sister was allowed while I was expected to study Latin and mathematics. We never took well to being separated, so we schooled together. When she sat in on my lessons, she called herself Liam. When I take art seriously, I sign Dawn."

Ulysses studied Leigh for a long time, expression softened by contemplation, as if he heard everything Leigh wasn't saying and was taking it in.

Leigh experienced another attack of vulnerability like the one that had struck when confronting the reflection in the window, as though all shields and efforts at pretense were futile, especially with Ulysses. He saw all.

It was an intensely defenseless sensation, but exhilarating at the same time.

"It's beautiful. Dawn." The sincerity, the intimate and warm acknowledgement in Ulysses's voice was deeply moving.

Leigh could hardly hold his gaze. Could hardly speak. "You don't find it...odd?"

"I find everything odd," Ulysses assured wryly. "I'm a curious fellow by nature, always researching and reading essays or philosophy. I absorb religious texts with sacrilegious ones, conservative views with libertine. I'm not distressed by what others might call unconventional. I simply want to know more. Understand better."

"I see." Leigh should have seen that from the beginning, perhaps.

"Why are you dismayed?" Ulysses narrowed his eyes.

Leigh swallowed the knot of disappointment and forced an unbothered smile that was completely false. "I had hoped I was more than a curiosity to you."

"Leigh." There was a note of insult and a sting of admonishment in Ulysses's deep tone. A light flared in his eyes that caused a heart-stopping lurch in Leigh. "You are."

•••

"I want to know everything about you," Ulysses said quietly, aware of the people around them. "I want to meet your sister, see more of your sketches. I'm honored that you've explained to me about Dawn."

Leigh's gaze dropped and pink stained elegant cheekbones the way morning sun left a rosy glow on snowy mountains.

Ulysses ached to caress that blush and set his lips against the warmth there. "Do you have somewhere you need to be? Come home with me. We'll have dinner."

It was the middle of the day, but Ulysses was gripped by that greedy possessiveness of their first meeting. He wanted Leigh to himself, where they could talk freely. Be themselves without fear of interruption. More. He simply wanted *more*.

"I was going to call on my cousin." Leigh's eyes were the clear blue of a morning sky in spring, bursting with potential. "But I can send regrets."

They gathered their things and walked, since it was only a

short distance. When he entered his townhome, Ulysses handed off his writing things to his butler, instructing him to put them in his library, then introduced Leigh.

"Lord Somerfair may be shown in at any time. No one else today, though. We'll be in my sitting room. I'll ring you when we want a meal."

"Very good, sir."

"This is my brother's house," Ulysses said as he led Leigh up the stairs to the comfortable room that adjoined his bedchamber. "Left to him by our uncle, but he's in Upper Canada and knows I can't live with our father for more than a day, despite their address being significantly better than this and my—"

Ulysses hesitated as he closed the door and turned the key. If he wanted to know everything about Leigh, it followed that he would have to open himself. That wouldn't be comfortable, but it was necessary.

"My son is staying with my parents. My sister is there with her children. They're all very close, otherwise I'd have him here with me."

"You have a son," Leigh said with astonishment. "I was planning to look you up in my sister's copy of Debrett's when she arrives in town next week. How old?"

"Ten."

"Ten!"

"I made an error in judgment as a young man," Ulysses confessed as he unstoppered the brandy and splashed a measure into two glasses. "Which isn't to say I regret anything about him. I would have a dozen more children, I love him so fiercely, but his mother died giving birth to him. It didn't occur to me that it could happen, certainly not while we were fucking the daylights out of each other."

Leigh took the offered glass with a solemn expression. "I'm so sorry."

"Thank you. I shouldn't speak so crassly of her. I loved her

very much. In the way of a young man in love for the first time,"
he allowed retrospectively. "It all happened very quickly. Passion,
pregnancy, *marriage*."

"You've been married." Leigh lowered onto the divan.

"She was the daughter of a clergyman. I had to. I didn't tell
my parents until it was done. They were furious. Mother was
plotting a far better match. Then it was over just as quickly. I left
Oxford, buried my wife, and took a house near my sister. She had
recently given birth to a son herself. She's had two more since."
Ulysses sipped his brandy. "I live in terror that something awful
will happen to the people I care about. I try not to add to the list."

"Ah." Leigh's voice panged with understanding.

Ulysses lowered to the divan and touched Leigh's elbow,
gently insisting Leigh meet his gaze. "Sometimes people arrive
on my list whether I intend them to or not."

Leigh's pretty mouth—yes, it was a very pretty mouth—
trembled toward a rueful smile before it was bit back.

"I wanted to write, or call on you, but I didn't know what to
say," Ulysses admitted. "When you left the carriage so abruptly,
I thought you might be offended. Then there you were today, so
different, and my head was elsewhere. It wasn't until I heard your
voice…" That husky edge of emotion sent tingles of awareness
down his spine each time he heard it. "I've thought about you
constantly. I was dying to see you again. Kiss you again," he
admitted as want rose like a tide within him.

Leigh's shoulders softened. "Me, too. I've wanted all of that
and—mmm."

CHAPTER FOUR

Ulysses smothered whatever Leigh might have said, but his mouth was so powerful, so deliciously confident and sensually hungry, Leigh's mind blanked to all but the glorious feel of him. The softness of his lips, the damp slide as they angled their heads and consumed one another.

They were picking up exactly where they'd left off, but this time sober, which took all the loose, fuzzy memories of that night and sharpened them into a thrilling point that filled Leigh with scorching heat.

Leigh welcomed the stab of Ulysses's tongue, which sent sparking sensations from lips to chest to the swelling, throbbing flesh below. When Ulysses's strong arms swept Leigh up, Leigh went into his lap, twining arms around his neck and tangling tongues and sharing groans of pleasure as their bodies pressed.

This was everything Leigh had been imagining for days. An urgency to touch and kiss and caress every part of Ulysses consumed Leigh. While Ulysses's wide hands pressed Leigh's ass against the hardness in his lap, Leigh spread open-mouthed kisses across Ulysses's jaw and throat, peeling away his cravat and stealing fingers beneath his jacket.

Ulysses was equally quick to slip free the buttons of Leigh's jacket and waistcoat, to sweep long strokes from Leigh's shoulders to waist to thighs. When his hand moved inward, though, Leigh's knees instinctively locked.

Ulysses dragged his head up, breath panting as he searched Leigh's gaze. "No?"

With a small head shake, Leigh said, "I've been thinking about touching you. Can I?"

"Anywhere," Ulysses invited expansively. When he cupped

the side of Leigh's neck and lowered his head, his kiss changed to one that was much less aggressive. Tender now. "But we can stick to talking if you'd prefer. We don't have to do this."

"I do," Leigh groaned ruefully. "You really are all I've thought about. You'll tell me if you like it or not?" Leigh skimmed a greedy touch beneath the layers of Ulysses's clothes, dragging shirt tails from his breeches to find warm skin.

"I already like it." Ulysses lifted his hips to help with the freeing of his shirt, steadying Leigh with a cage of his hard arms. "But tell me first. Are you a virgin?"

"It's obvious?"

"It's fine." Ulysses smiled with affection, then his grin grew more wicked. "I love to educate as much as I love to learn."

"You're very arrogant. Has anyone ever told you that?" Leigh pushed at jacket and waistcoat until Ulysses's arms were free, then dragged his shirt over his head. A noise of admiration parted Leigh's lips when Ulysses's muscled chest was revealed. "Perhaps you're entitled."

Ulysses's flat, dark nipples were already hardened to small beads, but Leigh played with them, lightly pinching and sucking until Ulysses's fingers were digging into Leigh's back. With a private smile of accomplishment, Leigh slid from his lap to kneel between his thighs.

"You're sure?" Ulysses asked as Leigh flicked open the fall of his breeches.

"Very su— Oh." It wasn't as if Leigh didn't know what a cock looked like. School had been a parade of them. Soft and hard, pale and dark, circumcised and not.

Ulysses was definitely allowed some arrogance, possessing such a proud specimen, but there was something in knowing this incredible hardness was in response to *Leigh* that made this erection particularly spectacular.

Leigh gave into the wild impulses that had been so constant in the last week, sweeping a wet lick from the base up Ulysses's length to his tip. He would want to be enveloped, Leigh instinctively knew, and clamped a firm fist around his shaft before closing lips over his turgid, wet head. So smooth and velvety against the tongue. Salty and leaping in reaction while a long groan of pure lust sounded in Ulysses's chest.

"Christ, Leigh. Dawn," he corrected on another groan. "What do you want me to call you, love? Fuck, that feels good." His hands moved across Leigh's shoulders and he opened his thighs farther.

Leigh glowed under that word. *Love.* It made Leigh want to give Ulysses as much pleasure as possible. Leigh abandoned all restraint, kissing back down to his balls, nuzzling and sucking and teasing, then continued to fondle him while licking all the way back to his head and trying to swallow him whole.

As spittle gathered, Leigh was able to pump a firm fist in concert with a head bob that had Ulysses's cock straining and twitching, the taste of him growing sharper.

"Oh fuck, love. I'm going to come. You don't have to— Oh, fuck, darling. I'm— Oh fuck. Yes. Fuck, *yes.*" In the final throes, Ulysses bucked his lips, fucking the mouth that suckled him, releasing a hot pool of come that was swallowed down.

● ● ●

Leigh was dizzy and trembling with arousal, but so proud it was silly.

Even so, when Ulysses lifted heavy lids enough to offer a smoldering stare, Leigh had to ask, "Was that…nice?"

"Nice?" Ulysses choked. "You tore me in half." His firm hands caught Leigh's upper arms and dragged Leigh to straddle his thighs. "I want to do that to you." He dragged Leigh's mouth to his own for a long, hungry kiss.

Leigh couldn't let him, though. The thought of being naked caused a head shake that was pure instinct. "Not yet." Maybe not ever. Leigh wasn't sure. This was all very new.

"I don't want you to be hurting." Ulysses's gaze went down to the hard shape pressing against his belly. "What if you do it?" he suggested.

"I don't really..." Leigh didn't like a hammering touch. In fact, as a child, Leigh had learned to finger a secretive canal that had never once been mentioned by any of the most coarse or flagrant boys at Eton, so Leigh had never spoken of it, either.

Today, gripped by even more urgent arousal than the night at the Cocksblood, Leigh was compelled to loosen a trouser button and slide the tips of two fingers inside. Anatomy textbooks called this a frenulum, but Leigh preferred "clitoris."

Either way, the first grazing touch had Leigh's breath catching, which caused a blush at the carnal way Ulysses smiled. "Let me kiss you while you do that."

Leigh allowed passion to take over, teasing that delightful spot while kissing Ulysses with abandon, biting at his lips when climax bore down with quick, unerring strength.

Ulysses massaged Leigh's ass, lightly rocking so even though Leigh's hand was trapped between the press of their bodies, the stimulation continued, slick and urgent as Leigh was overcome. There was nothing to be done but lock one arm around Ulysses's neck and shout with release into his open mouth.

● ● ●

"I made a mess," Leigh mumbled some minutes later.

Ulysses was well aware of the damp patch on the clothes still between them but didn't particularly want to lift his weighted body off the warmth of Leigh's. The bed would be more comfortable, he acknowledged distantly. The divan was creaking beneath them, but he'd only had the strength to tip them onto the cushions after Leigh had shuddered in his arms.

He stole another long, satisfying kiss before recovering the ability to speak. "I offered to let you come in my mouth," he reminded. "You made your choice."

Leigh dropped a lazy clap on his shoulder, but smiled. *So* pretty with that self-conscious flush of pleasure and husky laugh.

"I liked feeling you come like that," Ulysses said, nuzzling beneath Leigh's ear.

"You don't feel… I don't know. Cheated?" Leigh asked warily.

Ulysses quirked one brow in the imperious glare he'd learned from his father. It was cruel to scold, he realized when Leigh's mouth tightened. Leigh was very inexperienced.

He set a kiss of apology on the chin that had set with defensive annoyance.

"What I told you before, about my wife? It left scars on me." He played with a short lock of Leigh's hair. "Much as I'd love more children, I haven't come in a woman's pussy since. Rather than feel cheated by a lack of conventional fucking, I've learned there are infinite varieties of lovemaking that are every bit as satisfying. Everything feels natural to me. *Everything.* What we did today and anything else you might imagine."

Leigh's gaze widened.

Yes, Ulysses conveyed with a steady look. He would love to fuck Leigh's ass if that's what Leigh wanted.

The speculative look that arrived on Leigh's face was the most beautiful thing Ulysses had ever seen.

•••

They saw each other nearly every day for a fortnight. Each time, they stayed in each other's company for hours, talking, kissing, exchanging books and teasing barbs, stealing away to make love in one inventive way or another.

When Devona arrived in London, Leigh proudly introduced Ulysses to her and they played cards with their cousins. Everyone loved him, of course. He was charming.

Ulysses also introduced Leigh to his son, calling Leigh his "very dear friend." Leigh liked the boy immediately, and they all laughed until their cheeks hurt, batting a shuttlecock for an afternoon.

Everything about this affair was pure magic. It was exactly the intoxication poets had always promised.

Leigh wasn't sure how long it could last, though, not after receiving a letter from the viscount. Much as it grated when Leigh was called "son" or "my boy," the viscount used those words with genuine love and pride, not intending to demean or hurt Leigh by it. Even so, it was a reminder of their "man-to-man" chat when Leigh had been about to leave for Eton.

"If I could go back and make you exactly like your sister, I would. If I could have more children with your mother, another son, I would. But the two of you nearly killed her. This is who you are, Leigh. I *need* a son. We need you to be the next viscount."

It hadn't been a request or a demand. It had been a statement. And there had been Devona, furious she couldn't attend school, restricted from her own aspirations by her lack of a cock.

The world was not a just place. Leigh had done what had felt morally right at the time, if not right on a deeper level.

Since the night at the Cocksblood, however, Leigh had been spending more time with Dawn, trying to understand the split-soul that had been suppressed for so long. Reason had begun losing the battle to more intrinsic yearnings. Dawn's feelings for Ulysses put pressure on the sense of duty and love Leigh had always felt toward family.

When a knock came at the door, catching Dawn with pastel-stained fingertips, there was nothing that could be done except to resume Leigh's persona and call out a deep-voiced, "Yes?"

"It's me," Ulysses said.

A leap of excitement sent Leigh's heart knocking, but uneasiness chased it. Ulysses hadn't seen Leigh in a gown since the night they'd met. This was only the fourth time Leigh had put one on since childhood games with Devona had ended with a carriage ride to Eton.

This absolutely wouldn't be the last, however. That made this moment an inevitable turning point in their affair. Leigh swallowed nervously on the way to the door.

"I thought you were tied up today and I was coming to you. Later." Leigh spoke through a crack in the door, ensuring the landlady wasn't hovering, then stepped back to invite Ulysses in.

"My appointments were cancel— Oh, hello." Ulysses smiled in warm surprise as he took in the blue hair ribbon Leigh wore, the rouge and lip salve, the string of coral beads, the dark blue silk gown with its silver embroidery in the sleeves and across the bottom of the skirt. "That blue is stunning on you. Your eyes are dazzling. Where are you going?" His gaze sharpened to a frown.

"I'm exploring self-portrait." Leigh defensively waved in the direction of the easel.

"Good God." The tension across Ulysses's shoulders melted away. His eyes briefly closed in relief. "I was experiencing the worst case of jealousy you can imagine, fearing you were meeting another man."

He gathered Leigh close for a brief kiss of greeting, drew back, then came in for a longer one.

The feel of his lean strength, the heat and hunger in his kiss, dismantled the guard Leigh had instinctively raised.

"It doesn't startle you to find me like this?"

"I'm delighted by every facet of yourself that you show me. You know that. You should," he admonished with a light caress against Leigh's cheek. "I think you're adorable in breeches and you know I'm partial to you wearing as little as possible." He winked slyly. "But you are a very beautiful woman. Dawn." He lifted Leigh's hand, noting the stained fingertips. "May I see what you're working on?"

This dress and that portrait weren't simply an artist's experiment. This wasn't a game played as a child that was part defiance and part exploration of the person who had always lurked inside the shell of a boy. This was a moment that could cause a schism in both of them. One that might never be repaired.

Despite those high stakes, the word, "Yes," passed Leigh's nervous lips.

As it did, a tremendously heavy shield, one that had been crushing Dawn for years, was set down. She drew a relieved breath, able to shine unrestricted.

Ulysses didn't seem to comprehend the magnitude. He tugged Dawn by the hand through the modest suite of rooms in search of the easel.

Leigh wasn't at Ulysses's level, occupying one of many properties owned by the family. This comfortable apartment of four rooms was built on a second floor in a well-located town house. It offered a small breakfast room, a bedchamber, a bathing closet, and this reading room with such good light, Leigh had converted it into a studio.

Ulysses halted, seeming startled by the nearly-finished image of Dawn framed by the same mirror that stood at an angle to the easel.

"This is beautiful," Ulysses said with awe. "Subject and execution." His enthralled gaze lingered, taking her in, then scanned to the stacks of canvases against the walls. "I want to see everything. Will you show me?"

Dawn couldn't speak. She was transfixed by their image in the mirror.

"We make a handsome couple," she said huskily, stepping even closer to him, experiencing a catch in her heart when he looked at them and smiled with deep affection.

He drew her closer and tilted his head so his cheek rested on her hair. "We do."

Then he turned her to face him and touched her chin, looking deeply into her eyes. "You know I'm falling in love with you."

The sensation truly was one of falling. Dawn had to cling to his waist while the floor seemed to disappear from beneath her slippers and wind seemed to rush in her ears.

"I love you, too," she whispered, moaning when Ulysses dropped his head to capture her mouth with his own.

The familiar flood of passionate heat his kisses always caused carried a swell of something bigger and more profound, something that made the delicate threads of trust and caring between them forge to bright golden chains that bound them tighter.

"I want you to make love to me," Dawn said against his mouth.

"Always. Any way you want," he whispered, trailing his lips down her neck.

"I bought oil," she said, and took his hands as she backed toward the door to the bedchamber. He had used some to finger her ass a couple of times while licking her. She had liked it very much. It made her wonder what the rest might feel like.

His pupils flared behind his slitted eyes. "For you or me? Don't look so surprised," he scolded with a hot smile. "I told you I'm open to any variation."

"Well, since I'm the virgin…"

"So am I. There."

"You're such a tease!" She nudged his arm, then said tartly, "Show me how it's done and perhaps I'll take a stab at it."

He barked out a laugh. "Who's the tease?"

They were nearly at the bed and he lunged close enough to catch his hands under her ass and drag them into a soft collision. His mouth claimed hers for a long kiss.

"Anytime you want me like that, I'm yours," he broke away to say. "Any way you want me, I'm yours. But if you want me to fuck you, I would love to come inside you."

"I do," she moaned.

They kissed with a tangle of tongues as they undressed one another. He was as adept at skimming away a woman's clothing as a man's and she was equally familiar with removing his. They were quickly naked. The brush of his skin against her own made her shiver with pleasure. She knew the firm strokes he liked, and after days of getting to know one another so intimately, he knew the soft, muted caress she liked. Knew how to find the lovely spot and gently finger it until she was trembling in his arms.

Ulysses had been surprised to learn it could be such an erogenous zone when explored like that. His balls were so sensitive he couldn't stand more than the pressure of a tongue against the place where his testes retreated when he was cold.

When she broke away to lie back on the bed and crooked her knees, comfortable exposing herself to him, he said, "You're sure?"

His hesitation felt like unnecessary teasing.

"Very."

He covered her and she hugged him with her knees as they kissed. His cock was so hard. So *hot*. They moved against one another, enjoying the friction of skin on skin, hair-roughened spots on smooth, heat and firm muscles and the small dips and valleys on each other's bodies. Their hard flesh bumped and nudged deliciously.

When he drew back, he did what he'd done twice before, poured a little oil in his palm and used it to work a finger into her arse. This time, however, he soon worked a second after it. That, coupled with the flick of his tongue on her clitoris, had her quivering and moaning, "Ulysses. I'm close. I'm ready to come."

"I know. I can feel you gripping my fingers." He left her in a state of utter abandonment as he reared back on his heels, kneeling between her legs while he applied a generous coat of oil to his stiff, bobbing cock. "If it hurts, tell me to stop," he said in a voice thick with need.

She wouldn't. She wanted this too badly. It felt overwhelming, yet sweet and right and—

"Oh fuck," she breathed as the breadth of him pressed the rim of her arse, stinging with demand for entry.

"Stop?"

"No. I want this. I want you— Oh fuck," she couldn't help exclaiming as discomfort stretched into a brief moment of pain, then became an irrevocable feeling of fullness.

He paused.

"Is that all of it?" Dawn asked breathlessly.

"No, love." He sounded both tender and amused. He slicked a finger in the oil on his cock and massaged the tight purse that was gripping him with nervous resistance. "Tell me when you're ready for more."

His touch felt lovely, and soon flutters of urgent desire quivered in her belly, softening her tension.

"More. Give me the rest," she breathed.

The oil allowed him to slide in and in and in. Gentle, but relentless until the heat of his abdomen was crushing the taut, aching sac above her hole.

"Okay?" he murmured, bending to kiss her softly. "You feel so good around me."

She had never felt closer to anyone in her life. She closed her arms around his head and kissed him deeply, trying to convey how much she adored him.

A noise that exactly echoed her joy reverberated in his chest. "Touch yourself," he coaxed and drew back enough to hook his arm behind one of her knees.

That small shift caused his cock to caress something inside her, something that made her cry out at the sharp streak of pleasure it sent straight to the tip of her clitoris.

He froze, then started to withdraw.

"No." She clung to him with arms, legs, and the tight ring of her ass. "Fuck me. It feels so good—oh!"

He sank back in and there was that transfixing sensation again. As he thrust, that joyous vibration struck like a sensual hammer, making everything in her sing.

"Fuck me hard," she pleaded.

He did, with barely restrained strength. His fingers dug in at her shoulder and his other arm hugged her thigh and his hips slammed into her with shocking power that gave her such clashing pounds of pleasure she was suddenly soaring, coming in a burst of ragged elation.

He came at the same time, shuddering and bucking with the force of it, his long shout of gratification probably heard by the scullery maid three floors below.

CHAPTER FIVE

Ulysses wasn't sure how to take the silence afterward. They'd both risen to wash then returned to bed to cuddle and doze, but the person beside him was so quiet and somber, he experienced an uncharacteristic tug of insecurity.

"Are you hurting?" he asked, searching out warm skin beneath the sheet.

"A little." A sensual smile crept across the lips he loved to kiss. "I like it. It's like I have a secret I share only with you."

Ulysses liked that sense of intimacy, too, but— "I don't want us to *be* a secret, though. When I saw us in the mirror... I want to be that couple."

"Me, too." Warm fingers found his and interlaced them, drawing his hand up for a kiss. "But I'm not sure how."

Ulysses curled his arm under his pillow. "We could take a Grand Tour. Leigh might decide to stay in Italy? Dawn could return as my wife." Even as he suggested it, he knew it wasn't right. He would miss Leigh.

Leigh looked at him. Ulysses had been trying to work out which one of them was beside him, but that was definitely the cool practicality Leigh exhibited, revealing less of the empathetic artistry of Dawn's personality.

"The entailment system is bullshit," Leigh said with weary disgust. "Devona is older than I am, but I get everything because—" Leigh's nod indicated the flesh they both shared beneath the sheet. "I can't throw away what I've been given when it should be hers. At least I look the part. I *have* to be Leigh. Some of the time. I don't resent it. Perhaps I should, but Leigh gives me things that Dawn never could. And vice versa."

"I know." Ulysses cupped Leigh's face. "I love Leigh as much as Dawn. I wouldn't turn my back on my own legacy, so I can't ask you to do it, either."

"Speaking of legacies." Leigh frowned with consternation. "You realize I'll have to produce my own heir at some point."

"I know." Ulysses rolled onto his back and threw his arm over his head. "I've been refusing to think of it. It's not like you'd be the first to marry for progeny and maintain an affair on the side, but nothing about you sharing someone else's bed appeals to me."

"You're possessive?" Leigh curled into his side, sounding delighted.

"I'm afraid so, love." He tugged one of Leigh's curls. "You'd think I'd be willing to share at least one side of you, but I'm a greedy prick. I want all of you."

"It means the world to me that I can *be* all of me with you."

They shared a tender kiss, then one with more passion. Soon they were making love again and this time, Leigh was there. *There.*

•••

"I have good news for you," Devona said a few nights later, kissing each of Leigh's cheeks when Leigh arrived with Ulysses for the evening. "Lord Mesterlyn," she greeted Ulysses warmly. "How lovely to see you again. You're so kind to attend our little soiree."

"I'm honored you thought to include me."

"Of course." Devona sent Leigh a look, since the invitation had been extended at Leigh's request. "Will you forgive me if I steal Leigh for one moment?" she begged. "Let me find my husband to introduce you around."

Moments later, Devona had pulled Leigh into the library.

"Good news?" Leigh prompted.

Devona cocked her head, eyes narrowed with suspicion. "What exactly is between you and Lord Mesterlyn? You're very close these days."

"We are," Leigh confirmed. "I've… Well, I've introduced him to Dawn."

"Oh." Devona slapped her hand over her mouth and sank into a chair. "Now you're making me cry. I don't see her enough myself! I'm so glad you feel so safe with him. You deserve to be happy, darling. You know I want that for you. If he makes you happy and you can be all of yourself with him…"

"You're being a bit silly." Leigh drew a kerchief from a pocket and handed it to her, but was very touched to see the tears brimming in Devona's eyes.

"You're being rather dismissive of something that's monumental!"

"Because you've left the man I love downstairs with three matrons shopping for husbands for their daughters," Leigh pointed out.

Devona chuckled and sniffled into the handkerchief, then managed to collect herself.

"I thought you'd want to know that I caught a whiff of gossip that might buy you some time from Mother's attempts to find *you* a wife. You remember that house party we attended last summer at the Jaspers?"

"Of course." Their mother still thought the Jaspers' daughter, Cora, would make a fine daughter-in-law. Leigh had found her nice enough, if perpetually distracted. They'd had little in common and she had no interest in visiting London.

"Apparently she's madly in love with a footman. That's why she's refusing a coming out. She doesn't want to marry because she'll have to give him up."

That would explain why she'd looked past Leigh whenever a servant entered the room.

"Is she pregnant?" Leigh asked.

"How would I know?"

"Hmph. I'm just thinking of timing. It would save me some

trouble and her some heartache, wouldn't it? Does the footman love her back? Would they be happy, do you think, if they were left in the country while I was here with Ulysses?"

"You want some footman's baby to inherit our father's title?" Devona sputtered with exasperation, then sagged as she gave it more consideration. "I suppose it makes as much sense as the current system. I don't imagine it's never happened to other families."

"Would you write to her? Tell her I'll be in the area and would love to call in? Perhaps this *is* good news." Leigh bent to kiss Devona's cheek. "Thank you. I love you."

"I love you, too." They linked arms and walked down together. Devona leaned close when they arrived at the drawing room, nodding at Ulysses's tall frame in a tailored jacket and closely fitted trousers. "He's very dashing and handsome, your Lord Mesterlyn."

"He is." Dashing, handsome, and *mine*.

Ulysses sensed their return. His head turned. *There you are*, he seemed to say, adding a concerned quirk of his brow that asked, *All is well*?

Dawn smiled. *I'm perfect*.

●●●

Six years later...

While retreating to the country for the summer was a longstanding tradition in any noble family, the month of August had become a sacrosanct time for Ulysses and Devona to bring their children to Lord Somerfair's estate, especially once Leigh assumed the title.

Cora, the viscountess, was a gracious hostess despite the fact she lived most of her year very quietly in this manor house while her husband stayed in London or traveled with Lord Mesterlyn.

The viscount and viscountess stayed in close touch through letters and were very good friends. The heir and the spare, Tate and Everett, were always beside themselves with eagerness to spend time with their cousins. They were fond of their Papa if slightly more partial to the doting Brooks. Brooks, a one-time footman, had proven himself an extremely capable estate agent. He always joined the family for meals and outings and any other adventure or pastime.

Most importantly, Dawn felt comfortable making an appearance whenever it suited her. The children loved to draw and play cards with her and sometimes she talked for hours with Cora and Devona, drawing and drinking tea and laughing over things the children had said. Other times, Leigh walked the estate with Ulysses and Brooks, discussing yield improvements or repairs to cottages or the like.

It was as content a life as Dawn could have imagined.

"Good night," she said with a friendly nod at Brooks as they passed in the hallway.

"Sleep well," he said with an equally congenial nod.

She reached Ulysses's door and tapped, then let herself in, glancing along to see Brooks do the same at Cora's door.

Very content indeed.

The End

Love Letters
with a Governess

Love Letters with a Governess is a playful, witty bout of sexual banter between husband and wife via letters while the husband is away on business, however, the story includes depiction of alcohol consumption and the sexual use of objects not intended for such use. Readers who may be sensitive to these, please take note.

---·ᴇᴧᴏᴏ⅓·---

To my beloved Lord K,

I am in receipt of your letter and I am shocked by the proposal your letter contains!

Do you really expect me to write to you of such intimate things? To tell you in, as you request, "explicit detail" how we came to be in each other's arms one late night in your library? My lord, you scandalize me! English is not my first language, nor even my second. I should be crestfallen to attempt a romantic narration only to learn later that you found my rendition wanting due to some grammatical error or missing punctuation. If I am to take on this assignment, you must promise to forgive such small crimes. (Greater ones were committed, as we both know!)

Since it was the written word that brought me to the library, and thus to you and these, the most joyful and fulfilling days of my life, I feel obliged to record for you those happenings in hopes you can be persuaded to give me your side of it?

I will start by saying a fire of rebellion brought me to your library every night that you were away from this beautiful house. It was a terrible waste of your expensive spermaceti candles to roam through the halls with one, but I couldn't risk detection during daylight.

(Is this foreshadowing? Perhaps my literary skills are not so poor after all.)

I feel obliged to explain the fire of rebellion that I carried within me as brightly as the candle. It was not always there. It sprang forth after years of my growing dry and brittle, then enduring constant friction while smothering my will beneath layers of piety and obedience.

You know the unfortunate details of my first marriage. I must forgive my mother for matching me with a naval officer. She thought an absent husband would be a blessing.

(I can tell you in this moment, an absent husband is a terrible punishment. I miss you dreadfully and urge you to hurry your return.)

In those years of having a drunken, neglectful husband, however, and a father who left our family's fortune to my brother's perfidy, I felt very helpless and at the mercy of men's self-serving decisions. When my mother passed, I was a childless, destitute widow of thirty-one. Had I not quickly secured employment as a governess, I believe I would have resorted to prostitution.

Educating young women served me well enough, but as I approached my thirty-fifth birthday, I was about to enter my third strange household, this time in a country where I was treated with varying levels of tolerance. Pity, because Spain is still fighting for independence from the French, and suspicion, because radical ideas continue to spread across the continent like smallpox, disrupting the social order your countrymen cling to so fiercely.

But I have never been one to remark on politics. No, I fully understood my *raison d'être* was to fill another girl with all the useless accomplishments that had failed to serve me when the life I anticipated turned to ash. I would teach her court manners and dinner conversation. Languages were my asset and, because you had no wife, you wished your daughter to have a chaperone and female counsel on those intimate topics specific to our sex.

I found you to be a very contained man in those early meetings, not easy to perceive. I imagined you were still grieving your wife, though I later learned it had been a decade since her passing. This made me wonder why you hadn't remarried. You are fifteen years older than I, and you may have already had those telling lines beside your green eyes and silver at your temples, but your hair remains thick and full. Your tall, trim bearing makes you exceptionally handsome. You also never wear the flush of a drunk and are always in demand socially. You are a man many women still want, my lord, even without the seat in the House of Lords and the business interests that have, even today, pulled you to London.

At the time, I couldn't possibly betray that I harbored feelings of attraction toward you. A governess has to be above reproach. Any sign of loose morals would be my downfall. (Are you smiling as you read this? I imagine you are.)

I was convinced that if I failed to secure the position in your household, I would be forced to give up the few scruples I had left. I played the demure widow and tried to convince you I was an irreproachable guide for your daughter.

Your boys were at Eton, but you soon introduced me to H, who was then twelve. I liked her immediately. You installed us in this country estate where I endeavored to prepare her for life as a titled lady.

I, however, soon began to behave in a most unladylike manner. Certainly, I discovered a taste for the forbidden fruit of knowledge after years—an entire marriage, in fact—of wondering how women ever became pregnant when lying with a man was such an unpleasant experience.

I know you are frowning with pity for me, reading that. I am sorry to say, I believed it with my whole heart. I had not yet learned that, lying alone with the right words tantalizing one's mind, a most pleasurable activity could be enjoyed.

Where did I find those words? Well! I discovered that the staid-looking, infinitely well-respected Marquess of K— possessed a rich library of erotic literature!

Your library is a thing of wonder, my lord, even without the sensational additions. I sit here now, where H and I were spending much of our days then, combing through peerage ancestries, browsing novels, and referencing botany catalogues. We read plays aloud and solved equations from your mathematics tomes from Oxford.

When curiosity would have sent me up the ladder to the corner over the mantle, H dismissed the books on those shelves, telling me they were old account books that her father kept because his father had.

Indeed, they were. I can't tell you what possessed me to investigate them. A governess above reproach would have disregarded them completely. There was certainly no value in imparting to H the price of hair powder from a decade ago. That product is not even in fashion any longer.

No, I had a desire to pry, my lord. I will confess that. The day was a rainy one and H was in her room, afflicted with monthly cramps. I was bored, so I climbed the ladder, wondering how far back the accounting went. I wondered what my employer's holdings were. My conscience twisted at poking into your private records, but I persevered.

I was most disappointed to find that yes, they were nothing but dusty accounting books with prices for horses and shoe nails. Aside from the volume of purchases, it gave me no sense of the man who continued to intrigue me. I pushed the book back onto the shelf, annoyed that I had taken such a risk for no reward.

Then, somehow, as I started down the ladder and caught my balance on a shelf, the shelf itself shifted slightly. I heard the faint *ping* of a spring. The shelf released and became fluid. I was able to pivot it and—

You can imagine the sight as you've seen it yourself hundreds of times. I was agog, however, by the array of books in a dozen languages that appeared on the hidden side of the bookshelf. Latin poetry and French novels and a series in English with scandalous titles in the theme of, "The Fifteen Comforts of—" Whoring? Cuckholdom? A Wanton Wife?

I can tell you I barely held my balance, I was in such shock. I guiltily cast a glance to the open door, fearful the housekeeper or a maid might happen upon me.

Until then, the most salacious work I had ever read had been the tragic *Noches Lúgubres*, which my mother threw into the fire when she learned its hero aspired to steal his lover's dead body so he could sleep beside it. (I should still like to finish that, if you are able to find a copy while you are in London.)

In that moment of discovery, my heart pounded with excitement and shame. I knew they were hidden for a reason, but it was as if I had found a window into your mind. I snatched a book at random and replaced the shelf, ensuring I left no fingerprints in the dust.

Within days, I had consumed *The Pleasures of Coition*, *A New Description of Merryland*—is there really an author named Roger Pheuquewell? And *A Full and True Account of a Dreadful Fire that Lately Broke Out in the Pope's Breeches*.

I felt irredeemably wicked as I read the prurient, sacrilegious words. The texts caused sensual stirrings that I had been schooled to ignore so long ago, I couldn't recall a time when I hadn't suppressed all hint of them. I knew it was deeply wrong to stoke them!

Those carnal stimulations began to overwhelm me, though, refusing to be quelled. If anything, my self-reproach in this sinful indulgence amplified my yearnings. Each page made me feel hot and pulsating. Each blunt phrase fueled the wrong type of revolt within me. I should have been disgusted, not provoked to continue down this path of iniquity.

By the time *Memoirs of a Woman of Pleasure* came to hand, I had been burning for days with what I now understand is sexual arousal. Within the earliest chapters, I was consuming a graphic account of a woman's hand exploring between another's legs. Voyeuristic passages culminated in the heroine, Fanny, encouraging the fire of anticipation in her own loins until a flood of satisfaction put it out.

For the first time in my life, my lord, I touched myself where I had only ever passed a damp cloth while bathing. With nothing between my fingers and my flesh, I did something that felt very dirty, yet brought me the most profound sense of exhilaration. I discovered slippery wet petals and that a finger into my passage could make me close my eyes in bliss. My explorations found a protuberance that sat proud and resistant to my touch. When I stroked it, I couldn't stop. The madness in me demanded more and more until a bursting sensation consumed me and I pulsed with the most glorious release and satisfaction!

I read Fanny Hill's adventures back to front and back again. I discovered that some of Ovid's original Latin had not been translated because he promoted passion "from a thousand ways." I had been taught to be repelled by love between men, but his exaltation of it made my "furnace-mouth" all the more furnace-like. Catullus was positively obscene at times, but my only regret as I explored your private collection was that I had never learned Greek. (Although, I must say that I shall never forget the night you read Sappho's poetry to me and translated her words of love with such passion and attention to detail!)

We come now to the night on which you observed me. I hope the above has made clear to you how a woman educated by Catholic nuns, whose position in your household was so important and precarious, could risk all in my abandonment of propriety.

I was returning a copy of *Harris's List of Covent Garden Ladies*. (I trust this directory from 1779 was a souvenir of your premarital years of oat-sowing. While the listing of the prostitutes' characteristics and proclivities made for enlightening reading—you'll recall the time I asked you what "bathed in a Cyprian torrent" meant and you demonstrated by coming all over my tits?—that was a phrase I had read in this directory. Enlightening as the pocketbook was, I found the notations in your hand to be the most fascinating aspect.)

I had by this time discovered my own capacity for pleasure and had begun to wonder if I might enjoy a man's attentions when I had previously concluded, due to my late husband's ineptness, that I preferred not to engage in marital duties.

I recall being glad as I entered the library that the fire still glowed in the hearth, taking the worst of the chill from the air. I hadn't slipped my robe over my chemise. I never stayed long and perusing your collection always caused a tantalizing warmth to simmer in my blood. Also, my short chemise was less likely to brush the flame of the candle in the sconce, once I used my own to light it and went up the ladder beside it.

I closed the door so I could access the space behind it, already wondering what scandalous work I might find. I climbed the ladder and replaced *Harris's* then quickly picked out a French work, *Vénus dans le cloître.*

I bent so I could read a page by the candlelight. A pair of nuns were talking. One seemed to have caught the other in a private moment of self-pleasuring. I decided it would do.

I closed the book and set it aside, then carefully fixed the shelf. My worst fear was always that I would be caught in this clandestine act!

I know you are laughing at me writing that. Perhaps it is an untruth. I can't say which excited me more, the books with their depraved contents or the act of retrieving them. I knew both to be immoral and enjoyed the mutiny in all of it. I wasn't even down the ladder and already my breasts were feeling heavy and my sex growing damp.

As I reached the floor, I passed my hand across one breast and squeezed the other, trying to ease the ache, then I cupped my hot mound through the light muslin of my chemise. My juices were already seeping at my slit. They soaked through cotton onto my palm. I couldn't resist pushing my fingers against the molten entrance where I was wettest. I was trembling in anticipation!

As I reached to relight my own candle, however, my eyes traveled the shape of the one I held. I had the most depraved thought. Its length and girth were a modest approximation of a man's equipment.

I knew I shouldn't consider doing such a filthy thing as to penetrate myself with it, but the moment I thought it, I had to try it. Alas, I only had the one candle. If I took the book back to my room, I wouldn't be able to read it and use the candle for other things.

I ensured the door was closed and locked, then crept to the wingback chairs before the fire. For added insurance, I set an innocuous novel on the table beside me so I could claim to be reading it if I happened to be interrupted.

My nether lips were tingling in excitement. My inner muscles clenched with indelicate eagerness. I could already feel that tiny knot of flesh pulsing and pulling all my awareness into it. It always swelled against my touch, refusing to soften until I lubricated it and massaged it and coaxed the release that left me groaning and pulsing and throbbing in relief.

I took a moment to hold my candle near the heat of the fire, softening the wax so I could shape it into a more natural taper. It gathered soot, so I had a moment of panic, but I always left my evening teapot in this room. That way, should someone question my being here after everyone was abed, I would have an excuse of retrieving it.

I dipped the candle into what remained of the brew so it was clean. Setting it to hand, I settled into the chair and began to read of one nun seducing another.

Now, my lord, you must tell me what you saw that night, for I confess I have always wondered what your impressions were.

Your loving wife,

T

To my dearest and beloved wife,

You do tease!

Indeed, I know you *very* well. Your denial of the full details and turning this back on me is your way of expressing that defiance you possess in great quantities and that I so adore. It will delight you to know that your brief but tantalizing account—which has not gone nearly far enough—has forced me to take myself in hand and stain my handkerchief.

I am already hard again as I write this, thinking of that night. My goal shall be to inspire you to rub yourself raw in my absence, as punishment for leaving me so inflamed with need for you.

I had not expected to be back at W— Hall that night, but my appointments in London were canceled, so I left on impulse, late in the day. I stopped at an inn, planning to stay the night. After I had paid for a meal and a room and my horse had rested, however, the inn became overfilled. It was raucous with noise and the innkeeper made the request that I share my chamber—and my bed—with a stranger. He offered me a bolster to put down the middle, as if I would sleep beside some snoring, farting baron with gout if I could avoid it.

Annoyed, I took myself back onto the road for the last few miles home.

I left my horse in the stable, telling them not to bother waking the house. I knew my way in the dark and kept a key outside my library doors for those occasions when I happened to be in the garden and too lazy to walk around to the front. (Does such a statement age me? I shall hope you overlook it.)

It was a cool night, clear with a bright moon. I lit a cigar that I puffed while walking off my saddle-ass. As I neared the library doors, I became aware of the glow of a bobbing candle within. The drapes had been pulled across the leaded glass, but not completely. Standing at them, I could clearly see through the crack that my daughter's governess had entered my domain. You wore only a thin nightgown. I could see your shapeliness beneath and lust struck like a saber in my cock.

This was an even more fierce reaction than the guilty attraction I had been trying to ignore from the time of our first meeting. Was I still grieving my first wife in those days? Of course. Always. Ironically, my greatest sorrow is that you two will never meet. She was also an avid reader of Wollstonecraft and had strong opinions on politics and women's rights. When I hired you, I was thinking my wife would have approved of you in every way, most especially as a guide for our daughter toward possessing an independent spirit.

You accuse me of being difficult to gauge at that meeting. My dear, you were so careful in choosing your words and projected *such* a reserved demeanor, it was as if you were one of those enigma puzzles in the ladies' journal that H challenges me to solve before her.

But you were much more well-read than any of the other women recommended to me. You carried yourself with a sophisticated worldliness that told me your education had gone beyond the calm and secluded life a young lady is taught to expect. You had experienced hardship, and rather than allowing it to break you, you had developed inner strength and resolve.

I have never told you this, but I was warned that you carried an air of superiority that I might find off-putting. You did wear such an air and still do. I have never been put off in the least. I continue to be delighted and intrigued by your aloof arrogance. (And I can hear your *tsk* of dismay as you read that, across the distance that separates us.)

The fact you are very comely did not escape my notice, either.

It caused me some conflict, I must admit. I am not the type to fuck a maid and put her on the street when she falls pregnant, but the whole time you were relaying details of your previous employment, I was thinking of fucking you. Standing, sitting, in my bed, on the floor... I was contemplating making you an offer to be my mistress.

I come from a line of abolitionists, though. The keeping of a woman is too much like owning slaves. Even my youthful foray into visiting prostitutes sat wrong with me. In those early years when I did briefly purchase time with a few, I only wished to learn how to properly fuck a woman, but along with fear of the pox, there was something in the transaction that failed to satisfy me.

Thankfully, I met the woman who became my (first) perfect counterpart. H's mother, for all her rhetoric and challenges to my authority and aggravatingly stubborn personality, fucked the devil out of me. We were adventurous and passionate, and I should pay my entire fortune to the man who discovers a cure for scarlet fever for it broke my heart to lose her.

After she was gone, I occasionally took up with a married woman among my circle of acquaintances, but I never found anyone with my same quest for novelty. I enjoyed a few long-term liaisons but had broken off my latest before returning home that night. My lover at the time didn't understand why I was dissatisfied with our arrangement and I didn't have a good answer for her.

As I stood at the doors to my library, however, I could see the reason with my own eyes. I was nurturing a very inappropriate desire for my daughter's governess.

I made no effort to hide the glow of my cigar, but you paid me no mind. You were on a quest of your own. You ignored the shelf where ample gothic and romantic novels are stored. You didn't take up a newspaper from the stack. No, like a bee visiting a favorite garden, you buzzed directly up the ladder and cracked into my private collection of erotic works.

That bold act in itself forced me to make an adjustment to my cock as it thickened and pressed against the restraint of my snug riding breeches. With the candle behind you, I could see the outline of your thighs. When you braced a foot to bend and read a passage, the fabric was drawn taut against the curve of your lush ass. The weight of your breast fell against the fine cotton. I could see your nipple was a dark, shadowed point. I nearly came right then.

When you stepped off the ladder, you touched each of your breasts, palming them as though to soothe them before you covered your mound. You closed your eyes as your hand clenched there.

I did the same, my dear. I crushed the flesh that was firm and ready to fuck. My cock throbbed with joy against the cruel squeeze I gave it.

Then you did something that baffled me. You went to the fire with the wrong end of the candle, molded it and dipped it into a teapot of all things, then set it aside.

I had finished my cigar and it was damned cold outside, but I couldn't move. I could hardly breathe until I'd learned what you were up to.

You settled into the chair, one hand absently playing across the gathered edge of your neckline as you began to read. Gradually, your fingers strayed lower, circling a nipple, pinching, teasing the other and eventually pushing inside your neckline to squeeze your own breast. You massaged and rubbed your nipples, continuing to caress them after turning a page.

I do not possess the words to describe how exciting this was for me. I had become a jaded man. I had enough appetite to want sex regularly, but it had been a long time since I'd been so titillated. So quickly and intensely aroused.

Though I didn't wish to take my eyes off you for a second, I moved to the window that was closer to the wall of the fireplace. The drapes there were also cracked and I had a much nicer view.

I ran two fingertips along the thickening root that was straining against leather, watching you bend a knee and set your foot on the cushion so your chemise fell to your waist and exposed your cunt. You shifted and your hand went down to the underside of the thigh you had bared, drawing little scrolls, inching ever so slowly toward the thatch of thick, black hair. Your slit was a shiny pink line and you began to trace it with your fingertip.

I don't know how you didn't hear me. My breath was ragged with desire. I unbuttoned my breeches and my cock flinched at the touch of frosted air, but I remained rock hard, especially when I began to caress up and down my length, two fingers and a thumb, keeping pace with you. Slow and steady.

When I saw your finger delve into your pussy, I had to bite back a groan, fearful you would hear me. You fucked yourself with lazy little pokes that slid into your passage and came out shiny and wet. You danced that finger to the top of your slit then drifted down again, down and in...

I wanted to lick you. Suck on your fingers and run my tongue in that path, up and down, in and out of your cunt.

Then you left the book open upon your breasts and picked up the candle.

This was when I realized what you intended. I held my breath with anticipation.

Your bent knee opened and you draped your calf over the arm of the chair. You slouched lower so you could stretch your thighs wide. You were affording me a tremendous view of your wet, lust-swollen pussy.

By now, I was clenching my fist so hard around my cock I was in a state between acute pleasure and unbearable pain. I could have come in two or three quick strokes, but I made myself wait for you.

With one hand, you spread your lips. The other worked the end of the candle, seeking your hole. You frowned as you sought the best angle and slid down the cushion, then bit your lip as your pussy swallowed the tip.

I was dying, my love. I set my hand on the cold, rough bricks of the window frame, gripping it to fight my urge to burst into the room, yank out the candle, and replace it with the hot wick in my hand.

You began to fuck yourself with the candle, moving it in slow strokes. I could tell by your furrowed brow that this was new to you. You were trying to read, but clearly distracted. You finally set aside the book and used your free hand to stroke from one breast to the other. You lifted your chemise all the way up so I could see all of you, bare from the armpits down.

You played with your brownish-pink nipples, tugging on each sturdy little tip so they stood up even harder. Hard as my cock. All the while, the candle moved in and out.

Soon, your free hand moved to assist. While one worked the shiny wax rod, the other traced the clinging lips around it. Down both sides and up to the top of your notch, falling into a pattern that I matched with the pump of my fist.

Your eyes were closed. Your back arched. Your thighs fluttered like wings and your breasts rose in heaving pants. Your face grew strained with agony.

The thrusting of the candle abruptly stopped and your free hand stroked faster. The flush in your swollen pussy lips intensified. I imagined your sheath clamping down on my cock as your mouth opened and your whole body convulsed.

My cock went off like a cannon. I could only hold fast to the base of it, trying to keep the fucking thing attached to my body as hot come spurted onto the wall with such force I felt it would take my balls with it. The roar I bit back filled my chest with a hard ache.

For long moments, I had to brace my forehead against my hand, overcome by the delirium of orgasm. All I could think was that I had to keep my heaving breaths silent, but there was nothing else in that cold night except the unforgettable vision behind my closed eyes. *You.* In the throes of passion.

When I could straighten and blink back my sight, you were curled in my chair, your legs closed with your hands still trapped high between your thighs. You were recovering, too. Your lashes were still fluttering and your uneven breaths were causing your breasts to hitch.

The look on your face was one of utter bliss.

I knew if I did nothing else in my life, I would fuck away the reserve you wore when you were with me and leave you with that dreamy countenance.

Now, my darling, indulge me. Tell me what happened next.

Your loving husband,

Lord K

Darling,

You are the most wicked man alive! You also have as much propensity to arrogance as I do, so I shall not scold you for accusing me of it. In this way, as in many others, we are impeccably matched.

You will be delighted to know my loins are tender from attempting to douse the fire lit by your description of observing me at my moment of sinful self-indulgence. No candle could compare to the inexhaustible engine I long so desperately to have thrusting into my aching pussy. You are cruel, my lord, to start this game. In retaliation, I must continue to torture you as you have me.

I take you back to the events immediately following my abuse of your precious candle. Once I had recovered myself, I stole your book to my room for further study. I awoke to the news that you had arrived in the night! This was told to me by the butler as I retrieved my breakfast tray from the pantry. Lady H would breakfast with you, I was informed.

This meant I would have the morning free from providing her instruction, which ought to have pleased me. Any employee is delighted by a free moment to pursue personal activities, like reading, but I was consumed by one thought: How might I return the book to your secret library before you noticed it missing?

I took my tray to my room, remorsefully aware that the purloined book was under my mattress. My chamber was on the level of the obsolete nursery. It was a plain room, holding only the bed and a chair by the small window with a table where I ate my meals. There were no floorboards or other places to hide the item I could rightly be accused of having stolen.

I was in such a predicament! The house was abuzz with your arrival. All the maids were rushing to ensure not a speck of dust existed in the lower rooms. I couldn't risk returning the book but also couldn't keep it in my possession.

After much consideration, I stealthily moved it to a neutral location. There was an unused dressing room near the back stairs, where I could slip in unnoticed. This way, if the book was discovered missing and a search conducted, it wouldn't be found in my room. I anticipated retrieving it and returning it while you slept that night.

With my mind slightly more at ease, I ate and returned my tray to the pantry.

There must be a part of you that continues to wonder how a well-bred woman could behave in such an unseemly way, stealing around with forbidden texts. It was dangerous, given the fact a governess is in a precarious position, turned out for any small infraction. Many in my position receive only meals and lodging, unable to purchase so much as a bar of soap. Thanks to your generosity, I earned a wage comparable to the housekeeper's, which I scrupulously saved, but it still would have been a hardship if I'd been discovered and dismissed. I had no allies below stairs to defend me or offer aid.

A governess is neither family nor servant, my lord. She exists like a ghost, haunting a home, looked through instead of at. Our role is to prepare a young woman for a full life while never dreaming we might have even a fraction of one for ourselves.

I took your books under the reasoning that, if I was relegated to observing life, I ought to observe something interesting at least.

Which lessened none of my dread when the butler informed me I was to attend you in your library after lunch. A scorching tightness of apprehension stayed in my chest until the appointed hour. Then, with my appearance as scrupulously collected and unremarkable as I could make it, and my face arranged in its calmest expression, I arrived in your library.

It was a fine spring day. You had flung open the doors to the garden and stood outside them, speaking to your steward. Bright sunshine poured through the tall windows on either side of the doors, filling the room with light.

My eye was drawn to the large folder on your desk. It had been opened by the breeze and the pages disturbed, as though the light wind had lifted a skirt to reveal nudity beneath.

Because those images were nudes. Not the caricatures of Rowland, either, showing a saucy view of a buttock. No, they were brazen depictions of sex acts in such realistic fashion, I felt embarrassed for the couples who had been caught so intimately.

At the same time, lusty yearnings overcame me. I tried not to stare, but how could I not strain my eyes to see and memorize the sketch of a woman who needed two hands to grasp the full girth of a man's member while opening her mouth over the purple plum of his tip? How could I not speculate how it might feel to have a man's two fingers thrust inside her the way I had penetrated myself with the candle the previous night?

In my self-consciousness, I edged toward the chair where I'd sat to ensure I had left no trace of my presence there. I tried to disguise my discomfiture by glancing over a book that offered treatments for consumption.

Outside, the steward took his leave and you came in. You called me Señora in those days. I turned to see you closing the file and setting it aside, topping it with a paperweight then flashing me a glance as if you hadn't meant for me to know of your proclivities.

I asked how I might be of service, and you told me that H would be leaving to visit her cousin as a birthday surprise. She was to leave in two days and Mrs. R— (the housekeeper) had family in your sister's household, so she would go as chaperone. You told me I might stay here in your home and my wage would not be affected.

I didn't know what to say except that it sounded like a lovely treat for her and that it would give me an opportunity to prepare future lessons.

What you said next put a chunk of ice in my heart. You asked if I'd been making "thorough use" of your library.

I was sickened with terror. I am certain my voice quavered when I admitted it was the most well-stocked I'd ever had the pleasure to browse.

That night I returned the book and H left as scheduled the following day. You said nothing more, so I began to believe I had gotten away with my crime.

Then you sent me a note that I do not need to find to transcribe. It became engraved in my mind the moment I read it.

Señora—
I am under an impression you and I share a common taste in literature. I will be out this evening, but I will leave a volume on my desk that may interest you. If you prefer not to take my recommendation, leave it where it is and I will drop the matter entirely.
Sincerely,
Lord K

I contemplated running away, I truly did. I was certain you were judging me as a criminal and a libertine. If I'd had to face you, I think I might have expired from distress, but you were out and I could only pace my small room, trying to decide what to do.

Curiosity eventually sent me to the library to at least see what you had chosen for me. It was *Thérèse Philosophe.*

It was an account of a woman's sexual adventures. There were illustrations, too. I tilted the page to the light and gasped with astonishment. It showed a woman on all fours. Her thighs straddled the face of another woman who was being penetrated by the man between her legs.

I was immediately struck by a flush of damp heat between my loins, by a strong desire to stroke myself. I had seen you leave in the carriage myself, but I looked around the room, sensing your presence. My ears pounded with my rapid pulse.

What would I consent to, if I took the book? I longed to, regardless of the consequences. I was already clamoring for its contents.

That's when I discovered another note tucked between the pages. It wasn't addressed to me, but it was in your hand. It read: *I will wait in the library every evening for the rest of the week. Return it when you're ready. I am most especially interested in your opinion of the scene at the end.*

What scene? Damn you, my curiosity was piqued beyond what I could bear. I slipped back to my room and was still awake and reading (and growing sore from my own attentions!) when I heard the crunch of carriage wheels on the gravel.

I stopped reading, imagining I heard your footsteps moving through the hall three stories below. In my mind, you brushed aside the hovering footman and strode immediately to the library to see if your desk was empty of the book you'd left.

What did you think when you discovered it gone? Did you picture me lying abed, as I was then and am now, wishing for a bedpost upon which to grind my pussy? Even though the heroine had bruised herself with that activity? Were you hoping that the Abbé's blessing of self-love in the book was overcoming any self-reproach I might have felt at stroking myself to fulfillment?

That night, I imagined you coming to me, two stairs at a time, falling upon me and thrusting into me without preamble. It was such a potent fantasy, I was forced—as I am now—to set aside the written word and lift my nightdress. I am so wet and aroused, my lord, exactly as I was that night. Aching with desire.

That long ago night, I had to appease myself three times before I could fall asleep. Tonight, it may take five.

• • •

The morning sun is pouring onto my page. I have moved to the library to finish this letter, but I wonder how you slept. I used the stone dildo you gave me at Christmas, but, even after several shuddering orgasms, had to wake in the night and slake myself once more.

I miss you so, my lord!

This craving within me, one I know will be wonderfully gratified on your return, makes me wonder how I could have avoided you for three days after reading the book you loaned me. I was too embarrassed for you to see me, convinced you would know what sort of reaction it had provoked me to undertake. That's why you had given it to me, of course, but I couldn't bear to face what I imagined would be your knowing smirk.

I was also terrified to face what it might mean for my employment! Would you dismiss me? Or have some expectation that I would be forced to fulfill?

Or did you really only wish to discuss the book in a scholarly manner? The scene with which you had teased me was straightforward. Thérèse was fearful of pregnancy and wouldn't grant her lover intercourse. He challenged her to spend two weeks with his collection of erotic books and art without touching herself. She lost the challenge within a few days and he became her lover in every sense of the word.

By the time I was reading that scene, I had already spent two months with your collection. My lord, the dullest, most inscrutable poems had not failed to keep me from groping myself into convulsions. At this point, however, I bemoaned ever taking a single book! I should not have put myself into such an untenable position.

Yet the book you had chosen for me was so heartening. It encouraged the acceptance of the sexual natures of men *and* women. I had taken no pleasure in my previous marriage bed.

Until discovering your books, I had never imagined wanting intercourse ever again.

I now found myself yearning to try it. With you. I wondered if I made myself juicy and excited, might I discover it could be pleasant? Surely, I reasoned (rationalized?) I ought to be allowed to know the difference, to make an informed opinion, despite the fact I was only a lowly governess with a very narrow place in this world?

I sat on the edge of my bed as the hour grew late, contemplating whether to use the candle in my hand or go below. Like the heroine in the book, my desires broke me.

I felt very plain and inferior in my simple gray gown. I paused at the bottom of the stairs before working up the courage to move silently down the darkened hall. I stood in the open door of the library, which was lit by three candles and the fire, for a long moment before you lifted your head to notice me there.

I caught my breath then, because you are such a handsome man with your strong shoulders and your distinguished winged brows and square jaw. You were authoritative and vital as you set aside your pen and steepled your fingers. With a nod, you indicated I should set my candle next to the one on your desk.

That brought me close enough to set down the book. I could not meet your gaze. I could *not*.

You told me that nothing would happen between us that I didn't wish to happen. It was both reassuring and distressing. Was I to ask for what I wanted? I didn't know how!

You said if I preferred nothing happen, I should rise and close the door from the other side. It was my last chance to run away, but that felt too cowardly. I had come this far, I felt compelled to see this through.

I locked us in. I was trembling, though, with anticipation and fear. I could hardly draw a breath. When I turned, you were ensuring the drapes were sealing out every possible crack of moonlight that might have entered.

You asked me what I had thought of the scene you mentioned. I could only shake my head in confusion because I didn't know what to think of any of this. I didn't know what to say. I was mortified. Appalled. Afraid of you and myself.

I admitted all of that and have a recollection of wanting to hug myself and become very small, but I made myself keep my hands at my sides and meet your gaze. I asked you what repercussions you planned for me.

I will never forget how you sounded when you said, "Hopefully pleasure. I want you to become my lover, T—."

No one had called me by my name in years. Never in such a crisp accent or sensual voice. The way you spoke caused shivers to prickle on my arms, all the way to the back of my neck and into my breasts. I think I was in danger of fainting from the sheer power you suddenly held over me.

And your words! Lover? I had recently learned how vast the possibilities between lovers could be. Wild, wanton thoughts began to strike me like arrows from Cupid's bow. They shot stings into my heart and belly and loins that caused lewd heat to emanate throughout my being.

You must have sensed my reaction, because the curl of your lips was a carnal smile of anticipation. It stirred me in ways I cannot describe.

You asked if I was fearful of pregnancy and said you would withdraw. You said you were good at it, that the three children you had were all deliberate.

I was struck dumb. I was convinced I was barren, since I had never become pregnant by my husband. It hadn't occurred to me to be fearful of it. I was far more fearful of something else. I admitted I was not good at performing conjugal duties.

I must have looked to the rug in shame, because I cannot recall how you looked. I can only picture the swirl of the rug's pattern. I told you how there had never been anyone but my husband, that he had been away much of our marriage and I hadn't found much joy in lying with him when he was home.

I expected you to judge me as a terrible wife, but you only looked very introspective and said something about your timing being off and perhaps we would talk another time. You started to put away the folder of drawings and I became very annoyed, feeling you had promised something you no longer wanted to deliver.

I accused you of leaving them out deliberately for me to notice and you admitted you had. You said you thought we might peruse them together, to discover where our interests aligned. However, since you were realizing how new this all was to me, you wished to make a different suggestion.

You pointed to the chair where I had sat a few nights before. You said you would sit there while I made a study of the prints. I was to imagine I believed myself alone and, if I was so inspired by the lurid drawings, I should touch myself. You said you would step in when you could no longer resist.

In that moment, I knew you had witnessed my libidinous act with the candle. The knowledge struck like a kick to my stomach. I covered my face with my hands, unable to bear another moment.

I heard you laugh, but gently. Tenderly. You approached and took hold of my wrist, drawing one hand from my face. I was surprised when I felt the press of your hot lips to my knuckles and even more surprised when you vowed you would stop anytime I told you to, but that if I liked what you were doing, I should let you continue.

I didn't know what to make of any of it. I stood there in mortification, eyes clenched shut even as I heard you walk away to the chair and settle into it.

I returned my hand to my burning face. I have no idea how long I stayed hidden like that. You must have thought me so silly. I kept telling myself to leave because of what you had seen, but then wondered *how* you had seen me.

That curiosity caused me to lift my head to peek at the drapes, which I realized must have been open a little. Why oh why had I chosen *that night* to fuck myself with a candle?

I was still tempted to leave, but turning would have risked facing you and perhaps making eye contact. Now my eyes were open, my gaze strayed unerringly to the desk.

My hand still burned with the imprint of your lips, but it slowly lowered to draw the folder a few inches closer, so the light from the candles pooled upon the images.

There was no theme to the artwork except that they were sexually graphic. They were all different sizes, some watercolors, others woodblock. There were charcoal and ink, etching and engravings. Some were an elaborate style, some very simple. In some, the subjects wore wigs, in others the figures were Chinese or Indian, Roman or European.

All of these details hit me in a very ancillary way. I was too busy studying the actions between the figures. One showed a woman in dishabille on a fainting couch while a fully clothed, wigged gentleman was about to press his swollen cock into her bright red pussy. The next was a menage of sex, ten bodies in all, everyone with hands and mouth and sexual organs connected. The next was two women with their heads on either end of the bed, their cunts pushed together, legs crisscrossed. There was a strapping man in a toga balanced on his tailbone, legs forced nearly to his ears while an equally muscular man fucked his arse.

I began to wonder why I did not have a fan on hand. I was very warm!

There was a couple fully naked, the man balanced over the woman, but lying opposite. His hard cock dangled into her mouth while he licked her pussy. There was a man spent on a bed, cock flaccid against his thigh while a woman straddled his head, her cunt on his face. One showed a woman taking a man's cock in her mouth while he peered through a window at a couple on a bed. Another showed two men taking turns with a woman, one departing with a softened, dripping cock, the other prepared to thrust his turgid one in.

I was so lost to the images, I barely noticed the faint creak in the floor. I remembered then that I wasn't alone. That's also when I realized I had begun to caress my breasts.

I grew tense with anticipation, aware of your presence behind me. I waited, but you said nothing, did nothing. I turned to the next image, a man fucking a woman from behind.

You touched my lower back. The weight of your hand gradually pressed. There was no force, just a light pressure that suggested I set one hand on the desk. I did, leaning forward a little. Like the woman in the image before me.

Through the blood rushing in my ears, I heard my breaths hissing. I drew that image to the side, where we could both regard it while I looked at the rest. Here was a lady in an elaborate gown, seducing a maid, hand buried between the other's naked thighs. Now a mostly naked woman was flogging a man tied to a couch.

I could feel my gown coming up as you methodically folded it in layers on the small of my back. Where were the kisses and seduction I had dreamed of? There was none, but I didn't care. I nearly died at the depravity of feeling cool air wafting up my thighs. When I felt the distant warmth of the fire on my buttocks, I knew I was fully bared to the glow of it—to your eyes! I became so weak with wanton delight I barely kept my knees from collapsing.

I turned to the next image. It was a line of Roman warriors contorting so one penetrated the man before him. That one reached to fondle the one before him and the next took another in his mouth.

I saw nothing then. I must have closed my eyes, because you began to touch me. I don't know what I expected, but it was nothing so gentle. It felt reverent, the way you caressed my buttocks and the backs of my thighs. That tickling touch sent fresh dampness wetting my nether lips. Slowly, so terribly slowly, you let your touch steal between my thighs.

I held my breath and finally, you brushed the fine wet hairs that protect my entrance.

In an attempt to keep myself from collapsing, I made my eyes open and turned to the next drawing. Here a brown-skinned couple fucked against a wall, the man's muscles straining as he held her up, her legs over his arms.

I wanted to do that. I wanted you to fuck me against a wall. If only I could have articulated it, but I was in a paralysis of yearning.

A long finger traced my seam. You pressed a little as you returned, expertly parting my lips so your next caress was deeper. Slicker. You found my clitoris and circled it.

The sensation was such a sharp knife of pleasure I let out a choked cry. You froze.

I waited, feeling as though my heartbeat was in your hand. I thought you must feel the pounding of my blood, how my little button throbbed in want against your fingertip.

Finally, you caressed again, tantalizing me toward such desire, it was all I could do to lift my trembling hand and turn to the next image. It was a man straddling a woman. She was propped on pillows and his cock was nestled between her voluptuous breasts while he reached back to finger her.

Your finger easily skated through my wetness and intruded into me.

I moaned. This was better than any candle. So much better. I missed your touch on my outer flesh, though, where the bellows of my fire are more quickly stoked.

My eyes were closed again. I tried to open them to look at the next drawing, but you removed your touch and knelt between my feet. Your hands on the backs of my thighs invited me to step my feet apart.

I braced two hands on the desk, eyes open, but blind. I was dizzy, not certain of your intention as you cupped my cheeks as though it pleased you to lift and fondle them, spreading me wide before your eyes. I had bathed, but I was still worried you would be put off.

The heat of your breath arrived on my tenderest flesh. Your tongue swept to taste and plunder, so much more thrilling and adept than a candle or even my own fingers! My elbows weakened and I let my arms fold. My face rested on the desk, which allowed me to tilt my hips and offer you more of what you were treating like the greatest delicacy.

Your tongue licked back and forth along my slit until my lips had fully flowered open. There was a wanton ache in my belly that made me groan, but you continued to claim everything, licking and nibbling and sucking, causing pulls and tugs within me that dragged me inexorably toward the culmination I yearned for.

But just as I thought I must snap from the tension within me, when my inner walls were beginning to quiver and my juices ran so freely they coated the insides of my thighs, the sopping movement of your mouth against my cunt stopped.

I think I nearly wept.

You came to your feet behind me and said you wanted to fuck me.

I felt the brush of wool trousers against the backs of my thighs, the hot, heavy weight of your cock in the crack of my spread bottom. You traced the wet tip down, seeking the hole you had anointed so thoroughly.

You moved your cock as though tracing a pestle against the rim of a mortar, but you refused to give it to me. You wanted me to say aloud that I wanted it.

If there were reasons I should have said no, they were beyond me. I ached with ardor and longing. That incendiary fire of rebellion within me dredged up a phrase from one of your books and I demanded you give me all of it. *Tip to feathers.*

The noise you made as you began to enter me was exquisite. Relief? Humor? Both. But also admiration and gratification. I heard the sort of pleasure and delight in your voice that was filling me as you invaded, inch by inch.

Your hand tightened on my hip and I recall bracing myself, waiting for the pain. There was none. Only a glorious inner stretch that made me feel taut and full and incredibly sensitive. I was so wet you arrived in one slow, inexorable thrust. Your bollocks nestled against my swollen folds. Your belly was pressed to my ass. Your thighs were almost bruising in their hardness as you used them to nudge my own apart, stepping closer as you did.

Then you began to move inside me.

My only thought was that this was what it meant to be fucked well. You were in no hurry. You were moving in a way that celebrated the sheer enjoyment the act gave both of us. It was extraordinary! You pulled out nearly all the way then pressed deep again, as far as you could reach within me. It was a magnificent, exalting experience. I couldn't resist rolling my hips to meet your return. My inner muscles clung as you left and clenched to amplify the sensation of your return.

I had thought your mouth had taken me to the limits of pleasure I could withstand. Now you brought me back to that plateau and held me there. The thick, hot, vital intrusion filled my entire body with a simmering need for release. I thought I would burst.

Then you spoke, saying filthy things that urged me to come. You moved faster, and one of your hands swept forward to play at the front of my pussy, redoubling my pleasure.

I couldn't take it. I cried out as the shuddering quakes overtook me with far more strength than I'd experienced in my short acquaintance with orgasms. The way you continued thrusting as I came apart took me to further heights, drawing out the sensations so I soon pulsed and clenched and came again.

I was weak when it began to subside. Helpless. I was one more libertine sprawled flagrantly upon your desk.

You were still inside me. Still as hard as when you'd first thrust that engine into me. You made soothing noises and caressed my ass, but kept me bent against the desk as you began to unbutton my gown and reveal my stays, which you unlaced.

Only then, as my clothing was loosened and my final trembles faded, did you withdraw and step back to help me straighten.

I was swaying, too weak to protest when you turned me to face you. I looked down at your wet, hard cock, with its bright head and nest of eggs, and wanted to touch it. I had never wanted anything so much in my life, but—if you can believe this, my lord—I was too shy.

When I looked to your expression, though, I saw only approval and such lust I nearly fell to my knees. My heart lurched in my chest, but you only cupped my face and brought your mouth down on mine.

For a moment, I was too surprised to recognize you were kissing me very sweetly. My hand found your neck, where your pulse galloped against my palm. We kissed like that a long minute, as though we weren't half dressed and your cock wasn't turgid and glistening between us and my taste wasn't on your lips.

Eventually, you touched my gown, nudging it to fall off one shoulder. You said you wanted me in the chair wearing only my chemise.

It was how you must have seen me with the candle. I might have ducked my head then, but you didn't allow it. You caught my jaw and forced me to hold your gaze. You were fierce as you told me I shouldn't be ashamed of enjoying the pleasure my body can give me.

I might have been intimidated or stung by your gruff tone, but you immediately gave me a much softer look and kissed me again, then asked me to explore with you how much pleasure we might provide each other.

I was certain I couldn't give you any. I was distressed that I'd been selfish when I was bent across your desk, reaching my peak when you hadn't.

When I said that, you chuckled and told me the sight of

my cunt clinging to your cock as you fucked me would sit in your memory for the rest of your life. (Are you picturing it now, my love? I hope you are setting aside this letter to stroke your splendid cock into spitting across the room.)

I confess that when you spoke so blatantly to me, you provoked a wish in me to see your cock moving in and out of me. Perhaps that was your purpose? Because as intimate as it seemed to allow you to witness my expression as you fucked me, I now wanted to see your face when you were inside me.

I let you finish undressing me and we moved to the chair. You arranged me with my chemise up to my waist and one leg dangling over the arm.

You removed your boots and breeches, using the folded wool to cushion your knees when you came down before me. Leaning in for more kisses, you exposed my breasts then suckled at my nipples, which caused me to jolt it was such a startling sensation.

You were surprised no one had ever sucked my nipples and soon proposed we determine whether I liked it. You spent much time playing with my breasts, plumping and massaging them, licking at one nipple, blowing on it, then sucking the other with increasing pressure. You stopped just short of pain and went back to the first.

It was heavenly torture. I ran my fingers through your hair, nearly driven mad by your attentions, but they sent tendrils of desire into my loins. Soon I was wanton with longing again. You drew back to look at my glistening, exposed pussy, seeming rather proud of what you'd done, making me so ready that your two thick fingers slid easily into me.

I could only moan with pleasure. I had lost all inhibition and picked up my hips to encourage your touch. When you asked if I wanted your cock again, I moaned that I did.

I guided you myself as you shifted closer.

You pulled my hips farther off the chair and held me at an angle that allowed you to drive in with smooth, gliding thrusts. I watched your cock moving in and out of my pussy with unabashed fervor. Then you suggested I touch myself the way I had while fucking myself with the candle.

How could I continue to be embarrassed when we were joined and giving each other such pleasure? I couldn't.

I kept one arm over my head to keep a firm grip on the back of the chair. My other slid between our bodies. My fingers parted around the base of your slippery intrusion. I soothed lips that had only known the width of a candle after years of neglect. They now clung greedily to your cock! It was indecent and debauched, yet I loved it. I tantalized myself and clamped down on you with all my strength, making both of us groan at the increased sensations.

You began to fuck me harder. Faster. My hand got in the way so I removed it, but I was so aroused that the impact of your pubic bone against my clitoris was enough to spin me toward fulfillment. I clutched behind your straining shoulder, spread my legs wide, arched to welcome your hammering thrusts and suddenly ecstasy engulfed me. I was utterly abandoned to pleasure!

I can't imagine how it must have cost you to continue fucking me as long as you did, but I was quite startled when you let out a sharp curse and pulled out.

I instinctively grasped your slippery cock, wanting it back inside me. You pumped into my fist three or four times, then a ragged sound left you as your cock pulsed with terrific heat and strength in my hand. The tendons of your neck stood out as your come spurted in scorching spatters across my belly.

I have taken another break after transcribing these details, my darling. I had to visit our bed and the dildo and cannot continue this game for fear of causing myself an injury.

I trust this account has been true to your own recollection and explicit enough that you will hurry your time in London so you may come back and relive our glorious night in person?

I remain your devoted and adoring wife,

T

---·❧·---

My delightfully audacious wife,

You have indulged me so generously, I am spent, much as I was after fucking you so resoundingly that first time in the library (and every time since).

I recall thinking at the time, and may have said aloud, that I was too old for fucking a woman in a chair. You make me feel young, though. I can still see you sitting there with your legs spread, my come cooling on your trembling belly.

I know I kissed you and dried you with your chemise, but climbing to my feet reminded me I am not a young man any longer. I somehow pulled you to your feet, as well, then dropped into the chair so I might hold you in my lap. I wish you were here now, just so, with your bare ass against my bare thighs and your satisfied smile tucked into my neck.

I would propose again today, were we not already married. I made the right decision when I proposed that night. I trust you would not try to persuade me again that governesses only discover love with the lord of the manor in romantic novels.

(I still enjoy how hard you laughed when I said that you are a well-born lady raised with all the morals and manners as befits our station, therefore I was completely within my right mind to wish to marry you.)

Your laugh is one of the most beautiful things I have ever heard. I can say of all the things I am missing right now, your wit and humor is definitely among the top three. (I am teasing. I miss every part of you as though my arm is gone. I feel as though my heart beats outside my chest. It is with you and I am empty, hurrying my business here now that I have an urgent appointment to keep with you in the library.)

I do think it amusing, however, that you fretted that night, worried our short acquaintance did not allow us to know each other well enough to marry. The truth is I knew you very well by then. The letters I received from H every other day always included something about you. *"Señora believes no education is wasted and has encouraged me to read the same schoolbooks as my brothers."* A demure widow indeed!

Truthfully, I think I began to love you when you told me you were fluent in Latin. Boys learn Latin because they're flogged if they don't. A girl learns it because she wishes to learn. Your curiosity and intelligence are some of your most appealing qualities. (I would drop dead of boredom if I had a wife who only talked of buttons and menus all day.)

I am glad for your streak of rebellion, too. Had you not been provoked into prying at my secret cupboard, we may not have found each other. I love you so!

My solicitor has arrived. I must sign off. I trust the baby is well. I will be home tomorrow night. If you are not too tired, perhaps you will await me in the library. If I do not find you there, you may trust I will take the stairs two at a time to find you.

With all of my heart and my deepest passion,

Your loving husband,

Lord K

The End

A Glimpse
of Her Groom

CHAPTER ONE

Octavia Blenham was a woman in possession of intelligence and ambition, but not much else.

She'd been taken in by her aunt and uncle after her parents died, despite their having six children already and her looking starkly different from the bunch of them. She had a shade of autumn grass in her skin and straight black hair and eyes that were a much darker brown than her cousins'.

Octavia's father had married her mother while working on a ship that had sailed to the Far East. Weeks after they returned to his home in Nollingshire with their infant daughter they had both passed from fever.

Bless her aunt, she had never acted as though she owed explanations to anyone for why her niece looked so different from the rest of her children, but she did occasionally accuse Octavia of having her father's outlandish ideas. "He wouldn't rest until he'd been on a ship and who goes halfway around the world to find a wife? Your mother brought him home to his roots so *she* had sense. No, these peculiar ideas of yours come from him."

Octavia didn't think her ideas were peculiar. She simply had a lot of them. And she'd witnessed how her aunt and uncle had struggled to feed and clothe their children on Uncle Gerald's modest income fashioning wheels for wagons and carriages.

It had made her feel like a burden and had spurred her to find ways to contribute. She took in household mending and kept the garden producing more than they needed. She pickled and preserved and made salves and ointments that she sold to shops and markets, determined to have something of a dowry by the time she found a husband.

Not that she had any assurances she *would* find one. She might not be illegitimate, but she was orphaned and odd and Nollingshire was known for its abundance of apples, *not* eligible bachelors. *She* couldn't hop a ship and search the world for her perfect mate.

Then the militia arrived for the summer.

"Silly girls think if they catch an officer, they're marrying a gentleman," Aunt Greta *tsk*ed one morning as a pair of giggling young women wearing their Sunday best on a Tuesday hurried by the garden gate.

"Would I be better off setting my cap for a Regular, Auntie?" Octavia asked, sitting back on her heels from her weeding. It was a bright spring day with warm sun on her shoulders and birds squabbling in the trees. "I'm good with nursing cuts. I can launder and cook. Perhaps I could go on the march. I could see something of the continent." Her heart lifted with excitement for adventure.

"If you think being a camp follower is a grand tour, allow me to disabuse you, my dear. They only allow a few brides, none with families." Aunt Greta sat on the bench with the mortar and pestle in her lap, crushing dried hemp from last season to infuse the oil Octavia used in her salves.

Much of the garden work was Octavia's now that her cousins were grown and gone, but Aunt Greta worked as hard as her aging body allowed. Her gray hair was fraying from its knot beneath her bonnet and her plump face flushed with exertion as she released an aroma of cold apples and dry, pungent wood into the air.

"Soon as you have a baby, you're lucky if they pay to ship you home," Aunt Greta continued. "Then you're living with the rest of the forsaken wives near the barracks."

Octavia, starting to lean into her weeding, paused.

"Doesn't that mean a man from the militia is better because they stay in England?" The regiments moved around to guard different parts of the coast but were guaranteed not to fight abroad.

"You'd like to think so, but the motivated ones move on to the Regulars." She tipped the ground hemp into a bowl, using her fingers to swipe the sticky residue out of the ceramic mortar before breaking more leaves and buds into it. "No, the militia is nothing but young men who've been drafted to avoid parish fines. They don't want to serve. They want a signing bonus and a pretty uniform to cover up a scurrilous past."

"But even a lieutenant would have a little land, wouldn't he?" That's how the men were awarded rank. Octavia could already see herself tending her garden while her husband was traveling about, collecting his allowance. It sounded ideal.

"Their father might have a plot, but that land isn't here," her aunt said with a point at the ground beneath the bench. She shook her finger toward the hills where the men were encamped. "Beware of these idle young men, Octavia. They have no ties to our village. They'll drink and gamble themselves into debt, seduce whom they please, then move to the next county without consequence."

"There are a thousand men in the regiment! They can't all be profligate."

"You think I can't see your mind storming with wild dreams? I'm telling you, they are not a life mate you should consider," her aunt warned with a dour ring in her voice. "I lost my dear brother to daft notions. I won't lose you, too."

It was a warm sentiment from the soggiest wet blanket in Nollingshire.

Octavia went back to pulling weeds. Vigorously. Her aunt didn't see that marriage to a soldier was Octavia's most promising path toward making a home of her own. To let this opportunity march away in a few months without making the most of it could leave her a spinster for life. She had to pursue it.

So, when her friend Jill, the daughter of the local haberdasher, asked for help in her father's shop the day after troop inspection, Octavia eagerly agreed. It was a chance to make a little extra money, but also to catch a closer glimpse of the men.

When she arrived, matchmaking mamas were already keeping Jill's parents hurrying about, searching out the latest fashion patterns and measuring out bolts for new gowns. Competition for husbands was fierce, but soldiers were overrunning the place, each needing a reattached button here or a mended braiding there.

Octavia judged there would be plenty to go around and happily joined Jill in the back room. They were meant to work behind the curtain and not even speak to the men, but Jill's mother was soon sending the men straight through. Each stood with a stiff posture and used the courtliest of manners, but wore tight inexpressibles that made Octavia and Jill sputter with giggles as soon as they left.

Many of the men left their items for picking up later, but a few hovered to flirt, mostly with Jill. She had an outgoing, funny personality and seemed to talk with them very naturally.

Octavia wasn't shy, but she wasn't sure how to flirt. Mostly her conversations felt as though she were trying to keep rhythm and tune with a song she'd never heard before.

Thankfully, they were kept busy enough she didn't dwell on it. The rush bled into the next day and the next. Since Jill's parents were paying Octavia in store credit and Octavia would need a gown once she found a suitor, she kept at it until the light faded and took extra work home to finish by candlelight.

When a particular pair of men came back for a third time in three days, Octavia took her cue from Jill and welcomed them with a great smile. One seemed to favor Jill's orange curls and freckles and, as he stood close to examine her firm attachment of his brass button, he asked if he could kiss her.

Jill flushed and smiled with pleasure, glancing to ensure her mother wasn't peeking through the curtain, then nodded. Jill drew him into the corner and they began to kiss passionately.

Octavia was so astonished by the fact Jill had agreed to the kiss and was doing it so enthusiastically, she pricked her finger. How did her friend know that's what she wanted? How did she allow it to happen so easily?

"Do you want to?" the other soldier invited, blushing furiously and looking very awkward and self-conscious.

His name was Lieutenant Reeve Quenton. He had blond hair and a boyishly handsome face, but he had barely spoken two words to her. Octavia had the impression he only turned up each day because his friend wished to see Jill and forced him to come along.

He looked about as comfortable with his suggestion as Octavia felt accepting it, but there was Jill, who wasn't nearly so desperate for a husband, making great strides toward landing one.

Octavia set her mending aside, resolving to master the skill of courtship. She had been kissed twice before, but only light pecks as part of a game with her cousins' friends. It was time to branch out.

Their kiss started out self-conscious and awkward. His mouth touched hers and his lips froze. She had the startling thought that perhaps he'd never kissed a woman before and it was up to *her* to teach *him*.

They found their way, though, allowing their lips to part and rub. The tip of her tongue accidentally brushed his bottom lip and they both stiffened slightly. It wasn't unpleasant. He had a strong form to lean against and it was nice to be embraced, but she wasn't swept away the way she'd been led to believe would happen. Jill was over there sighing blissfully, but Octavia felt as though she was observing herself and the lieutenant, not participating.

Perhaps it was because she didn't really know him. Reeve seemed kind and pleasant. He even lifted his head as if he sensed her reaction to be lukewarm. She smiled in encouragement, going along out of curiosity, not true desire, but she was *very* curious because there went Jill's hand into her partner's trousers.

Octavia drew Reeve into the rack where a number of gowns had been hung for finishing and alterations. Following Jill's example, she shyly touched her hand to the front of his breeches. Every whispered secret over tea with girls and every bawdy comment her male cousins had ever made led her to expect she would find something like a sapling branch pressing determinedly against a fence.

Reeve seemed to be stiff everywhere *but* his breeches. It was her turn to draw back. Did he not like what she was doing? Should she tell him she didn't *know* what she was doing?

On the other side of the room, Jill's partner gave a muted groan and said, "Squeeze me harder and rub— oooh *fuck*." His muffled groan was longer and more agonized, suggesting he was in a crisis of some kind.

Octavia might have checked on him, but here came her partner's member, nudging under her hand like a kitten under a blanket. She smiled, pleased with herself for inspiring it.

Reeve looked deeply chagrined, so she gave his willy a there-there pat and smiled to reassure him. On the other side of the room, the pair were panting and cooing softly.

"Quenton," Jill's partner asked in a loud whisper. "Are you done? We should go."

"Yes," Reeve said abruptly. His face was red and his expression apologetic as he turned away and swam out of the dangling gowns.

Octavia surfaced to see Jill wore a sleepy flush of satiation.

"That was a lovely surprise, wasn't it?" Jill said.

"Remarkable," Octavia agreed, smiling through her disappointment. "I hope they come again," she added, but it felt like a fib and she wasn't sure why.

CHAPTER TWO

A few days later, Jill suggested they walk into the hills above the fields of militia tents, joining the rest of the unmarried women who had suddenly found a desire to pick berries, gather wildflowers, or "enjoy a fine day."

After an hour or so, they came across their quarry in a small group of soldiers throwing an axe at a target. Introductions were made all around, then Jill mentioned the horseraces next week—which the men were planning to attend.

Octavia made a point of telling Reeve that she would be working a stall in the market tent. She secured his promise that he would seek her out, and she walked away smiling. Her aunt would meet him and see that marrying a soldier was an excellent idea.

Reeve made good on his vow, turning up at her stall at the races accompanied by a Captain Paine. The captain was in his thirties and possessed a rugged face, an abrupt demeanor, and a crutch he used to keep pressure off his peg leg.

Aunt Greta made quick work of learning everything about both men. Reeve hailed from Norwich. He was the youngest of four boys and his uncle was a vicar. He intended to become his uncle's curate once he'd been discharged from the militia and anticipated taking over the vicarage eventually.

See? Octavia wanted to prod her aunt. He was already respectable and would have a good position in society along with an income to support a wife. He was perfect!

Aunt Greta was pleased enough she gave Reeve a jar of pickled relish and suggested he call by the cottage for more when he was next in the village.

Captain Paine had served on the continent before returning home maimed. He hadn't been required to enlist in the militia, but a nobleman had paid him to take his son's spot when the young man was drafted.

Octavia hadn't known such a thing was allowed, but she noted Captain Paine's glower and restlessness with the crutch beneath his arm. She decided to impress Reeve by doing a Good Work.

"Captain Paine, does your leg cause you discomfort? Please try this soothing ointment I make." She offered one of her small sample jars.

"What's in it?" he asked, giving it a suspicious sniff.

"I can't reveal my secret ingredients. That's not good business, is it?" She smiled, but he didn't. "I start with olive oil and arrowroot," she conceded. "Are you familiar with that powder? It was named for its ability to draw poison from arrow wounds. I also use powder made from frankincense resin to thicken it and settle inflammation. If you return the jar and report back that this formulation helped you find relief, I'll tell you what else it contains."

His expression was completely unimpressed as he accepted the jar.

With luck it would improve his mood, she thought as he limped away. Was he a very close friend to Reeve? It would be nice to have a comfortable acquaintance with her husband's circle.

She was so happy to hear Reeve had such good prospects! She turned her mind to wedding gowns and a parsonage with a glebe that she could plant and tend.

Her future was falling into place!

• • •

Indeed, it was. After bumping into Reeve outside the bakery, she invited him to see her garden, being sure to point out she was very industrious and put up preserves and knew how to keep a home tidy.

She soon coaxed him into a proper courtship. He was shy and

they didn't have much in common, but she found him amiable and respectful if not very talkative. He barely took her hand, let alone encouraged her to touch his todger again. She presumed he was being a gentleman and appreciated his consideration.

When she nudged him toward marriage by asking if it might give him an advantage with his uncle, suggesting it might propel his uncle to give up the vicarage sooner if Reeve had a wife and family to provide for, he grew very red-faced and stammered agreement that it might.

A week after that, he had a private meeting with her uncle and her uncle subsequently had a private meeting with her aunt. Two days later, Octavia was engaged.

It felt so good to have her future settled! Perhaps she wasn't wildly in lust or love—as Jill and many of the other young women seemed to be—but Octavia had always been the practical sort. She was excited in her way and hoped Reeve felt as optimistic as she did that their union would be a happy one.

The bans were read at church that Sunday and the wedding scheduled so Octavia would be married before the end of summer. At that point, the militia would move closer to Bournemouth as there weren't enough rooms in the village to house them all.

Octavia was so buoyed by her good fortune, she wasn't the least put off when the odious Captain Paine turned up while she was in the garden. In fact, his sour demand to buy jars of her salve only cheered her further.

"You found it helpful?" she asked after fetching four from the cottage. He must have, if he had walked all this way to get it.

"Extremely," he said dryly. "I'm buying some for friends."

Octavia bit back a tart, *You have friends?* saying instead, "That's wonderful."

"You promised to tell me the secret ingredient," he reminded.

"Oh. Hemp oil, but it's an exotic variety. A tinker came through a few years ago with seeds a sailor had brought from India. He claimed they were medicinal. I was curious, so I traded him a jar of preserves. The plants aren't very hardy. I understand India to be much hotter than our climate. I start them in a window box. I moved this year's plants into the cold frame only a few weeks ago." She waved at the end of the garden. "Once the fine weather arrives, they grow well enough. The oil they produce has a heavy, sweet aroma, but my uncle says the salve helps his shoulder. The mercantile stocks a few jars."

"The mercantile carries it?" He gave a considering nod, one she didn't know how to interpret. He saluted her with a jar as he tucked them into the bag slung over his shoulder and limped away.

Octavia went about the rest of her wedding plans, which included stopping by the mercantile. She used her credit there to order a few things for her wedding breakfast, but the wife of the shop owner pulled her aside to say there had been a run on her salve.

"It's become very popular among the soldiers," she said with some anxiety. "I like having a jar on hand myself, so please restock it as soon as you can."

"I suppose the men are collecting bumps and scrapes during drills?" Octavia surmised, but she was perplexed at how quickly it was being snapped up.

She decided against taking payment in store credit for the rest of her stock. It made more sense to sell directly to the men and pocket all the profit herself. She had a wedding to pay for, after all. Plus, it was an excuse to see her intended.

She set aside a few jars for her uncle and took the remainder to the field where the militia was preparing a march they intended to demonstrate for a visiting general in a few days. Octavia promptly sold what she'd brought, but Reeve didn't emerge from the crowd, which was disappointing.

One of Reeve's compatriots offered to show her to his tent where she could await him. He waved her down a row to where a butt of wood had been set in the shade next to a tent with a shirt pinned and drying on one of its lines.

"If you sit there, you'll see him when he returns from wherever he's gone. I'm sure he won't be long."

She nodded her thanks, relieved to know they weren't concerned and therefore she shouldn't be. She made her way down the quiet rows. She heard the wring of a cloth in one and assumed a man was bathing. That caused her a small blush. Soon she might watch her own husband bathe.

Reeve had kissed her cheek a few times, now that they were engaged, but they hadn't stolen any moments like the one in the back of Jill's store. Jill had told her there were at least two women their age who would be nursing babies this time next year—with or without a husband to provide for them. Even with the prospect of being abandoned, Jill was lifting her skirts for the major who was pursuing her. Octavia felt very blessed that Reeve was disinclined to jeopardize her that way.

As she approached his tent, she heard a soft snore and bit back her smile. Another glimpse of her future, she supposed. Was that why he'd been absent from the marching? He was fast asleep?

She lowered to the stump in the shade and noted a small tear in the canvas that, if she angled just right, allowed her to see Reeve's bare back.

She jerked away from the sight as another heated flush overcame her, one of mixed feelings. Her aunt had taken her aside the other day and ensured she understood what to expect on her wedding night—the same thing Jill and others were doing without the benefit of a blessing from the church, she surmised.

Octavia was curious to know how that might feel but wasn't particularly excited by the prospect. It was strange to be so ambivalent, but she expected she would feel more drawn to Reeve once they'd fallen properly in love. He was certainly the sort of person she imagined she *could* love. She thought he would make a kind husband and father. They would have a good life, she was sure of it.

Wouldn't they?

There was much to be done for her wedding. She shouldn't be sitting here ruminating, watching bees visit trampled clover, but she was here now and thought it would be nice to see her groom one more time before they made things official. It would dispel these small doubts that were trying to creep in. Perhaps they didn't know each other very well, but few did when they married. A successful union was a matter of wanting to make it one. Wasn't it?

Just as she was considering loudly clearing her throat or some other interruption of his slumber, she heard the stretch and sigh of a body against bedclothes.

Then there was a soft grunt that became a low moan. Something that sounded like a long kiss. Like someone *else* had been disturbed from deep sleep.

He was with another woman!

Octavia glared with wide-eyed outrage at the tent wall. It glowed from the sunlight coming in from the far side, illuminating the interior.

"We should get back," a distinctly male voice rumbled. "Before we're missed."

"It's our last chance," a softer, but also distinctly male voice replied. Reeve!

Her hair stood on end. It was a symptom of a mind that had made an enormous, impossible leap. She could hardly comprehend the thought that occurred, let alone believe it. Were they...*lovers*?

"Ah, fuck, that feels good."

Her heart began to beat so loudly, she could hardly hear anything, but she could definitely hear quiet, wet kissing noises.

She looked around. The area was still deserted. Very slowly, she shifted on the stump, leaning forward until she was able to peer through the small tear.

There was Reeve, the man she was about to marry, abed with Captain Paine. Well, they *were* very close, weren't they?

She didn't know what shocked her more—two men together so intimately or that it was *those* two men.

The captain lay on his back like a sovereign being served while Reeve had his hand fisted about the largest cock Octavia had ever seen in her life. To be fair, she'd only ever seen a boy's flaccid one, but the captain's was majestic in length and girth, yet Reeve seemed determined to stuff the whole thing in his mouth.

Jill had confided doing something like that with her beau. Octavia had thought it sounded silly and wondered how anyone accomplished it without a fit of giggles.

Reeve managed just fine. He opened wide, then sealed his lips over the head. He began to move his head up and down while he strayed his hand down to stroke Captain Paine's bollocks, fondling and making the other man twist in pleasure.

She knew she ought to look away. It was wrong to watch anyone in such a private moment, even if it was *her intended* committing *infidelity*.

She couldn't make her eyes leave the pair, though. Making love with one's mouth looked like quite an endeavor. Reeve came up on his knees and shifted so he could better work Captain Paine's member into his throat. Captain Paine lifted his hips, thrusting his cock in and out of Reeve's clinging red lips. Good lord that was a lot of flesh!

They both seemed to be enjoying it. The captain ran his hand across his own chest, pinching his beaded nipples. Reeve pulled his own cock, which was hard and dark and bobbing. He moaned as he continued to swallow the captain's cock.

Then the captain took hold of Reeve's soft curls—hair she hadn't had the nerve to caress herself, but had fantasized of having the right to—and drew Reeve's head from sucking his swollen, glistening member.

"Turn around," he said in a gritty voice that caused a lascivious feeling to accost her. Her seat on the log was growing uncomfortable. It was hard against a bottom that had become sensitive and prickly. She felt restless and wanted to put pressure on places that were clenching of their own accord.

This was terrible of her to keep watching, she knew that. It was even worse to react with such sinful excitement, but she was only able to tear her glance away long enough to ensure she was still unobserved in her observing.

When she looked back, Captain Paine had sat up and reached for something.

Reeve moved into the spot where the captain had lain. He presented his ass to his superior.

No! She pinched her mouth to keep from gasping aloud, because surely he wasn't inviting the captain to—

He was!

Captain Paine opened a jar of *her ointment* and smeared a great gob onto his erection, greasing every inch of it. Then he proceeded to work his oily fingers into Reeve's arsehole.

"Be sure to thank your bride, hmm?" Captain Paine said with dark humor before he took hold of himself and guided the tip of his cock against the puckered ring of Reeve's ass.

"Oh fuck," Reeve rasped as the captain's cock invaded. "That feels so good. Fuck me hard. Really hard."

Where was the shy, stammering man who had barely spoken two words to her?

Captain Paine began to move with vigor. Octavia bit her lips in distress, waiting for screams of pain or, at the very least, outrage. But no. Reeve's whole body strained as he held himself still for the thrusts, encouraging in a muted plea, "Don't stop. Oh fuck, oh fuck."

The captain reached to take her fiancé's cock in his fist and began to work it. He seemed very adept at finding a rhythm between that and thrusting his hips. They reached a mutual crescendo very quickly. Reeve's cock spewed ropey ejaculate to the bedding beneath him. Captain Paine bucked two or three more times, then held himself inside Reeve while they both bit back muffled sounds of gratification.

They collapsed into a heap seconds later.

Octavia stood to hurry away, moving so quickly her head swam, but she was mortified by the thought she might be caught here, especially by them. It was a wonder she didn't trip on the tent pegs, but at one point, as her staggering shadow was thrown across another tent in her hurry, she heard someone inside it say, "Shh."

Farther along, she nearly ran straight into a young woman coming out of another tent.

"Visiting your fiancé, too?" the other asked with a throaty chuckle.

Fiancé? She couldn't marry Reeve. Not now.

The truth hit her so hard, the other woman's expression fell. "Are you all right?" she asked.

Absolutely not, but Octavia dredged up a feeble smile. "Of course," she assured her, but her stomach was in knots as she hurried home.

Reeve not only didn't want *her*, but he didn't want any woman. Why had he let it get this far? She felt so foolish! Was this why she'd felt so conflicted? Had she sensed it in some way?

It didn't matter why or how, she realized starkly. The hard truth was that her wedding was off. The future she had imagined for herself was gone.

CHAPTER THREE

The easiest part of calling off her wedding was drafting her note to Reeve.

It had been clear to her that the two men hadn't wished to be discovered, so she only said their wedding could not take place due to her learning that "recent happenings will forever call into question your devotion to me as your wife."

She used one of the coins from the very ointment she'd sold this morning to pay a boy to run the letter out to Reeve. Then she walked to the vicarage, each step weighted with ignominy. In stilted, painful words, she informed the vicar's wife that the ceremony should be called off.

Of course, the woman wanted to know why. Octavia mumbled something about it being for the best. She still hadn't fully made sense of it herself so how could she explain it?

Burning with humiliation, she returned to the cottage and broke the news to her aunt and uncle, by now wishing she could dig a hole in her garden and fall into it, perhaps emerging in an unrecognizable form a season or two from now.

"What happened?" Aunt Greta demanded.

Octavia didn't relay anything of what she'd seen, only that she had changed her mind. "I promise I will pay you back for the costs you've laid out on my behalf," she vowed.

"But Octavia," her aunt bemoaned. "You will be labeled a jilt. No man will propose after this!"

Octavia knew. She was distressed at the blight she had placed on herself, but the fact Reeve made no effort to write back to her, or appear with protestations or attempts to patch things up, told her he hadn't been as invested in their marriage as she was. No matter the painful consequences, calling it off was the right choice.

She didn't tell her aunt she'd been seen visiting his tent, hoping to avoid that gossip as long as possible. It would be assumed she had anticipated their vows and was very much shop-soiled. What passable reputation she'd had would be irretrievable after that.

She should have listened to her aunt and not looked twice at a man in uniform!

Miserable, Octavia asked to stay home two days later when her aunt and uncle left to watch the marching drills. They would suffer the discomfiture of having to explain her called off wedding, but there would be a mock battle and marksmanship contests. They were excited to attend and would be gone for the day.

Not only had Octavia been loath to bump into Reeve or any other man in regimentals, but the weather had been dry for days. She had to water her garden. That required carrying buckets from the pump beside her uncle's shop all the way around to the back of the cottage. It was hot, hard work, exactly the sort of punishment she deserved.

She was aching under the yoke, sweating, and confident her life could not possibly be worse, when Captain Paine turned up.

"Miss Blenham. That looks heavy. May I assist in some way?"

She looked from his crutch to his peg leg and back to his inscrutable stare.

"My uncle is at the fields. Should you not be there as well, demonstrating your ability to hit the center of a target with your arrow?"

He allowed a distinct pause before saying, "I saw your uncle. When I noted you weren't with him, I requested leave from my commanding officer. I wish to speak with you." He followed her around to the garden gate.

"In need of more ointment?" she asked scathingly. "I'm fresh out." Not true, but she would be damned if she would sell any to him ever again.

"Lieutenant Quenton shared your letter with me," he said,

following her through the gate without invitation.

"Why?" She slouched to carefully set the buckets on the ground, then turned a pithy look on him. "Are you particularly good friends? What else do you share?"

He narrowed his eyes in a way that suggested it was unwise to keep throwing challenges at him, but she was confident she could outrun him.

"He was told you visited his tent. He's of the impression you happened along at an inopportune time. Did you know that he is so concerned by what you may have witnessed, and what you might report to others, that he has requested a transfer to the Regulars?"

She paused in pouring water from a bucket into a watering can. "That could be dangerous."

"Yes, it could," he agreed gravely.

"He should have spoken to me. I would have assured him I have no intention of revealing he was unfaithful." She struggled to maintain a dignified tone. "Let alone with whom." Her face grew so hot, she had to look away. "But when I realized where his interests truly lie, it seemed obvious he would never come to love me. I broke it off because I didn't expect he would leave *you*."

Yet he had. The captain must be very angry with her.

He flushed a little and grasped the back of his neck. "We aren't in love. He's a...kindred spirit."

Was that supposed to make her feel better? That her fiancé hadn't cheated on her out of deep feelings, but purely for physical pleasure?

"Well, I'm sorry he felt it necessary to take such drastic action." She crossed her arms defensively. "I realize now I shouldn't have pursued him. I sensed he wasn't deeply interested in me. I thought it meant he was respectful and that affection would grow between us over time. Why on earth did he propose if women aren't his partiality?" That had been baffling her!

"To hide the fact that women aren't his partiality?" the

captain suggested dryly.

She'd seen the cheap religious pamphlets that derided men who took up with men, but, "You're not provoked to marry or leave. Are you?" She waved at him, very self-conscious of the fact she'd watched them. That had been *very* bad of her.

"Neither wife nor army will take me," he said dourly, then limped the half dozen steps to the bench and threw himself upon it, releasing a long sigh.

She regarded him, considering his disgruntled expression. Despite the fact that long walks must be excruciating for him, he'd been concerned enough to come learn how she intended to proceed.

"I always think men so much better situated than women," she said with compassion for the fact that he couldn't transfer to the Regulars to forestall potential scandal the way Reeve had. "Physically, more is expected of you, I suppose. You're called up to fight wars and such, but to me it looks as though you have so many choices. I'm expected to marry and produce children. That's the best future I should expect for myself."

"I'm taxed for being a bachelor. Did you know that? I have no income but this." He waved at his uniform. "If the militia is disbanded, I don't know what I'll do. I can't work in a field. Something in a factory, perhaps, not that I expect they'll want me, either."

"You don't have any land? That's why I wanted to marry Reeve," she confessed. "He said he'd have a vicarage eventually. I had plans to grow my herbs and sell my salves—"

She recalled what they'd done with her ointment and cut herself off to tinkle the watering can over the strawberries.

"You still can, can't you?" he said.

"What?"

"Make your salve. How much can you produce in a season? Because I doubled the price and could have got more—"

"Double!" She dropped the can and stalked over to him. "I

was offended by how you used it! And now you have the nerve to tell me you doubled the price and pocketed a profit that could have been mine? You are reprehensible!"

"I haven't claimed to be otherwise." One corner of his mouth twitched in self-deprecation. "But watching how I used it makes you reprehensible, too."

"Oh, shut your mouth." She went back to the can that had spilled over. "What does it even matter how much I could get from *certain* men— Good grief." She hushed her voice as she snapped a look at him. "Do all those men who bought it make love with each other?"

"No." He snorted. "They use it with women."

"Men do that to *women*?"

He gave her a befuddled blink. "Some do, I suppose. To avoid pregnancy, but they use it for conventional intercourse. Octavia— May I call you that? I feel we're becoming friends. You may call me Fulton."

She sent him a glower as she refilled her watering can.

"I understand you might have been saving yourself for marriage," he continued, "but have you not tried this salve on yourself?"

"I use it on my hands after doing laundry so my skin doesn't become chapped and cracked. Do not tell me you..." She couldn't say it, but her gaze dropped to the fall on his breeches. She was so scandalized, she didn't have words.

"It was the first place I tried it. One likes to stay supple," he said with a grin that would have been handsome if she wasn't so affronted. "It was very pleasant. So much so, I was compelled to share it with a friend."

"No." That's all she could say. She picked up her heavy can and marched to the far end of the garden.

He said nothing until she was back in earshot, refilling the can. "I'm under the impression the indignity of your groom's infidelity has been overshadowed by the indignity your precious ointment has suffered. Have you really never—"

"No! It's inappropriate. This entire conversation is *inappropriate*."

"We're discussing a potentially lucrative business idea. A moment ago, you mentioned that you can't approach men with a suggested list of *all* its uses. I could be a perfectly good agent for that, but I think you would be doing a disservice if you didn't explore how it might also help women. Spinsters and such."

"I prefer when you scowl and barely speak to me. Good day."

"I've been in a much better mood since discovering the reviving wonders of your salve," he said with a mocking smirk. "But I should start back." He rose and fitted his crutch under his arm. "If you care to research for yourself, I recommend a shilling-sized dab rubbed into the appropriate area for...a quarter hour? I don't know how long these things take for a woman. That's really why you should—"

"Would you please leave?"

"I'll come by the next time I visit the village. You can tell me if you're interested in a distribution agreement."

"I am not," she muttered at his back.

What an infuriating man!

●●●

Octavia lasted two trips to the pump before she gave in. The cottage was empty and her curiosity had grown to irresistible levels.

She took a spoonful of ointment from the jar in the kitchen and locked herself in the room she had once shared with her two girl cousins while the four boys had slept in the unheated loft in her uncle's shop.

What sort of rake was Captain Paine to recommend she try this? What sort of libertine was she to do it? A quarter hour of massage? Really?

No. She would try it for two or three minutes if only to reassure herself he was a fool.

She sat on the edge of her bed with her back to the door and lifted her skirts. She opened her knees and dabbed a bit of salve where the pinkish-brown inner lips of her slit were hidden by the short, black hairs of her mound.

Tentatively, she began to smooth it along that seam, enjoying the tickle. Soon her lips parted under her firmer touch. Her finger delved deeper of its own accord, slowly spreading the oily mixture between the soft ridges into moist, warm valleys.

It was pleasant. Not the same as when she massaged oil into her forearms after a long day of gardening, but relaxing and relieving in a different way.

It was also compelling. She began to vary her pressure, allowing herself to lose her thoughts and simply enjoy the lazy roll of her finger as she returned her touch again and again to a small nodule that grew firm against her fingertip. The more she circled and rubbed the ointment against it, the more inflamed and sensitive it grew. She *needed* to keep massaging it.

All of her was growing very warm, as though she was still working with all her strength to carry water. She broke away from her ministrations to sweep off her gown and loosen her stays. She hiked her petticoat higher, fully baring herself below the waist. She opened her legs wide to continue her steady massage.

Her thoughts drifted to the way Captain Paine had pushed his fingers into Reeve's arsehole and her lower muscles clenched as if calling to her touch. She wouldn't penetrate her bottom, but one finger stole to the front opening. It was slippery even without the ointment.

"Oh." Her sighing voice startled her. She bit her lip as she pushed her finger in all the way, as far as it could go, then withdrew it and easily slid a second in beside it.

Her body seemed to be producing its own lubrication to accompany the slippery texture of the ointment and did this all feel ever so luxurious! She could massage herself this way forever. In and out and around and back in. Deep and shallow, feeling stretched one second and sweetly fluttery the next.

Without thinking about it, she rolled onto her face on the bed, feet still on the floor and fingers still tucked deep inside her. Now she could rock her hips on the edge of the mattress while the slippery heel of her hand ground against the nodule that made her muscles clench around her fingers.

She was very sleek and slippery and she was picturing again the way the captain had fucked Reeve so vigorously. Reeve had said, *"Fuck me hard. Don't stop."*

Had he felt like this? All shivery and urgent? Because she couldn't stop what she was doing. She worked herself harder and faster, growing so tense she could hardly bear it, but she couldn't stop.

Suddenly a convulsive euphoria bathed her from the inside. She groaned into the bedding as pulses and twinges took over her nether regions, making all of her shiver while she kept rocking and rocking, playing out the sweet sensations.

She could hardly catch her breath afterward and stayed exactly as she was, limp and deeply relaxed. She might even have dozed, but she slowly came back to awareness when her knees sagged. She felt the most blissful and optimistic she had ever been in her life.

Her new friend Fulton was right. She was onto something.

CHAPTER FOUR

The first thing Octavia did was corner her Aunt Greta as they cleaned up after the evening meal, when Uncle Gerald had gone out to his shop.

"I think I might be able to make a living selling my salve," Octavia told her. "But I need more information first." Here came a small white lie. "When I was at the mercantile, the soldiers had bought them out. Mrs. Henfield seemed concerned. I'm under the impression it's being purchased for marital relations."

"Octavia!" Aunt Greta demonstrated exactly the level of outrage Octavia had shown Captain Paine.

"I'm not asking if you've tried it. Only wondering if you thought anyone would?"

"Are you looking for ways to be a less attractive marriage prospect? Even your father never came up with anything so bird-witted. No man would want a woman who sells such a thing."

"If I were successful, I might not have to marry at all."

"Octavia. We have given you a home and love you as our own, but you know we can't keep you forever. Your cousin will take over when your uncle is too old to work. He'll have his own family. There won't be room for you here."

Tight-lipped, Octavia nodded but took a scrap of newspaper to her room where she scratched out numbers in the white spaces, adding up the costs of her supplies and calculating how much ointment she would have to produce and charge in order to support herself.

She would have been disheartened by the results, but she used the salve on herself and fell into a tranquil sleep.

Later, she woke to a noise through the wall. It was the creak of her aunt and uncle's bed. Her aunt said, "Oh, Gerry!" with surprised delight. The bed groaned along with them as their pace picked up.

Octavia bunched her blanket against her mouth to muffle her laughter when they ended their lovemaking with mutual noises of fulfillment.

Her aunt looked very refreshed and chipper the next morning when she made a surprise announcement. "Having slept on your idea of recommending your salve to married women, I feel I should encourage you," Aunt Greta said. "There's always value in at least *trying* to open a door that appears closed. One never knows how well it could work. And if you had a stable income of your own, you might attract a decent offer from a practical man. Eventually."

"Your endorsement means the world to me, Auntie. Thank you." She didn't allow herself any smugness, but she was privately still laughing. She was also excited for the potential she suddenly believed she possessed. It was validating and thrilling. She couldn't wait to get started!

●●●

Octavia had a few more questions before she could fully commit to her venture, questions she couldn't answer for herself—partly because she had no man with whom to experiment and partly because her reputation would be completely eviscerated if she sought one out.

Jill had got herself engaged, though. She was more than happy to take samples for testing and return with a full and candid report.

"I tried this one first." She pointed to the salve that Fulton liked so much. "We didn't have much time and my fiancé is quite well-built, if you take my meaning. This worked a treat for getting us going on short notice, but I do prefer more preamble of kissing and such. I was only starting to appreciate his vigor when he pulled out. He has four years of service yet, so we're holding off on children," Jill mentioned in an aside. "I finished myself after he was gone and it was quite satisfying. The heavenly feeling lasted a long time, too. I quite liked it. May I keep it?"

"Of course." Octavia was so grateful that Jill was willing to be frank, she was considering offering a lifetime supply. "What of this one?" She pointed to a liniment she made for arthritis. It had hemp oil, but also mint.

"This was interesting. It made me feel very tingly right away. He *loved* the smell and started licking it off me, which was extremely enjoyable. I hit my peak quickly. Several times, actually. I thought I was done by the time he put it in me, but we were both very aroused by then and finished fast and powerfully. We took a rest, then I revived him and I found the taste pleasant as well. We did it again and it might have been all our activity, but I had a burning feeling down there after. I feared one of us had caught something from a previous encounter, but it soon subsided."

"It's the mint," Octavia confirmed, trying not to be self-conscious as she admitted, "I tried it on myself. Now you've said you experienced the same thing, I'm sure that's what causes the discomfort. It doesn't happen with the other two. Would you use it again?"

"Yes." Jill nodded. "But not every time." She put the jar into her bag.

"And this one?" Octavia pointed to one that didn't have any hemp oil at all.

"We used it with a sheath, one made from sheep gut. He wanted to know how it feels to finish inside a woman and it did seem to make all of that go well and feel very nice. I hit my peak first. By the time he finished, I was worked up again. We were kissing and cuddling and I still had quite a bit of this on me, so I was rubbing myself on his leg. It was quite nice, so we added a little more and I could have done that all night. After three or four peaks, I was sleepy and satisfied, so even though this was not my favorite, I would still keep it."

"Of course." Octavia invited with a wave of her quill for Jill to take it, then made her final notes. She had had no idea there were so many ways to enjoy intimate relations. It made her feel she was offering something many people needed and would use. "This has been so helpful, Jill. Thank you."

• • •

Captain Paine wore a smirk when he turned up at church the following Sunday and cornered her after the service.

"Have you given further thought to my proposal? Perhaps experienced an epiphany or two?" His smile broadened at his wit.

She narrowed her eyes. "I'm coming merrily along, yes."

He barked out a laugh and waved toward the path that led to the other end of the village, where her cottage was located. "Please. Allow me to walk you home. I'm eager to hear every detail."

She told her aunt that Captain Paine would escort her home, and Aunt Greta brightened.

That seemed to throw a blanket of apprehension over Fulton, but Octavia quickly reassured him.

"Don't worry," she said once they were out of earshot and able to speak freely. "I won't pressure you into a proposal. Lesson learned." She still felt remorseful about Reeve.

"He went to Canada," Fulton said, glancing at her. "As the aide to a colonel. Or so I've heard. If the report is accurate, he will enjoy certain favors that won't put him at risk."

"That's something," she said, relieved he wouldn't be in imminent danger. "Thank you for telling me."

He shrugged and took on a wicked grin. "Tell me how your experiment went."

"If you must know, I've tested different formulations. The

hemp oil definitely provides a prolonged afterglow, but the others are effective in other ways. That's reassuring, because it will take a few seasons to increase my hemp oil yields. Everything else can be purchased, but it's good to know I could offer a lesser product that is still efficacious."

"Efficacious," he repeated as though enjoying the sound of the word.

"I'm concerned that I haven't personally tested my formulas with a partner, though. It troubles me because, aside from the fact that I'm not the least interested in marriage or becoming pregnant... I just don't want to." She held her breath, awaiting his reaction.

"Then don't," he said with a shrug. "I've heard enough from men who are using it with women to know they find it completely satisfying. I can easily offer them the other formulations and relay their findings."

"It's not just that. I'm actually hoping you can help me understand something." She cast another wary glance around to ensure they weren't being overheard. "When you...think of making love with a woman, how do you feel?"

His grimace was not one of disgust, just refusal. "Nothing. Uninterested."

"Even if she's very pretty?"

"Look, I'm sorry if you've felt insulted by me in the past. It's not something I do deliberately. I just don't find women appealing," he said shortly.

"That's not what I'm asking. Tell me how you feel when you consider making love with a man."

He gave her a flat scowl. "You saw how I feel. I get aroused. Hard. Why? Is that how you feel about women?" he asked with a penetrating look.

"No." She crossed her arms even though the day was very warm. "I don't feel that way about anyone. I feel curiosity, but it's more like the interest that would make me watch a pair of snails in the garden. Then I remember I don't want snails in the garden and throw them over the fence," she added with dark humor.

He cocked his head inquisitively. "But you've tested the ointment on yourself. You enjoy sexual pleasure."

"That's different, isn't it? Being alone. I find it satisfying, yes, but I don't feel a need for anyone else to be there." She was blushing, half expecting he would tease her, but he only gave a considering, "Hmph."

She waited, but he said nothing more.

"Do you think it's wrong of me to sell something for marital relations if I am unmarried and not interested in having a partner?"

"How many bald shopkeepers sell hair ribbons?"

"I suppose," she agreed.

"Does it bother you? This absence of desire for a partner? You might meet someone who makes you feel differently. Don't go by your experience with Reeve." It was the kindest tone she'd ever heard from him. Concerned. Bolstering.

"Maybe." She shrugged. "I don't know that I care one way or another. I thought marriage was the only way I could have a future. I'm very excited by the idea of supporting myself without relying on anyone else. Well, I suppose I must rely on you."

"I have to rely on you, too. I can't make the ointment, but I have hundreds of contacts through the army and the militia that will help us sell the hell out of it. I believe we could earn a living if we bring our strengths together."

She stopped and held out her hand. "Then I formally propose we embark on a business partnership."

"It would be my honor to accept your proposal." He shook her hand. "And if it doesn't make us rich, I'll marry you myself. How's that for incentive to work our asses off?"

She laughed aloud. "I could think of worse fates, but you're right. It is very motivating."

He kissed the back of her hand with a loud smacking noise.

• • •

Fulton left with the militia a few weeks later. He soon had barrels of olive and coconut oil shipped to her along with some other ingredients, all paid on credit.

This terrified her, motivating Octavia to risk a few precious hemp seeds on a second, late planting. It resulted in a few more ounces of oil and a few more seeds for next year, which was heartening.

She then began to work so incessantly, her aunt begged Uncle Gerald to build her a shop to get Octavia out of her kitchen. Her uncle erected a small structure where Octavia installed a cookstove, anxiously aware she owed them for the costs of both.

Fulton wrote sporadically to request a dozen jars here or there. She was using their modest profits to pay down the bill for the oil, but eventually used some of it to pay a local boy to chop wood because a Christmas rush left her without enough hours in the day.

Things fell off after that. It was a blessing and a curse. She had nothing but time to put up nearly two hundred jars. Sadly, it was a very wet spring and roads had washed out in every direction. Her crates of ointment piled up in her room while Octavia kept telling herself that once the stages were moving again, things would improve.

Then a letter from Fulton arrived and, while his letter started out cheerfully, the news soon became grim.

Miss Blenham,

I have purchased another barrel of coconut oil at such an excellent price, I had to use what profits I've made lately to secure it, so I enclose no funds and hope you will forgive me. I was promised the oil would be forwarded to you the moment the roads have improved.

I am also pleased to report that I have lately enjoyed the company of a naval officer who has recently spent time in the Caribbean but also traveled extensively in the Far East.

He is familiar with the exotic hemp you cultivate and assures me that the enclosed seeds from the colony of Jamaica will provide an excellent addition to your extractives. Given his knowledge and enthusiasm on the topic, the cigarillo we shared, and the price he extorted from me when I requested he gift these seeds to me—I shall not regale you with the details of our negotiations, but I did have to demonstrate the efficacy of the salve itself—I believe you will be pleased with the potency found in these plants.

This might be a good time to point out that it does take time for a man to work through a jar and arrive at needing to purchase another. I urge you not to lose faith in our venture.

Octavia—

Since writing the above, I have learned something that may already be in the newspapers by the time this letter reaches you. Napoleon has left Elba and has begun mobilizing troops.

As you can imagine, things have become extremely tense within the militia. I cannot in good conscience promote our product. It would not be used regardless. Many of the men who might have purchased it are being sent to the Netherlands.

I am sorry if you find this distressing. I am extremely worried on many fronts, most especially for the safety of my fellow soldiers. The Regulars have refused me, so I remain with the militia and am being moved to Dover.

Yours sincerely,

Captain Fulton Paine

CHAPTER FIVE

One year later...

With Napoleon's defeat at Waterloo and the Regulars back on British soil, the militia was disembodied. Fulton wrote from London to say he was making their pitch to several key warehouses that carried soaps and other beauty products.

Octavia wrote back, advising the state of things since his dire letter last year. As the summer had waned and interest in her ointment had seemingly died off, she had had a difficult decision to make—pay down their debts or throw away her last bit of cash on advertisements.

Fulton didn't respond with an opinion on the actions she'd taken. In fact, she didn't hear from him again until he strolled into her new shop on a soggy spring morning.

She was on the outskirts of Nollingshire now, where a small dairy farm had fallen into disrepair. Her uncle had helped her patch the barn when she leased it with the pasture for a very affordable price. It had come with a modest cottage where she lived now and had six ceramic barrel churns that were ideal for mixing batches of salve. Her first seedlings were ready to transplant into the fields as soon as she hired a farmhand to turn the soil.

Fulton was still limping but needed no crutch, only a handsome walking stick. He had a proper prosthetic leg with a wooden foot that wore a matching shoe.

"Fulton." She beamed as she came forward to greet him. "You look so well! But how...?" She glanced at his leg, guiltily aware she had reinvested everything she'd made last fall to expand their business. She hadn't sent him money or ointment in months.

"I'm extremely well. This"—he tapped his wooden shin with his stick—"is thanks to the deposit I have received on the orders I secured while I was in London."

"You've been in London? When I didn't hear from you, I wasn't sure where you'd gone." She'd entertained every thought and worry, even wondering if he had judged their venture a lost cause and moved on. "That's quite a deposit if it affords you a new leg. I'm encouraged."

"You should be." He showed her a list of shops and the numbers of jars they'd requested.

"Goodness!" She took the list, staring at it agog.

"And this is your share of the deposit."

She was still taking in the number of jars on order, mentally adding them to the orders she had from other venues. When she looked at the bank draft, she nearly fell over.

"This is a lot of money. A lot of ointment!"

"*Octavia's Restorative Ointment* is gaining a reputation, ducky. A *good* one. If you had told me five years ago that I would one day be so successful at selling strangers on friction-free fucking that it would buy me a new leg, I would have told you to pull the other one."

"I cannot believe I will say this after you just spoke like that, but I have missed you." She kissed his cheek, laughing with disbelief and delight.

Could she fill all these orders? Yes, if she started more seedlings and aimed for three plantings this season—

Her whirling thoughts were yanked to a halt as she noticed a man had come in behind him.

"Hello," she called. "Are you here about the ad for a farm-hand?"

"Pardon?" He jerked his head up from studying the way the barrel churns were set up to be rolled by a pulley system and a single crank. He was quite attractive, perhaps twenty-five or six, very fit with darkly tanned skin even though the sun wasn't out much yet. He had straight black hair and very serious, very dark brown eyes, and a quick, bright smile.

"Naseem is with me," Fulton said, urging the man forward and making introductions. Something in the way the men's eyes met told Octavia they were kindred spirits.

"Fulton has told me wonderful things about you," Naseem said warmly as he bowed over her ungloved hand.

"Naseem is very mechanically minded. Did you know Napoleon's army was eating food out of tins? Naseem thinks there's potential there. Less chance of breakage during shipment. We'll have to investigate," Fulton said.

"That's how I'm currently filling the jars," she said to Naseem, nodding at the modified wagon wheel her uncle had helped her fashion, one with a reservoir and funnel suspended over it. It could be closed off after it blobbed enough ointment into a jar. The next empty jar easily swung into the space below the spout. "My friend Jill and my Aunt Greta help if I fall behind."

Naseem moved to examine it.

"We're here to work, Octavia. I felt terrible, stopping cold on you last year."

"It was war, Fulton. I understood."

"You became wildly successful anyway." He looked around the barn with wonder. "I wish I could take more credit, but I knew you were onto something. That's why I hitched my wagon to you."

"I'm fairly certain your wagon is hitched elsewhere." She slid a look to Naseem.

"Does that bother you?" Fulton asked, sobering.

"Not at all. If you're happy, then I'm happy for you."

"I am," he said with a nod and a glance at Naseem that bordered on sentimental. He swung a curious frown back on her. "You, though? Still no husband?"

"I've had two offers. Nice as it feels to be courted, I've been clear to both that I'm not interested. I have too much to lose."

"I'm hardly the one to extol the virtues of commitment, since I only recently came around to the idea, but..." He shrugged. "You really don't feel a desire for a partner?" It was the same concern Jill exhibited sometimes, the fear of leaving a friend behind.

"I have a partner." She touched her elbow to his. "Does this new arrangement of yours mean you're throwing me over?"

"Hell, no," he said with an amused curl at the corner of his mouth. "I clearly remember vowing to marry you if this business venture didn't make us rich so I'll be working harder than ever."

"That prospect keeps a fire under me as well," she said, holding his laughing gaze with her own. "Why do you think I took out all those advertisements?"

"How do you think I got all those orders? I think it's safe to say, Octavia, that you and I will *never* marry."

• • •

MATRONS of a certain age may experience friction in what had previously been a happy marriage, one that has resulted in an UNWILLING DISTANCE between spouses and may even cause GENERAL MARITAL DISCORD. This can be attributed to the lingering effects of CHILDBEARING YEARS. If instructions are closely followed, those ladies suffering a withering malaise can be SWIFTLY RESTORED to a YOUTHFUL ANTICIPATION and a HEALTHY GLOW with only a few applications of OCTAVIA'S RESTORATIVE OINTMENT.

NEW BRIDES may easily become OVERWHELMED by UNFAMILIAR RESPONSIBILITIES. Therefore, it is HIGHLY RECOMMENDED that a jar of OCTAVIA'S RESTORATIVE OINTMENT be kept nearby for any small injuries or discomforts that require SOOTHING. New husbands are encouraged to gift this comforting yet BOLSTERING BALM to young wives, to keep on hand for the REGULAR NEEDS of both parties. This young groom wouldn't do without it: "We are freshly married and things are VERY TIGHT, but we make room in our budget for OCTAVIA'S RESTORATIVE OINTMENT, which we could not manage without."

Are you a SPINSTER? You are likely well-versed in taking care of your own SMALL NEEDS, but when a woman does not have a spouse, various aches can arise that must be managed alone. OCTAVIA'S RESTORATIVE OINTMENT has been extensively tested and proven to deliver SUPERIOR RELIEF when self-applied exactly as directed. VIRGINS may be comforted to know that a CERTAIN SUPPLENESS can be maintained whether or not a marriage is in your future. The only thing that should be ON THE SHELF is OCTAVIA'S RESTORATIVE OINTMENT.

GENTLEMEN of all ages, MARRIED or BACHELORS, may have occasion to suffer SPECIFIC TENSIONS that are difficult to alleviate. When one is FRUSTRATED by a lack of a more stimulative therapy, OCTAVIA'S RESTORATIVE OINTMENT can provide immediate relief. This specially formulated compound has been found useful in those situations when pinching or other PROTRACTED DISCOMFORTS are also experienced, particularly when the ointment is applied PRIOR to VIGOROUS ACTIVITY. Daily use is perfectly safe. THIS IS NOT A CURE FOR POX.

The End

A Lady for a Highwayman

A Lady for a Highwayman is one woman's thrilling venture into discovering her sexual preferences with someone of the same sex, however, the story includes a detailed account of a highway robbery that includes "stealing" a kiss. Readers who may be sensitive to a person initiating such contact without permission, please take note.

CHAPTER ONE

"I don't wish to marry Lord Quarrymire," Annabelle said calmly and firmly. "I would prefer you call things off."

She hadn't once raised her voice or sniffled a tear from the moment she'd been stuffed into a gown and paraded through London like a broodmare at auction, but her mother's reaction was still condescending.

"It's a lovely day for a drive. Don't spoil it with tantrums, Annabelle." The countess lifted her nose to the fine country air. "We're meeting his mother in two hours. I don't want to appear cross when we arrive."

They were in a rented barouche en route to the property the marquess owned in the district. It was a small manor the family rarely visited, Sherwin Bickford had told Annabelle's mother when they had met him in London last season. He had promised to call on them when he was next in residence.

Indeed he had, much to Annabelle's profound disinterest. He had soon made an offer for Annabelle that her parents had snapped up, paying no mind to her objections.

"Mama." Annabelle had spent hours rehearsing this argument. "If I'm too childish to have a discussion about marriage, surely I'm too immature to marry."

Her mother sent her a stony look at that irrefutable logic. "Take it up with your father."

Annabelle turned her attention to her father. He was also pretending great enchantment with the rolling hills, so he didn't have to look his daughter in the eye. He gave her no opportunity to speak.

"I am beyond exhausted with the topic. Ask Quarrymire while you're on honeymoon."

Mrs. Hargrove's Academy for Female Learning and Scientific Study didn't take married women, or she would have made it a condition of accepting his proposal. And Annabelle didn't *want* to marry.

"I can pay for it myself with the money Auntie left me." That was not entirely true. The moment she had received a letter granting her admittance, she had forged a note from her father to the family's solicitor, urging him to prepare a draught for the funds. It was hidden in her room at home, unbeknownst to anyone including her aunt.

"I do *not* understand why you think boarding school is a better option than marriage," her mother said with genuine bafflement. "It's no better than a convent. People would talk about why you had to go. All you'd gain is a reputation."

"And an education."

"You want to think so, but those schools are rife with social climbers," her mother said disdainfully. "Young girls who think they can better themselves by balancing a book on their head. You've been presented at *court*, Annabelle. You're about to marry a marquess."

"Some girls *read* the books. They want to learn how to support themselves so they don't have to marry."

"You're speaking nonsense. Your father supports you very comfortably." She waved at the barouche. "So will the marquess. Someday your brother will be the earl and he'll appreciate the valuable connection you're providing him. You're doing this for all of us, Annabelle, as I did for my family."

How was Quarrymire a valuable connection? He was nearly forty and thought Wollstonecraft was a type of wool from the north. When she had expressed her reservations about marrying, he had made a demeaning comment about trusting men to know what was best for her and then got foxed with her father.

Annabelle had tried to tell her mother how unpleasant she found him, but her mother kept insisting this was *a very good match*.

"I've taught you how to run a household and move in society," her mother continued. "You already know the harp. Those are the skills a woman needs. You're being silly."

And here she was reduced again. It was so infuriating.

"I'm only asking for one year at school before I marry. Tom and Freddie get four." And another decade of leeway after that, but a year was the thin edge of the wedge she would use as a starting point.

"I told you it was a mistake to allow her to sit in with Freddie," her mother muttered to her father. "That tutor put ideas in her head."

Was it so impossible these ideas could be her own?

When they'd sent her younger brother, Freddie, off to Eton two years ago, they'd let his tutor go and pushed Annabelle into gown fittings and a coming out ball. That had been insult to injury when Freddie's tutor had always praised Annabelle's grasp of Greek and Latin, mathematics and engineering. He hadn't urged her to press flowers as a botany study the way her governess had done. That grotesque inequality between the sexes fueled Annabelle's ambition to become a teacher. She wanted to provide what she'd had to fight so hard to attain.

Her mother would fall right out of this barouche if she revealed that was her goal, though. No, she had to pretend she wanted to better her French and study music.

"It's all arranged, Annabelle. Men of the marquess's caliber don't wait a year while his bride cloisters herself with social inferiors. You're marrying him and that's the end of it."

"I don't wish to marry *anyone*," Annabelle burst out.

"I've said—" Her mother cut herself off and looked past Annabelle, leaning to see why the barouche was slowing. "What is happening?" she asked the earl.

"A lady in distress, m'lady," the driver said over his shoulder.

"Drive past," Annabelle's father said. "Quickly."

"Oh, *Papa*." Annabelle twisted to see a woman in a blue

riding habit on the tree-lined lane ahead of them. She stood in a shallow ditch, looking worse for wear, attending her horse that must have thrown a shoe. The plume on her wide-brimmed hat bobbed as she bent over the animal's raised hoof. "She's a woman alone. At least ask if we can take a message into the village for her."

"Do you see others?" Craning his neck to see if there were thieves awaiting them in the trees, he allowed with a grumble, "Oh, very well, then. Stop and ask if she needs assistance."

The driver came to a stop alongside her.

"Thank you!" the woman said with breathless gratitude. She kept her head down to watch her footing as she came out of the ditch, hands in the full skirt of her habit. "I was hoping someone like you would stop."

She caught the reins of their nearest horse beneath its bit and lifted a pistol at the driver, finally tilting her hat enough to show her face. She wore a black kerchief across her eyes and had disguised the shape of her mouth by wearing heavy powder and painting a pert red kiss on her lips.

"Step down, driver," she said with congenial authority. "Make yourself comfortable with your nose to the dirt while I acquaint myself with your passengers."

A highwayman? *Woman?* Annabelle was frozen with astonishment.

"Drive on!" her father shouted.

He was too late. The driver had leaped from the barouche and run into the trees.

"Was he your accomplice?" The earl stood and shouted after him, "Get back here, you coward. Are there more? Show yourselves!"

"Just me, my lord. But now you're up, I'll have you step out. All of you, please. I have three pistols, one bullet for each if you grow frisky."

Annabelle could only stare at this *vision* of boldness.

"It's the middle of the day!" Her father was apoplectic.

"Ah, the gentleman can tell the time. You won't need that pocket watch, then. Your girl can bring it to me along with your cufflinks, my lord. And all those baubles the lady is wearing."

"I will not." The countess placed a protective hand over her grandmother's broach.

"I usually start with shooting the men," the robber said as though she were talking about her favorite part of a meat pie. "But I can make an exception today."

"William," her mother said weakly.

The earl hesitated. He was still standing in the barouche, but he was red and perspiring with distress.

Oddly, Annabelle didn't feel frightened. She ought to. No one had ever pointed a weapon at her before. The danger emanating off the woman was the kind that might come off a tiger or she-wolf. Annabelle would be very wary if she came face-to-face with one of those.

But she only said, "I suppose we ought to do as she says. Give me your watch, Papa."

"A sensible young lady you have there, my lord. Yes, that pin from your cravat, too. Well done. And now you come down here and kneel on the grass where I can keep an eye on you."

Annabelle's mother began to weep. Annabelle didn't like to see her upset, but it also made her realize that her nerve was actually much stronger than her mother's. Why did she allow her mother to bully her when she was the one thinking most clearly right now? She helped her mother shakily remove her earrings and necklace and rings, then supported her as she stepped out of the barouche.

"Oh, your poor mama looks as though she could use your father's handkerchief. I'll have you take it, though, love. Make a pouch for all that booty, if you please, and be sure to add that pretty locket you're wearing. Mama, you can settle on the grass beside your husband. Give her a cuddle, my lord. She's distressed."

Annabelle's mother fell into her father in a heap of shaken tears. He wrapped his arms around her protectively. Annabelle felt him watching closely as she brought the heavy package of silk-wrapped loot toward the most dazzling person Annabelle had ever encountered.

"Annabelle," her father said urgently. "Don't get too close. Leave it on the ground."

She faltered to a stop just out of the other woman's reach.

"Put it in your bonnet and tie it off, Annabelle. A pretty name for a pretty woman."

She wasn't. She never had been. She was plain featured and her common brown hair refused to hold a curl for more than five minutes. The fashion for high-waisted gowns disguised the fact that her figure was boxy and her bosom modest. That's why her parents were so thrilled she had caught the eye of a marquess.

She managed to yank off her bonnet with one hand and do as she was told, aware the woman still had her pistol trained on them. When she looked up, she was startled to find the woman's golden-brown eyes taking her in the way her brothers looked at housemaids.

The way *she* sometimes looked at the maids.

Seeing that speculation in this woman's gaze sent Annabelle's heart into somersaults. Her body flushed with heat and an inexplicable smile of discovery tried to break on her face.

"Hold tight, love."

That was all the warning the robber gave before she released the horse and gave its haunch a terrific slap while yelling, "Hiya!"

The barouche took off, driverless and horses out of sync. It rattled wildly, kicking up rocks off the rocky lane. Annabelle's parents cried out while Annabelle was briefly accosted by the highwaywoman. The stranger's free hand stole the bonnet from her startled grip while her pistol arm wrapped around Annabelle's waist and squeezed her tight.

She kissed her!

It was a single, hot, damp sweep of her lips across Annabelle's mouth, which was parted in shock. Her tongue brushed her bottom lip once and it was over.

The woman leaped onto her steed—astride!—and spurred it into the trees.

While Annabelle stood there in a moment of tremendous epiphany.

That's why I don't wish to marry. No man will ever *make me feel like she just did.*

CHAPTER TWO

In the aftermath, Annabelle did something even her mother didn't stoop to. She claimed to be completely overset and debilitated by the robbery.

None of them had been harmed and they'd only had to walk a small distance around the bend to find the horses had stopped on their own. Annabelle insisted on going home, though. She even managed to conjure a damp lash to emphasize her distress.

Her father drove the barouche back to East Grinsley himself and had one of their stablemen return it to its owner. Her mother sent a note to the marquess that they had been set upon and would not be visiting as expected.

"Don't ask him to come, Mama," Annabelle beseeched her. "I couldn't possibly hold my composure. He'll think me hysterical. Give my nerves time to settle before we continue with wedding plans." She barely resisted rolling her eyes at herself, playing the helpless female so baldly.

In reality, she was invigorated. Not only was she more resolved than ever to forgo marriage and go to school, but also she kept wondering about the woman who had awakened her to such surprising self-knowledge. This was why she found men so dull and women so fascinating, be they parlor maid or married mother of two. Men didn't possess a combination of curves and lightness of step and a voice that was alluring and soft. They didn't understand her intuitively or see the injustice of the world being slanted sharply in their favor.

Annabelle became obsessed with seeing the highwaywoman again. She wanted to ask her why she had kissed her. She wanted to know if it had been a lark or something more meaningful. She wanted to understand how a bandit could become such a beacon of enlightenment in the fog of gray that was her life. She *needed* to see her again.

Those in the habit of robbing carriages weren't given to handing out calling cards, however. They were hanged if they were found and her father had hired an investigator to make inquiries. If the woman was smart—and she clearly was—then she was in another district by now.

Annabelle knew her quest to find her was futile, but she couldn't stop thinking about her anyway.

It made standing with her mother in the hat shop a week later more interminable than usual. One of the local gentry, Lady Henshaw, was receiving a blow-by-blow account of their harrowing adventure, murmuring, "My word. My word!"

Annabelle had heard the story a thousand times by now, each of her mother's retellings more dramatic than the last. She dragged her gaze off the cobwebs in the ceiling beams and asked, "May I visit the necessary?"

The shopkeeper was listening avidly to her mother, determined to hear every word so she could repeat the tale herself. She pointed to a curtain and said, "My daughter will assist you."

Annabelle went through to a back room filled with bolts of ribbon and faceless wooden heads covered in scraps of wool and partially woven straw fibers.

The daughter was absent, but Annabelle spotted a boat-shaped tin pot on a low shelf. The pungent aroma when she lifted the fitted lid assured her she had found the proper device.

She lifted the front of her skirt and held the pot between her thighs to relieve herself. Then she pushed open the door into the back alley to look for the night soil bucket.

The hatter's shop backed onto the lane that served the stables of the Stag and Sorrow Inn. The manure collector had his wagon parked there, stenching up the area. He also had the hatter's daughter pressed against it. They were locked in a passionate kiss. His hand was splayed over her breast.

Annabelle always thought, *Ugh*, at the idea of being pawed by a man. Before she looked away, however, she had a flash of *her* hand on that ample breast and her mouth on that girl's lips and a very different reaction swirled through her. One that warmed her blood with possibility and caused a lovely tingle through her pelvis.

That delightful and singular reaction was immediately wiped away by a jolt of shocked recognition. She *knew* that young man.

"You!" she said, dropping the piss tin in her hurry to get across to them.

They broke apart and the young man staggered backward with alarm at how fast she was advancing. The young woman tried to hide her face and slink behind the wagon.

"Your mother wants you. Go," Annabelle told her with a point that sent her running. "You. I want to talk to you," she said to the young man, narrowing in on him as he searched for an avenue of escape. "You know her. I was there when my father rented the barouche and so were you." She'd wasted an afternoon and all of her breath trying to talk the earl into calling off the wedding. "You overheard where we were going and when. That's how she knew to be at that particular bend in the road. You told her. Didn't you?"

"I don't know what you're talking about, Miss," he stammered, lips white with terror.

"Tell her I want to see her." She advanced on him. "Tell her I'll be on the hillock of the green near the Earl of Unstead's estate tomorrow night, soon as the moon rises."

He was about fourteen and was shaking his head so hard his shaggy hair was falling in his eyes. He nearly tripped over his feet as he continued backing away. "I don't—"

"*Tell her* the girl with the locket wants to see her. Or I will send my father's investigator to find you both."

As he went deathly white, her mother's voice screeched from

the hatter's door. "Annabelle! Have you lost your senses? What on earth are you doing out there?"

With a final glare at the young man, Annabelle turned to her mother.

"Seeing if it will rain. We should make our way home or we'll be caught in it."

•••

*A*udentes fortuna iuvat. Fortune favors the brave.

It had been Velvet's motto long before she'd been thrown all the way out on her ear, left with no means of supporting her sick mother and baby sister.

Was it brave to break into the Earl of Unstead's stately house, though? Or the height of foolishness? She had watched to see the earl and his wife leave in their carriage. A number of servants had made an exodus afterward, all in high spirits for what looked to be a night off.

As far as Velvet could tell, that left only the daughter in residence, but a few servants would be lingering and could pop out of the woodwork at any moment. Here came one up the back stairs behind her.

Velvet hurried to slip into what looked like the bedroom of a young man and left the door cracked as the maid bustled by. The maid tapped on a door farther along and a muffled female voice discouraged entry.

"Your mother asked me to bring you this towel and jar of hot water, Miss. I have a draught of laudanum as well. Is there anything else I can get you to make you more comfortable?"

The door was opened and a distinct *tsk* of dismay sounded. "Thank you, but it wasn't necessary. I'm lying down. Are my parents away to the Henshaws?"

Annabelle.

Her voice put a smile on Velvet's face even though she had no reason to like her, especially since she'd put the fear of gallows into her brother yesterday. But they'd had that brief moment on the road outside of East Grinsley. Velvet had sensed something in her, an air of assertiveness that had been smothered in ribbons and layers of silk, but it had plucked a string in her heart she couldn't explain. When their eyes had met, Annabelle had worn the most wondrous look that also had enough carnality to wet Velvet's pussy with excitement.

She shouldn't have kissed her. It had been an impulse, but she couldn't regret it. Not when Annabelle had kissed her back. At least, she might have, if Velvet had been able to linger and explore her startled response further. Annabelle certainly hadn't pushed her away or stiffened in rejection. And damned if that didn't feel like unfinished business between them.

"They're gone, yes," the maid was saying. "Cook said she'll have your tray ready whenever you'd like it."

"I'm not hungry. I'll ring if I want it. Don't disturb me unless I call for you."

She sounded every bit as snotty as Delilah had been. Why on earth had she come here, buckling to the demands of someone so arrogant?

The maid wished her good night and carried on to the stairs at the other end of the house. The chamber door closed.

Velvet glanced around the room she was in, looking for an easy steal. Before she could decide whether to pocket that ivory handled shaving brush or rummage through drawers for something more valuable, she heard Annabelle's door open again.

Through the crack, she saw the uppity Miss Annabelle look both ways, then start down the hall in the direction the maid had gone. She was dressed like a lad in knee-breeches and a coat with a cap.

Velvet stepped into the hall and walked silently behind her until she was even with Annabelle's door. "Psst."

Annabelle swung around. Her startled expression became

wide-eyed shock. Her mouth hung open and Velvet braced herself to run back the way she'd come.

When no scream came, she smiled and wiggled her fingers in a flirtatious wave, then stepped into Annabelle's bedroom.

CHAPTER THREE

S he was the most audacious person ever created!

Annabelle hurried into her room and snapped the door shut, locked it, then pressed her hand over the crack as if she could seal them in.

"What are you *doing* here?" she hissed.

"I was invited." The woman wore her riding habit again, but a much smaller cap and she hadn't bothered with a mask or powder.

She was perhaps twenty or twenty-one. Definitely only a handful of years older than Annabelle's cusp of eighteen. And genuinely pretty. Her hair was caramel, her nose playfully tilted up, her wide mouth pursed in a thoughtful pout.

Her snug coat gave her the most gracefully feminine silhouette. Annabelle found herself quite distracted. She watched her walk around the room, touching her things—her hairbrush and her bathing sponge, her bottles of scent and her painted fan and the deck of fortune-telling cards her cousin had sent her. She read the title on the novel at the bedside.

Annabelle half expected her to pocket everything she touched and didn't care if she did, she was so happy to see her. Ridiculously glad.

"Why are you dressed like that?" the woman asked with a curious cant of her head.

"They're my brother's." Annabelle ran a self-conscious hand over the riding coat and down to the baggie-seated breeches. "I was headed to the stables to ride out and meet you." She'd wanted to try riding astride. "It's surprisingly comfortable." No corset. No swaths of skirts to manage. Why had she never tried his clothes before?

Oh, right. Because her mother would throw herself from a

window if she saw her in them.

"It suits you." Her mouth softened and her gaze traveled over her with a curiosity that was so sensual, the air was squeezed from Annabelle's lungs.

She touched the jar with the towel wrapped around it. "Monthlies?" she guessed, wrinkling her nose in sympathy.

"I told my mother that's why I wanted to stay home. I—" She took a couple of steps forward. "What's your name?"

"You can call me Velvet."

"Is that your real name?"

She smiled.

Annabelle wanted to know what it really was. She wanted to know everything about her. She shook her head in wonderment, even as Velvet looked Annabelle right in the eye and slid her silver letter opener up her sleeve.

"What is it *you* want from *me*?" she asked.

Annabelle was speechless. "This," she finally sputtered, waving a helpless hand. "I wanted to see you again."

"Why?"

To see if she would feel the same as she had the first time. She did. Emotions were accosting her a hundred-fold. She was physically sensitive in a way she hadn't known was possible. She could feel every dust mote, could smell the fresh air that clung to Velvet's skin, could hear the other woman's heartbeat alongside her own.

She didn't know how to say all that. It felt far-fetched and juvenile. It felt like a risk.

"I was hoping you would know," she hazarded uncertainly.

Velvet held her gaze with a brassy stare. Her brows went up and her lips formed the question, "Know what?"

So she was wrong. All Annabelle's buoyancy evaporated. Maybe what she was feeling was more than a mistaken impression. Maybe it was wrong. Morally. How embarrassing. If she was lucky, Velvet would plunge that letter opener into her chest and put an end to this strange angst that had gripped her since they'd met.

"Annabelle." Velvet came to stand before her, making Annabelle lift the lashes she'd lowered in torment. They were of a similar height and she cupped her cheek. "*Audentes fortuna iuvat.* You were brave enough to tell me you wanted to see me again. Now tell me why."

As words swelled in her chest and throat, she blurted her truth. "I want to kiss you again."

She didn't know what happened then. She might have pressed her mouth to Velvet's or perhaps Velvet drew her in. Annabelle would never know. Either way, her mouth was suddenly against Velvet's and she was discovering she was aptly named.

Her lips were luxurious and soft. Warm. It made no sense to her that such a small action, so gentle and tender, could feel so big, but it did. As their lips worked against one another's, Annabelle felt as though this was the only place in the world she was ever meant to be, right here, sharing this sweet sensation with this woman.

Every emotion in the world flavored Velvet's lips, without a single word spoken. As though Velvet was celebrating her, telling her she was lovely and perfect and everything she could ever want. They were kindred spirits who had found one another.

Slowly they inched closer, arms sliding around one another until they were in a hug that was the most cherished Annabelle had ever felt. Revered, even though Velvet's tongue slid between her lips in a very lascivious way that sent a jolt of power into her loins.

Out of sheer instinct, Annabelle closed her mouth over Velvet's bottom lip and sucked it into her mouth, savoring her the way she might play with a spoonful of warm custard as it melted on her tongue. A pliant feeling settled in her hips and she adjusted her stance so their curves fit together like puzzle pieces. Then she did what she'd been thinking of doing since seeing the pair outside the hatters. She moved her hand to Velvet's breast, palming the outer curve. Oh, heavens, she was alluring.

Velvet sighed and her arms tightened around her, reassuring Annabelle she liked her touch, but she moved her damp mouth to Annabelle's cheek and whispered, "Rub my nipple."

Annabelle didn't mean to freeze, but it surprised her. She hadn't thought of doing *that*. She instantly wanted to, but Velvet drew back a little and blinked her eyes open. A puzzled shadow moved behind her brandy-colored eyes.

"Have you never been with a woman?"

"No," Annabelle breathed, stricken by inadequacy.

"With a man?"

"*No*." She choked on a laugh of repulsion. "I didn't know I could feel like this about *anyone*. It's certainly never happened with a man. My fiancé tried to kiss me and I ducked."

"I'm your first kiss?" Velvet's smile was unsteady, as though she was moved to hear it. "Did you like it?"

"So much," Annabelle said with a bashful laugh. "Have you? Been with women? Men?"

"I prefer women."

That answer suggested experience with both, which might have intimidated Annabelle, but she was mostly reassured to hear there were other women who felt this way. The church made anything to do with sex outside of a union between a man and a woman sound sinful, but how could this be sinful when it felt so natural?

They were still in an embrace, and it was the furthest thing from awkward to simply hold one another while they talked.

In fact, it gave Annabelle all the courage to confess, "I wanted to see you again so I could ask...*everything*." She laughed at herself, at her confusion and enchantment. "But now I just want to keep kissing you."

"Oh yes. Let's do that." Velvet took her by the hands and drew her to the bed.

They lay across it and rolled into one another, pressing their happy smiles together. It felt like coming home. Annabelle didn't want to stop tasting her lips, but Velvet ran her mouth down to her throat again and she couldn't help arching her neck to let her. It felt so good!

"I never want us to leave this bed," Annabelle gasped.

"Me, either." Velvet lifted her head and her hand paused in opening the top button that closed the collar of the shirt Annabelle wore. "Will you let me show you?" She looked so earnest, so eager.

"Show me what?"

"How it is to make love with a woman."

Annabelle blinked. "You want to do that with me?" She could hardly think through the wash of ecstasy that overcame her. "Yes. Please show me."

With a glowing smile, Velvet opened the shirt buttons and spread the collar as much as she could, then pressed kisses across Annabelle's upper chest. Soft, damp kisses that she paused to blow across.

"Oh." Annabelle sighed. Her breasts swelled, growing so tight it was a painful ache. A dull thudding arrived between her legs. It was exquisite. "Can I touch you, too?"

"Of course." Velvet stopped long enough to remove her jacket. The letter opener fell to the floor as she threw the jacket away. "I'll get that later," she said and they both chuckled.

Now she was only in her muslin bodice and began kissing Annabelle's chest again, pulling the shirt free of the breeches at the same time.

Annabelle ran her touch over Velvet's shoulders and the back of her neck, thinking she'd never felt skin so soft. Never understood that she could make someone shiver and doing so would make her shiver as well. Velvet's hair loosened from its pins and Annabelle played with the tendrils in fascination at how soft and silky it was.

When Velvet's hand roamed beneath her shirt, caressing her

stomach and ribs, Annabelle was paralyzed by the sheer pleasure of it. She kissed all over Velvet's temple and cheek and shoulder, wanting her to know how lovely she made her feel.

Then she remembered that Velvet had urged her to rub her nipple. She clasped her breast and discovered her nipple was poking sharply beneath the muslin. She wasn't sure what she wanted and rubbed her middle finger against it, like smudging a crumb of pastel.

"Like this," Velvet said. Her warm hand swept up beneath the shirt to cradle Annabelle's breast. That in itself caused the hairs on the back of her neck to lift. Then her thumb flicked roughly across Annabelle's nipple.

Annabelle jolted at the sharp sensation. It bordered on pain, but Velvet only smirked and said, "It's okay. I won't do that again if you don't like it. How is this?"

Her touch shifted so her fingers were lightly tracing either side of the distended point, sawing back and forth, causing little shudders of ecstasy to work through her.

"That's lovely," she sighed.

Velvet changed to circling her thumb around her nipple, then gave it a small pinch that made Annabelle jump again.

"This one?" She went back to the sawing motion that only grazed her nipple.

"Yes. I like that." Annabelle was trying to get her rubbing of Velvet's nipple right, but Velvet distracted her further by lifting Annabelle's stolen shirt all the way up to expose her breast to the fading light.

"What about this?" She lowered her head and danced her tongue in circles around Annabelle's nipple.

Annabelle's skin shrank and her nipple felt as though it would burst like an overripe berry. That wet stimulation, so gentle, so right, made her *burn*. Her loins were a very private place that she instinctively protected, but intimate muscles clenched of their own accord there. Her flesh grew distinctly wet.

It was disconcerting, but each time she tightened, the longing inside her was both satisfied and frustrated. The longer Velvet licked at her nipple, the more a web of hot wires seemed to pull at her inner flesh. She almost feared she was getting her monthlies, the trickle of dampness became so abundant. She pressed her thighs together.

"That's how you're supposed to feel," Velvet said in a voice that was a caress. "Lie on your back. Let me have your other nipple."

"I want to make love to you, too."

"I want to show you first."

Annabelle let her press her onto her back and tantalize her other breast. This time, Velvet closed her mouth over her nipple and sucked.

A sharp sensation in her middle struck with such tight power, Annabelle's toes curled in her boots and her knees came up.

"Too much?"

"I don't know. I don't know what you're doing to me." She brought Velvet's mouth back to hers and kissed her, needing to calm her raging senses. Even so, she couldn't help using her tongue. She wanted to incite her. She needed to express this passion and urgency and deep, deep hunger that had her in its grip. She was in a state of abject joy and gratitude that Velvet was here with her, drowning her in sensations she hadn't known were possible, but she was anxious, too. She needed her to come with her into this new place.

"You don't touch yourself here?" Velvet's cheeks were flushed and her eyes bright with passion as she set her fingers on one of the buttons that secured the fall of the breeches.

"Only to bathe."

"Will you let me stroke you? It's so lovely, Annabelle. I promise you."

Annabelle had a fleeting thought that she barely knew this woman. Velvet had held a pistol on her, robbed her family, and was likely to rob her again. If Velvet ever revealed to anyone what Annabelle was allowing her to do to her, she would be ruined.

But all Annabelle could think was, *I want to know. I need to know.*

She offered a jerky nod and Velvet released one button, giving herself enough room to slide her hand inside.

She kissed her again, lazy, sweet kisses as she drew the most exquisitely light caressing tickles on Annabelle's upper thighs and stomach and the fine hairs of her thatch.

It made tingles run down her spine while her body went lax the way a kitten did when picked up by the neck. Velvet petted her like that for a long while. They kissed and Annabelle stroked her cheeks and her hair and adored the way Velvet let her breast sit so lovingly in her hand. She rubbed Velvet's nipple and they both moaned.

The only thing that spoiled this perfect moment was an echo of her mother's voice in Annabelle's head, telling her this was very wrong, but nothing about it *felt* wrong. It felt like swimming or dancing. The sort of movements that were graceful and joyous and slow and flawless.

She felt as though she were on the verge of a great understanding. The anxious throbbing was still there, fed by Velvet's feathery touch, but she was *happy*. Enthralled. Velvet was right. It was the most incredible thing in the world to be touched this way.

As if she knew exactly what kind of infernal itch had arisen in her, Velvet traced one finger against her flesh, sawing with a little more pressure. She parted her intimate flesh and suddenly grazed a spot that caused a sensation so piercing Annabelle gasped and clasped Velvet's shoulders in a silent message to stop.

Velvet broke off kissing her and moved her hand to the quivering tension in her abdomen.

"It's like another nipple," she said with a small, reassuring kiss against the corner of her mouth. "I'll go slow, but you'll like how it feels. Can I?"

Annabelle offered a hesitant nod and Velvet drew her hand out of the breeches long enough to lick her finger, moaning, "Mmm," as if she liked the taste.

When she slid her hand into her breeches again. This time her damp touch parted Annabelle's flesh more easily. She explored gently and discovered more moisture that she spread around.

As her finger began to move with less friction, Annabelle writhed in paradoxical torture. The sensations were profound and so alluring, she could hardly bear it. The petals of her sex felt as though they quivered. Velvet found that spot again, circled it, and made a sort of music within Annabelle that made her open her mouth, but no sound came out.

"You're so swollen, it's like you're rising to my fingertip. I barely have to touch you. I would love to roll this pearl on my tongue."

"Velvet," she gasped, clinging to her.

"Feel it. Let it fill you. Do you like it better here? Or here?"

Annabelle didn't know what she was doing to her. One moment it was side to side, another it was circles, then like a tickle under a chin. She varied the pressure and it was all mind-boggling and lewd and delectable.

Then her fingertip settled into a place that made a strangled noise leave Annabelle's throat.

"There?" She did it again.

"It feels sharp. Strong." She could hardly speak. Behind her eyes she saw sparks of fire and flashes of gold.

"Let it build, love. Move your hips with my hand if you want to."

She did. Somehow Velvet's caress became a pinpoint on which the entire world balanced. It was a world where thrashing storms and blistering heat and every rainbow color reigned. The sensations grew more acute and her tension increased and the breath in her lungs ceased to move. She couldn't bear it!

Rapture struck like a crack of thunder and lightning.

Everything within her turned and tumbled and her throat unlocked with a shaken cry. Her pelvic muscles spasmed and a burst of perspiration coated her skin. All of it caused a soaring euphoria that convinced her she was flying. She was a kite that had lost its string and was tumbling adrift through endless skies.

Warm, wet lips settled over hers, grounding her as ripples of joy continued to accost her. Velvet continued her caresses between her legs, encouraging the pulses and waves as they slowed and faded.

Annabelle curled her heavy arms around her, thinking, *I love you*.

CHAPTER FOUR

Velvet had told herself she hadn't come here for this, but she had. Not that she had expected to seduce a novice, but she had wanted to see Annabelle. Kiss her again. The possibility of a torrid, passionate clash had not been out of the question.

Heaven above, she was so aroused after frigging this young woman, she could tear her apart, but there was something deeply endearing and satisfying in watching her eyelids flutter as she came back from the throes of climax and turned her head to reveal such satiated joy. Such gratitude, as though Velvet had given her the greatest gift imaginable.

"You have answered questions I didn't know I had," Annabelle said in a husky, shaken voice. "Why aren't all women married to women if we can make each other feel that way?"

Velvet snorted. "Some women feel like that with men. Some don't," she allowed. "And they're stuck married to them anyway. You can do it to yourself, you know. You don't need me."

"I don't think that would be nearly as wonderful." She bit her lip, growing shy, but excited. "Can I try to do that to you?"

Velvet had thought she'd never ask. She lifted the skirt of her habit—they did have a lingering trust issue. She wouldn't be caught naked and unable to run if she had to.

With a small rearrangement, she was on her stomach next to Annabelle, whom she told to stay on her back. She brought Annabelle's hand into place between her legs and kept her own there to guide her as she began to grind against her touch. Then she slid her free hand into Annabelle's breeches so she could caress her again.

They kissed and Annabelle moaned, kissing her back with great passion, telling her how exquisite she found this.

So did Velvet. She was so aroused, it only took her a moment before she was coming wetly in a powerful release, muffling her cries of ecstasy against Annabelle's mouth.

"Oh," Annabelle said with a wisp of desolation when Velvet broke away to catch her breath. "I thought we would do this longer."

"We will." She smiled and kissed her again.

• • •

Annabelle was so replete she was nearly unconscious. Her loins were nearly rubbed raw, but she didn't care. She was far more hurt by the fact Velvet hesitated when Annabelle asked, "When can I see you again?"

"I don't think we should." She was lit only by moonlight. "You could ruin me, love."

"You could ruin me, too." Annabelle sat up, dimly aware the blankets smelled of their erotic fondling and powerful releases.

Velvet was buttoning her coat. She had picked up the letter opener and secreted it back up her sleeve, Annabelle noted as she slid to the edge of the bed.

"Why do you do this? Steal?" Annabelle asked.

"Because we're not all given everything we need for the hard work of looking pretty," Velvet said with a spark of resentment.

"Not all of us *are* pretty." Annabelle had reached her limit on accusations of being a spoiled child. "And I'm expected to pay for my upkeep by giving my virginity to a man who leaves me cold. In fact, I'll have to submit to him for the rest of my life, providing as many children as doesn't kill me. But you *are* pretty. So why do you steal?"

Velvet said nothing. Annabelle noted her hands had closed into fists.

Annabelle rose and didn't bother searching out the breeches. She'd removed all but her brother's shirt and it hung long enough to cover her bare ass. She found her candle and then took a spill from the cup on the mantle. She used the fire tongs to rummage for an ember among the ashes in the fire.

"Don't say you're not pretty," Velvet said when Annabelle rose with the flaming spill and lit the candle in its holder.

"I don't care about being pretty." Her mother had hammered into her that she ought to, but she only went through the motions. "You seem to have some education. You speak like a lady. Are you..." She hesitated.

"Fallen?" Velvet sat at the dressing table and started to fix her hair, removing what remained of the pins and smoothing it with Annabelle's brush. "Yes. Obviously. Except I wasn't a lady; I was in service. I'm trained to be a lady's maid."

For some reason, Annabelle wanted to scold her for using that word. *Fallen*. It seemed cruel, even though a woman who was making her way by stealing had clearly lost her honor somewhere along the way.

"My first employer didn't want her daughter to pick up my low accent, so she made me read books aloud to correct my elocution. I didn't mind. Some of the stories were good. Then the young lady married and didn't wish to bring me along. I think her mother-in-law knew the housekeeper and I were close."

Annabelle inhaled sharply.

"Jealous? Don't bother. She was much older and we were friends, not lovers. I was sorry to say goodbye to her, though, when I found a new placement."

Velvet's hair was very long. Annabelle used the excuse of plaiting it to touch it, and her. Velvet lowered her hands to let her.

"My new mistress loved horses, so I got to ride with her. I did fall in love with her. I thought she loved me back, but when her cousin tried to seduce me, and her mother saw him groping me, my lover didn't stand up for me. She didn't have to reveal we were involved. She could have set things right out of decency, but she was afraid of upsetting her family. She let her mother turn me out without a reference. She's married now, getting royally fucked by a man. I hope she's happy."

She didn't sound it. She sounded pensive and cross and sad. Deeply hurt. *Betrayed*.

Annabelle coiled Velvet's length of hair and held it while Velvet pinned it. When it was secure, Annabelle opened the wooden box on her dressing table and took out one of her pearl earrings. She offered it to Velvet.

"You can have the other one when I see you next. I ride on Friday mornings with a footman. There's an old henge near the millstream. Do you know it? I'll be there at ten."

Velvet looked up at her, very somber in the flickering light of the candle. "If you have me arrested, my mother and sister will starve. I'll be hanged and my brother as well."

A pang struck deep in Annabelle's heart that Velvet still didn't trust her after all they'd shared this evening. Even deeper was a knife of concern for the very real straits Velvet seemed to be in.

"I want to see you. That's all," she vowed.

Velvet took the earring and stood.

Annabelle set her hands on her waist and pressed a tender kiss to her lips. Velvet's lips trembled slightly.

"Thank you," Annabelle said. "Truly. I didn't know who I was before I met you."

Velvet cupped her cheek and kissed her with more heat, saying with affection that warmed her through, "We've barely scratched the surface, love."

• • •

"You are not riding astride. Marie Antoinette did it and look where that got her," the countess said frostily when she caught Annabelle instructing the footman to forgo a side-saddle. As the footman scampered away, her mother added in a hiss, "Your bridegroom expects a virgin, Annabelle."

Annabelle clenched her teeth against stating that, while the unbroken state of her maidenhead might technically make her a virgin, she had the experience of someone who definitely was not.

She refused to fight with her mother and lose her chance to see Velvet, though. She agreed to the side-saddle and took her leave.

She couldn't wait to tell Velvet that even though she was right, Annabelle *could* pleasure herself to orgasm, extensive testing had proven Annabelle was also right. It wasn't as sublime as when Velvet did it, even when she pretended it was Velvet's hand.

Annabelle was so anxious to see her again she arrived at the henge thirty minutes early. She had to pretend she was collecting wildflowers, not that the footman cared one whit.

When Velvet turned up, she was on the other side of the stream. She waved and called, "I want to sketch at the millhouse. There's a lovely prospect from the upper floor."

With their alibi firmly in place, Annabelle told the footman to amuse himself for a couple of hours and hurried downstream to urge her horse across.

This tiny millhouse had been abandoned when the water upstream had been diverted for a canal. Its millstone was long broken, the wooden stairs rotting and missing treads. The few windows were covered in dust. Some were broken out, and brown leaves had blown in and feathers drifted across the floor from birds that had nested here over the years.

But it was cool and quiet and Velvet kissed her as soon as they were inside.

"I've missed you."

"I've missed you, too."

Logically, Annabelle knew she couldn't have fallen in love so quickly, but she didn't know what else to call this wild excitement, this urgent desire to be with this woman.

She removed her cloak and wafted it out to make them a

place to sit on the dirty floor.

"Here," she said as they knelt upon it. She removed the pearl earring from her ear.

"That's not the pearl I want, love."

Annabelle's breath stopped and she had to set a hand on the wool of her cloak to keep herself from falling over. "I kept thinking about you saying that," she confessed. She'd imagined it a thousand times while caressing herself. "Do you really want to...?"

"I do, my love. Ever so much." Velvet pressed her onto her back and kissed all over her face, but she soon began lifting Annabelle's skirts and kissing the legs she bared.

It felt too fast, but they only had an hour and she was very eager to know—

The soft, wet dab of Velvet's tongue wriggled into her folds. Annabelle sucked in such a sharp breath it was like glass breaking.

Velvet looked up at her with knowing laughter dancing in her gaze. Her mouth went back to Annabelle's pussy and her eyes rolled back in her head, then she moaned as if she were consuming the most exotic treat. Annabelle stopped thinking. She could only feel the swift build of arousal. The nipple-like bump that was so sensitive she had to be careful how she touched it grew fat and ripe beneath the ministrations of Velvet's tongue.

Annabelle pressed the back of her wrist to her mouth, muffling her moans as she spread her legs wider, wanting more. Everything Velvet wanted to give her.

Apparently, she wanted to give her a finger, because along with that luscious ablution of her tongue came a firmer touch, one that circled her opening and caressed and gently sought entry.

Annabelle had a fleeting thought that virginity meant keeping that place untouched for her groom, but she gasped, "Oh yes. Oh, please."

She wasn't even sure what she was inviting, but Velvet's finger slid in and out. As Annabelle clamped down on her muscles, all the sensations within her seemed to shoot outward like flames from a grass fire, swift and hot. Velvet kept anointing the little bud as she fucked her with her finger—because that's what she was doing. Annabelle was so joyously thrilled she was soon cresting and thrashing under the onslaught of an intense orgasm.

She came back to herself a few minutes later with the sensation of Velvet lazily continuing to lick her. It was divine and Annabelle could easily lie here basking in Velvet's attentions all day, but she set her hand on Velvet's hair.

"Please, can I do that to you?"

• • •

Annabelle was a very quick study and an avid pupil. Three fingers and four orgasms later, Velvet came to her senses enough to whisper, "Is that your footman?"

Annabelle lifted her head from between Velvet's thighs and they both pushed down their skirts. It was only the wind rustling a tree branch, they determined a moment later.

"I have something else for you," Annabelle said, digging through the slit of her habit into a pocket. She brought out a small purse of coins and offered them.

Velvet knew women who made their way like that, some because they wanted to, others because they had no choice. She wasn't either of those, so she refused to take it. "I'm here because I want to be, not because I expect compensation."

Annabelle's spine stiffened. She plopped the purse on the floor between them.

"That's not what it is. It sounds as though you have a difficult situation with your family, but I don't want you to steal to look after them. I'm afraid for you." Her brow pleated with worry, then cleared as a small, rueful grin took over. "Besides, I stole it from my brother's room."

Velvet looked at the purse, very tempted, but what did it make her if she stole it secondhand? What was she already? It hadn't mattered when only her brother knew. One day his job with the shit wagon might lead to stable boy work, but honest labor was so poorly paid, he barely kept himself clothed and fed. He couldn't help with their mother and sister. Velvet had resorted to doing what she had to.

"I keep thinking—" Annabelle scowled and looped her arms around her upraised knees. "My parents have engaged me to a marquess. He's horrible. *So* old and condescending and loves his port. I can't stand him. I've been trying to convince them to let me go to school."

"Finishing school?" Velvet wrinkled her nose at the thought.

"Mrs. Hargrove's Academy for Higher Learning and Scientific Study. She runs it from a house in London that only has rooms for two dozen. I had to write a long exam on multiple topics to get in."

"What do you study there?" Velvet lay down with her head propped on her hand, genuinely curious. "And why?"

"To learn what men know! Would you be stealing pocket watches if you knew how to make them? What if you could read Latin and learn medicine? What if you could invent a—a formula that keeps women from having babies they can't afford?"

"I think that's called 'succession powder' and you put it in a man's tea."

Annabelle's face closed up. "Please don't mock me."

"I'm not. I promise." Velvet set her hand on Annabelle's knee, growing more enamored with her the more she learned about her. "I've always wished I knew more about the law. When my father died, we were turned out of our cottage, but Mama was sure it was arranged for her to use for her lifetime. She had no way to prove it, though."

"Where do you live now? Wait, don't tell me. It's better if I don't know."

True. Velvet appreciated that she understood why.

"It's not nice," she admitted with a grimace. "My sister takes in mending, but she's only eight and has to care for our mother. She's sick." Velvet would take those coins. She already knew she had to.

"I keep thinking..." Annabelle dropped her face onto her knees, seeming quite tortured before she lifted her head and rushed out the rest. "I keep thinking that if I married the marquess, I could hire you as my lady's maid."

Velvet snorted. Nobs were always so *arrogant*. "You want to install me under your husband's nose and fuck me behind his back?"

"I don't *want* a husband," Annabelle spat. "I sure as hell don't want to fuck him. I only thought having you there would make that bearable, at least." She sounded miserable.

"It's a kind offer." Insulting, but kindly meant. She could see that. "But I don't want to be paid to be your lover, Annabelle."

"I knew you wouldn't trust me to look after you. I don't blame you." The corners of Annabelle's mouth went down and she set her chin on her knees, frowning dolefully. "This is why I want to go to school and become a teacher who teaches other young women. We ought to have more opportunities to better ourselves. We shouldn't have to resort to stealing or rely on someone else's good graces. We should have the ability to become self-sufficient, not be deliberately held back from it."

Velvet had tried to resist meeting Annabelle again. She had known the sensible thing would be to move her mother and sister to a new room in a new village and take whatever drudge work she could find.

Instead she found herself compelled to see her and admired her all the more. She was the sort of noble that the nobility ought to be.

Unable to resist, Velvet leaned forward to nuzzle Annabelle's cheek, seeking out her ear to nibble the shell-like rim, tilting toward falling in love with her.

Oh, that was dangerous. She already knew their worlds were

too far apart for this liaison to last. At best, she would only have her heart broken when it ended. At worst… Well, she didn't dwell on that. Not when, "We only have a little more time. Would you rather be self-sufficient at home? Or talk me into getting you off here?"

"I want to taste your quim again." Annabelle turned her head and lust colored her cheeks. "I really like it."

Her words hit like a sensual punch to her stomach, making Velvet's heart soar at being wanted so blatantly. *Don't fly so high, Velvet. The fall will be fatal.*

Ignoring her inner voice of warning, she said, "Seeing as I am highly trained in giving a lady what she wants…" She lay back and lifted her skirts.

CHAPTER FIVE

Annabelle was playing a dangerous game. She saw Velvet as often as she could and gave her money when she would accept it. She wrote her a letter of reference and Velvet nearly broke down in tears.

She had confessed her real name was Vera, explaining that Velvet was a nickname her family called her. It made Annabelle feel special to be allowed to use it.

The letter was hogwash, of course. Annabelle claimed that Vera had worked for her cousin who had recently died. *While I cannot speak to her daily work, she was well liked in their modest household. My cousin never spoke a word of criticism of her conduct in my presence. Vera brought my cousin great comfort through her protracted illness and has been helpful at all times as we put my cousin's final affairs in order.*

She signed it, *The Future Marchioness of Quarrymire.*

"I can get proper employment with this, Annabelle." The page shook in Velvet's hand.

"Yes, I know. That's why I did it."

They celebrated by getting naked and finding inventive ways to rub their pussies together.

But in order to allay suspicions and have opportunities to rub up against Velvet, Annabelle had to go along with her mother and the wedding plans. It was like a ball of yarn that kept rolling down the stairs. At some point, it would fully unravel and run out.

She kept thinking marriage might not be so bad, now that she understood how her body worked. How sex worked. Maybe if Velvet got a position with someone she knew, they could still see one another.

By the time her brothers came home on school break and

other family arrived and her parents invited the marquess and his family to meet hers, Annabelle had convinced herself she should go through with the wedding.

Sherwin, though more than twice her age, was not bad-looking. He was opinionated, but he was also rich. Was there not some influence to be had for her, if she became the wife of a man with influence? Annabelle had never been the sort of daughter her mother wanted and the countess was so *happy* these days. It made marrying Sherwin seem like the right thing to do.

"We're engaged now, Annabelle," Sherwin said a week before the wedding. "We can walk in the night air."

She let him draw her from the laughter of cards and the lively music drifting from the open doors of the parlor out to the garden. He wanted to kiss her, and she was going to let him because, well, this was her life now, wasn't it?

When they were a little way from the well-lit house, he turned her to face him and drew her into his arms.

Her own arms bent themselves between them, forcing a space. His chest seemed displeasingly flat and hard. He was very tall and loomed in a way that irritated her and put a crick in her neck. He had a smell about him, too. It wasn't unpleasant, but it wasn't soft and appealing. It made her head turn itself away.

"Come now," he said in that *awful* tone, as though she were a child to be scolded into kissing him. He took hold of her chin and found her mouth with his own.

She tried, she really tried to relax. He wasn't being violent, just proprietary. As if he had a right to thrust his tongue into her mouth and wiggle it around.

Trying to enjoy it, she sucked on his tongue and swirled hers around his. It disgusted her a little and made her feel as though she was cheating on Velvet.

Thankfully he put a quick end to it. He jerked back and his hands went to her shoulders to clench a little too tightly.

"You kiss like a whore," he said flatly.

Annabelle was stunned speechless, then blurted, "How do you know how whores kiss?"

"That's none of your concern." He dropped his hands from her and wiped them on his silk breeches.

"I think it is," she reasoned. "I've seen the advertisements in my father's *Gazette*." The ones for medicated soap aimed toward men who visited *unfortunate* women driven to *illicit commerce.* "If you're suffering a 'horrible consequence' from an 'indiscreet connection,' I certainly don't want it." There'd been whispers of her father's cousin being driven mad by the mercury treatment for his venereal infection.

"I'm more concerned something like that might come from *you*. I was told you're a virgin. Are you?" he demanded.

His question left her utterly agape with offense that she was being made to answer for herself while he had no intention of doing the same. Her response was out of her mouth before she'd fully thought it through.

"The state of my hymen is not your concern. I will not marry you." She hurried into the house.

•••

"Annabelle," her mother said in hushed horror as she burst into her room. "Tell me you were lying. You aren't *ruined*."

She looked up from changing into a simple travel gown, mind whirling with how she might get a message to Velvet. "I don't believe I'm ruined, no."

A wavering moment of silence, then her mother said in a trembling voice, "Don't be coy. I won't stand for you claiming things that aren't true so you can throw a man over. This is a *good match*."

"For whom? He consorts with prostitutes. Would you like me to catch a disease?" she asked with disbelief.

"You don't know that!"

"He didn't deny it."

"So you lied and gave him the impression you've been having relations as well? That is an outrageous lie, Annabelle. Go tell him it wasn't true." She pointed to the door. "Beg him to reconsider because he is telling your father right now that the wedding is off."

Annabelle's only regret was that Velvet wouldn't be able to use her reference letter. She would have to write her a new one and, given how things were sounding with her father, might not be able to sign it as "daughter of an earl," either.

Even so, she instinctually knew that Velvet would understand and support what she'd done here.

"I never wanted to marry him in the first place, so no, I will not ask him to reconsider." Annabelle rolled up the clothes she'd stolen from her brother and stuffed them into a leather satchel.

"You're *bluffing*. Aren't you? *Is* there another man?? What if you're..." She could hardly whisper it. "Expecting?"

"I'm not," she assured her and pushed her jewelry box into the bag. It already contained more of her brothers' possessions—a gold tie pin, a silver snuff box, and two gold guineas to match the one she'd been given last Christmas from their uncle. She retrieved the bank draft from the drawer of her dressing table and tucked it into the snug confines of her bodice.

"Your father will turn you out," her mother charged. "Are you *that* set on making your own way?"

"I'm packed and catching the mail coach to London so the answer appears to be 'yes.'"

"Do not do this, Annabelle," her mother said in a death-knell. "We will not see you again."

"You never did anyway," Annabelle said as she brushed past her mother and left.

• • •

Annabelle had to wait half the night outside the inn for the mail coach to come. One of the hostlers eventually appeared. She asked him if he could relay a message to the young man who took away the manure.

"Could you ask him to tell his sister that I've gone to London?" Annabelle asked.

"Who are you, then?"

"She'll know."

He shrugged and told her the stage wouldn't be by for hours.

"I'm catching the mail coach." It was cheaper and East Grinsley was one of the easier places to get an impromptu seat on one.

Annabelle was prepared to be ousted at one of the towns between here and London if the space was needed for cargo. She almost wished it would happen. She spent the entire bone-rattling journey listening for hoofbeats in pursuit of their coach, yearning for a certain highwaywoman to catch up to her. Much as she wanted Velvet to give up that dangerous profession, she wouldn't mind one last robbery!

Then what? Would they live like fugitives, robbing coaches together?

Annabelle wasn't the weepy type, but she had to wipe away a few tears as she traveled. She wished she could have said more to Velvet before she left. She wished they could be more to one another. She wished and wished and wished.

•••

Ten years later...

"Here she is," Velvet said, standing proudly behind the young woman she had just brought into Annabelle's office. "The most promising and outstanding student who will ever grace the halls of Westbourne Women's College for Science and Engineering."

Jenny rolled her eyes to the ceiling and slouched her shoulders beneath her sister's hands. "Do I have to call you Mistress Belle?"

"I'm not one to insist on conformity for the sake of it. If you have a good reason not to, by all means, make your case." Annabelle waved her hand in invitation.

Jenny pushed her mouth to the side in consideration. She was bright-eyed and good humored these days, far different from when they'd first met a year or so after Annabelle had come to London.

Velvet had turned up first, excited to have a position with a family in London. She and Annabelle had rarely been able to see one another, but they'd been heartened by the proximity. When Velvet's mother had passed, she had talked her employers into allowing Jenny to be an unpaid apprentice. Jenny had been very withdrawn and grieving, but the sisters had been together and it had given Jenny a proper start in service.

Not long after that, Annabelle's father had passed. Her mother had slowly come around to speaking to her again and, when Annabelle was ready to open her own school, her eldest brother had been persuaded to give her the funds that would have been her marriage settlement.

By then, Jenny had a good situation in another house, so Velvet had given up her position and come to run the dormitory of Annabelle's college. She ensured their students helped with meals and the daily upkeep of the house while Annabelle ran the school side, recruiting students and teaching the lessons. They shared a small suite of private rooms where they slept together in the sort of marital bliss Annabelle had thought she would never want. It really was about finding the right person, she had concluded.

"I guess the other girls would tease me if I called you 'Auntie,'" Jenny said. "They'd say I didn't have to study as hard as they had to be invited to attend."

"They had better not," Annabelle said firmly. "I expect my students to show each other respect at all times."

"And I will cut their throats if they say that, because I know how hard you worked to earn your place here," Velvet said against her sister's ear.

"Your sister will not cut any throats. Criminal behavior of any kind is highly discouraged. We've talked about that." Annabelle leveled a mockingly stern look at the woman who was her breath and blood and bone.

"And yet she stole my heart," Velvet said with a dreamy smile at her over her sister's shoulder.

"Sounds a bit hypocritical," Jenny whispered as she drew her sister's arms around her like a cloak.

"No one is perfect," Velvet commented with a shrug. They wore matching smiles of laughter at Annabelle's expense.

"I'm going to regret having two of you in the house, aren't I?" Annabelle said with a curl of her lip, but she was so elated, there was a small ball of sunshine in her throat. She adored them so much! "You'd better settle in before I change my mind."

"You're in room six with Constance," Velvet said. "She's a dear. Go make friends." She shooed Jenny out and closed the door, then widened her eyes at Annabelle as she hissed, "A *boy* walked her here. He carried her *bag*."

Annabelle gasped in mock outrage, clutching at an invisible broach the way her mother used to do. "We have a young woman under our roof who possesses *sexual feelings*? What *shall* we do?"

"The same thing we do with all of them, I suppose." Velvet came across to snuggle herself into Annabelle's lap. "Tell her how it all works, then assure her that if someone truly loves you, they'll wait until the time is right before demanding intimacy."

"The way you did." Annabelle caressed Velvet's hip. "When you stole a kiss along with my locket."

Velvet looked down at where said locket hung around her own neck. "You can have it back anytime. I've told you that. I'm an honest woman now."

"I like it better on you." Her wearing it reminded Annabelle that

Velvet was still the charming, audacious, unbreakably self-possessed woman who had given her far more than she'd ever taken. She'd given Annabelle the confidence to be who she really was.

"Me, too," Velvet said with an impudent smile and kissed her.

This was turning into the type of stolen moment they typically kept inside their private rooms. Their students were intelligent. They figured things out quickly. Some of them even felt drawn to fellow students and opened up with a heart-to-heart conversation with Velvet and Annabelle as they figured themselves out, but Annabelle and Velvet knew the school's reputation could not afford a scandal, so they didn't flaunt their relationship.

That didn't mean Annabelle didn't love to push her head up Velvet's skirt midday if the opportunity presented.

"What time is our other new student arriving?" she asked.

"Not for a few hours. Her parents are bringing her."

"They'll expect to see me in a gown, won't they?" Annabelle far preferred the comfort of men's clothing. Corsets and lace did not lend themselves to demonstrations in bricklaying and long walks to observe waterways and working near open flames for chemistry experiments. She kept her hair short for the same reason.

Velvet always said she looked dashing in men's clothing and there wasn't a person in this world whose opinion mattered more to her, but there was an expectation that a headmistress of a *women's* college would look like a lady at least some of the time.

"I'd better change."

"You'll probably need the help of your lady's maid." Velvet rose to offer her hand. Her lashes slanted in coquettish slyness.

"*Such* an honest woman," Annabelle teased. "But yes. I couldn't possibly manage without you." She led her to their bedchamber.

The End

An Evening
of Cards

Simone LeBlanc had been her mother's eldest daughter of three, all by different men. Her mother had grown up in the miserable poverty that led to the revolution. She had survived by any means necessary and had been determined her girls would not "become like me."

It was a noble aspiration that she pursued wrongly, in Simone's opinion. Her mother's first and worst mistake was believing marriage would elevate her in any way. They'd had a roof over their heads in the brothel and the overbearing lout she married denigrated them far worse than anyone on the street ever had.

Simone couldn't blame her mother for seeking any sort of betterment, though. The revolution had been a terrifying time with heads rolling in the street, but Simone had been far happier when she'd had to keep her younger sisters quiet while her mother entertained lovers. She had learned much, eavesdropping on those interactions, and even more by listening to her mother's conversations with other prostitutes.

Her nostalgia for that time increased when the mood in Paris settled under Napoleon and her mother decided her girls must learn a trade. She sent Simone to sew, which wasn't a terrible education. She had some talent for it and was taught letters and sums. She also learned about elegance and fashion and heard the latest gossip about the influential and wealthy.

Sewing was a demanding, wretched way to earn a pitiful wage, though. The more she observed the clientele, the more she aspired to be like the women who were called courtesans.

Prostitution was legal and yes, still regarded by many as a debauched way to make a living, but courtesans held an accepted and respectable place in society. They were invited to parties and talked of books and bought beautiful gowns and traveled. More important than the silk that draped them, however, was the demeanor they wore. They were like the wealthy aristocrats who had returned from exile without money or possessions yet maintained an air of confidence in their own worth.

Simone was fascinated by that assurance. She *wanted* it.

So, when her mother died of influenza and her stepfather began arranging a marriage for her, Simone took her fate into her own hands. She knocked on the servants' door of a well-known courtesan's town house in Faubourg Saint-Germain. According to gossip, Zarina had traveled Europe with the circus from St. Petersburg for many years. She was past her prime but had lately begun an affair with a general in Napoleon's army.

Simone was deflowered under Zarina's roof on her fifteenth birthday. Zarina, who mentored her for several years as she embarked on her new career, allowed Simone to take over her town house when she retired to warmer climes, afflicted with a lung ailment.

Simone was approaching twenty-five now, and, even though she had only ever been considered passably pretty and not truly beautiful, she was among the most well-known and esteemed of the demimonde. She hosted a salon twice a week for men and women, one where she maintained her own literary library that included a compilation of love letters she had exchanged through the years—names withheld, of course. Painters and poets and composers attended with aristocrats, doctors, lawyers, and a particularly astute banker who had steered her from speculating in the stock market to purchasing real estate that she rented to textile mills and other industrious enterprises.

With Zarina's guidance, Simone had climbed her way beyond needing a benefactor, but she enjoyed the support and attentions of a Romanian prince anyway. He was not her only lover. She didn't rely on any one man. She never fell in love, either. That would give a man too much power over her. She was even cautious about taking a lover who held too *much* power, as that would require she be constantly on guard against losing that man's favor.

Besides, she was a woman with an insatiable sexual curiosity and a desire for variety. Perhaps it arose from her early childhood in a brothel. Perhaps her conception as a result of her mother's profession imbued her with a sexual nature. Either way, she enjoyed the attentions of men. Not just rich and influential men, either. She was known to impulsively invite a musician or shopkeeper into her bed purely for the pleasure of it.

And she didn't confine herself to men. She had enjoyed affairs with women at different times along with men who dressed as women and the other way around. She had once spent a rapturous night with a street performer who had utterly charmed her despite refusing to speak a single word. She still didn't know if they'd been a man or a woman, but they'd slept well and smiled when they parted, which was all that mattered.

So, when Prince Yurik informed her he would leave Paris for a spell, Simone suffered no anxiety. She lived comfortably on her own terms. Her bed would not be cool for long.

Yurik, however, urged her to let him choose his successor.

"Don't sit on the face of a starving artist. Let me find a benefactor who will be as generous with coins as climaxes. I have contenders in mind. In fact…" And here Yurik proved why he had been a good match for her while their affair had lasted. "We could play a game that will introduce you on a more intimate level, so you could be sure of the match. And I'll know he won't mind sharing your favor when I return."

When he told her what he planned, she narrowed her eyes with suspicion even as titillation began fluttering behind her navel. "How long have you been plotting this?"

"It's the sort of request that can end a liaison very abruptly. It seemed best to wait until we were near the end regardless," he said with more amusement than rue.

She told him she would think about it, but she was intrigued, already wet with anticipation. He turned to licking her pussy as persuasion and within moments she cried, "*Oui!*"

So it was that she arrived in Yurik's town house on the rue du Faubourg Saint Honoré for an evening of cards like no other.

•••

S imone had prepared herself with a leisurely morning, a light meal, a quiet bath, and perfume that was prepared for her alone. The secret formulation carried the fragrance of jasmine, clove, sandalwood, and aphrodisiac herbs from Africa and Asia. These same enhancing herbs were in the cognac the men would sample through the evening.

A servant showed her to Yurik's library. The polished floors reflected the firelight. Candles added warmth and glow to the quiet room. The velvet drapes were closed. A wooden box sat on the mahogany desk. A round table had been brought in for cards and already had stacks of coins in front of four chairs. As she entered, the four men rose from sitting near the fire.

"Beloved," Yurik said, coming forward to kiss her cheeks. "What aren't you wearing that you refused to give your cloak to my servant?"

He took it, revealing her gown with its high waist and low neck in diaphanous mousseline. She kept her cashmere shawl in ruby red, but made no effort to disguise where the brownish pink of her nipples and the dark thatch of her mound were as visible as the shape of her legs and the roundness of her derriere.

"It's a long-accepted fact that fashionable dress in today's Paris is no dress at all." It was the sort of witticism men loved, having no idea she had lifted it from the *Lady's Monthly Museum* long ago.

All the men chuckled, eyeing her with such unabashed carnal interest she had a moment of unease. Like Yurik, they were all dressed in stylish comfort with buckskins and white muslin shirts tailored to accentuate their wide shoulders and trim waists. One had a pair of dark breeches with a bulge already pressing against his front fall. Another set down his drink and buttoned his dark velvet coat to greet her.

"Introduce me to your friends, *mon amour*," she urged, attempting to take control.

"Comte de Gautier, recently returned from America." The first man kissed her cheeks as though they were well acquainted. "Longing for a return to beauty and refinement." He had a charming curl to his hair and a wicked gleam in his eye, exactly as she enjoyed in a lover.

"I promise one or the other, *mon chéri*. Not both," she said smoothly.

"Marchese Renzo." He possessed a velvety Italian accent that slid into her blood like mulled wine. He bowed over her hand and pressed his lips to her knuckles. "I look forward to an enjoyable evening."

"I have arrived. Your wish is granted," she replied with a squeeze of his hand.

"Marquis de Beauvais, French by way of Mauritius." This man's hand was very warm, as though he carried the sunshine of the tropics in his blood as well as on his skin.

"Parisian by way of preference?"

"It's growing on me." He kept her hand while grazing her cheeks with his lips.

"Is that what is growing on you?" She flicked him a coquette's glance and his white teeth flashed in unabashed humor.

"He's starting without us," Gautier drawled. "What are the rules, Yurik?"

"Beloved, let me show you how the game is played. I made them wait to see everything until you had arrived." Yurik opened the box on the desk.

They all gathered around to watch as he removed the contents, laying each item on the desk.

There was a selection of *godemiché* in polished rosewood. One was *very* long and robust with a sizable pair of *couilles*. There was a pretty glass one that Yurik had used on her once, a couple of smaller plugs for the arse and one made from leather with two heads. He set out a stack of sheaths still in their envelopes. There was a stoppered bottle of oil, scarves for binding and blindfolding, a riding crop, and a strap of leather.

Those last made her nervous. Pain and submission were not the stimulant for her that they were for some.

"I'll explain the rules, then Simone, you may put anything back in the box that you don't wish to be included in our game." Yurik moved to the table and splayed out a deck of cards so remarkable, they all murmured in surprise.

It was based on the typical thirteen that went from ace to king in four suits and two colors, but each card was painted with a blatantly sexual image.

The ace showed a man's fist clutching his own erect cock mid-release so his come dribbled down his knuckles. The two was a voluminous pair of breasts gathered by their owner's hands, topped by plump, turgid nipples painted a ripe rouge. The three was a woman's glistening pussy. Her folds were spread by her two fingers from one hand, one from the other. The four was a man's hand touching a woman's pussy. His finger and thumb held her plump outer lips open while two fingers of his other hand were partially inserted. His fingers glistened so brightly, she thought the paint was still wet.

"Where did you get these?" she asked in fascination. Her loins were growing slick just looking at the flagrant images.

The other men were examining them just as closely. The five was a woman's delicate hand wrapped around a very engorged cock. The six was a round ass spread by a woman's hands. A man's finger explored the puckered bud of her arsehole.

"I was invited to a ball in the English countryside," Yurik said.

"The artist paints them on commission. Notice the lower cards show a man touching a woman or a woman touching a man? On these higher cards, lips and tongue are used."

The seven was a pussy, wet with lust, positioned over a man's chin, his tongue extending. The eight was a woman's mouth about to close over the tip of a man's cock.

"Higher cards, higher stakes?" Renzo noted, shifting himself behind his breeches.

The nine showed the tip of a cock breaching the entrance of a splayed pussy. The ten was a man's hands on the spread cheeks of a woman's ass, his cock buried inside it.

Simone was growing hot despite the thinness of her gown. She heard one of the men clear his throat. All of them were breathing more deeply.

The jack wore a smug, laconic expression. His clothing was disheveled and he had his leg thrown over one arm of his chair to negligently expose his flaccid cock. The queen was also half dressed, breasts exposed and legs open as she slouched in careless satisfaction. The king sat in a regal pose with a chalice in his hand and his cock thick and ready where it peaked from the drape of his robe.

"The game is to collect and play three of a kind so you may enjoy the act." Yurik demonstrated by gathering three fives and motioning the pull of a hand on his cock.

"While the rest of us watch?" Renzo asked.

"Of course."

Renzo's cheeks darkened with a flush of excitement and he nodded approval.

"A roll of the die will determine how long you enjoy it. This timer is marked with the minutes," he noted, pointing to the small hourglass. "If you want to enjoy something to completion, you must play your jack." He dealt one to each of the four seats. "Those are not in play. Leave yours on the table until you wish to use it."

"Hold out because we can only come once?" Gautier clarified.

Yurik held up a finger to indicate he would explain further.

"The queens are Simone's." He handed her all four. "For each climax she enjoys, she must give up a card to the man who provoked it. Be judicious, beloved. If a man wins a queen, it sits with his jack as a wildcard. He can add it to any pair he holds if he is impatient to enjoy a certain act."

Her gaze flickered over the delectable possibilities and her inner muscles clenched with intrigued anticipation.

"And the kings?" she asked.

"The man who collects all four kings will win the privilege of becoming your benefactor in my absence."

"For however long I wish to bestow that privilege," she warned.

"My *bon amis* know they will have to impress you with their prowess or your favor will not last long," Yurik said in mild warning that this was a game of pleasure, not power.

"How many cards do we hold?" Beauvais asked.

"Four. We each start with a king and three from the pile. We discard as many as we like to the man on our right. Since I cannot enjoy Simone's company for the next while, I will always discard a king."

"But if we hold onto a pair of kings, there will be no room for three of a kind," Beauvais deduced. "Not unless we've won a queen."

"Exactly. You may play for immediate gratification or prolonged, not both. We ante each round and the pot will go to Simone for her generosity in providing us this evening."

All the men gazed on Simone with such consideration, her nipples rose up against the fine fabric of her gown.

"What of the ace?" Gautier touched the image of a hand pulling at his own rod. "Surrender?" he guessed dryly.

The other men chuckled and Yurik made a noise of iniquitous anticipation.

"The ace is our *tabou*. Add it to a hand and you may up

the play to something that is not represented." He set an ace alongside three sixes, where the image showed a man fingering a woman's behind. "Perhaps use one of the items on the desk or something else that pleases. Are there any cards you wish to remove, beloved? Any objects you'd rather were left in the box?"

She put away the crop and leather strap, the bindings, and the largest of the carved phalluses. She allowed the blindfold and the smaller implements and left all the cards in play.

"As host, I hold you as we start." Yurik drew her into his lap with the casual ease they had enjoyed for the last months. "Kisses and caresses are allowed when you are in possession of our prize, gentlemen, but stay above the skirt unless you have the cards."

Renzo was quick to take the seat on Yurik's right, ensuring he would have first crack at Yurik's discarded king. Gautier sat across from Yurik and Beauvais on his left.

With the face cards and aces dealt, Yurik shuffled the numbered cards, dealt three to each man and set the remaining face down on the table. "Once you've played a hand, you'll set it aside and take fresh ones from the stack."

Sitting in Yurik's lap, she was able to see he passed off his king to Renzo along with a five, retaining a pair of threes. He shared tender kisses with her, playing his hand over her hip and waist while the other men deliberated.

He added the cards Beauvais sent him and asked if anyone had three of a kind. No one did, so they anted another five francs into the pot and circulated another round of discards.

They had to ante once more before Yurik received a three to match the pair he'd been holding. "I'm about to win a queen right off the top," he declared, laying down his matching images of a woman caressing herself.

Simone's heart swooped with excitement, but she only gave him a haughty look. "That will depend on your roll."

It was a three.

"Do I stay here?" she asked.

"You do." He pushed back his chair to afford the other men a better view.

She rearranged herself so she had her back to Yurik's chest and let her legs fall on the outsides of his knees. She glanced around briefly to ensure she had the full attention of the other players before she slowly lifted her skirt to reveal her pussy.

"The timer, Beauvais, if you please."

With a nod, Beauvais turned the timer.

Simone licked the tip of her middle finger and lightly teased along her slit. All the men's eyes were fixated on the slow measured way she began to stroke herself.

Simone always enjoyed the power of arousing a man with an action like self-pleasuring. It was no surprise her pussy grew wet very quickly. She'd been stimulated from the first mention of this night, so it took nothing for her lower lips to blossom open and the little nub at the top to grow firm and sensitive.

She taunted them further by exposing one breast and playing with her nipple, pinching and rolling it to increase her own pleasure and theirs.

"Push a finger inside you." Gautier threw a coin into the pot. She did as he asked, clenching her inner muscles around her own finger and enjoying the light ripples of gratification that resulted. Her slickness increased as she slowly fucked herself.

"Two." Beauvais threw a coin into the pot.

She watched the sand in the hourglass through her lashes. It was only about halfway and she was growing *very* aroused. She occasionally took two men to her bed. Her appetite was such that she enjoyed being fucked in turns, but she had never felt one at her back, caressing her waist and setting kisses on her nape, while three others waited in anticipation of ravaging her. It was a potent prospect.

Her fingers slid easily in her abundant juices, making a muted, sopping sound.

Gautier licked his lips and Renzo said in a voice ringing with a lover's solicitude, "Would you like to play a queen, *cara*? Touch your *perla*. Let us watch you come."

Pearl. She didn't know much Italian, but she knew what he meant. Her breathing was growing uneven and the little nubbin at the top of her sex clamored for her touch. She rolled her two fingertips around it and then ran her fingers down either side of her swollen inner lips, spreading herself for the enjoyment of her audience.

Beneath her hip, Yurik was rock hard and his breath animalistic against her ear. Just as she began to think she might have to play one of her queens or die of need, the final grains of sand in the hourglass fell through.

With a careful exhale, she removed her hand and closed her thighs. She offered her wet fingers to her lover. Yurik sucked them clean and settled her more deeply in his lap. The feel of his cock against her ass, so hard and currently off-limits, made her pussy throb with such need she felt it as an ache in her belly. They kissed deeply as play resumed.

Three rounds of discards added coins to the pile before Beauvais made a noise of triumph. He set down three eights with the depiction of a woman's mouth settling over the tip of a cock.

"Fucker," one of the men said under his breath.

With a shiver of anticipation, Simone gave Yurik a parting kiss and rose. Beauvais pushed back his chair and unbuttoned the fall of his breeches. He was already very hard. His skin was even darker on his cock and balls, like the rich brown of the rosewood *godemichés* and equally pleasing in size and shape. This would be a delight for both of them.

He rolled the die and came up with the four. The other men hooted and placed a few side bets on whether he would lose his jack.

Simone reached into the small drawstring bag she had brought and produced a tin of lip color. "Shall I?"

"Oh yes," he assured her. "I am quite sure that shade will suit me."

She made a small ceremony of rubbing the brilliant red over her lips in preparation before she knelt between Beauvais's feet. She glanced at Gautier, who took charge of the timer. As it hit the table with a quiet *thump*, she lowered her mouth to the base of Beauvais's cock and ran her tongue slowly up the pulsing vein underneath until she found the sensitive point where the head formed an arrow.

His cock bobbed in reaction and he gave a low noise of pleasure. She took him in hand and, for the enjoyment of the other men, spent some time playing the flat of her tongue around the crown and diddling the tip of her tongue into the salty pool of fluid that leaked from the eye.

He was very hard and twitched and pulsed in her hand as she hit certain spots. His breath grew ragged and he looked to the ceiling while the other men gave husky laughs edged with envious enjoyment at his suffering.

Slowly, with her gaze raised to ensure Beauvais was watching, she licked her lips and set a kiss at the very tip, then held her lips firm as she allowed the head of his cock to force its way in. With the crown filling her mouth, she used her tongue to press him to the roof of her mouth and applied gentle suction, letting her spittle collect in a hot pool as she did. Her tongue worked again to caress and explore and make him clutch at the arms of his chair.

As the moisture in her mouth began to leak out the corners and run down his shaft, she drew more of his cock into her mouth so the tip nudged the back of her throat. Her hand gripped him firmly, pulling back the skin to heighten his sensitivity. His taste grew sharper as his arousal increased. He was hard as a flat iron and twice as hot. Perspiration stood on his upper lip. He glanced with concern at the sand in the hourglass.

She used her other hand to fondle his bollocks while applying more suction. Just enough to make him catch his breath and grit out a curse from between clenched teeth.

As he spread his thighs and lifted his hips in a reflexive gesture, she began to bob her head with more purpose. Her clenched fist followed the movement, lubricated by her spittle. She stroked his shaft as she fucked him with her mouth, sucking hard each time she drew back. He made noises of supreme torture and she was bracing herself for his thick come to slide down her throat when Gautier said, "That's four or your jack."

Simone lifted her mouth and set her hands in her lap, staying on her knees while she looked up at Beauvais, awaiting his decision.

His chest rose in uneven pants and his cock was twitching and leaking fluid. She saw the intense conflict in him. The frustration that he shook off with a rattle of his head. He lifted a hand to indicate she was done and she rose.

"A marvelous show of courage, man," Renzo said.

"Indeed. You've earned our respect," Yurik said.

"You've earned me. For now," Simone said, not giving him a chance to put away his straining cock before she went into his lap.

A growling noise of pleasure-pain sounded in his throat as he pulled her bottom hard against his damp, straining cock. He ran his hands over her with brazen greed, kissing her passionately and thrusting his tongue into her mouth, paying little attention to the cards he drew to replace his eights. They were a three, which was played out, a six, and a five. He still had his king, she noted.

Gautier handed him another six and Beauvais sent his five to Yurik. A moment later, that card had transferred to Renzo who set it down with a shrug that said, *I'll take it.*

"*Avec regret, mon chéri.*" She had been enjoying Beauvais's petting and kissing. They shared one more lengthy, passionate kiss before she rose and walked in a small daze of arousal behind Gautier. She traced her fingers along his tense shoulders as she passed, holding Yurik's gaze, then settled into Renzo's lap.

They exchanged one friendly kiss of greeting, before Renzo rolled a two.

"This may not be my lucky night," Renzo said fatalistically. He didn't pause the game, only opened his breeches so she could fondle his cock while the men continued the play.

Which wasn't to say Renzo wasn't aroused or that no one took notice. The eye of his cock leaked a steady stream that soon had her grip sliding freely over the head, greasing him well, but she was no sooner making a show of it when the clock ran out.

Which was when Gautier made a triumphant noise and set down three sevens.

"Prick," someone called him.

Gautier rolled a five before she'd kissed Renzo goodbye.

"I will have my meal here, thank you." He pushed aside his own coins and reached to the pile of coins in the middle of the table to spread them into a bed.

All the men secured their own coins and cards as Simone sat on the edge of the table in front of Gautier. He guided her slippered feet to the arms of his chair and she bent through them to play with his hair.

"Hello, new friend," she said with a light kiss.

"Goodbye, sweet thing. I am not sorry to cause you the small death you will now endure."

"We will see." She lay back, but she was very aroused and always enjoyed a head between her thighs.

"The curtain rises on a wet delta where the scent of the sea is ripe in the air," Gautier proclaimed as he ran his hands from her ankles to her knees and higher, taking her skirt up. "The queen shall surrender or I cannot call myself a man. The timer, if you will."

Gautier hitched his chair forward, which forced her knees to bend higher. He pressed them open and dipped to steal a long taste from the sensitive skin behind her entrance through the slick hole that had been teased by her own touch earlier and up to swirl around the nub that throbbed with latent desire.

A small quake went through her abdomen and she released a moan.

It could be said that enthusiasm counted for much when a man went down on a woman. In Simone's opinion, skill was far more important. When a man had both, as Gautier seemed to, she was lost. His mouth heated her sensitive tissues, making her melt at her very core, sending her quickly into the throes of acute pleasure.

Through slitted eyes, she saw the other men watching, which increased her titillation.

Her breasts ached so, for her onlookers' pleasure as much as her own, she exposed her chest and began to massage and pinch her nipples. Sharp talons of sensation dug deeper into her loins, tightening the coil of tension in her abdomen.

"No, no, beloved." Yurik took her hands and held them above her head. "He must achieve it himself."

If anything, the constriction of being held and forced to endure the ministrations of Gautier made the eroticism even more piquant. He was fucking his tongue into her hole, making her nub ache with longing for him to return there.

Her breasts quivered in the cool air as she panted, trying to resist her mounting climax yet aching for it to arrive. When she moaned her tormented frustration, Beauvais sweetly stroked her hair from her forehead while gazing down on her with cruel, lascivious delight.

"What's wrong darling? Can't take it?" She had tortured him in exactly this way. He was enjoying her agony, especially as she had to endure it a full minute longer than he had.

She rolled her head to see that only three minutes had passed. She wouldn't last, not when the light constriction of her hands stimulated her darkest desires. Not when being observed like this had her loins welling with excitement. Not when Gautier ceased attempting to reach into her very depths with his tongue and returned to swirl her neglected nub and suck it with brazen purpose.

A fresh, hot flush suffused her. A rolling sense of pressure flew into her loins while an internal expansion hollowed her breath. A bolting strike of sharp pleasure hit so hard it hurt. Ecstasy crashed over her very suddenly, like an unexpected gust of wind. It tumbled her senses, buffeting her in rippling sensations from her toes to her straining fists to her throat and breasts and down to her belly and loins again.

Wave after wave moved through that way, hot and cold and disorienting and delicious. Moans and cries of delight spilled from her lips as he continued laving her, setting his tongue firmly against her pulsing flesh, unrelenting and forcing her to stay in that state of pleasure even as her climax receded. He didn't stop until the last grain of sand had fallen.

When it did, she was nothing but shaking bones and melted flesh, both gratified and freshly aroused.

"*Merci, ma chéri.* It is wonderful to have the taste of home on my lips once again." Gautier planted a tender kiss against her trembling belly as he reached over her to take a queen from where she had left her stack of them. "Mine, I believe."

He stayed over her long enough to drop a kiss on her lips. His were still glistening with her juices before he swiped the back of his hand across his mouth and retook his chair.

All the men sat back and eyed her like wolves wanting to tear her to pieces as she lay with her legs still splayed to Gautier's gaze. Slowly she managed to collect herself and sit up.

"Poor angel," Gautier murmured as he gathered her into his lap. He sounded very solicitous, but his body was tense and hard, not nearly the soft cushion a man could be when he'd spent himself. His cock pressed insistently into her ass, but only ruthless control showed in his hardened features. If she were a betting woman, and she only gambled very lightly and on very sure things, she would put her money on Gautier to win tonight.

She was not as relaxed as she could be, either. He had licked her enough to freshly stoke her desire. If they were alone, she would demand he fuck her right here and now, she was that charged with lust.

They had to make do with a lengthy, tongue-sharing kiss, one that still held the taste of her pussy. She curled her arm around his neck and cuddled her head into his shoulder while he fondled her breast as play continued.

Conversation was less convivial. The silence was tense as the coins rattled, hitting the pot for several hands before Beauvais said a smug, "Ah-ha." He splayed his hand of sixes.

Ooh. She was about to have her arse fingered.

"Play your *tabou* if you want to spank her," Yurik advised.

"For how long? My hand is liable to get as sore as her ass." He rolled a two and made a disgruntled noise.

"I'd rather see the fingering," Renzo said, throwing coins into the pot.

"Same," the other two men agreed. More coins jingled.

"Holding onto my jack when I had my cock in your mouth might have been the wrong move. I'm liable to spill all over you while I fondle that pretty ass of yours."

"A gentleman uses a generous amount of oil," she advised as she left Gautier's lap and brought the small vial from the desk.

"Maybe the chair without arms," Renzo advised with a chuck of his chin.

The chair by the fire was brought over and she draped herself across Beauvais's lap, balancing herself with her hands on the floor.

He drew her dress up, exposing her ass and giving each cheek a squeeze of greeting. The timer must have been turned, because she felt a cool dollop of oil land in the crack of her ass beneath her tailbone. It ran in a trickle as Beauvais's firm hand pressed her cheek open. The fingertips of his other hand delved between her thighs. He grazed his touch along the fine hairs of her mound just enough to send a quiver of anticipation through her pussy before he traced up to her arsehole. He began to firmly rub the oil around the tight purse.

She enjoyed having her ass toyed with, but like all the other aspects of her life, she limited how much access she gave a man. She didn't ever want them to become possessive or believe they owned any part of her.

But as Beauvais's long finger worked its way past her body's natural apprehension and gained entry, her pussy responded with a throbbing clench of delight. She couldn't help releasing a small moan of pleasure.

"You like? We don't have much time, *chere*," Beauvais murmured. "Will you take two? Tell me what you like."

"Slow and deep. More oil if you're going to give me another finger."

He kept his single finger inside her as he dolloped more oil onto her. She grew more and more restless as he worked it against her hole and forced a second finger inside her.

She groaned at the ache of it. At the way he seemed to touch a hidden part of her—

"That's your two minutes. Play your jack if you want more," Yurik said.

Beauvais removed his finger from her arse and gave her the chair as he rose to wash his hands in the basin.

Simone was lightheaded and shaky. She sent a look around the room at the men watching her with their avid, feral expressions. She wanted to take all of them, one after another, each of them grinding into her pussy until this infernal fire of desire was quenched.

Beauvais returned and took his proper chair, inviting her into his lap with a tilt of his head. She went and stroked her hungry hands over his shoulders and chest, dislodging buttons so she could feel his skin.

"I would keep my fingers in your ass all night," Beauvais

said as play resumed. "You would have come in another minute, wouldn't you?"

She nodded, nuzzling her face into his throat and wishing his fingers were still there.

"Now, it gets interesting," Yurik said with a licentious curl at the corner of his mouth. "No one has played his jack. Someone is holding a pair of kings." Simone knew it was Gautier but didn't say so. "No one has used his *tabou* and only Gautier has earned a wildcard. Our dear Simone is ready to spend another queen, though. Aren't you, beloved?"

She was. This game was most stimulating, filling her with nothing but salacious thoughts and a willingness to submit to nearly any debauched request.

A few minutes later, Yurik set down his cards and said with a matter-of-fact nod, "I can finish what I started at least." He had three fours, each carrying a picture of a man's hand pleasuring a pussy.

She said her goodbyes to Beauvais and moved into Yurik's lap. He rolled a four and smiled with wicked satisfaction. "That's enough time for a queen. Possibly two." He lifted her dress to expose her and hooked her leg over the arm of his chair. As the timer was turned he combed his fingers into the soaked curls between her thighs. "Oh, I very much smell a queen and I have deeply sinful plans for it. Show them how you cream for my touch."

She responded to that commanding tone with a small wriggle. She liked a man with sexual confidence, and Yurik had spent the last months learning how best to reach two long fingers deep into her pussy and lightly stroke while rolling his thumb around her nub. They had started many a morning in exactly this fashion and she always came into his hand.

But she didn't wish these other men to see her as easy to conquer. She was ending her relationship with Yurik, but starting fresh with one of them. It would be wise to prove she was not as malleable as Yurik made her sound.

Nevertheless, her stomach quivered in familiar anticipation as he worked two fingers, then three, deep into her slick channel. Her thighs twitched and she bit her lip and struggled to resist the effect he was having on her.

She couldn't prevent the way her pussy clenched on his fingers and released juice that fairly ran down his wrist, though. She didn't have it in her to reject his kiss when he captured her mouth and slowly fucked his tongue between her lips, mimicking the rhythm of his fingers moving inside her. She couldn't control the instinctive lift of her hips into the roll of his thumb across her nub. Climax beckoned and she very much feared she would succumb.

"You're running out of time to win a queen." Gautier warned Yurik, voice tense with the rising stakes.

No! She couldn't wait for another hand. Simone pushed his touch deeper between her thighs and clutched at the back of his head to hold him in their passionate kiss.

One more flick of his fingers inside her and she was moaning with abandon. The walls of her pussy shook in ecstasy as she poured her gratification into his palm.

The timer finished and he removed his hand. She was still shivering and sucking on his tongue in gratitude.

"That is how it is done, gentlemen," Yurik said in a voice low with guttural arousal as he rested his wet hand on her inner thigh, leaving her plump, shiny pussy exposed for all to see. "A queen, beloved?"

She couldn't speak, she was so overcome, but managed to shakily drag one from her stack to sit next to his jack.

Yurik closed her legs for her. This time he offered *his* wet fingers to *her* and she delicately licked them clean as the game resumed.

Despite the two orgasms she'd enjoyed, she was far from satisfied. If anything, she was nothing but sensitized skin, paying little attention to the game, preferring to slide her hands beneath the edges of Yurik's shirt to play with his nipples and pet his chest hair while she set kisses under his jaw.

A few moments later, Renzo set down three twos. As they all regarded the images of plumped breasts, Gautier remarked, "You can always add your *tabou*."

Renzo moved to peruse the selection on the desk. With a nervous flutter in her belly, Simone joined him.

"What are you thinking?" she asked.

"That I'd rather fuck your tits than fuck you with one of these. A blindfold would be interesting if I had any patience left, but all I want is to come all over you."

"That will cost your jack."

"But seeing it will make them wild with lust and I'll be able to think again, yes?" he said dryly.

The men at the table chuckled at his strategy.

Simone moved to the divan where she shed her gown completely.

As she reclined, Renzo brought the oil. He stepped free of his buckskins and set his knees on either side of her chest, then poured oil onto her breastbone. Simone gathered her breasts to capture it, using her fingertips to smear it so her globes gleamed while creating a slippery channel between.

His weight settled on her a little more as his cock and balls came to rest against her skin, warm and firm. His narrowed eyes ate up the vision she made as he began to fuck her tits. The hair on his balls abraded her breastbone and their friction heated the oil coating her skin. The divan rocked and creaked.

The other men came to watch. Simone felt a light touch on her knee, one that opened her thighs to grant them an even more libidinous sight.

Touch me, she thought longingly. The pressure of her hands on her plumped breasts and the jiggle as Renzo fucked them created a hot massage that made her nipples prickle and sent a sensation like heated wires into that place weeping with need.

"I could eat that cunt all night," Gautier mused.

"I have," Yurik said smugly.

Unsurprisingly, the filthy talk had an effect on Renzo. They'd been playing this game for nearly an hour and he was so ready, he came suddenly and powerfully. His hot cream hit the underside of her jaw and pooled in her neck, dripping across her collarbone and down her shoulder into her hair.

Renzo was heavy on her, still panting and bracing most of his weight on his heels while staring at her. In a tender gesture he touched his thumb near the corner of her mouth and slowly smeared a fleck of his come across her bottom lip.

She dabbed the taste with the tip of her tongue.

"Fuck, that's beautiful," Beauvais said with gruff admiration and slapped Renzo on the shoulder. Someone offered a towel. As Renzo weakly moved off her, Simone sat up and cleaned her neck and throat. When she would have moved to the basin for a proper wash, Renzo stopped her.

"Leave the smell of me on you. It will make them jealous and stupid."

The men chided him, but she found her shawl, not bothering to dress again as she went into Renzo's lap at the table. He seemed to enjoy sniffing at her neck where the scent of his come was musky and strong.

On the very next hand, Renzo picked up the discard from Yurik and made a noise of annoyed disbelief. "What are you holding that you gave me *two* of these?"

With disgust, Renzo showed his hand of three nines. "I just came all over her. I'm not ready to fuck her, you prick." He didn't have a jack left, either.

With a smirk, Yurik said, "It seemed a safe discard, given you're spent and can't use them."

Across the table, Beauvais said, "I'll trade hands with you." He showed his pair of tens, a seven, and a king.

Yurik was instantly annoyed. "I've been waiting for those

tens." He had been holding onto a pair of them from the time she had been in his lap and his fingers up her cunt. "I was about to play the ones I have with the queen I got last round."

"Unfortunate," Beauvais said without any regret as he exchanged his hand for Renzo's.

"A proposition," Yurik said. He added her queen and his *tabou* to his two tens. "Use your ace and we'll enjoy her at the same time."

Simone's heart took a wild leap and drop. She accepted a man's cock in her arse when the mood struck, but she'd never been fucked in her cunt while she did.

The men looked to her.

"If we do it right," Yurik coaxed, "we'll each earn a queen."

"And you'll lose your jacks," she noted pertly. "Into a sheath." She might be impulsive and willing to engage in the most wicked dissipation, but she was also smart about it.

She moved back to the divan. Beauvais undressed and sheathed his cock, then lay down at a slight angle so Yurik would be able to brace himself with a knee on the edge of the cushion and a hand on the back of the divan.

With some apprehension, Simone straddled Beauvais and slowly impaled herself upon his erect cock. It felt incredible to finally feel a stiff heat in her aching pussy. They both enjoyed a few light pumps as Yurik greased his sheath with oil and watched.

"Lean forward," Yurik urged Simone and began to work fresh oil into her arsehole.

Before he positioned himself, Yurik looked at Gautier and Renzo, both standing on either side of the divan to watch. "You both have a *tabou* left."

Gautier and Renzo held a long stare as if waiting for the other to give in to temptation. Gautier said a quiet and challenging, "I plan to win."

Neither man played his card and Yurik got himself situated so he could line himself up to pierce Simone's arsehole. He worked one finger in, ensuring she was relaxed enough to take him, then the tip of his cock pressed with determination.

A shiver of trepidation washed over her, but her pussy was clenching in reaction around Beauvais's intruding cock. Yurik's position pressed her more fully onto Beauvais's chest. They were all perspiring with nervous excitement.

As Yurik gave small pulses of his hips, urging her to take another increment and another, Beauvais played with her nipples. It was the oddest sensation, bordering on pain, trying to fight her own instinctive resistance while being toyed with in such a lewd way. She grew more laden with desire even as she bit her lip to bear the ache.

The divan creaked under their weight and someone stroked her hair. The scent of sex permeated the air. She could hardly breathe, but she thought that might be because she was forgetting to. The sheer sinfulness of what she was doing was as profound as the act.

The heat of Yurik's abdomen pressed her bottom cheeks, spreading them that tiny bit more as he forced the last millimeter of himself deep into her back channel. She was so full, she couldn't make sense of it, could only hold very still and try to endure the magnitude.

"I can feel his balls against mine," Beauvais murmured with a lazy grin. He tucked a tendril of hair off her face. "What does it feel like for you?"

"Too much," she breathed. "So hot. Like I'm being hugged by both of you." Tenderly cherished, yet caught like a butterfly on a pin and utterly helpless.

"Like we both want you and couldn't wait to have you?" Yurik suggested against her nape. "I've always wanted to share you with another man like this, so you would experience as much pleasure as possible."

He carefully pumped his hips.

Beneath her, Beauvais groaned, reacting to the muted

movement of her pussy on his cock as Yurik's thrusts rocked her on him. They fused their mouths in a passionate kiss and he took hold of her breast, pinching her nipple. His other arm went around her waist, trying to keep hold of her while Yurik pressed down on them. Beauvais found Yurik's rhythm and lifted his hips to work with it.

She made a high, keening noise, unable to express herself any other way. She was trapped in a vise of absolute pleasure. She had never wanted for love, but she had never felt so loved by any man as she did while caged in this sensual pinch. Her entire lower half was on fire. Part of her wanted Yurik to move with vigor and hurry the sensations to their ultimate culmination. The other part reveled in the way he moved with gentle, steady purpose, holding all three of them on a plateau of want.

When she managed to blink open her eyes, Beauvais wore a barbaric grin.

"I can feel him moving in you. I want to fuck you so hard, but I want to stay exactly like this." He combed his fingers into her hair and brought her mouth to his to stroke his tongue deep into her mouth. Yurik's steady fuck of her ass quickened.

"I should've played my *tabou*. I want in on this," she heard Renzo say. "Look at her. She's in heaven."

Behind her, through her convulsive trembling, she felt Yurik's body shuddering with his effort to maintain control. He was stroking faster and harder, which shifted her sopping pussy on the incredibly hard cock lodged within her.

Beauvais's arm around her waist tightened as did the hand he had clenched in her hair. It stung, but she liked it. She liked being held very still for the hard fuck of her ass and the buck of his hips beneath her.

Simone was in a state of complete euphoria. It was the place she touched when she was at the very peak of pleasure, right before she tipped into orgasm, but she was held there for what felt like eons as the men took their pleasure in her.

When Yurik cursed, it seemed a signal for all three of them. The tiny ripples of near orgasm that had been playing through her loins and ass narrowed to a concentrated point.

Yurik made a harsh animalistic noise and his hips slapped hers in a final, rough thrust. As a hot burst of heat filled her ass, her own orgasm exploded like a flashfire. The waves of pleasure that had been running through her like a current hit her in a splash of supreme, glorious joy. She screamed into Beauvais's mouth while his body went taut beneath hers. His hips rose beneath her and his cock pulsed in hot spurts, pooling heat inside her pussy.

Her ears felt as though they filled with water. Their mutual cries of release arrived from a distance and their combined orgasm went on forever, retriggered by a twitch or a shift or a pulse from another. She may have had the breath pressed out of her, because she almost felt as though she fainted.

When she became aware again, all she heard was the harshness of all their panting breaths. Her breasts were adhered to Beauvais's damp chest. It rose and fell beneath her while Yurik was sweaty and heavy on her back.

"If I only had a queen, I would switch out with you, Yurik," Renzo mused. "I seem to have recovered very quickly from my recent enjoyment of our sweet Simone."

He had his cock in his hand, unashamedly stroking himself as he watched them. Gautier was squeezing himself through his buckskins, but she thought he remained dressed for control, not modesty.

They began to recover themselves. Yurik slowly withdrew from her ass and moved to the basin where he washed and discarded his sheath. Gautier offered her a damp rag and she tidied up while Beauvais also dispensed with his sheath.

When they returned to the table, Beauvais and Yurik lounged with the relaxation of men who had spent the entirety of their strength. They clinked drinks in a self-congratulation and took deep swallows.

Renzo said something rueful about the dangers of sitting while stiff, but his mood was light. Gautier was the only one who had not used his jack yet. He had a *very* tense look about him. Determined.

Having discarded their played hands, Yurik and Beauvais drew the last of the cards from the pile. Simone was sitting with Beauvais and saw he only had orphans. Yurik was likely the same. Both men were essentially out of the game.

It had come down to Gautier and Renzo and they didn't bother hiding what they held. Renzo had two kings and the two tens he had taken from Beauvais plus his *tabou*. Gautier had a nine and a three with his pair of kings, plus the queen he'd won, his jack, and his *tabou*.

"I'll give you my two tens for your kings," Renzo suggested. "With everything else, you could enjoy something very special."

"With four kings, I could enjoy something very special every night," Gautier responded. "Suppose, Simone, that I fuck you while you suck Renzo's cock. I propose we throw our kings together. Whoever comes first loses."

Renzo had come all over her neck and Gautier not at all. "You think you can last? I *can't* come," he pointed out somewhat facetiously. "I no longer have a jack."

"Then you accept the terms," Gautier presumed. "If you come, you lose."

"If Simone is amenable, then yes. Winner takes all," Renzo agreed and moved his chair back, opening his buckskins to expose a cock hardened by watching her with Yurik and Beauvais.

Still shaking from that experience and curled in Beauvais's warm lap, Simone hardly had the strength to find her feet and stand.

Gautier gathered cushions and set them on the floor at Renzo's feet.

As Simone knelt and braced her arms on Renzo's warm thighs, she was still trembling. Gautier knelt behind her and lightly embraced her. He kissed her neck.

"Are you up for this, *ma chéri*? I'm going to make it good for you. I hope you'll make it good for him so I can win you."

She thought of the way Gautier had eaten her and rather liked the idea of taking him as her next lover. They were all skilled, though. She would be happy with any one of them.

She nodded and shared a kiss over her shoulder before she turned her attention to Renzo. He might have come a short while ago, but he quickly responded to her caress of his balls and light squeeze of his thickening flesh. As Gautier was fondling her still sensitized pussy and pushing his sheathed cock inside her, she began to suck firmly on the tip of Renzo's cock.

Gautier did indeed mean to make it good for her. He was very hard. And hot. He must be dying to pop the cork on his pent-up desire, but he slid his hand around to smear her juices between her thighs and into her folds, spreading them and paying particular attention to reawakening her desire.

As those flickering flames began to lick at her, she grew more attentive to ensuring Renzo's pleasure. Much as she had with Beauvais, she played her tongue over his ridges and the salty indent at his tip, allowing spittle to leak out of her mouth so her hand moved freely on his shaft as she began to bob her head and suck.

Renzo groaned and spread his knees wider.

"*Oui*, hmm?" Beauvais said, agreeing with Renzo that she was very skillful at pleasuring a man this way.

Behind her, Gautier was in no hurry. His strokes were lazy, his caresses moving to less sensitive territory before returning to pluck at her nub. He should have been lost to the moment, but even though he was hard as marble, he was not urgent. His hands moved from her waist up to her breasts to caress then back down to squeeze her ass then they were again spreading her folds while he pressed deeper within her.

It was such a delicious sensation, she hummed in response.

Renzo's cock happened to be touching the back of her throat as she did. His cock twitched in her mouth and he let out a strangled noise.

"There we are," Gautier murmured, as if that was exactly what he had planned. He did it again as she went down on Renzo's cock, making her moan when he was deep in her throat.

"You bastard," Renzo gasped.

"You could've had your cock in her mouth while she was taking both of them," Gautier reminded. "You wanted to."

Renzo made another agonized noise as he was reminded. The salty flavor of his fluid intensified in her mouth.

Gautier swept his fingers across her nub again. This time he pressed firmly against it. At the same time, he moved faster, thrusting deeper and harder so that orgasm was suddenly upon her.

In reaction, her hand tightened on Renzo's cock. She moaned lustily, cock deep in her throat as an incredibly satisfying orgasm took her.

"Fuck!" Renzo's cock swelled and hot come spurted into her mouth.

She was so startled, she swallowed, but she was also trembling with the fresh climax that crashed over her, topping the first and making her groan even louder. Come leaked out of her mouth down Renzo's shaft.

"Ah, my sweet queen. Thank you for that." Gautier's hands clenched her hips and he began to fuck her so hard, she had to release Renzo and press her face into his tense stomach, clinging to his hot thighs as Gautier finished lustily with a crow of triumph.

He came so long and hard, she felt it as her own, prompting latent twitches and echoing ripples of pleasure inside her. He held her in a crushing grip, cock buried deep inside her while his hips pulsed against her ass.

"That is the most exquisite defeat I have ever suffered," Renzo said whimsically, head lolling on the back of the chair.

He stroked her hair. "I am sorry to lose you, *cara*, but I am not sorry to have had you."

She was surprisingly comfortable leaning into his stomach this way, pussy still full of Gautier's cock, breasts nestled against Renzo's thigh.

With a deep inhale, Gautier withdrew and tossed away his sheath. He returned to gather her up. "I believe she is mine?"

"For now," she said as he settled into his chair with her in his lap.

All the men lifted their drinks in a toast to a fine game. Gautier offered his glass to her and she sipped before she looked to Yurik.

"May I keep the cards as a parting gift?" she asked.

"Of course, beloved. I'll order a fresh deck for myself. And for you, gentlemen, if you'd like?"

"Will that be necessary?" Simone asked with an ingenue's flutter of her lashes. "When we'll continue to play together?"

The End

The
Baker's Man

The Baker's Man is a delicious treat you can enjoy slowly,
bite by bite, or devour it all in one go, and you're always
welcome to come back for seconds, however, the story includes
classicism and references to outdated views of homosexuality,
so readers who may be sensitive to any of these,
please take note.

CHAPTER ONE

Hugh Norton heard the swish of his sister's skirt as she entered the bakehouse, but he kept a close eye on the loaves he was forming. The assize here in Queenslie Hedge left no room for generosity while the village would riot if they thought they were being cheated. Making bread was the bulk of his day, but it was a zero-sum-game. Cakes, pies, and the use of the oven were how he kept himself and his sister's family from starving.

"I'll need you to keep an eye on my sweet buns while I fetch water," he told her.

A throat clearing, distinctly masculine, made him glance over his shoulder. Honey-ale eyes kicked him in the heart, and lower, but he pushed his gaze to the lady beside him, a chestnut-haired pain in his ass who was already batting her lashes in a way that probably worked on other men.

"Lady Beatrix." He grabbed a towel to wipe his hands. "Beg your pardon. My sister and the lads are the only ones coming into the bakehouse." Which was how Hugh liked it.

"She was fussing with the baby. I should remember her when it comes time for a wet nurse," she said to her companion, tapping her chin thoughtfully.

Hugh bristled. Fuck, he hated quality.

"Cart before the horse, isn't it?" The man's hair had the same rich color as hers with a shorter curl. His jaw was wider and he was much taller. He gave her a pithy look down a nose that held a bump that also matched hers. "Unless you have something to confess, dear sister?"

"Ugh. No. Why did you call me that? You never do. But here, let me introduce you to our *master baker*, Hugh." She made it sound as though Hugh was putting on airs with the title. "Meet my brother, Kip. I'm the youngest, but he's next and the one I love the best. Aren't you?" She hugged his arm.

"Sir Christopher," Hugh recollected, because this woman never shut up about herself.

"Kip is fine." He held Hugh's gaze in a way that could have been a challenge. Felt like something else. Something that put tension in Hugh's spine and tickled at his balls.

"He's not going to call you Sir Kip." She joggled her brother. "Can you still use Colonel? Kip was in the militia. Like you."

Kip glanced to Hugh for confirmation.

"Army," Hugh corrected.

"That's why he looks so frightening."

"Bea." Kip scowled at her.

Hugh had been called worse and wasn't sure if he was flattered or insulted that the brother thought he had to stand up for him.

"I only mean he's very big and serious. He came to the house when he arrived and insisted on speaking with Papa. Papa said he didn't look the type to be messed with. You've missed so much! It was all very dramatic. Oscar, the man who has been leasing this bakehouse for ages, and whom we all trusted—you know how hard it is to find a baker you can trust. Well, he was struck by a carriage! He broke his leg and it was very gruesome. There were boys who were helping Alice. You saw her with the baby. She was increasing and the boys were useless. Bread sellers were coming from all over like flies to a carcass, bringing the most stale, awful stuff."

Hugh had learned that Lady Beatrix Marchington was like a clock wound too tight. You could only listen to the rapid ticking while waiting for her inner coil to spin itself loose.

His own sense of time was firmly on the batch in the oven. He would excuse himself when he had to.

"Papa didn't want to turn out a cripple and his wife with their new baby, but what was he to do? The village needs bread! He was looking for a baker to take over when Hugh turned up. From *Waterloo*. Except you were somewhere else before."

"Vienna," Hugh supplied.

She tucked her chin. "No, it was Paris."

"I think he knows where he was, Bea," Kip said.

"In any case, he came straight to the house and said he would take over the bakehouse until Oscar heals, but Papa thought he looked like a ruffian."

Hugh was aware of Kip searching his expression for signs he was taking offense. Mostly he was just fucking tired of it, but he was well-practiced at hiding such things.

He was *very* aware of Kip's lean build and clean-shaven jaw. His well-tailored breeches showed off his thighs—meaty and firm, as if he spent a lot of time on horseback. The white lace cuffs poking from the sleeves of his coat put a knot of apprehension in Hugh's gut, though. He used to love the feel of that against his skin.

He hid all of that, keeping his polite attention firmly on the babbling Lady Beatrix.

"Hugh said he would prove his worth and went to the kitchen, where he made the most scrumptious crescent rolls. Mama insisted he teach Cook. That's what we had this morning, but she hasn't got it right. Hugh's are much better."

"Oh? I should like to try one," Kip said, forcing Hugh to look at him.

That's when Hugh saw the glints of apology in his golden-brown gaze. It caused a punch of affinity under his rib cage.

Hugh firmly ignored it and said blandly, "I'll have Alice set aside a batch in the morning. They go quickly."

"I'll be here early, then," Kip promised.

The knot in Hugh's belly twisted, but in a way that wasn't entirely unwelcome. Fuck. Being used by another dandy was the last thing he needed, but it was also something he *really* needed.

"Oh!" Alice burst in with a flustered *swish* of her gown. "I apologize for making you wait, Lady Beatrix. I hope we haven't got flour on your gown. This is why I said I would fetch Hugh myself. Please let me bring you back to the shop where it's cooler."

"But it's Hugh I came to see. I have very exciting news." She paused for dramatic effect, hands clasped. "I have decided to let you bake my wedding cake!"

Fuck. Me.

"That *is* an honor," Alice rushed to say, not meeting his eyes.

She didn't have to. They were both thinking the same thing. What had they done to deserve the shit that kept befalling them?

It wasn't shit, though. It was a feather in his cap from a patron who would, God willing, move away after her marriage to antagonize innocent bakers elsewhere.

"I look forward to it, Lady Beatrix," Hugh made himself say in his most conciliatory tone, which probably still sounded like he was telling her to shove it, but he was what he was. "If you could have Alice write down all the details, size and ingredients and such, I'll work up a price for your approval next time you come in."

"I'll show you some recipes we've done in the past," Alice promised, holding the door to escort them out. "We can tailor any of them to your satisfaction."

Hugh turned away to check the rolls, releasing a beleaguered "Christ Almighty" under his breath when the door shut.

"Not to your liking?"

"Fuck." Hugh snapped around. "I thought you went out with the ladies."

Kip's brows went up as if to say, *Not ever.*

Right. The knot in Hugh's belly clenched again. Some other force in him wanted to reach out to grip the man and pull him in. He wanted that man. Kip was pure temptation, but promised hellfire.

Hugh looked to the shelves of bowls and sieves, scrapers and pans so he wouldn't notice Kip was immaculate and shiny-jawed and had the sort of lips that gave him wet dreams because he also had that air. Kip had purchased his way up to colonel, for Christ's sake. Or his father had, which was worse.

But Hugh didn't want to lose the cake order over his lack of patience with his betters. "Rolls aren't browning. I need more wood. Was there something else I could get you?"

Kip was studying him with interest. Possibly invitation. "You fought in Waterloo?"

"I slept on sacks of flour with a knife in my hand."

"Ah. And Vienna?"

"It's a long story."

"My sister will be here for hours."

Jesus Fucking Quality. How bored was this prick?

"And if I have to listen to her debate currants over candied lemon zest one more time, I'll spoon my brains out my ears," Kip drawled.

"I use currants and lemon zest along with orange. Would you like to hear why?"

"I do not." Kip's mouth twitched. His shoulders relaxed as he leaned on his boot heels, arms crossed, enjoying the fact that Hugh was teasing him. His eyelids drooped as his gaze went over Hugh's chest like splayed hands. He gave up on subtle, going for suggestive. "Would you like me to watch your sweet rolls while you get the wood you need?"

"I do not," Hugh repeated Kip's words, but more gruffly, dispensing with what levity he'd allowed to creep in.

Hugh was always serious when it came to his baking. He was supporting his sister until her husband could do it himself and couldn't afford missteps. He'd almost forgotten what a mistake men like Kip were. They were distracting and had the power to make him feel important when he would never be as important as they were.

"No one is allowed near the ovens but my sister. She knows how to stay out of my way."

"I see." Kip cooled so fast he should have cracked. "Good day, then."

Ah, hell. Hugh felt as though he'd stepped on the tail of a puppy. And possibly lost the cake that might give Alice and Oscar future referrals.

But it was probably for the best, so he didn't call him back to apologize.

• • •

"Excuse me, Lord Byron, but what are you doing down there?" Bea's voice came from an upper floor.

Kip lifted his gaze from the notebook balanced on his knee to see his sister half hanging out her bedroom window, still in her nightcap.

"I'm attempting to capture the scent of morning dew with my pen." He hadn't been able to sleep and thought it better to smell the roses than sift through the flour of one-sided lust.

"You're supposed to be capturing the scent of crescent rolls. You said you would fetch us a batch. They're much better than Cook's. Don't tell her I said that."

"You're shouting like a harridan. Every servant in the house can hear you." He dropped his attention back to his line about bees in coats of lifted gold.

"Kip! I am a bride who is soon to be married. I must have my crescent rolls!" She withdrew from the window, then poked her head out again. "Mama says get two dozen."

Fuck.

He closed the bottle of ink and left it on the bench but tucked his notebook into his pocket. His brothers had always thought reading aloud his heartfelt musings was the height of entertainment, the pricks. Bea wasn't much better. She'd embarrassed him yesterday, treating Hugh with such oblivious lack of respect.

The walk into the village wasn't far, but Kip drew it out, taking the longer path through the woods so he could brood as fiercely as all the best poets over his broken heart.

Which wasn't broken, precisely. It was slightly scuffed by a glancing blow of unrequited attraction. Hugh's thick shoulders and barrel chest and rugged jaw belonged on a pugilist, but he'd come off sounding very soft at heart, saving his sister in her hour of need.

Kip was an incurable romantic, so susceptible to heroic tales, his gloomy mood slipped away as he began to fantasize that Hugh's brawny arms were crushing him while his mouth was smothered by Hugh's full, wide lips. He probably had a massive cock, but Kip imagined a gentleness in his heavy hand as he cupped Kip's cheek while lovingly fucking his face.

Bollocks. He had to make a sharp turn down the track that wound behind the front street so he wouldn't walk into the shop with a raging erection.

Which was how he came upon Hugh outside a shed in a fenced garden. He stood with a boy of twelve or thirteen. The lad had a sack of flour in his arms like a sheep that was on its way to shearing. Hugh held one corner, keeping the boy from taking it inside, though the lad clearly wanted to turn and carry his heavy load into the bakehouse.

"Have you got it?"

"*Yes.*"

"Are you sure? Because if you drop it and it breaks, I'll grind *you* into flour."

"I *know.* You do this to me *every morning.*"

"To build your strength. My pa did it to me and I could swat you into next week, couldn't I? Say 'thank you' and mind the backchat."

"Fuck's sake," the kid groaned, then stiffened as Kip's snort alerted them to his nose peering over the fence.

Hugh might have grimaced when he recognized him. Or

brightened. Whatever it was, it caused a skip in Kip's chest, but the moment was gone before Kip could interpret it.

Hugh released his hold on the sack. "Tell Alice to box a dozen of the crescent rolls for the big house. And none of that language around her."

"I know."

Kip held up two gloved fingers.

"Two dozen," Hugh corrected as the boy hurried away.

Hugh moved to unlock and open the gate. "Mostly only have peddlers back here. They're trying to steal as often as trying to sell."

"Are you still sleeping on the flour to keep it secure?" It was a poor attempt at wit and Kip was sorry the minute he said it because Hugh nodded at the shed to indicate it was, indeed, where he slept.

"I have a bed, though."

Show me, Kip wanted to say. He couldn't help it. Gruff as Hugh had sounded with the boy, his affection had been obvious. There was tenderness beneath his toughness. Kip wanted to see it. Find it. *Feel* it.

He glimpsed it again as he took in Hugh's dark brown eyes and spiky lashes and thick brows. There was a far-off flame there. Cautious consideration. Possibility.

It caused a yank on the subsiding thickness in Kip's trousers.

Hugh quickly turned away to the water pump, leaving Kip's breath punched out of him, wanting that moment back.

"I didn't mean to be rude yesterday," Hugh rumbled. "I've seen bad burns. Fires. Makes me an arse about who's near the ovens."

Kip wanted to say it didn't matter, even though a nameless, stinging hurt inside him eased on learning the rebuff hadn't been personal. Hugh had been watching out for him, which filled Kip with a soft glow.

Whatever he might have said in response dried up as Hugh

began working the pump. He thrust his bared forearms beneath the flow, gave them a scrub, then splashed his face and neck, shuddering at the cold. His shirt became drenched and his lifetime of moving sacks of flour was evident in the way the rough cotton clung to the flex of his thick muscles.

While Kip stood there, Hugh commenced filling wooden buckets with water, glancing at him in a silent question as to why he was hovering.

I'm a poet, Kip wanted to say. *I'm studying the human condition and the beauty of the common man.* But Hugh wasn't common. Not in the least. And Kip really wanted to be noticed by him while maintaining a right to watch him.

"Are you not going to change into a dry shirt?" *Please let me watch.*

"It'll dry in the heat of the bakehouse."

"Right." Kip wasn't usually at a loss for conversation. He almost brought up the militia, but it was hardly common ground. It had been full of landowner sons like himself. They'd been guaranteed they wouldn't see active service while Hugh had shadows in his eyes that suggested he'd seen terrible things.

"I'm still curious how you went to Vienna? Was it with the army?" He couldn't help it. He wanted to know everything about him.

Hugh straightened and started to say something, glanced back to the bakehouse and the door to the shop. When his attention came back to Kip, he gave him a measuring once-over, tongue set against his bottom lip, forcing it against his teeth.

Kip's cock wept. *Yes, fucking please.*

"If you're really interested—" Hugh left the smallest pause there. "I finish around six. I'm asleep by eight. Early start."

His steady gaze and confident, no-nonsense tone reverberated behind Kip's breastbone.

"I'm interested," Kip assured him.

Hugh seemed skeptical, but his gaze flicked downward and

came back edged with cynical amusement.

"Use the path at the side to get to the front of the shop so you don't have to come through the bakehouse. When you're ready. The cold water helps," he added as he tipped a nonexistent cap and disappeared.

Kip looked down at the pole tenting his trousers and swore.

CHAPTER TWO

No matter how he tortured the numbers, Hugh couldn't find a way to take a profit for himself that wouldn't cause the shop to suffer. What little he'd had when he came home from the continent had gone to keep Alice and Oscar from debtor's prison.

Since then, he'd had bed, meals, and the satisfaction of knowing he wasn't a shite brother and uncle. Oscar had been feverish with infection when Hugh arrived, but he'd since recovered enough he was coming into the bakehouse for short periods, working as much as his stamina allowed.

They got on well enough. Oscar had apprenticed under Hugh's father, which was how Alice had met and married him. Hugh was teaching Oscar all he'd learned in Vienna. Once Oscar was fully healed, Hugh would move on. It was Oscar's shop and Hugh wasn't of a mind to be a journeyman beneath him.

He wouldn't have a farthing to get himself started in his own bakehouse, though.

A quiet rattle at the gate had Hugh perking up like a wolfhound. He'd left it unlocked and his usual leap of aggression was tempered by a branding iron of hot desire pressing right into his cock.

Was it him? Had he come? Hugh hadn't let himself believe he would, still convinced it was a bad idea, but he slipped out of the shed to see Kip Marchington letting himself in with that annoying air nobility possessed, the one that was confident they belonged anywhere.

When he saw Hugh, and smiled as though he was genuinely happy to see him, fuck if Hugh didn't feel flowers bloom inside his chest.

Kip spared a glance upward to the small apartment where

Alice and Oscar made their home above the shop, but they'd already pulled the shade on the single window.

Hugh had more concern about Kip's sister's reaction to their trysting than his own. The back lane was private so, unless Kip had announced where he was going, no one would know. Still, Hugh wordlessly held open the door to the shed so they were quickly out of sight.

The shed's musty smell of spilled grains and old flour didn't seem to give Kip pause. He entered the small room where Hugh slept and looked around with more interest, taking note of the pulled curtain on the small window and the candle glowing on the tiny table next to the meat pie Hugh hadn't finished eating yet.

"I expected something spare and military, less cozy." He nodded at the mismatched colored squares of wool in the quilt on the bed.

"My sister." Hugh shrugged. Alice had insisted on making it as homey as she could, but it was very small. They were face-to-face unless Kip chose to take the single chair.

He didn't. He stood right in front of Hugh, head tilted back to meet his gaze. He licked his lips, seeming nervous. "So. Vienna."

"Is that what you really came here for?"

A brief hesitation, then a quiet, "No."

"Good. Come here, then."

• • •

His touch was everything Kip had dreamed it would be. Hugh hooked his hand behind Kip's neck, drawing him in, not rough, but firm. His other hand landed on his hip, guiding their bodies into a crash while his mouth landed upon Kip's lips with purpose.

Kip groaned, not intending to be so unconstrained, but any composure he aspired to was gone. His own hand found the back of Hugh's thick neck. He wrapped his free hand behind his back and used his own strength to pull himself into the layers of ropey muscle that seemed to envelop him.

He wanted closer to Hugh's kiss. The brawny man seemed intent on consuming him and Kip was more than happy to be his meal. He welcomed the lick of his tongue and sucked it, grinding his stiff cock into the ridge of Hugh's.

Urgency gripped him. Kip didn't know if they were in a hurry, but his desperation was more than that. He wondered if it had been as long for Hugh as it had been for him. He also wondered if Hugh shared his frantic, *It has to be you. It has to be now.*

This craving had hit him so hard and fast yesterday, refusing to leave his mind, it was unnerving.

But the pace of Hugh's hand as he swept it across his back and down to his ass was calm and deliberate, seeming to ask if this was really what he wanted.

Kip's cock was leaking inside his breeches. His answer was a firm, fucking, *Yes.*

"What do you like?" Kip asked, drawing back enough to work his hand between them and squeeze the girth of Hugh's cock through his trousers.

Hugh grunted and said, "That."

His strong hands were kneading Kip's ass, making him all the more frenzied.

He worked Hugh's brace off one shoulder and stuck his hand down his trousers to grasp Hugh's naked girth, damp silken heat over powerful strength.

Hugh's chest swelled as he dragged in a breath.

The tip of his cock was wet and grew wetter when Kip lightly crushed it in his fist. He watched Hugh's nostrils flare. His mouth trembled.

"Do you want me to suck you off?" Kip wanted to taste him. So much.

"If you want to." He almost sounded dispassionate, but his slitted eyes glowed and the way his hands clenched into Kip's cheeks told him he liked the sound of that. A lot.

"I want to do what you want." He was shaking with it. "Do you want me to fuck you?"

"If you want." This time Hugh's voice wasn't quite steady. His cock flexed in Kip's grip.

Kip laughed jaggedly. "If you want to do what I want, then I want you to fuck me."

"Yes. That." Hugh's broken voice was like the roar of a lion as it leaped for a kill. He kissed Kip again. Hard and deep. Like he wanted to own him.

It was so exciting and encompassing, Kip didn't realize he was being undressed until the chill of the air filtered up his back from his untucked shirt. His coat and waistcoat were open, his lips wet and stinging, his knees unhinged.

"Should you lock the door?" Kip managed to ask.

"I locked the outer one when we came in. Is that why you're shaking?" He lifted his head to look at him with concern. "We're fine here. Completely safe."

"I just really want this."

"Me, too." Hugh's mouth moved onto Kip's throat. He opened his teeth against the point where his neck met his shoulder, making Kip shudder.

"Hugh," he protested. Kip was going to come if he kept that up.

"I won't mark you. I just wanted to see if you like a bit of rough."

Did he ever. They kissed once more, then began pulling at their clothes in earnest.

Hugh was magnificent. Kip had known he would be. He wanted to take bites out of his chest and rub his face on that line of hair down his hard stomach and—

He dropped to his knees, unable to resist tasting that spear of a cock. It was thick and red with an engorged vein on the underside that drew a line from his heavy balls to his dark, bulbous tip.

Kip sucked him in like a scoop of ice cream on a hot summer's day, loving the way Hugh groaned, as if Kip had pulled him from a blizzard into the sun. Kip cupped his sack and fingered his behind, caressing and drawing forth another groan. Another shudder. More of his salty taste in his mouth.

When Hugh set the weight of his hand on his hair, he didn't pull or force. He combed his fingers through the strands restlessly. As though he couldn't get enough of how soft his hair was while ever so slightly coaxing him to bob and take more.

Kip did, wanting all of him. He opened his throat and angled to take all of his fat cock, until his lips were tickled by Hugh's wiry hairs and Kip's nose grazed his belly.

Hugh was looking down at him with the intensity of light through a magnifying glass, burning the memory into Kip's mind. Hugh caressed his brow, the side of his mouth where his lips were clinging to the root of his shaft.

"You're incredible," he said in a voice graveled by fraying control. "But get on the bed or I'm going to spill in your mouth."

Yes, Kip thought, sucking hard. But Hugh lost some of his gentleness as he fisted his hand in Kip's hair and carefully withdrew from his mouth with a wet *pop*.

Kip started to put his elbows on the mattress, not sure how Hugh wanted him, then he remembered the tin in his coat pocket.

"I brought this." He showed him the ointment. "It was popular in the militia."

Hugh sat on the foot of the bed and opened it, sniffing warily at the greasy balm. It had an herbal scent that wasn't floral but held an underlying sweetness.

"It doesn't prevent clap," Kip warned.

"I don't have clap. Do you have clap?"

"I barely get cock."

Hugh snorted and jerked his head. "Lie back."

"On my back?"

"Yeah." Hugh shifted so he was still on the foot of the bed, but with his legs off the side so he half faced him as Kip settled his head on the pillow.

"Will this bed hold us?"

"I made it myself with the possibility of an occasion like this in mind." He set the cool tin on Kip's quivering belly and smoothed his rough palms over Kip's thighs, pushing one of Kip's knees up to his chest to expose him right down to his arsehole.

Kip had only ever bent over for this. He hadn't realized what a nerve-rackingly intimate experience it was to watch another man look at him like this, as though he liked what he saw. As though he wanted him on the most carnal level, yet his touch gentled into a caress that made Kip feel almost cherished.

Kip clenched his fist in the blankets, paralyzed with lust, yet terrified at how much emotion Hugh was stirring in him.

Abruptly Hugh shifted. His head went down and the wet rasp of his tongue worked against Kip's arsehole.

Fire licked through him, making his cock leap against his shaking belly. Kip made a noise so helpless, Hugh lifted his head.

"No?"

"Yes," Kip said in a voice still strangled with want, mind so melted he could hardly speak. "It feels really good."

"I know. That's why I did it." His hard mouth was skewed off-center with a knowing grin. "The rosewater scent is a nice touch. Thanks."

He went back to eating his ass and Kip had to clench his fist around his cock to keep from losing control. As it was, his stomach was smeared with leaked fluid and his balls were so swollen, they felt as though they would burst.

The heat of Hugh's mouth enveloped his sack, sending a burn through Kip's entire body. Then cool air doused him as his wet balls were released. His cock was given the same treatment and the contrast in sensations nearly undid him.

"Fuck me," Kip said, one arm thrown over his eyes. He didn't know if it was a plea for the action or for deliverance from this agony of pleasure being visited upon him.

"I will," Hugh promised.

The weight of the tin left his stomach and Kip uncovered his eyes in time to watch Hugh take a gob on his finger. He began rubbing it against the ring of Kip's arse. Hugh pushed a finger into him and lightly explored.

Kip bit the back of his wrist and used his free hand to grip Hugh's thigh. Hugh shifted so Kip could take hold of his cock. Kip's breath was wheezing. Hugh's cheeks were dark, his face carved with intense focus.

When he began to work a second finger into him, Kip gave Hugh's cock an insistent pull. "Fuck me. I'm dying."

Hugh moved with surprising agility for such a huge man, suddenly over him, knees splayed under Kip's thighs to bracket his hips. He bent Kip's knees up and out, then watched as he lined up and leaned in to push past Kip's instinctive tension.

Kip could have used a little more massage, because the ache was intense as Hugh got his thick head into him, but they both groaned with delight. Kip reach up to set his palm flat on the wall over his head to give Hugh leverage to plow into him with a steady thrust.

Then he was full. Aching and pinned and slipping into that space where he was so aroused, he balanced on a razor's edge, unsure if he was coming or about to.

Hugh planted a hand near his shoulder and hovered over him as he offered a shallow thrust. "Good?"

Kip could only make another garbled noise of agonized ecstasy.

Hugh's growl was somewhere between satisfaction and agreement. He dropped a single kiss on his lips then began to fuck him proper.

Kip was pretty sure he would die, taking the firm crash of Hugh's hips and splendid cock into his ass, but what a way to go. His cock was leaking, his body one golden ball of joy, his arse a pinpoint of intense sensation that left him unable to see or hear and incapable of thought. He didn't realize he'd reached to jerk his own cock until Hugh brushed his hand away.

"I'll do that when we're both ready." He was still braced on one hand by Kip's shoulder. The other went back to Kip's knee, holding him open, holding him steady for his quickening pace. His skin was dark with lust and sheened with sweat.

"Do it harder. Hard as you want." He wanted *all* of him.

Hugh's pace quickened and the bed creaked as he held nothing back.

He was beautiful. So powerful and exciting, Kip didn't need a hand on his cock at all. Suddenly there was a shot of lightning down his spine and a burst of scorching heat through his cock. He was coming in such hard pulses, his spurt hit his shoulder.

Hugh tipped back his head so the tendons in his neck stood out. His grip on Kip's knee tightened and, with a final slam of his cock deep into his ass, he released a shout of abject pleasure and bathed Kip's insides with heat.

•••

I *want to do what you want.*

Hugh still didn't know what to think of that. Which wasn't to say he allowed himself to be bullied in the bedroom, but he had spent too long tangled up with a man who had had too much control over his life. What he had wanted had never mattered.

Hugh dropped the cloth he'd used to wash his cock and wet a clean one, taking it to the bed where Kip was trying not to shift too much while he worked a handkerchief from the pocket of the waistcoat on the floor.

Hugh gave his chest a swipe and handed off the cloth to let him finish tidying up.

"Thank you," Kip said.

"My pleasure." He began pulling on the clean clothes he'd

put on after washing up before dinner.

"Oh." Kip sat up and his lazy satisfaction turned to a more pointed search for his clothes.

"Take your time," Hugh said, shifting to take the chair so he was out of the way but could still watch Kip. He rather liked the look of him befuddled and too weak to move very fast. Hugh was in a stupor himself, more lighthearted and satisfied than he'd been in years. "I sleep in my clothes in case I have to get up to brain an intruder."

"Ah. I'll be sure you expect me before I turn up next, then." Kip paused and rolled his lips together. "That is, if I'm invited?"

Hugh didn't give himself time to think on it. He should. Kip was shaping up to be all kinds of sweet trouble, but he said, "It's a quiet village. A man needs his amusements. I don't mind being yours so long as you respect my need for sleep. I'm up before the birds."

Kip paused again, sending Hugh a sharp look.

Hugh quirked a brow. Did he think Hugh didn't know that's exactly what he was for a man in Kip's position?

Kip didn't get a chance to say anything. Something dropped out of the coat he was holding. It landed with a soft *thump* at Hugh's feet.

They both reached for the leather bound notebook. Hugh got it first and heard Kip's inhale of alarm before Hugh gave it up to him.

"State secrets?" Hugh was trying not to be intrigued by him. This was a temporary arrangement and Kip would move on, but his blush had Hugh wanting to know more about him. All his secrets.

"I write poetry," Kip admitted so defensively, Hugh felt a pang behind his heart, not that he knew any beyond the rosy rhymes his sister pattered at the baby.

Kip struggled to keep a strong grip on his notebook while trying to put on his coat.

Hugh rose to hold the coat, partly for the excuse to touch him. "Your valet is going to think you're seeing a wig powderer behind his back." He brushed away the traces of flour that coated every surface and crevice of Hugh's life.

"I don't have a valet. Or wear wigs. Or pay for powder. Do you know what the taxes are on that?"

"Let me check with Her Grace, Lady Norton. I'm sure she'll know."

"I have the sense you're a bit of a snob, Hugh."

Hugh stopped buttoning Kip's coat and pushed his hands into his pockets. He did not drop his gaze from staring straight into a gentleman's eyes, but his heart wanted to shrivel.

"Do you take issue with the fact I was born into a family of rank?" Kip demanded.

"On the contrary, Sir Kip. It's like the ovens. You get burned badly enough, you learn to be very careful around them." Hugh met his gaze, letting that settle between them.

Kip's brow lowered in a glower, but his mouth softened with compassion.

Which was so disturbing, Hugh was forced to look away to hide how it affected him.

"I don't think of you as an amusement," Kip said quietly. "I want to know you."

Hugh bit back a disparaging, *To what end?* But he only said, "It will have to wait. I'm barely standing upright, thanks to you. I have to lock the gate behind you. I'll kiss you here?"

Kip gave a small nod and they shared a delicious kiss that Hugh was still thinking about when he fell asleep a few minutes later.

CHAPTER THREE

"I've been thinking of you," Hugh said, snatching Kip from behind a few nights later.

He was already naked. They had a routine now, making no ceremony of undressing the second they were inside his room so they could fuck like feral cats as fast and hard as possible. Yesterday, Hugh had bent him over this chair.

Kip threw his shirt onto the back of it and grasped at the arms banding him. Hugh's impatience was everything he wanted. Kip had been the amusement that Hugh feared he was. He didn't want that for either of them. He wanted to be thought about. He wanted to be the chest and stomach Hugh couldn't wait to roam his strong hand across.

He savored the way Hugh plastered him closer, trapping his trousers up so Hugh's ready cock nestled against Kip's ass through the wool. He sucked on Kip's earlobe and Kip melted.

"I've been thinking of you, too." He'd written a poem about him. It was very ambiguous and most would interpret it as blossoming love for a woman trothed to another, but it had come from the deepest part of Kip's heart.

Was it foolish to believe they had the seeds of a future together?

"What have you been thinking?" Hugh's hand went down to his trousers, unbuttoning Kip's fall to expose him.

Kip's thoughts splintered. He gave a muted shrug so Hugh would ease his hold enough so Kip could turn around.

He savored that, too. The way Hugh playfully pinned and had the strength to force, but always released him at the first hint of a nudge. Their ability to communicate silently was as special as the rest.

Before he could tell him what he'd been thinking, Hugh licked his palm and gathered both their cocks in his loose, damp grip, gently bumping their engorged, weeping heads against one another's.

"Fuck," Kip said dumbly, bracing a hand on Hugh's shoulder and watching.

Hugh's rough thumb grazed across the eyes and worked the slippery fluid all over so they were both soon giving slow, muted pumps into his hand.

Kip heard noises, knew distantly they were emerging from his own throat, but all he was really aware of was how screamingly erotic this was.

"I've been thinking of the way you swallowed my cock the other day," Hugh said in a low, jagged rumble while the slide of his cock hit perfectly against the sensitive notch in the arrowed head of Kip's. "All I think about is coming down your throat. Would you want that?"

The quivering in Kip's balls erupted against his will. He was suddenly coming all over both of them, wordless and racked by pleasure.

Hugh could have laughed—Kip expected him to—but instead he crushed Kip close. Kissed him hard. He ran his hands all over his shivering, shuddering body while the final throbs and pulses prompted Kip to give a few thrusts of his cock into the slick puddle sealing their bellies.

When his orgasm subsided, Hugh was stroking his hair and kissing his neck, making Kip feel safe and treasured and hot behind the eyes.

Then Hugh's mouth brushed his ear. "Is that a yes?"

They both broke into laughter and stepped apart. Hugh grabbed a towel and ran it between them.

Then Kip sank to his knees. "Fuck, yes. Let me have it."

• • •

Kip felled him like a tree.

Hugh was so wrecked, he couldn't remember how he'd wound up on his bed, but he strained to commit to memory everything Kip had just done to him. The lick of his tongue around and behind his bollocks, every noise he'd made that told Hugh he was enjoying it as much as he was, the way he'd taken his time as though Hugh was something he wanted to savor. The drool that had coated his fist as he twisted and sucked and worked his shaft, then his steadying grip on Hugh's hips as he bobbed his head.

Hugh hadn't been able to help himself. He'd started meeting him with thrusts of his hips, watching his cock disappear into Kip's mouth, his tongue slithering around his head on each withdrawal. The urgent way he'd sucked to keep him in.

Kip had looked up at him like he was the happiest man alive. Hugh was.

He heard the rustle of clothing and dragged his eyes open. "Where are you going?" He held out his arm to invite Kip onto the bed with him.

Kip gave a small chuckle, looking shy as he settled atop him. "You don't usually ask me to stay after."

"I don't usually break my arrow five minutes after you get here. You, either," he teased.

They pressed their smiles into a kiss that turned into another and another, long and wet and lingering, tongues brushing. As they did, they shifted so Kip was aligned along Hugh's side. Hugh couldn't recall the last time he'd simply held a man. It felt nice. Relaxing.

"I may not be able to come for the next few nights," Kip said as he settled his head on Hugh's shoulder.

And so it starts, Hugh thought.

He must have made a noise or stiffened, because Kip lifted his head. "What? I have family obligations."

"Of course."

"Do you get any days off? I keep thinking it would be nice to walk along the river—"

Hugh did snort openly at that.

"What?" Kip narrowed his eyes. "Not even Sundays after church?"

"I don't go to church. I mind the stews and joints that the villagers put in our oven so they'll have something to serve their families after *they've* been to church."

"I hate when you take that tone." Kip sat up and reached for his shirt. "If I don't understand your life, it's because you refuse to tell me about it. I ask, in case you haven't noticed. I come to you on the schedule you set, but I'm the villain for having obligations? I'm paying the price for the oven that burned you in the past, aren't I?"

Hugh wavered, feeling like a shit. He told himself to let this be the end of it, quick and neat, but he knew deep down he wasn't ready for this to be over. He caught his fist in the finely woven linen of Kip's shirt, keeping him sitting on the edge of the bed beside him.

"You are," he agreed. "And that's not right of me."

Kip let his hands settle in his lap. "Was this oven in Vienna?"

"He took me to Vienna." Hugh moved his hand to Kip's thigh, giving a light squeeze, because those thighs of his were as tasty and irresistible as drumsticks. "I was meant to take over my father's bakehouse, but I was persuaded to accompany him to the continent. He was an officer with charge of the commissariat."

"Oh," Kip said with grave knowledge. "You were in front of every battle."

"Into villages to arrange for rations, yes. They barely had enough for themselves and didn't want to sell what they had. They feared and resented us. It wasn't pleasant."

Kip's warm hand settled on his chest, and Hugh used his free one to play with Kip's fingers, skipping the midnight attacks and other hellish memories as he continued.

"I would have left. I wasn't enlisted, but I had no wages, no means to come home. Nothing to come home *to*. He kept promising me there would be compensation, that I would be able to have my own bakehouse one day, but that never came about."

"Who was he?"

"The son of a duke. Very well off. He liked that I was reliant on him, though."

"For this." Kip's thumb traced a line down Hugh's middle to his navel.

"For this and getting the work done. He didn't know how to settle a fair price with a butcher or miller. He had a silver-tongue in other ways, though." Hugh curled his lip at the double meaning in that. "Talked his way into the Foreign Secretary's entourage."

"You went to Vienna as part of the congress? I've heard it was a spectacle and a half."

Hugh's contempt came out as a choke. "You have never seen such excessive waste on the select few while the peasants were gnawing the meat off their own limbs."

"And you?"

He grimaced. "I was given the honor of ensuring the bread for the English wasn't tampered with by baking it under the eye of a master baker in the baron's employ. Franz. He would have sooner killed me in my sleep, but our delegation had a taste for the Viennese delicacies. I was ordered to learn how to make them and Franz was ordered to teach me. He refused to translate, hid ingredients from me. Worked too fast for me to grasp it, then berated me for my failures. I was so homesick."

"Hugh." Kip's tone was so filled with pity, Hugh could hardly stand it, but he'd been drowning in self-pity at the time and would have welcomed a compassionate ear.

"I felt like the biggest fool alive," he admitted, voice as low as he'd been then. "I'd allowed myself to be talked into giving up a good living. I was beholden to men who cared nothing about my well-being. I had no means to get home. Nothing to come home *to*."

"And your lover?"

"Was fucking Franz on the side." His jagged laugh held no humor, but there'd been a part of him that was relieved to learn it, even though it had made everything that much worse. "It was his idea I learn to make sugar twists and strudel so he could enjoy them once we left Vienna. Then word came that Napoleon had escaped Elba. We were ordered to Waterloo, and when that was over, I had to beg him to arrange my passage home. He was reluctant, afraid I wanted to maintain our association here. His family expected him to marry, so he had been prepared to leave me in the Netherlands."

"Fuck, Hugh."

He nodded. "It was lowering. I got him to put me on the ship and found a silver coat button rolled into a corner while we were out. I felt like the worst thief, keeping it, but it was all I had. I sold it when we docked, bought a coach ticket here, and the rest went to settling Alice's debts."

"I'm so sorry, Hugh. But listen, if wanting to believe the best in people makes you a fool, then you are looking at the biggest fool alive."

Hugh gave a dry chuckle, but he was touched Kip had listened. He'd spent a lot of time blaming himself for all that had happened, but maybe the truth of it was he'd tangled with a manipulative prick and not all gentlemen made such a mockery of the title.

"What's his name? I'll challenge him to a duel," Kip said.

That did make him laugh, because, softhearted as Kip was, "You could defeat him with my bread spade. He was fucking useless." He moved his hand to Kip's side. "Come here," he said gruffly.

Kip leaned down and they shared a few warm kisses that closed old wounds and made Hugh sigh with contentment.

Kip stroked his cheek when he lifted away. "I'd stay longer, but you need your beauty sleep."

"Such a mouth you've got on you."

"You approve of this mouth. I know you do." Kip rose to finish dressing, but the mouth in question curled coyly at the corners.

"I very much do." Hugh made himself rise and begin dragging on his clothes. "And I want you to enjoy your time with your family. I shouldn't have been an arse about it."

"I won't," Kip said flatly. "My brothers are arrogant pricks. The eldest stands to inherit everything, so he insists we all kiss his feet. The middle was a captain in the navy and spent more time smuggling than protecting our shores. Bea is the best of the lot, I'm afraid, and I can only imagine what you think of her."

"Only that she's second best." He touched Kip's chin to lift his mouth for a kiss. "The best is right here."

"Flatterer," Kip accused. "But I'll take it."

● ● ●

Kip was the happiest he'd ever been in his life.

His entire day revolved around awaiting the end of his mother's afternoon tea party in the garden, when he could embark on his "constitutional." Sometimes Bea tried to invite herself along, but he claimed it as his composing time and she would petulantly pick up her embroidery.

He would ramble his way to the back alley behind the bakehouse and get himself royally fucked. Sometimes Hugh was urgent, particularly if they hadn't seen each other for a few days. Then Kip could count on coming away sore, but the furthest thing from sorry. He loved when Hugh acted as though he couldn't survive without him.

Other times, Hugh was more tender. Yesterday, Kip had lain upon him, both of them naked and kissing and fondling. Kip had lazily rocked his toes between Hugh's spread feet. The motion had stimulated their cocks in the press of their bodies, the fluid they both leaked providing lubrication so the sensation was heavenly.

When Kip had made a helpless noise in his throat, unable to hold back any longer, Hugh had said, "Don't stop. I'm almost there."

They'd come in unison. It had been both quiet and powerful, messy as hell and damned near reverent.

"Kip," his father said, dragging him out of that delectably filthy memory and reminding him he still had to get through this interminable tea before he knew ecstasy again.

"Yes?"

"What of politics?"

"What of it?"

"How have you never grown out of these daydreams?" his father barked with impatience. "I asked if you made connections while you were in the militia. Is there someone who might get you in with the diplomatic service?"

Oh, Christ, this again. His father wasn't wrong. Kip needed a living, but the way Hugh had felt so maltreated by the Foreign Secretary had Kip making a dismissive noise. Hugh wouldn't have anything to do with him if he went into something like that.

"You should get married," Bea said. "To an heiress. A sister of a duke."

"Because those grow in fields like daisies?" He didn't even like daisies. How had no one realized that?

"I thought you were going to be a barrister," his mother said. "And look after the property in Newcastle."

Kip's enthusiasm for becoming a barrister or going to Newcastle was about as strong as his passion for daisies.

"Ask your brother when he arrives," his father said. "He'll have some ideas where you could seek a position."

Kip had an idea of his own, one that was so new and shiny and delicate, it was fragile as a bath bubble. Hugh was an integral part of it, so he waited until he was with him to explore it further.

• • •

"What will you do when your brother-in-law is well enough to run the bakehouse by himself again?"

"Hmm?" Hugh lifted his head from where he was playing his tongue against the sharp bead of Kip's nipple.

They were sitting on the bed, half facing one another. His mind was firmly on the man he was trying to pleasure and Kip seemed to be enjoying it. His cock was appetizingly hard in Hugh's hand. Hugh was thinking of shifting off the side of the bed to kneel between Kip's open legs, but Kip had hold of his own cock and it felt too good to give up.

"Will you stay here and work with him? Or look for something else?"

"I don't know." He ran the edge of his finger up to the taut bit of flesh under the tip of Kip's cock, making Kip's breath stop. Kip clenched his fist harder around Hugh. Hugh smiled and buried his mouth in Kip's throat, licking up the side of his neck.

"Hugh. I want to know," he said, but his hand gave a restless pull on Hugh's cock.

Hugh thought he understood what Kip was really asking. He cupped his face and gave him a kiss of reassurance.

"I know you're only here until the wedding. The village will quiet once the nobs leave for the season. Oscar won't need me. I might be persuaded to look for a situation in London." He caressed Kip's cleanly-shaved cheek. "If that's where you'll be. And you want to keep seeing one another?"

"I do!" Kip's expression brightened so fully, it caused a kick of pleasure in Hugh's chest. Who knew he had the power to make a man that happy?

Really happy, Hugh realized as he kissed Kip and Kip threw his arms around him, squeezing tight. His weight pressed Hugh back onto the mattress and he wound up with Kip sprawled across him.

"Don't get too excited," he cautioned, though he was coming to care for Kip enough he would hate to disappoint him in any way. "There are a lot of men still coming back from the continent. They're all looking for work. I don't know how I'll fare."

"It's okay. I have the perfect plan." Kip was kissing across his chest in eager pecks. "We'll open a tea salon. Like a coffee house—"

"Those were closed for sedition." Hugh pressed his shoulders, forcing him to stop kissing him and look at him.

"This won't be political. It will be for literary clubs, but a public room. We'll invite men *and* women, then bring in poets and bards for recitations and readings. We'll serve tea and your lovely rolls…"

"Kip." Hugh rolled him away so he could climb from the bed.

Arousal was still simmering in him, especially as Kip looked up at him with the fog of lust and the brightness of excitement lingering beneath his confusion. "What's wrong? I have a little money from my aunt, enough to get us started. We'll find somewhere we can live above the way your sister lives here. Near Covent Garden, I think—"

"Kip," Hugh said again, hardening himself against the innocence in Kip's expression. This was too much like the way he'd been manipulated in the past. It was damned hard to think straight when he was stricken with lust and he resented that Kip had brought it up when they were naked. "I've told you what happened to me in the past."

"This is different."

"How?" Hugh demanded. "I'll be doing the work and you'll be collecting the return."

"I'm not *him*, Hugh. This will be a partnership. We'll benefit equally and we'll be *together*."

"And what happens when you start fucking someone else? Where do I go then? How do I get my money and start over?"

"You don't trust me at all, do you?" Kip said with stunned realization.

"No." He'd said it more as a weapon, to hurt him, than out

of truth. Because he was hurting. Because he had to get in front of the hurt that would be done.

Kip's eyes began to gleam. He rose to hurriedly dress.

And Hugh felt as though he'd taken a horse kick to the chest. His mouth kept opening, trying to take back what he'd said, but Kip spoke first. And made him feel worse.

"I've been hurt, too," he said with dignity as he closed the buttons on his coat. "I've been toyed with and treated like an amusement. Unlike you, I'm *not* happy to have been *yours*."

CHAPTER FOUR

Kip was in the untenable situation of having to spend time with people he didn't particularly like and watch them celebrate a type of happiness he despaired he would never have. Hell, the few times he saw his sister with her intended, he had to wonder if they had even a tenth of what he had had—what he had thought he had—with Hugh.

Now his eldest brother was engaged and his fiancée had joined them for the wedding. The house was swelling with extended family all brimming with, "When are you going to find yourself a wife?" and "What are you doing now you've been discharged from the militia?"

He kept telling himself he only needed to bear up until the wedding was over. Then he could stay with a friend in London and lick his wounds.

"Kip!" Bea called from the other side of the rose garden. She was with her groom, their eldest brother, and their future sister-in-law. "We're walking into the village to check when my cake will be ready and pick up some ribbon for the cutting knife."

Happy day. "Do you realize that if you leave him to it, instead of interrupting him, he has a better chance of having it done?"

"For God's sake, man," his brother called. "Read us some of this poetry that's more important than your sister's wedding cake."

Much as Kip had no desire to spend time with his brother, the excursion was a chance to see the man who had taken his heart and snapped it across his knee like kindling for his oven. Kip couldn't resist and closed his ink bottle. He left it on the bench, pocketed his notebook, and trailed after them as they took the short path onto the front street. They entered the bake shop a quarter hour later.

"Alice. I've come to check on my cake," Bea announced.

"Lady Beatrix. You have a merry party with you today." Alice was about to send one of the lads off to hawk yesterday's stale bread, but took the crate from him and said, "Go fetch Hugh. Stay to watch what's baking if he asks."

"Yes, mistress."

"My own husband has assisted by assembling all the ingredients," Alice said happily. "I must thank you for giving him such a sense of purpose, Lady Beatrix. He walked to the miller himself to purchase the cake flour and ensure its quality. Such good exercise for getting him back on his feet. Oh! And I've written out the recipe for your records." She moved to a back shelf to fetch a slip of paper. "I don't have a hand for calligraphy, I'm afraid."

"I do," Kip said, moving around his brother to take the slip of paper she offered. "I'll turn it into a keepsake."

"Thank you, Sir Christopher."

He was anticipating seeing Hugh, though. It made him distracted and he was feeling obvious for turning up here at all. He took the folded sheet and it promptly fluttered from his numb fingers.

"Oh, I'm so sorry—"

Kip waved off Alice and bent. Of course, that caused his damned notebook to tumble out of his pocket. He grabbed it as he straightened, but his brother snatched it out of his hand before he got it tucked away again.

"Hoo, hoo, hoo!"

"Albert," Kip warned through his teeth.

Bea laughed and clapped her hands. "Read some, read some!"

Kip closed his eyes in frustrated, blistering anger.

"'Be large or small, those weights upon thine heart...'" Albert said with melodramatic feeling. "'Be mine, whether thou be mine not ever, or only for a day, or one lost hour—'"

A creak of a floorboard and, "Hey!"

•••

Hugh didn't think, he only reacted to Kip's cringe of humiliation and the cruel way the other man was taunting him. He snapped the book from him and held it out to Kip without breaking his eye contact with the bully.

"Thank you," Kip murmured, taking it.

"I don't know who the hell you think you are," the man said, trying to straighten tall enough to look down his nose at Hugh's superior height. "But do you know who *I* am?"

A pompous fucking ass, not that Hugh said it.

"This is Hugh. He's making my cake," Lady Beatrix said, taking a few uncertain steps forward so her skirts were rocking in Hugh's periphery.

"Is he?" the other man asked in the sort of lofty challenge that tried to exert power over Hugh.

Hugh had had enough of that shit years ago. He didn't flinch, only asked with equal condescension, "I don't know. Am I?"

Because he didn't have to.

Alice gasped, but the bride's horrified rasp was louder.

"Yes! You most definitely *are*!" Lady Beatrix hurried up to them. "Don't you dare ruin my wedding because you want to act like a schoolboy." She batted the other man's arm, then stood in front of him to face Hugh, saying with contrition, "I only came to ask what time the footman should collect it?"

"It will be ready by eight," Hugh told her and flicked a final look at the other man that said, *If he behaves himself.*

"Excellent! And have you met my bridegroom, Barton?"

They exchanged nods and the bridegroom said a nervous, "We should let him get back to work."

"Yes, I suppose." Beatrix turned. "Oh, quit looking so constipated, Albert. Once you taste it you'll understand why we put up with Hugh being such a curmudgeon."

For Alice's sake, and Kip's, Hugh pretended he didn't hear it.

The party all shuffled toward the door.

Kip stayed where he was. When Hugh looked at him, he half expected to see a reprimand or alarm at Hugh challenging a man so far above him.

Instead, Kip wore a smile that seemed to glow with pride. In him.

Hugh swallowed the ache that had been sitting in his throat since they'd argued. He'd been an arse again and was sick with himself over it. Kip was better than that prick who'd tried to break him. Kip was far better than any man Hugh knew.

And even though rage had knocked out most of his senses when he had walked in here, he had heard the deeply sensitive lines of poetry that had come from Kip's heart. He was a man of compassion and kindness who wouldn't hurt him. Not on purpose.

Hugh would be the biggest fool if he didn't try to patch things up with him.

"I've given a lot of thought to your proposal," he said solemnly. "I'd very much like to discuss it further if that's something you'd still like to entertain."

Kip's smile broadened, but whatever he might have said was drowned out by his sister's very nosey, "What proposal?" She came back through the door her bridegroom was holding.

"A tearoom," Kip informed her. "Hugh will make his specialty biscuits and pies. I will bring in poets to recite their verse for people who actually appreciate it." His gaze slid to the window where their brother stood outside with a spanked look on his face.

"Here?" Bea's bridegroom asked skeptically.

"London." Kip glanced to Hugh and he gave a small nod.

"Will I be able to visit this tearoom?" Lady Beatrix asked with a make-or-break tone.

And Hugh thought, *What have I done?*

"It will be a salon for men *and* women to discuss the arts," Kip informed her. "So you will have to elevate your conversation skills."

She waved her hand to dismiss his teasing. "I think it's an excellent idea. Papa will hate it, but Mama loves her tea parties. Everyone will want to try it. And I will have so many contacts once I'm married and we're spending the season in London. Won't I, Barton? I will make everyone come with me and tell everyone how I discovered your *master baker*."

I am so sorry, Kip said with his eyes.

Hugh bit back the smile that was pulling at his mouth. "And here I thought I wouldn't see you again after you were married, Lady Beatrix."

"Some relationships are meant to last a lifetime," she said loftily. "But come, Kip. We really must leave Hugh to it. I want my cake ready on time."

They left and Alice came up to lean into his upper arm.

"Are you really going to London with him?"

"Yes." He nodded, promise and excitement growing in his belly by the minute.

"Good. I like him. I was worried when you quit leaving the gate unlocked for him."

He looked down at the top of her head and couldn't resist kissing her hair with affection. "You're a good sister."

"You're a good brother. But you really should get back to work. *The cake.* Do you realize what you've done?"

"Christ, I know." But the mosquito-like annoyance of Lady Beatrix was a small price to pay if he could see Kip every day.

CHAPTER FIVE

Fourteen months later...

Hugh had Kip exactly where he loved him most, writhing on his knees in the middle of their bed, biting the pillow while making noises like a wounded animal.

Hugh mercilessly swept his arsehole with his tongue, loving that he could still make him shake more than a year after the first time he'd done this.

"Fuck, Hugh. How does it keep getting better?" Kip groaned, voice muffled.

He didn't know, but it did. "Do you want to come like thi—"

"No! Fuck me, you fucking tease."

Hugh laughed and reached for the tin. He used the fat pad of his thumb to grease him, being just a tiny bit rough because he liked to watch the shiver flex through Kip's back.

"I was going to offer to let you fuck me, seeing as it's our anniversary," Hugh said as he knelt behind him. Their shop had been open a year today. "But I got distracted."

"I will if you want me to."

"I like this." He played the tip of his cock against the hole he'd stretched and lubricated.

"Me, too," Kip said, then groaned as Hugh buried himself balls deep inside him.

Hugh covered him, nipped his earlobe, and said, "I fucking love this. You. I love you so fucking much, you don't even know."

"I do. I love you, too." Kip sounded half delirious, which made Hugh smile against his nape. "Now fuck me 'til there's nothing left of me."

Hugh did. They both fell into a hard sleep afterward and

Hugh didn't realize Kip had left the bed until he came back when it was time for Hugh to rise.

They had a funny schedule. Hugh was up before dawn to light the oven and begin his daily baking. He had a journeyman and a couple of lads to help, but they were thinking of hiring more, since the deliveries were growing so popular.

Hugh was very scrupulous about the budget and was waiting to be sure they could keep the handful of women they had hired over the last weeks. The one selling the morning baking to foot traffic could already use a hand. They could also use a third in the tearoom during the day. Word was out among the ladies that the Queenslie Hedge Tea Room was *the* place to revive oneself—and catch up on all the gossip—amid a busy day of shopping.

In the late afternoon, as the crush was winding down and Hugh was cleaning up, Kip would open the doors to his more exclusive salon. These were the cream of the *ton*. They ate the least and paid the most. Hugh honestly didn't understand why they were willing to pay a membership fee simply to sit in a room and ignore his scones, but Kip never had an empty seat.

When that most pretentious lot left, Hugh and Kip would enjoy a private hour or two. Kip often left Hugh sated and snoring in their bed. Kip would then open the doors for the actors and playwrights who had finished their performance at the theaters for the night. He would sell off the day's leavings at half price and schedule which ones might come in to offer a soliloquy to patrons. They were a colorful bunch of night owls and Kip often came to bed as Hugh was rising.

At which point their day would start all over again.

This very early morning that was still the middle of the night, Kip sat down next to him in the candlelight and said, "I meant to give you your anniversary present before you fell asleep, but I got distracted."

"I thought that was my anniversary present."

"No, it was mine. But look at what I've got you." Kip showed him a rolled and sealed document.

"My poem?" Hugh took it with a swell of emotion coming into his chest.

"No." Kip's eyes widened and grew glossy. "I didn't know you would want that. Of course, I'll write it out for you if you like." He blinked fast and his smile wobbled. "You're such an easy man to please. But no, this is something else. And it's not official. You'll have to go to the barrister to sign other papers if you want to accept it."

Hugh was still half asleep, so nothing about the document made sense as he unrolled it and scanned his eyes across the abundance of words. "Is this some sort of debt notice? Why is my name on it?" He was waking up fast, growing alarmed.

"No, it's the deed to the bakehouse in Queenslie Hedge. You and I talked about investing our profits into purchasing this building, but we would have had payments for years. This way, if anything happens, you will always have something to go back to. Plus, you can set a more modest rent for Alice and Oscar so they can build their own nest egg."

"I don't understand. You bought me this? Kip, I can't."

"No." He pushed his hand back from trying to return the document. "I only sent a letter to my father and made him an offer. The purchase will be made from your half of the profit from the salon, but it will be yours free and clear."

"The bakehouse doesn't make this kind of money, Kip. You're supposed to be paying the lease out of the salon intake." Pressure was beginning to build inside his chest. Hugh trusted Kip, but Kip hadn't grown up in the reality of a common man's life. Had he not understood that the wages they took were for small necessities like clothes and soap, not for hiring barristers to write up papers that could never be finalized?

Hugh was suddenly wondering how far he'd have to stretch the few coins he'd saved in the money jar beneath the floorboard.

"The lease is paid." Kip was taking a *calm down* tone. "I've set aside what we'll owe for the next two years. I know how closely you watch the numbers on the bakehouse to keep it profitable, Hugh. I love you for that. It means our membership fees for the salon are pure profit. Everyone has just renewed and we had so many applications, I doubled the fee and still couldn't chase anyone away. I've set a little aside as contingency, but once I thought of buying the bakehouse, I had to write to Papa to see what sort of offer he might accept. It's a very good price, Hugh. And it gives you another reason to go back to visit when I have to visit *my* family."

Hugh couldn't make sense of this. "I need to sit down."

"You are sitting down. Do you want to lie down?"

He did, but he only sank his face into his hands, trying to catch his breath. "What about... Did you say this is my *half*? You also have this much?"

"Yes. And I've been thinking of investing in a publishing house so I could compile a book of my poetry with some others, but it's a tricky business. I know you'll have some good ideas, but we'll talk more once you've had time to let this rest and rise."

"No baking puns. We've talked about that."

Kip was grinning.

Hugh was on the verge of crying. "Kip, are you sure about this?"

"Hugh." He took his hand. "The first day we met, I realized you were capable of great love. I walked away thinking, 'If only I could get him to love *me*.'"

"I do." He crushed Kip's hand in his. "I don't need..." He flipped his other hand toward the paper that had somehow drifted onto the floor.

"I know. But I want you to feel secure and loved and valued, too. The way I feel when I'm with you."

"You're going to make me cry, you fool." He cupped Kip's face. Kip's eyes were wet, so he was in good company. They were both grinning wide. "I do love you. A great sodding lot."

"I know. Me, too."

They kissed and passion rose to match the intensity of their emotion.

"Am I going to be late starting the ovens?" Hugh asked as Kip's lips went down his throat.

"You tell me."

"Definitely." He brought his mouth back so he could suck on Kip's pretty lips until they were both hard. "Do you want to fuck me? Your ass must be sore."

"I want what you want."

"I want to sit on your cock. Drop your trousers and get onto this bed."

Kip smiled and began to release his buttons.

The End

ACKNOWLEDGMENTS

Thank you to my agent for connecting me with the team at Entangled. Thank you to all the incredible, hardworking people at Entangled Amara and Macmillan who helped make this collection as strong as it could be on every level. Some of you remain anonymous to me, but I'm deeply grateful to each and every one of you. Most of all, a humble and loving thank you to the only person I confided in while working on this project for endless patience, understanding, and for making me laugh every single day. I love you.

Looking for more romance?
Entangled brings the heat.

FOLLOW ME DARKLY

One chance encounter is all it took for Skye to find herself in the middle of a Cinderella story…but self-made billionaire Braden Black is no Prince Charming, and his dark desires are far from his only secret.

THE SPINSTER AND THE RAKE

The marriage game is afoot in this clever blend of *My Fair Lady* meets *Pride and Prejudice* with a twist!

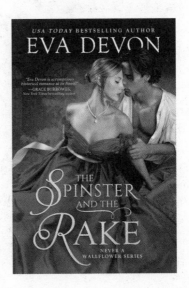

Entangled brings the laughs.

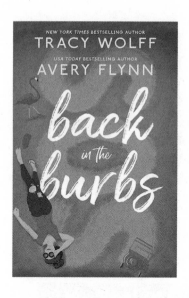

BACK IN THE BURBS

After a nasty divorce, Mallory's ready to leave NYC and start over. She decides to live in the house her aunt left her...in the suburbs. First rule of surviving the burbs? There is nothing that YouTube and a glass of wine can't conquer.

THE REBOUND SURPRISE

Carefree bachelor Aniel is the perfect guy to have a rebound fling with after organized and predictable Libby finds her fiancé defiling her linen sheets with the maid. Except, the fine print that says condoms aren't 100 percent effective is unerringly accurate.

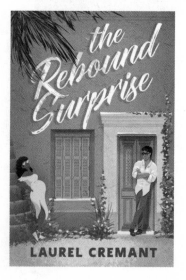

Entangled brings the heart.

THE BEST KEPT SECRET

After she rescues her sister's ex from a loopy response to pain meds, Nyla has to keep Leo's biggest secret while trying not to fall for him.

THE BRIDES OF LONDON

Enjoy two stories in one! From an arranged elopement with one of London's famous actors, to a story about the resurrection of first love after being widowed—this Regency romance collection is perfect for *Bridgerton* fans.

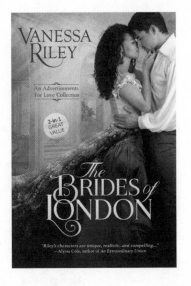

Don't miss any of the
exciting new romances
Entangled has to offer.

Follow @Entangled_Publishing
on Instagram and join us at
Facebook.com/EntangledPublishing